xx Rebecca Sharp

the
BOOKWORM
box

Helping the community, one book at a time

Beholden

A **CARMEL COVE** NOVEL

DR. REBECCA SHARP

Beholden (Carmel Cove, Book 1)
Published by Dr. Rebecca Sharp
Copyright © 2018 Dr. Rebecca Sharp

All rights reserved. No part of this book may be reproduced, distributed, or transmitted in any form or by any electronic or mechanical means, including information storage and retrieval systems, photocopying, or recording, without permission in writing from the publisher, except by reviewers, who may quote brief passages in a review and certain other noncommercial uses permitted by copyright law.

This is a work of fiction. Resemblance to actual persons, things, living or dead, locales or events is entirely coincidental.

Cover Design:
Cover Designer: Kris Hack, Temy's Designs
Exclusive for The Bookworm Box

Formatting:
Stacey Blake, Champagne Book Designs
champagnebookdesign.com

Editing:
Ellie McLove, My Brother's Editor
mybrotherseditor.net/

Printed in the United States of America.
Visit www.drrebeccasharp.com

To everyone who has lost someone,
Though the morning light conceals the stars,
it doesn't stop them from shining.
They watch over our brightest days just as
they guide us through our darkest nights.
They're always with us even when we can't see them.

To everyone searching for a path through grief,
Start where you are. Use what you have. Do what you can.
One day at a time.

And to Larry,
I love and miss you.
This series is for you.

Beholden

Prologue

Laurel
Fifteen Years Old

"You okay, Ishkey?" My grandfather's voice, roughened from smoking for almost forty years, rang out from the kitchen. He hadn't smoked in a long time. Not since I was born. But it still had a scratchiness to it like the worn top of a dining room table, sturdy but weathered.

My dad says I was the one who got him to quit—that when my dad handed me to my pap for the first time, it came with a wordless accusation: it was his choice to smoke and risk dying before I had the chance to grow up.

Rumor had it he quit cold-turkey the next day.

Knowing my pap… knowing Larry Ocean, I believed that rumor.

For as long as I could remember, he'd always called me Ishkey. I had no idea where the name came from or what the name meant; it certainly sounded nothing like Laurel.

"Yeah." My sore throat croaked out just loud enough to provoke another coughing fit.

Ducking my mouth into the crook of my elbow, I let out a few nasty coughs that sounded like they took a part of my lung with them.

I blamed Jane for this.

She showed up to school last week, sick, and coughed right into the open—no elbow, no hands, no nothing, like the posters plastered all down the hall about flu season didn't matter. Next thing I knew, my throat went from scratchy to feeling like any food was made of pure fire as it burned all the way down to my stomach.

I was supposed to have a sleepover with my cousin, Jules, tonight but when I started coughing yesterday, my mom said no. And when I woke up with my right eye all red and gross from bursting blood vessels, my dad decided school today was a no-go too. Instead, he dropped me off at my grandparent's house on his way into town to our family's coffee shop, Ocean Roasters.

Picking up *The Lion, The Witch, and the Wardrobe* from where I'd dropped it in my lap in order to cough, I thumbed through the pages trying to find where I'd left off. I'd already read the book last year and done a book report on it, but I loved *The Chronicles of Narnia* and my well-read copy had come with me earlier as a comfort.

"Let's go, Ishkey," he said gruffly, motioning to me with one hand, a cup of coffee in the other. "Outside."

I looked up at him with a blank stare from my perfectly warm and comfortable pile of blankets and fantasy book that I really didn't want to leave.

"Don't make me tell you again," he scolded with not even a hint of real anger, pushing his reader glasses up onto his full head of hair—an accomplishment for a man in his seventies.

I knew my mane of hair came from the Ocean side of my family, but its red tint? That came from my mom's Irish roots along with my unable-to-tan pale skin. It made me stick out like a sore thumb against the rich brown locks and sun-kissed complexion of the very Italian Oceans; Jules had inherited those genes and I was kind of envious, especially since we lived in California where pale wasn't popular.

My pap whistled and the short, shrill sound pulled me back from my rambling thoughts. "C'mon, Ishkey, before your grammy is done making the salads and dinner."

I let out a small moan at the reminder. I loved my grammy's salads. I'd watched her make them a hundred times—a simple mix of red wine vinegar and oil and spices—but still, no attempt at home on my own ever came out as good. And dinner… my pap had made his famous spaghetti and meatballs with his magic red sauce. There was nothing in this world that I loved more than this meal… and that magic sauce.

I shoved my sock-covered feet into my sandals and followed him outside.

It was fall, but up in Northern California, in Carmel Cove where we lived, it was actually pretty warm during this time of year. Unfortunately, even warm air made me chilly since I was sick.

"Over here, let's go," my pap insisted, wrapping an arm around my shoulder as we walked on grass-covered ground that was still spongy from the rain last night.

Our shadows began to blend in with the darkness as the outside lights of the house faded. The sliver of the moon out tonight played hide-and-seek behind a few scattered clouds, slacking on any substantial illumination. Thankfully, we'd walked this path so many times that we could find our way to the edge of their property even in the dusky darkness.

For most people, the edge of one property meant the beginning of someone else's. Not my grandparents'. At the edge of their land began the sea—right after a huge drop off a rock-face cliff along the Big Sur coastline. I wasn't allowed to go outside alone until I was almost twelve because my mom was afraid I'd get too close to the cliff.

"What are we doing here, Pap?" I grumbled when we came to a stop a safe several feet short of the edge. Here, without the house or trees to block the ocean breeze, I was starting to feel the real chill from the wind. I huddled in closer to his side and his hand instinctively squeezed on my shoulder as he sighed.

"Just breathe. Nice and deep," he instructed, and I rolled my eyes into the darkness.

My pap was convinced the sea air could heal anything. I told my dad it was like the grandfather from *My Big Fat Greek Wedding* who thought that Windex was a cure-all.

At least my pap wasn't spraying Windex down my throat. Although, at this point, I doubted it could make it any worse.

"I don't think this works. It's just salty air," I grumbled in protest. "It's not going to fix my sore throat; it could make it worse."

"That's the thing about healing, Laurel," he clipped, taking a sip of his coffee. "Sometimes, to get better, you have to risk getting worse."

There was no point in arguing. My pap had a thing about this town right down to the air in it.

"I want to tell you something, Ishkey," he began as he squeezed me to him. "Now, I don't care what your father says, but I want you to know if you don't want to take over the coffee shop, you don't have to."

I shifted uncomfortably on my feet, pressing one then the other onto the soft, grassy earth and listened to the soft hush of the waves below, wishing they could answer him instead of me. I knew why he was saying this.

Last weekend, I'd been at Roasters studying for my biology test when Mrs. Grace, one of the tellers at Cove Bank, stopped in for her afternoon coffee. She asked if I liked science, and considering how much I struggled to keep the flowers my dad always got me and my mom for Valentine's Day alive, let alone understand how photosynthesis worked, I answered with a firm no.

With a smile, she then informed me that I must be happy to not have to worry about science since I'd be the owner of Ocean Roasters one day. I think she mentioned something about being the fifth Ocean to do so after that, but I couldn't really remember. I just stared at her with bugged eyes; I was already freaking out about a test and then she'd gone and brought up what I was *supposed* to do with my life—like my future was as clear and outlined as Dorothy's yellow brick road.

Of course, everyone assumed I'd be next in line to take over Ocean Roasters; it had been in the family for four generations. In my opinion, the second generation had a choice whether they wanted to continue the legacy, the third, only a questionable escape, and the fourth, an unadvisable abdication, *but the fifth?*

I shuddered.

Excommunication would have been less shocking than if I decided to walk away from the family business. It was the center of town and the center of the community—basically the center of the world for everyone in Carmel. My great-grandfather from his dad, my pap after him, and now, my dad and mom handled most of the work even though my pap was still there almost every day. He wasn't ready to give up roasting the beans quite yet— or talking to the patrons.

"I don't know what I want to do yet. I haven't thought about it," I mumbled, my voice falling off over the edge of the cliff to be swallowed up by the waves.

Okay, that was kind of a lie.

I had thought about it after that day and all the times Jules wouldn't shut up about how she wanted to go to nursing school and then kept trying to make me say I'd go with her if I couldn't decide. We were only in ninth grade. We couldn't even drive yet, I wanted to scream at her.

How was I supposed to know what I wanted to do for the rest of my life?

"Well, I just want you to know that no one here will be mad or upset if you decide you want to do something different with your life, you hear? No one. Or they can answer to me," he said gruffly with that tone he took whenever anyone gave him a problem.

"So, you wouldn't be upset even just a little bit?" I clarified hesitantly, looking up at him in the dim light coming from the house several yards away.

"Doesn't matter what I'd be, Laurel," he grunted sternly. "Only matters who you *want* to be. Most important thing in life is to be you, not who everyone else wants you to be."

"But I'm an Ocean," I offered hoarsely, only a small cough escaping this time. "Roasters is our legacy."

I guess if I stopped to think about it, I did assume that running the coffee shop is what I would end up doing. Maybe that's why I didn't stop to think about it. It's not that I didn't love Roasters or my family or this town. I loved them more than anything. But it was also my life and I wanted to do something that I loved with it... I just wasn't sure that thing was Roasters.

I shivered when his arm dropped so he could turn me to face him. Even in the darkness, I could see the steely, stubborn glint in his eyes as he made sure he had my full attention before speaking.

"Who told you that?"

I tried to swallow over the sore lump in my throat but it

wasn't happening. "I... uhh... No one. I just... it just is." I didn't know how to answer because I felt like I was somehow in trouble.

What did I say wrong?

"Roasters is not our legacy. It's our business, not our legacy," he explained firmly, waiting for my weak nod before he continued. "You know how Mrs. Covington comes in every morning and stays for an hour while she drinks her small coffee with one sugar and a dash of cream and chats with your grammy?" I nodded, unsurprised that he remembered her exact order. "That's because she's home with those four kids all day and for that hour, your Gram reminds her she's a good mom and that she's doing a good job at raising those kids even when it doesn't feel like it."

I stared at him because I didn't know what to say. Four kids *was* a lot of kids. Was that his point?

"And you know how your mom always sets aside two apple fritters for Sister Margaret every Sunday afternoon even though she only ever comes in asking for one? That's because Sister Margaret's young niece, Brandy, has cancer and your mom knows those fritters are her favorite and will brighten Brandy's day when Sister Margaret brings her one."

My chest tightened. I'd gone to elementary school with Brandy before she got sick.

"And Josie? She stops over every morning not just to bring over the day's specials from their bakery, but because she likes to hear my stories from when her dad and I were in the service together; he didn't make it back home with the rest of us so those stories and my old photos are all she's got left to know him." His voice somehow got harder yet shakier each time he spoke. Even the ocean breeze picked up around us, like it was stirred by all the emotion in his words.

Somewhere in my mind I knew about all these things. I mean, I'd heard them all. I'd heard the conversations between my gram and Mrs. Covington; I'd even see her break down and cry a few times because she was so overwhelmed. I knew about Sister Margaret's niece; I'd been the one to share my apple fritter with her and it was the first time she had one—but I didn't think my pap knew that. And yeah, I'd seen my pap look through the same old photographs from the war with Josie, and I remembered wondering who would want to look at the same pictures over and over again? Now, I was glad I'd held back from making a comment.

Now, I connected all the dots. Each moment like an individual star in the sky but it wasn't until now that I could see the picture that formed once they were connected into a constellation of compassion.

"Every single person who walks into our business isn't coming just for their daily coffee, Laurel. They're coming because they know we care about them and their lives. They know one of us will be there as a friend to laugh with, an ear to listen without judgment, or a shoulder to cry on," he pressed on firmly.

My pap didn't cry, but for the first time in my whole life, I thought I saw him getting close to it.

He let out a long shaky breath, pulling me hard against his chest as he finished with, "That's our legacy, Laurel… being there for the people in this town, being there for someone in need. Our legacy is about loving people, plain and simple, because it's the most noble thing you can do in this world—love one another, especially someone who's struggling. And there are a million and one good ways to go about helping people in this world, so don't think your legacy has to be tied to brewin' a cup of coffee, understand, Ishkey?"

I nodded against his chest, breathing in the faint smell of fresh-cut grass that clung to his shirt.

"Larry!" We both turned at my grandmother's voice coming from the front door to the house. "Dinner's ready!"

"You understand?" he asked again, fully prepared to ignore her until I answered him.

I nodded again quickly. "Yeah. I understand."

I knew this was one of those moments I'd never forget. It wasn't a big moment either—just a few minutes spent standing out in the darkness, breathing in the ocean air. Still, I just felt it somewhere deep inside that this was something that was going to change me.

My mind flicked back over probably hundreds of similar scenes I'd witnessed at Roasters with my parents and grandparents and the people of our hometown, only now I saw them all the way he described them—and I couldn't *unsee* it; I couldn't undo the constellation.

"Good," he said with relief and turned us back toward the house. "And remember, Laurel, love is a two-way street. The only way to really be there for someone else is by knowing that at some point, you're gonna need someone to lean on, too. Love without vulnerability is only frivolity."

Love without vulnerability is only frivolity.

My brain traipsed over the phrase several times, imprinting it into my memory because it felt like one of those things that should be there.

"Love without vulnerability is only frivolity. Got it…" I murmured softly and felt the scale inside my heart that weighed my future begin to tip just a hair.

Hearing him talk made my decision about more than just choosing to brew coffee; it made me want to be a part of that something more—not because I was expected to, but because I *wanted* to be a part of something that could go so unnoticed and yet be so profound.

It was like a butterfly effect. One kind word. One kind action. *A world of difference.*

"We're coming, we're coming," my pap announced as he held open the door for me, the smell of spaghetti and meatballs immediately drowning my senses.

I took one last deep breath just before we walked back inside and oddly enough, my throat didn't hurt as much as we sat down to eat.

One

Laurel

Welcome to Carmel Cove.

To everyone else, the large weathered timbers of the sign signaled a warm welcome to the small town on the Pacific coast.

To me, they signaled a warning.

And instead of the comfort of arriving back in my hometown, I felt the dread as though I'd crossed enemy lines.

Open-heartedness. Charity. Perseverance.

The words were etched into three massive pieces of ruptured stone just behind the welcome sign. From their broken-open center, the dense trunk of the iconic Monterey cypress rose, irregular and tipped forward from the steady force of coastal winds, and the thick, bright green foliage fanned out with a flat-top for the same reason.

The stone had once been a platform for a non-existent statue which had toppled and shattered from a massive earthquake in the early nineteen-hundreds. The shocks were also responsible for fracturing the massive stone platform, angling up the pieces in pyramidal fashion like a rocky funnel with a jagged hole at the top.

In the aftermath of the destruction the quake wreaked on the town and the environment, that lone cypress had sprung from the center of the stones. *New life from the ashes.* Since then, the rubble had been reborn, the stones polished and carved with words that symbolized this town and the people in it, and the tree had flourished.

It remained a monument to those characteristics. And a testament to the good that could grow after disaster.

For everyone except me.

"I'm so sorry for your loss, Laurel."

Though the words were shined with sorrow, their sharp, cold reality was still another shot to my heart. I was sure everyone thought it was a restrained sob that shook me and brought me back to the present. *It wasn't.* I was just reeling from one more blow.

One more loss.

"Thank you," I murmured, hardly seeing the person who'd spoken as my attention turned to the plain bronze urn that reflected my face instead of his.

Veteran. Coffee shop owner. *Grandfather.*

Larry Ocean.

Pap.

He was my hero—the man who ate four donuts every morning before going to the gym and half a Hershey bar before bed. The man who made sure the small cliff-side cabin I'd spent so much time at was always landscaped to perfection. The man whose steely kindness and unending compassion was famous in our small, Italian-immigrant town long before I left it. *And now, he was gone.*

May he rest in peace.

Because there was no peace here for me.

"It's so good to see you again, Laurel. I'm sorry about your grandfather. He was such a good, kind man. I can't believe he—" the older woman broke off with a fluttering hand to her chest, losing her words to overwhelming emotion.

And another shot of sympathy speared through my chest.

Names. Faces. They were all familiar yet foreign. Pieces of a past I'd rather forget were now jammed into all my broken cracks as though they were meant to fit.

They weren't.

The losses I'd lived through left irreparable wounds.

"Yes, he was. Thank you," I answered blindly, my insides twisting in knots underneath the prim and pressed black suit I'd worn to the viewing.

How did one grieve for someone who took their own life?

How did one grieve for someone who couldn't bear to stay?

I knew the sorrow of losing a loved one—the sorrow that shattered my life when my parents were killed in a boating accident. And again, when my grandmother's health gave way to her broken heart.

But this sorrow was different...

It had the same excruciating sensation of a knife sliding in between my ribs, only the blade was hot. Sharp sorrow seared with an anger that didn't feel right, yet was *felt* all the same.

Anger that he'd chosen to leave now.

Anger that I'd chosen to leave then.

Anger that this was how it all ended.

And that anger scrambled my grief. Like a word-search in my heart, I knew all the letters were there, I just couldn't find them together. Every expression of sorrow twisted the hot knife deeper, cauterizing as it went and sealing my grief inside to eat away at me as it grew.

"Just be comforted in knowing he's with your grandmother and your parents," the elderly woman murmured before she moved on.

Once again, I was the center of my hometown's sympathy. I could see it in every gaze that was on me.

Poor little Laurel.

One more loss.

Loss was what drove me away and what brought me back. In my world, home was a four-letter word spelled L-O-S-S; loss was all it could mean because loss was all it had ever given. *And asking for anything different would be as fruitful as asking the sun to set in the east.*

Someone else hugged me—a smaller middle-aged woman who then reached up and cupped my face with tears in her eyes to give me her condolences. I recognized her but couldn't remember her name—just like most of the people in the room. She hugged me like she'd known me my whole life—*like I was family*—and I fought not to jerk away; I didn't have family here. *Not anymore.*

"That was Josie. She owns the Carmel Bakery," Diane whispered under her breath as she resumed her perch at my side.

Diane was one of our oldest family friends. An unforgettable face with jet-black eyelashes that reached her eyebrows and a giant perm of blonde hair that framed motherly eyes and a compassionate character.

Josie. Now it clicked. An image flashed in my memory of her and my pap looking at old photos from during the war, and the words *'it's all she's got left'* flitted through my mind before I shoved them away.

"Thank you," I said hoarsely.

'Thank you' was about the only thing I'd said to her since she'd picked me up at the train station in San Francisco yesterday, her tears an uncoordinated accessory to her bellbottom jeans and tight pink shirt for the hour-long drive south. Now, they accented her long black dress perfectly.

"I'll be right back, dear. I see some of the students from my studio. They would always stop for coffee after class and show Larry their projects," she murmured sadly and gently squeezed my shoulder with her warm grasp before stepping from my side.

Diane owned an art studio a few doors down from Ocean Roasters, my family's coffee shop. I watched her massive bleach-blonde hair that could only have been blow-dried by a jet engine weave through the crowd, rising above the rest on platform shoes that made step-stools look like technology from the past.

She finally disappeared and I assessed the receiving line that seemed to be both never-ending and self-generating. And as soon as she was out of sight, dozens of grief-laden gazes stacked solely on my chest like iron weights, making each breath harder and harder to take.

Poor little Laurel.

The prodigal granddaughter.

In their eyes, mourning mingled with confusion and, in some cases, resentment like oil dropped in water. I was supposed to be the fifth generation of Oceans to inherit Roasters. *Instead, I'd been the first to renounce it and leave town altogether.*

It was no wonder they couldn't decide whether to console or curse me.

"That's a lot of history right there." My eyes flicked to where Josie had reappeared by my side, a heartfelt smile gracing her kind features.

I dragged my eyes to the photo display Diane had created, standing to the side of the table holding the urn.

The snapshots of generations of Oceans past: my great-great-grandfather on the docks in San Francisco before he quit being a fisherman and moved to Carmel Cove, him and my great-great-grandmother in front of Roasters the day it opened as the first coffee shop in town, pictures of my great-grandparents, my grandparents when they were younger, and finally, a photo of them with my parents and me.

"Yes, it was."

But no longer.

Generation after generation had run our coffee shop, now on prime real estate in a town that was famous for the golf and wine as much as it was for the ocean and the family-roasted coffee.

Every generation.

Until me.

The weight on my chest grew heavier and hotter. More people—more pieces—from a past I was desperate to forget.

"So, you're still living in Los Angeles then? I think that's what your grandfather told me," Josie continued with a soft voice.

She seemed like a nice woman—she *was* a nice woman, from what I remembered—but I didn't come back to this town to get close to all the reasons I'd left it. I came back to pay my respects, make my peace, and move on.

Still, I politely replied, "Yes. I'm the executive assistant to Rachel Moss, the Menswear Merchandising Manager at Ralph Lauren."

It was a good job. *Interesting.* Not what I'd dreamt I'd do, but that made it safe. I wouldn't take a chance of getting close to anything I truly wanted, knowing what it felt like to have it ripped away.

"Good for you, dear." She nodded and then reached out to briefly touch one of the photos of my pap, my dad, and me in front of Roasters… and then brought that same hand to my arm—*searing it like an unwanted brand.*

"We're glad you're back." She squeezed my arm with an encouraging smile before turning and walking away.

Back.

I hadn't returned to Carmel since the day I'd left it… *along with the possibility of taking over my family's coffee shop.* I'd left and worked my ass off to make a life for myself somewhere else, and I wouldn't be ashamed of that. No matter what they thought I was here for or how they might judge me for it, I wasn't staying.

I couldn't stomach living in the town that had cost me so much.

My eyes narrowed on the urn, like he could see me glaring at him through the simple, polished exterior.

I didn't know he was sick like this.

But I guess no one had.

Those who knew he'd been on medication for depression assumed he was taking it. Until it was too late and too clear he wasn't.

Until he'd taken his own life.

I closed my eyes, needing a respite from the crowd; their silent and stark grief was more overwhelming than the black they wore or the tears they cried. It was palpable in every look, every word; it painted the walls and covered the floors. It was inescapable.

I took a deep breath, hoping to inhale enough determination to get through this. Instead, I choked on the suffocating scent of lilies.

I hated lilies.

Lilies always accompanied loss.

And the rooms at Fiori's Funeral Home were filled with them. The entire bottom floor of the old, ornate Victorian home had been opened up for the memorial to Lawrence Ocean in order to accommodate not only the suffocating flowers but the swarms of people who came along with them.

Every person within a twenty-mile radius of Carmel Cove would be here today to pay their respects. Because that was who the Oceans were: *Carmel's legacy.*

I groaned under my breath. *Funeral home.* Home should be a place of love and life and family. 'Funeral,' though, seemed to be a more appropriate descriptor of home for me. First, my parents. Then, my grandmother. Now, my pap.

I shifted as a sudden wave of heat came over me. I unbuttoned my black blazer, wishing I could take it off. I turned to look for Diane and instead came face-to-face with the balding, bearded, George Covington—a name and a face I knew because he was the plumber who showed up at Diane's house last night to fix the toilet in her guest room. I only had memories of his wife from *before*, and how *'she was a good mom.'*

"So sorry again about Larry," he murmured with the exact same bereaved tone he had yesterday when we met.

Déjà vu.

I hadn't been crying then either.

I murmured my thanks as one of his hands left its perch on his decently sized gut to clasp my shoulder in support. Immediately following him were three younger men—all so stoic and well-built it looked like the town plumber was traveling with his own special-ops unit. *Which could only mean they were his sons.* The men who became of the boys their mother used to talk about. Maybe if I planned on sticking around, I would have bothered to remember their names.

But I wasn't going to stay.

So, I accepted their condolences in the same subdued manner as I had the rest.

Alone again, I dragged in a deep breath, but the oxygen only fueled the fire that was sweltering me. Ducking my head, I abandoned my designated post and waded through the sea of black, accepting apologies as I went like they were candy being given out on Halloween.

"Laurel." My head jerked up as Diane found me in the corner I'd retreated to and wrapped me in another hug. "You okay, honey? Can I get you anything?"

Out of here.

"I'm fine. Thank you," I lied numbly instead.

"There are a few more people who want to offer their condolences," she said softly as her hand rubbed up and down my arm, like it would make me feel better about the proposition. "And I want to introduce you to Eli; he just got here. You need to meet Eli."

Eli? I started.

Who was Eli?

I was almost curious enough to ask. *Almost.*

The name wasn't completely unfamiliar to me. I'd heard several people mention this *Eli* from where I stood, watching the world happen around me. They said his name almost as many times as they said mine. They said his name with a magical mix of reverence and awe, and I fought to not be intrigued as to who Eli was… *and who he'd been to my grandfather.*

She dabbed her eyes again with her handkerchief, the ringmaster of this grieving circus, and declared, "Let me go find your Aunt Jackie and Eli, and I'll be right back."

I didn't respond. I didn't want to see my aunt or uncle right now. *But Jules…* My stomach twisted at the memory of my cousin. We'd been so close when we were younger, and then she'd left for boarding school and forgot I existed. *Another loss.* None of this was right. *He shouldn't be gone.*

He wasn't supposed to die.

He wasn't supposed to leave me.

Not now.

Not yet.

My name being called broke through my thoughts. Diane motioned for me to join her and my Aunt Jackie who dabbed her eyes with a rehearsed motion and was unsurprisingly, even after all these years, dressed to the nines in black and glittering jewels as though she were walking the red carpet rather than the processional at her father's funeral.

Jackie Vandelsen stood next to her husband, Rich, who appeared to be eagerly awaiting the moment when it was appropriate to leave, holding his arms tight to his chest like even a brush with middle-class was infectious. They owned the Rock Beach Golf Club and Resort right on the ocean and were always mingling with celebrities and politicians—social classes that required a respectable distance from her working-class family.

Since she'd married him—and into the upper crust of Carmel, my aunt decided that the rest of town, along with her own family, were beneath her.

Ironically enough, since I'd left Carmel with no intention of returning, she was probably going to inherit Roasters even though she'd never wanted anything to do with it.

I stood frozen, unable to bring myself to join them. And then I heard it, the whispers between two elderly women off to my right.

"*The poor girl. First, Mark and Fiona, then Helen, and now, Larry.*"

The words were so quiet and yet detonated like a bomb inside me.

Poor. Little. Laurel.

It had been almost thirteen years since the boating accident that took my parents' lives. The last thing I wanted or needed right now was to remember that day. *Or that funeral.*

I gave Diane and my aunt a weak smile and instead, one-eightied and made for the bathroom with my head down to avoid the pity-filled eyes of everyone in the room.

I was practically running by the time I whipped around the corner to the hall where the bathrooms were located and plowed directly into a manmade wall.

Or a wall made of man.

I let out a loud gasp as my hands instinctively planted on the hard muscle of his chest. Large warm hands closed around my upper arms, holding me steady—*and holding me close.*

"Woah, there. You okay?" the wall asked with a warm voice that purred down my spine. Like the frequency of a whistle only dogs can hear, the rough timbre called to a part of me I didn't know existed and that begged me to run to him.

Which was exactly what I'd inadvertently done.

Slowly, I dragged my gaze from my hands that were curled into the pressed black lapel of his suit jacket, up to the collar of his pressed white shirt that cut in a bit too tightly on his neck, and then paused on the pulse that thumped against his rich olive skin; the vibration seemed to be in sync with my own. Snapping out of it, my eyes jerked up at least another foot above my five-foot-one frame to see who possessed the paired pulse.

To see who was holding me.

Wood-burnt eyes greeted me, their deep brown streaked with red and gold and flickered with recognition and something more... *something hotter and darker.* But only for a second.

I sucked in an unsteady breath.

Those twin embers roamed my face, searching out and claiming anything to fuel their fire. *As though he could burn anything wasted into something new and bright and full of promise.*

"I'm so sorry," I heard myself say though I couldn't drag my gaze from him.

He had, by far, the most perfect face I'd ever seen. And I let myself make that assessment with confidence, knowing the scores of male models my department at Ralph Lauren went through each season.

Strong cheekbones balanced out a sculpted nose, its precise planes marred by the slightest shift at the top where it had been broken and then healed almost perfectly. And his lips... their fullness was confidently masculine. His were the kind of lips that would be so devilishly skilled as to make you forget your own name, and then gentlemanly enough to remind you of it afterward.

My tongue slipped out and moistened my own, craving an amnesiac taste.

The rapid flutter of my heart in my chest adorned how my body burned for a whole different reason—*a reason I couldn't understand.*

But this... this was an everyday sight for me: the hard, sculpted jawlines... eyes that could strip you in a blink... hair perpetually sex-tossed... I'd seen so many handsome men I didn't *see* them anymore... like living in Paris, at some point even the Eiffel Tower becomes blasé.

But not him. I'd never been so affected by this kind of ordinary perfection before.

His eyes raked over me, their pulsing warmth stripped me of something other than my clothes. Something that allowed him to see far more.

Maybe into my soul.

Maybe past the walls I'd put up around my heart.

I swallowed over the lump in my throat. "Y-Yeah. I'm fine. I'm sorry."

His body tensed against my hands. *He didn't believe me.* And his expression didn't bother to hide it.

His stare enveloped me like a blanket on a cold winter night: comforting and protective, some place safe to let go of my troubles and let down my guard.

My attraction to the mysterious model confirmed he was different. But this... *this man's ordinary perfection was dangerous.*

I murmured another apology before he could say what was on the tip of his tongue and pulled completely out of his grasp.

I had to escape his warm embrace.

I had to escape those ember eyes.

Bolting into the women's restroom just a few feet away, I immediately splashed cold water on my face, though it did nothing to hide the heat in my cheeks.

My father had married an Irish girl, and one would think the pale, red-haired genes would've lost the battle against the dark Italian ones, but they hadn't. My hair was a duller version of my mother's vibrant red and my freckles easier to conceal as long as I stayed out of the sun. The only thing I managed to get from the Ocean side of the family was the coffee-roasted brown eyes—more along the lines of a French Roast than a breakfast blend.

Dark. Strong. *Bittersweet.*

I washed my hands and spun right into my cousin when I went to reach for a paper towel.

"Oh!" My hand smacked against my chest before rising to pinch the bridge of my nose. "Jules. Hi. I-I didn't see you there." I gaped at the woman who'd been my best friend—*a woman I hadn't spoken to in over a decade.*

I hadn't seen Jules since her parents sent her to Our Lady of Mount Carmel, the private Catholic high school just on the edge of town… since she'd left and hadn't returned my calls.

"I'm so sorry," she mumbled and ducked her head. "I didn't mean to startle you. Are you alright?"

My eyes narrowed as they quickly scanned her, filling in all the holes a decade created in my memory. I always thought she'd been the prettiest out of both of us; now, she looked like she was trying to appear anything but.

Her dark brown hair was pulled back tight into a bun. Combined with the formless black dress that covered every inch of her and lack of makeup, she was halfway to passing for a nun—*a chic one*—only lacking the veil and head-covering.

But it was more than that. She appeared a shadow compared to the sunshine personality that I'd known. Jules had been the kind of person who'd greet you with a smile on her face even at a funeral. But things happen. People change.

Maybe because this was a funeral, Laurel.

Her expression... her emotions... she looked how I should. Tears streaking her face. Her skin pallid with pained sadness.

"It's okay." I sighed and shook my head. "I'm... I'm fine."

"I can't believe he's gone," she murmured in a daze.

He chose to leave, I wanted to scream, the anger and confusion rising inside me again. *Why did he want to leave?* I bit my tongue before the acerbic words leaked out.

The bathroom suddenly felt a lot smaller and about a thousand degrees hotter than the crowded room had. Sweltering, really.

I had to get out of here.

I put my hand to my clammy forehead and groaned, "I'm sorry, Jules."

Leaning in hastily, I hugged her for no real reason other than it seemed like the right thing to do. *Other than all my senses seemed to be failing.* Her entire body tensed in response, far from the welcoming warmth of how we used to embrace. "I-I have to go. If anyone asks, just tell them..." Any further explanation I planned on offering was lost.

"I'll let them know," she said with this soft, eerie calm, as though the thought of escaping was the only luxury her well-off life couldn't afford.

I nodded and fled, holding my breath and praying that the hard, handsome, and completely off-putting obstacle I ran into on the way in was gone. *And only partly hoping for one more glance at his un-ordinary perfection as I fled...*

Two

Laurel

I didn't release my breath until I pushed outside, audibly gulping down fresh funeral-free air, exchanging the suffocating sadness in my lungs for cool Northern California oxygen.

None of this was right.

The thought was like a soundtrack in my mind, repeating louder and louder the longer I stayed. I needed to get out before it made my head explode.

I couldn't go back there.

The thought willed my feet forward while my emotions floundered. The crunch of the sandy gravel grating on asphalt alerted me that I'd reached where the side street intersected with the coastal highway.

I glanced back at the elaborate Victorian building, grateful to see no one had followed me. Because I'd ridden over with Diane, in order to leave, I'd have to go the good old-fashioned way: on my own two feet.

"I'm sorry," I whispered to the wind, a blanket apology while continuing to walk away from all the people the apology was for.

For Diane, for leaving the funeral.
For Jules, for brushing her off the first time I'd seen her in a decade.
For everyone I'd let down by leaving.
For my pap... for everything.

Grief was a great irony. In the same way the body was made of ninety-six percent water, yet a few well-placed cups could kill you, grieving was both the thing I needed to do to survive yet felt as though one more breath of it would drown me.

There was no way Poor Little Laurel was going back inside to ask someone for a ride.

The ornate funeral home stood a few blocks up from Ocean Avenue, the main drag which ran straight through Carmel to the beach and cove. I shoved away the many memories of countless tourists who met my grandfather and asked if the street was named after him. He'd always deny it—*the road did lead right down to the Pacific after all.*

But I knew better.

The Oceans had been here for five generations—back before the streets were paved and the streams were sifted for gold. And this was just one more example of how my family was woven into the very fabric of this town, like the roots of a multi-generational tree, twisting and wrapping around everything it came into contact with.

I tugged my blazer tighter over my chest, ignoring the fine grains of sand in my flats as I walked toward town—*and the nearest bar.*

I wasn't much of a drinker. Aside from the work-related martinis I shared with my boss once every few weeks and the glasses of wine I consumed on even sparser disappointing dates, my Life-Alcohol-Content was zero-point-zero percent. But it was the only idea I had: to get my grief just drunk enough to stumble out of me so we could get this over with.

I stumbled and slowed about a quarter mile up the road as an extra-large white Ford pickup pulled off to the side of the road in front of me. I stopped warily and coughed as a wave of dust kicked up. As the debris settled, I saw the maroon emblem, *Madison Construction & Masonry*, on the side of the truck first before my eyes squinted to look at the driver as he rolled down the passenger window.

At least he wasn't a tourist.

"Good evenin'. Y'all right there, miss?" The distinct Southern drawl was impossible to ignore. Just like the kind smile and benevolent hazel eyes it belonged to.

What was it about Southern accents that were instinctively trustworthy?

"I'm fine, thank you," I said, still staying a safe distance from the passenger door.

"Well, this here is a pretty busy road drivin' right along Big Sur with tourist season and all. Any chance your walk got a destination in mind?" he asked and, as if to prove his point, a red convertible flew up behind him, horn blaring as it blew by him.

"In town." I looked down at my once-black shoes that were now a sooty gray.

He checked both directions down the road with worry. "Well, I'd be much obliged if you'd let me give you a lift, otherwise I'm goin' to have to drive alongside you until we get into town. Can't let you be walkin' the whole way without some sorta protection."

I didn't move at first, taking everything about him in. "Are you from around here?" He didn't look or sound like it.

"Moved up here about a year ago from Texas." His kind grin faded. "Was just leavin' a viewing for a good friend…" He gave my all-black outfit a once-over before continuing, "And I live right in town, so I can take you wherever you need."

Good friend. Funeral.

My breath faltered.

My grandfather knew I'd needed to leave all those years ago, and now, standing on the side of the road, I wondered if he somehow knew I needed to leave the funeral... leave the focal point of my past... and had sent this friendly Texan to make sure I went safely.

"I would appreciate that." With a grateful smile, I opened the passenger door and climbed up into the giant Ford, realizing why such a large vehicle was necessary beyond its owner's occupation when I saw the friendly Southern driver was also a giant.

Okay, not really. But he filled every inch of that seat and tested the limits of the seams in his clothes. Objectively, I could say that he was handsome in the fresh-off-the-ranch way, but my appreciation was tainted by the vivid memory of ember eyes and ebony hair and the tingle which lingered on my arms from where the perfect stranger had held me.

"Thank you," I murmured, buckling in and giving the cabin a once-over.

It was clean inside, the fresh evergreen scent hitting me as I noticed the air-freshener attached to the vents. But it was the open can of La Croix in one of the cup-holders that convinced me I was safe.

Serial killers didn't drink water that sparkled.

Noticing my stare, the friendly giant grinned and said, "My younger sister got me on this darn kick." He chuckled and picked up the can of 'Tangerine' water. "I don't want to like it, but for some reason, I can't stop drinking it."

This time I laughed with him in a way that was *almost* not completely forced.

"Name's Mick. Mick Madison," he said with a lopsided smile as he extended me a hand. "Pleasure to meet you, Miss..."

"Laurel," I said hesitantly. "Laurel Ocean."

His eyebrows rose as darker clouds shadowed his previously sunny demeanor. "Oh, damn. You're Larry's granddaughter?"

I nodded. *No point in lying now, I'd already come this far.*

"And you're leavin' the viewing?"

I swallowed hard, searching for any whisper of judgment in his tone but came up empty. "I can't be there anymore."

His lips pursed as he gave a slow nod, like he was processing what I'd said and what he wanted to say next.

"Your pap was a good man," he finally murmured with a remorseful nod. "A real good man."

For the first time all day, the knot of trapped emotion in my stomach loosened, ebbing a little closer to escape.

He didn't offer me the requisite 'I'm sorry for your loss,' and I could've kissed him for it. I didn't want to hear that right now. It reminded me that loss was my life. Loss after loss after loss. And right now, *this* loss wasn't real. But 'a good man'... now that was something I could agree to—something I could process. *Something I could feel in the very fabric of my soul.*

"You were friends with him?" I prompted as he turned onto Ocean Avenue, preferring to turn the conversation to the fact he'd admitted to a few minutes ago.

It was his turn to nod. "Of course. I don't think anyone lives here without getting to know Larry Ocean—and I don't mean just because he brews the best coffee on this coast," he chuckled. "My brother, Miles, and me moved from Texas 'bout a year ago. Larry introduced us to Eli and, well, that was the beginning of our construction business."

There was this Eli again... along with the inexplicable shiver up my spine.

"We woulda been back to Texas with our tails between our legs if Larry hadn't put the word out for us. I owe that man...

well, I owe that man more than I can ever repay," he finished quietly.

I ducked my head, turning to look out the window as we drove past the shops on the main street. *Crap.* I hadn't given him a destination.

"Thanks, Mick," I said hollowly, hardly recognizing half the businesses on the street anymore. "Right here is fine. You can just—"

"I owe your grandfather a lot, Miss Laurel," he interjected with a pinched smile. "And I'm going to start by takin' you to the best watering hole in town and buying each of us a shot for him." He grimaced. "I think we could both use one today."

A weak laugh escaped my chest. Maybe I really was going crazy with grief—letting a stranger pick me up on the side of the road. Letting him take me to a bar to buy me a drink.

But it made no sense why my pap had died.
It made no sense why he left everything—and left me.
And that meant I didn't have to make sense right now either.

"Another, please," I said with a polite smile to the bartender I'd met earlier this afternoon; *he was one of the plumber's boys.*

This was the musky and pervasive essence of a small-town—being unable to escape those who knew you and your story.

Poor little Laurel.

Concerned eyes gave me a hard once over, assessing if another drink was going to be one too many, before looking to Mr. Friendly Giant sitting to my left as though Mick had the final say. I may have had a few drinks, but I did *not* have a keeper.

I chewed on the empty toothpick, my head resting on one hand, my elbow propped on the rich wood bar as I slumped over the edge. My black jacket was shoved haphazardly up my arms, and the stain decorating the front of my blouse was a battle scar from where an olive had tried to escape my last drink.

I was quickly approaching a carrot-topped mess, so it was only out of guilt and grief that Mick grunted, "One more, Benny."

Benny.

A heavy sigh escaped. At least one of the plumber's three boys had a name I would now remember.

With a nod that made a stray curl fall in front of his face, Benny-the-Bartender poured me another dirty martini. *My fourth.* An easy number to remember.

Four.

For the number of funerals this town has cost me.

"Maybe after this one it's time to call it a night," Mr. Friendly Giant—*Mick*—suggested gently.

My body revolted in a way that had me grabbing my new martini and gulping down a large sip. *I didn't want to call it a night.* Doing that meant I had to go to bed. And going to bed involved finding a place to sleep—a situation that only gave me very limited and equally unwanted options.

One, going back to Diane's and subjecting myself to the tears and pity for a loss I wasn't sure I was strong enough to face.

Or *two,* returning to my grandfather's house and sleeping with ghosts. *All of them.*

Option one was completely out of the question. And as for option two… well, I was going to spend as much of the night with the Goose—*the Grey Goose*—before I moved on to ghosts.

Mick looked at his watch again. He'd done that every time I ordered another drink. Maybe I turned into a pumpkin on the fourth one or at midnight, whichever came first.

"You don't have to stay with me," I said slowly so I wouldn't slur. "My friend can pick me up and take me home."

His disbelief arched one of his eyebrows. Alcohol made me an even worse liar.

"I'll stay for a little longer, Miss Laurel." His determined smile practically blared the announcement that he wasn't leaving me alone until someone else came to be responsible for what happened when the drinking stopped.

"I appreciate that, Mr. Friendly Giant, but really, I'm fine," I insisted, this time letting his nickname slip from my lips.

I squinted at the clock on the far wall. *Good Lord, how long had I been here?* The hands on the clock seemed to sway and shrug like even they didn't know the answer. I probably should call a cab soon…*ish*.

"It's more than bein' friendly, Miss Laurel." His Southern drawl was even more pronounced—whether from his alcohol or mine—as it rolled up and over his laugh. "Larry would have my hide, even from the other side of the pearly gates, if I left his granddaughter alone—and sloshed—in a bar. Even Benny's bar."

I shuddered. *I was not sloshed.*

"I'm just gonna go make a phone call real quick. I'll be right back." Mick stood from the stool that squeaked in relief with his weight removed. I caught how he nodded to Benny-the-Bartender to keep an eye on me and swallowing my smile of annoyance burned more than the alcohol that washed it down.

I didn't care if I was the Pope's granddaughter, couldn't a girl just get piss drunk in peace? Couldn't I just be left to my own devices to find a way to grieve?

I groaned.

Whoever said grief was the price of love was a liar.

Grief was the interest. The tax. The additional, invisible cost added to love that was only collected in death.

It was everything you never expected to pay and more than you ever thought you could owe.

And I was afraid the cost might be too much for my heart this time around.

Shuddering, I lazily scanned the rest of the bar from the corner where I sat. TVs crowned the top of the wooden shelves of liquor behind the bar. The shelves... actually the whole bar... *if I could focus on it for long enough...* was a rich mahogany, weaving around in a giant L to easily accommodate twenty-five people seated around it. The wood of the shelves had carvings at the edges—the kind of handmade design work that made me think of Viking ships.

There were a few high tops with good views of the TVs and the far wall was broken up into several booths, deep green cushions covering the seats like thick moss.

And the lights, they all had green lampshades. Like a leprechaun had come in demanding only green illumination.

Carved wood. Thick moss. Leprechauns. *Apparently, I was getting drunk inside a fairy tree.*

This bar was strange though; it smelled like mint. Not smoke. Not beer. Not liquor. Minty-fresh. It was the first thing I noticed when I walked inside before a single drink had been ordered. And it caused a peculiar alertness to my stupor as though even here, even under the influence, I couldn't escape the crystal-clear confines of my new reality.

I shook my head—another mistake as everything immediately spun and swayed.

My hand slapped down on the bar to steady myself.

"You alright?" Buzzkill Benny—*both of him*—slowly came into focus.

"Yep." I grinned. "Just... ahh... remembered something..." I hit the top of the bar again as though that would make it seem more normal.

Yeah, I was getting cut off. Dammit.

That was about as clear from his expression as my drunkenness was from mine.

My head dropped, feeling like a belt was tightening around my chest. My hair that had been as straight as a sunbeam earlier now slipped in frizzy, strawberry waves over my shoulders. This is what happened when I came to this place—*I unraveled*. Right down to my roots.

I didn't want to leave the bar. I didn't want to have to go back to reality—to the memories. *To the obligations and expectations.*

I drank tonight for a lot of reasons, not in the least of which was trying to forget that I was angry with a dead man. I shouldn't be. It was *wrong* to be. But I was. I was angry that he hadn't left me the option to just calmly sail from a shore that was always stormy.

No, I'd come back and grief threw anchors over me like chains. Heavy, imprisoning anchors. Not the kind that kept you steady. *The kind that took you down.*

Pull it together. Loss has been scarred into your bones. You'll survive this like you survived the ones that came before—alone.

Straightening my spine, I looked up to see Mick had returned and was talking to Benny, both of them looking at me.

But there was someone else with them.

And then the friendly, frustrating giant moved, and the scorch from those blazing embers trailed up my spine once more. *The perfect stranger from the hallway.*

I'd recognize him anywhere—and if not from his looks, from the way his presence was like lightning through my body: the bright energy on the horizon that warned me of the impending storm.

Even though the pain was distant, I bit down hard on my tongue, searching for something to jar me from my trance.

From far away—a safe distance from the protective and

distracting warmth that I'd crashed into earlier, I took in the rest of him, everything from the neck down, for the first time.

Black suit pants that clung to him like night and his white shirt strained slightly over his chest with the sleeves rolled up to his elbows revealing forearms that had far too many veins to be legal. *Then again, I was sure they were; this was California, after all.*

My crossed legs cinched even tighter as heat flooded between them. *All because of those eyes.*

The corners of them were tipped down slightly, giving them a naturally serious stance. Not serious as in angry or somber, though. They were serious like Clark Kent searching for the nearest phone booth—*seriously determined to save the world.*

I doubted my model was about to pop the buttons on his shirt to reveal blue spandex, although I wouldn't complain if he did, but that didn't change the look that said he was coming to save me.

My whole body tingled like it should after four martinis, only this tingling had only just started. He might not be a superhero but there was something about him that felt like magic.

I groaned. *God, I hoped my friendly giant didn't bring him over here.*

A pitiful laugh escaped my chest like I'd given it a 'Get Out of Jail Free' card as they moved around the bar and began to head directly for me.

Even drunk, it seemed I never had any kind of luck in this town.

"Miss Laurel," Mick's genial tone rung next to me.

I was in trouble.

Like I was trapped in some sort of myth—definitely a Greek one because they always seem to end tragically—the giant spoke but I couldn't seem to take my eyes off the model-god who stood silently next to him.

"Let me introduce you to Eli Downing. He was a… good friend of your grandfather's."

I turned my head slowly as he spoke, knowing the face and the wood-burning eyes I was about to become officially acquainted with.

"Good to meet you, Laurel." His voice warmed me again like the heat from a fire, slowly and steadily working its way first through my clothes, then into my body, and finally settling in my bones, making me never want to move away. "I'm so sorry… about your grandfather."

My head tipped to the side like the thoughts in my brain were uneven.

And they were.

Those were the same words I'd heard from more people than I cared to remember in the past few days, each repetition digging deeper into the hurt of my heart. But when he said them, they weren't laced with pity, they were laden with regret. *Real regret.*

My brow scrunched.

Why did he sound like he was apologizing to me for my grandfather's death? Like he was the one responsible?

For the first time since I'd gotten the news, I felt the first prick of tears in the corners of my eyes. Like a mosquito bite, the sting was all it took for my body to try to fight off the foreign feeling, to swell and itch and eliminate it.

What if I gave in and it never stopped?

What if I scratched the itch of sadness and it never eased?

What if I couldn't stop scratching my heart until it was open and bleeding and unable to heal?

"Thank you," I mumbled, ducking my head and searching for something else to say. "I think… I have to pee."

Mostly, I just needed to get away from Mr. Model-Magic who was making my brain even foggier with things like emotions. I didn't like emotions. That's why I moved to L.A.

The Land of Acting. Lacking in Authenticity.

His voice strummed through my body all the way to the bathroom—which was thankfully about three steps to my left.

Just like the last time, I didn't have to pee. I did, however, need to put a stop to the crazy desire that was practically impossible to control at Martini Level Four.

With another groan, I splashed some cool water on my hot mess. Looking in the mirror, I realized it did about as much for me as a squirt gun used to put out a forest fire. My makeup was streaked, my hair was a frizzy mess, and my clothes looked like I'd just worn them to a spin class.

I covered my mouth, laughing at myself.

I might not be able to stop wanting him, but if I looked even half of what the mirror showed, that would be plenty to deter him from wanting me.

I reached for a paper towel, startled by an old photograph of the town hanging on the wall. It was of Ocean Avenue back in the sixties. My grandmother and grandfather were standing outside Ocean Roasters, the hand-carved wooden sign hanging above them, with their son, my dad, Mark, and their daughter, my Aunt Jackie, in front of them.

I gave up with a long groan. Maybe it was time to go. All I had to do was go back out there, call Diane and ask her to come pick me up, thank my Friendly Giant for the drink and his concern and Model Magic for his condolences. *Easy.*

Too easy, I thought.

Until it wasn't

I stumbled to a stop in the doorway realizing that there was only one male left standing. This wasn't how drinking was supposed to work; they were supposed to *multiply*, not *divide*.

"Where did—" I broke off because 'Friendly Giant' was the only thing that came to mind, the martinis making me blank on his real name.

"Mick had to go pick up his brother," Model-Magic replied and my body started to vibrate again. "I'll take you back to Larry's."

There were several parts of me that urged yes. Fortunately, the hardened part screamed no.

"Thanks, but my friend is coming for me." I patted my pocket like I was just waiting for my cell to ring that my ride was here.

"It's almost midnight, Laurel; Diane is sleeping."

My mouth opened and closed several times. Four martinis made forming words the newest Olympic sport.

"How do you know?" I demanded, defiantly reaching for my phone.

Who did this guy think he was?

When I tipped to the side, one of those warm, strong hands clasped my arm and held me up straight. His grip was like a lightning rod, a metallic center for all the electricity he created in my body to strike and the force of it sent me reeling.

And when I steadied next to him, the first breath I drew was brewed with the fresh scent of coffee. Even stronger than the mint of the bar, he smelled like fresh ground beans with a hint of lily.

God, I hated lilies. But I liked the smell of him. And the warmth from his touch.

I winced, seeing several missed calls from Diane along with a final text that said Mick called to let her know he'd picked me up and that Eli was going to come get me and bring me to Larry's.

Wait… this was…

Like the key to a safe, all the tines clicked into place. The funeral. The friend of my grandfather's. The coffee and the lilies. *This was the Eli I was supposed to meet.*

How had I not realized?

There were *four* answers to that question, and they were all the same.

My head snapped up to confront him and the alcohol hit me like a home run, tearing through the dizziness of first, the nausea of second, and the blackness of third, sending me sliding—or rather sinking—into home that just happened to be *his* arms.

Three

Eli

Swearing hoarsely, I caught Laurel's compact curves just as she went to tumble to the ground. *Mick was going to hear it tomorrow.* I didn't give a shit if Larry's viewing was today, he shouldn't have brought her here; he shouldn't have let her get this drunk.

Her Friendly Giant.

I huffed. If Mick was a giant, then Laurel had found the perfect sentimental stone to sling at his heart because the man had completely caved to whatever she asked.

I should've come sooner.

I didn't expect the viewing to go on for so long, and I didn't feel right leaving Diane there alone without Laurel. I reasoned Mick could handle Larry's granddaughter for a bit, but I was wrong.

"Thanks, Benny," I said tightly, adjusting my hold as he put her purse in my open palm.

What a damn day…

I'd been caught up at Roasters this morning, subconsciously

waiting until the very last moment when I'd have to face the finality of Larry's loss. Even though I'd been the one to find him in his garage. Blood everywhere. Gun resting in his limp hand. Today was the day I'd had to face his loss and the world at once. *And all the reminders of how I should've done more.*

Maybe if I had, he wouldn't be gone.

I grunted, shifting her soft, sleeping weight against me. This was the second time I held her against me, and it was just as memorable as the first. I recognized her earlier at the funeral home. It had taken a moment, her familiarity obscured by the decade that had passed since any of the photos hung in Roasters were taken.

Yet, my impression of her hadn't changed. From the photos to in-person, *she was mesmerizing.*

And infuriating.

A feat for a woman I'd known all of thirty seconds. *What the hell was she thinking, hitchhiking into town?* Christ… Thank God it was Mick who'd picked her up and texted me to let me know. The thought of her in anyone else's care made my grip tighten her against me.

"You got her?" the youngest Covington brother asked, ready to jump over the bar and lend a hand if necessary.

At that moment she sighed and burrowed her face into my chest. A burn of possessiveness shot through me. Yeah, I had her. *The problem was the unexpected notion that I wanted to keep her.*

"Yeah," I grunted roughly, glancing down at my precious cargo. "Yeah, I do."

Mesmerizing.

Her hair was the color of a burning sunset—*a warning sign of the fire that burned inside her.* And her eyes? Even though they were closed, I'd drifted so far into their rich ocean blue earlier I wasn't sure I'd be able to make it back to shore.

She breathed softly against me, so relaxed compared to what she'd been a minute ago. I shouldn't have, but I let my eyes stray down from her hair, over her freckle-studded cheeks, taking note of her adorably pert nose, and lips that were full and lush now that she wasn't frowning at me and my body began to harden.

I didn't know what hurt more: wondering how long it had been since she'd smiled, or wanting to be the reason she did.

Focus, Eli.

I gritted my teeth. I should've looked away; she was Larry's granddaughter—she was still passed out for fuck's sake.

But she was fascinating, and I was weak.

My eyes drifted rebelliously along her pristine pale neck that disappeared enticingly beneath the collar of her shirt.

Her black suit was wrinkled and covered with a fine film of dust, as though it had been balled up, run over by a bulldozer, and then put back on. But even dishevelment couldn't detract from how the fabric clung to every curve.

Maybe it was her clothes or maybe just the look in her eyes, but Laurel Ocean had a presence that felt larger than her size. From the second I met her, I noticed her strength before her stature. I noticed for being so small, she carried so much. Not like the god, Atlas, who held the world, but like an ant who, without myth or magic, carried ten times her weight in loss without batting an eye.

But holding her now, sedate and serene, I realized just how small she really was—smaller than even the photos had let on. And I'd looked at those photos for a long time... I'd looked at *her* for a long time trying to understand why she never came back.

Now, I wondered if it was the same reason she fled the viewing today without a word.

Because the strongest people would rather break alone in the shadows than risk reflecting any weakness in the light.

That truth was all too clear to me now. And it was why I told Diane I'd find Laurel and bring her home.

I might not have been able to help Larry out of those shadows, but Laurel was here and I wasn't going to let her out of my sight; *I owed him that.*

Still she fought me with a fire that bled into her thick, silken hair that draped over my forearm, right up until she passed out, all soft and warm and woman into my arms. My body—*especially my cock*—really took notice of that. My heart though had me holding her like I could hold her troubles, even just for one night.

"See you tomorrow," Benny said with a heaviness in his voice. It was a hard day for the whole damn town, there was no denying that.

Tearing my eyes from my warm cargo, I grunted goodnight and carried my passed-out princess over the threshold and out to my truck.

"Where... am I?"

My eyes flicked to the passenger seat as Laurel shifted, dragging her gaze from the black outside the window over to me.

"W-Who are you?" Her blue gaze was a tempest. *The perfect storm: beautiful and tragic.*

I slowed, turning onto the gravel drive that led off the cliffside highway down to Larry's cabin that sat both in the mountains and by the sea, looking out over the rocky cliffs down to the Pacific.

"We're almost home," I answered quietly, belatedly realizing this wasn't actually her home.

"Don't have a home." Her head slumped back to look out into the night.

"You do now," I informed her, turning on my high beams because the brush had grown thick over the drive even in just a week.

"Don't want it," she argued weakly.

Intoxicated *and* intractable.

I bit my tongue, wanting to remind her that it had been in their family for centuries—just like the coffee shop. Today, it was worth millions even though it was small.

She needed to want it.

I needed to make her want it.

"Well, you're going to want it for tonight so you have some place to sleep," I said, throwing my truck in park right next to Larry's old Nissan and came around to the passenger side.

My whole body jolted to a stop when I opened the door to see how her very business-like black blazer was caught tight up under her chest, popping two of the buttons open on her white blouse, and pushing the almost glowing white swells of her tits up.

Fuck.

Again, I found myself ogling the questionably-conscious granddaughter of the man who'd been like a father to me. My gut clenched as another wave of guilt and grief came over me.

Larry Ocean had been the closest thing I had to family.

He'd given me a home when I had none, taught me how to work at the coffee shop and then how to run it until I'd made enough of my own money to start my construction business. He gave me a place, a purpose… he taught me what it meant to be a part of this community: *to help others*. Birth, race, sex, background, education… none of it mattered to Larry because it didn't matter to the important things in life—like how to treat people with kindness and respect, to love your neighbor when they need it, and let them love you when you did.

There was a reason the line into the funeral home stretched for miles earlier: when a good man dies, the whole world felt his loss.

Like a natural disaster, only the permanent scars left from the destruction were all held internally by everyone who knew him.

And *this*—I looked down at the bulge in the front of my pants—was how my body decided to repay him.

Groaning, my fist slammed into the side of my truck like that would stop my dick from hardening or convince my eyes to look away.

If Larry knew, he'd smite me. Then he'd kill me.

What happened next wasn't exactly in that order, but with a miserable groan, Laurel turned to the side, her arm falling from the edge of the seat to swing right into my already painfully hard nuts.

And if doubling over in white-hot pain wasn't enough satisfaction for that man, Laurel's head tipped to the side as she vomited down onto my shoes—*shoes I would have to put on again for the funeral tomorrow.*

"Point taken, Larry," I rasped weakly, looking up to the clear night sky, the stars twinkling with laughter like he really was watching.

I barely got a minute to recover from the assault before she angled farther out of the door.

"Shit." I caught her and pulled her out into my arms.

"Where am I?" she murmured again, wiping her face of I-didn't-want-to-know-what on my shirt—*also to be worn at the funeral tomorrow.*

"Home," I bit out again, fumbling for the spare key that Larry always kept hidden underneath the coffee bean container disguised as a planter.

"Don't want a home," she murmured again and I winced at the hurt-filled sentiment. I opened the door and carried her down the step, tossing my keys onto the dining room table. "Hate the word home. Homes are hollow. Hollow hurts."

Christ.

The strain on my chest had nothing to do with her weight in my arms or maneuvering her through the door.

I wondered if Larry had known. All the times when he brought her up, when the look of it-was-for-the-best regret came over his face, I wondered if he knew how she hurt.

"Let's get you to bed," I said hoarsely, turning on the dim light in the bedroom.

I felt like Peter Pan capturing Tinker Bell, her sprite-like form and whimsical hair, caged in my arms. Maybe her magic would help me finally catch all my shadows that had been eluding me.

All I'd ever wanted was a home and this girl wanted to give hers away. I prayed that sober Laurel was less stubborn than her pap because she needed to stay. She couldn't just give all this up and walk away. *I wouldn't let her.*

"Have to pee."

Biting back a curse, I walked over to the bathroom door and carefully set her down on her—bare—feet. *Dammit. Where were her shoes?*

"You okay?" I asked, holding her by the waist to make sure she was steady all the while trying to ignore how I was holding her very soft, warm waist the same way I would if I were going to kiss her.

I wasn't.

But I wanted to.

"I know how to pee, Model Magic," she retorted with an exaggerated eye roll.

"Model... magic?" I stared dumbfounded only to be answered by the slam of the door in my face.

Running a hand through my hair, I let out a long, strained groan and went to the kitchen in search of paper towels to wipe off my shoes. Maybe Diane would know what to do with them after tomorrow.

Grabbing a handful, I walked back to the bedroom, and sat on the edge of the bed to wait for Laurel to finish, not trusting her to make it the five steps from the bathroom to the bed without falling and hurting herself.

My whole body ached like I'd run a marathon. The viewing had been more of an emotional strain than I ever could've anticipated. The only thing I saw in Larry's urn was his face when I found him in the garage, lifeless and bleeding from the self-inflicted gunshot wound... and all the ways I hadn't done enough to prevent it.

All the ways I'd failed him.

I shuddered and willed those thoughts from my mind; those demons were only allowed to haunt me when I was alone.

But Laurel, she was here, and I had a chance to make this right. I could prevent her from leaving. I could prevent her from giving this town one more loss it wasn't ready to deal with.

I could and I would. I promise, Larry.

As if bidden by my thoughts, the bathroom door opened and my redheaded pixie stepped out.

Wearing nothing but her underwear.

"Jesus Chri—where are your clothes?" I stood rapidly and demanded even as my gaze roamed down her body. Black bra and matching black underwear were hard to miss against skin that was the color of moonlight and starred with freckles.

"I think..." she began, turning back to the bathroom and allowing me to correct myself—black bra and matching black *thong*—before shrugging, "Did I throw up on them?" Her head cocked. "I think I threw up on them."

Fuck. "Right, yeah, you did a little, but—"

"I'm not sleeping in puke," she cut me off and unsteadily sauntered toward me.

Groaning, I tried not to look. I tried to quell the strain against the front of my pants while she passed by in my periphery. *Do not touch.*

Don't even think about it...

She almost made it to the side of the bed before her sway tipped the scales from upright to topple.

Fuck. I wasn't going to survive long enough with this girl to convince her to stay.

My arms shot out and hauled her back steady against my chest, all those warm and soft curves from earlier back to torture me. *Only naked this time.*

"Why do you keep catching me?" she muttered as she leaned against my chest, my grip on her upper arms steadying her.

"Because you keep falling." Why I didn't let go right away or sit her on the bed... those were questions I hoped weren't coming next.

Her head tilted and need shot straight to my dick as pale blue orbs looked up at me—barren on the surface but promise held deep underneath.

"I don't drink," she mumbled, her eyes swimming as she swayed closer to me.

"I figured." My voice was hoarse.

I felt every movement, every breath as it pushed her breasts against my chest. I felt the soft skin of her arms underneath my fingers and wondered if her nipples were just as velvety. I saw the dark spark of lust in her eyes and the way she licked her lips as she stared at mine. The pink tip of her tongue a cruel tease on my cock that wanted to be licked too. Mostly, I felt the way she leaned into me and not just with desire, but because without all her walls, the weight of her worries was too much for her to bear.

"Don't want to be here," she continued softly, a wash of despair falling over her beautiful face.

God, I'd do anything to take it away. In the same way I'd do anything to bring Larry back.

Laurel Ocean had always been an enigma. She'd left Carmel at eighteen for school after her parents died. I knew Larry had paid for it. I didn't know why she'd never come back. I didn't know why she didn't keep in contact with her grandfather or the rest of her family.

I wanted to know. I *needed* to know.

I'd never had a family. Larry... the people I'd met here... were the closest I'd ever come. I needed to know because I couldn't fucking fathom why you'd turn away from that—from people who loved you.

Her eyes flitted shut and she sagged against me only to jerk back the next second awake again.

She was going to have a helluva hangover tomorrow.

"Why?" I rasped. This might be the only time I'd get an honest answer from her.

She looked at me like her answer was as obvious as gravity. Tipping her head to the side, a sad smile tugged on lips that were too beautiful to say something so despairing.

"Every time I come here, I lose something. Don't want to lose anything anymore."

My jaw tightened and desire dulled against the utter bleakness in her voice.

Beautiful and beholden.

That was how she looked in the bar. She came here out of obligation, knowing this town would take something else from her before she left, only the hollowness in her eyes confessed she didn't have anything left to give.

I wanted to hold her. I wanted to show her that there was something here for her to fight for. She may have lost her grandfather, but there was still a family—a community here that would *give* her something and not take anything away.

I felt her uneven breaths, her softness molding against me. My cock throbbed against her thigh, imagining her bare skin against it.

Wide eyes fluttered to mine.

"Are you going to kiss me?"

There are moments in life where the smallest thing—an action, a word—course-corrects the path you'd been on. And with that question, everything about the path I'd been taking suddenly shifted.

The turns, the choices, the desires... they now all pointed to this woman.

Finding her secrets. Healing her hurts.

Making her mine.

I dragged in a heady breath. Her pink, lush lips remained parted as the words floated unevenly in the air between us. It couldn't have been more of an invitation if there'd been an RSVP line attached at the end—one that my dick was ready and waiting to sign.

My head dipped.

There were so many things that felt wrong about today. But this... her... it was the only thing that seemed right.

I wanted to kiss her. *I wanted to know what mesmerizing tasted like.*

She shivered ever so slightly, but it was enough to remind me where I was—*and who I was with.*

Tightening my grip on her arms, I pushed her back. I

couldn't kiss her now; *I wouldn't*. She hardly knew me—and if she did, well, she might rather kill me than kiss me for the role I'd played in the loss of her grandfather.

With that sucker punch of guilt slamming into my gut, I grunted, "No, I'm going to help you into bed."

The unearthly trance held for another second before her head fell—whether from a nod or because she couldn't hold it up any longer.

"Good, because I think I might—" And then she threw up on my shoes. *For the second time.* Thankfully, this time there wasn't much left in her to lose.

I looked up at the ceiling. *Was that my punishment for wanting to say yes? For wanting her?*

Ignoring the way my body throbbed, I lifted and put her in the bed. Grabbing one of the paper towels I brought in with me, I pushed back her hair from her lips and cheeks and wiped her mouth. She was completely out now. It hurt to see how, even in sleep, there was still a sadness that lingered on her face like dew on the grass after a storm.

"I won't let you lose anything, Laurel," I rasped with a low voice even though she wasn't listening. "While you're here, I won't let anything else be taken from you, I promise."

I sat there, to the detriment of my dick, until I felt sure she wasn't going to be sick again. Then, too exhausted to remember the regrets this house held for me, I kicked off my shoes, walked out of the bedroom, and dropped onto the couch.

Before she left, Laurel would know just how much there was here for her—and that if she still decided to go, any loss would be by choice and not by chance.

Four

Laurel

It wasn't a dump truck that rolled over my head, it was an eighteen-wheeler. Oversized. Little flags of warning waving off the sides and everything.

I peeled my eyes open like I was pulling a Band-Aid off a raw wound. Slowly. Painfully. Too scared to rip it straight off.

With tunnel vision, I scanned my surroundings. There was a small nightstand next to me, but it had no clock to tell me the time. A dark mahogany dresser against the far wall next to the bathroom door and, in addition to the bed, that was the extent of the furnishings and decor.

White-washed wood walls… surfaces… everything was bare. *And familiar.*

My eyes dropped to the floor, speed-bumping over the pair of dirty black shoes that were unlaced and left by the side of the bed.

Black shoes.

Men's shoes.

I sucked in a breath, my hand covering my mouth. Worse

than a walk of shame, my head tipped down to confirm that I was, in fact, in just my underwear.

Had I slept with someone?

Oh, God.

I couldn't remember much after the second martini with the Friendly Giant… *Mick*. He'd been telling me about the town, trying to gauge how long it had been since I'd been back. I didn't have the heart to tell him how each story only made me drink faster. But being drunk was a better alternative than having to think about my past.

Peeking over my shoulder, I let out a breath I didn't realize I was holding seeing the empty and untouched space next to me.

Whose shoes were they?

My head pulsed like there was a rave going on in my brain. Wincing, I fought through the party I regretted RSVPing to and slid out of bed.

Unsteadily, I made my way out of the room, stopping with a gasp in the doorway to the living room. *I'd been so focused on the mystery shoes that it hadn't hit me where I was… where I'd slept.*

My grandfather's house.

Suddenly, the eighteen-wheeler in my head was nothing compared to the tank that rammed into my heart, throwing all of its nostalgic firepower against an already damaged and retreating organ.

Memories fought through the hangover fog to remind me of Sunday pasta dinners with my whole family, the days Jules and I had sleepovers in the living room snacking on jellybeans and watching the latest Mary-Kate and Ashley movie.

Those were days when my grandmother was still alive, and Jules hadn't been sent to boarding school. Those were the days before my parents had died.

Those were the days before I realized love and loss would always go hand in hand.

I dragged in a huge breath, the familiar scent of dark coffee beans mixing with nostalgia and twisting the knife.

Before I could get irrevocably lost down the rabbit hole of reminiscing, my head turned and my heart skipped at what I saw.

The perfect stranger from the viewing.

Model Magic.

Like one of those old slide reels, snapshots of the night before filtered into my mind. The giant leaving me with this man—the one who looked like a god and acted like my savior. Drink after drink. A ride that wasn't called. The tall, dark stranger carrying me inside, tucking me into bed.

And a question that could've led to something more...

I shuddered. That one couldn't have been real; it couldn't have been more than a drunken dream.

Tousled hair framed his sculpted face, his broad, bare chest rising and falling softly as he slept. He looked exhausted, like down to his soul exhausted. My mouth watered, seeing the smattering of dark hair decorating his muscled chest and abdomen. One arm rested on his stomach, the other draped over the side of the couch, both laced with a map of veins that led my body into dangerous territory.

My eyes lingered a little too long at the black pants that were tight all the way down his legs, but especially by his waist. And then my perusal abruptly stopped at his feet.

His shoeless feet.

Anger flashed through me. *How dare he undress me?*

Rounding the corner, I yanked the first kitchen utensil I could find and stalked back into the living room. My emotions and less-than-conducive hangover blinding me to the fact that I was still undressed—*and that I was poking his chest with a whisk.*

"Hey." The thin metal tines bent and caved against the solid male chest.

Warm brown eyes shot open as I jabbed his muscled peck again.

"Laurel." His morning voice was like salted caramel—smooth, with just the right amount of roughness.

"Who are you?" I demanded, poking him again.

His eyes flicked down to my embarrassing, in hindsight, choice of weapon.

"Eli," he replied, dragging his gaze slowly back to mine. "Eli Downing."

Eli. I blinked as more tiny pieces from last night came back.

This was the man everyone murmured about with rich reverence, who commanded so much authority and admiration. He was the one Diane insisted I meet, and who she'd sent to bring me here.

Where he'd stripped me and almost kissed me.

"How dare you?" I bristled.

His eyebrows rose. "How dare I what?"

"How dare you bring me here and undress me?" I poked him again. "I don't know you. You don't know me. I don't care if you knew my grandfather, that gives you no right To. Take. Off. My. Clothes." Each word was punctuated with another jab into a chest that seemed to grow harder with each assault.

A fact my lower body took particular notice of.

"Okay," he grated, one hand shooting up to grab the whisk, his forearm flexing. "First off" —he tugged and the utensil slipped right from my grip—"what were you really planning on doing with this? Whisking me to death?"

I glared at him and crossed my arms. *Okay, I could've chosen a better weapon.*

The metal clattered as he dropped it onto the couch and rose in front of me.

"Second" —his head angled just inches from mine—"*you*

were the one who took of your clothes... clothes you're still missing, by the way."

I sucked in a breath and glared at him, refusing to look down even though I felt my face heat.

"And why would I take off my clothes? Were you really trying to get some from a drunk chick? Seriously? Picking up a chick from a viewing is low," I accused tartly.

His growl was feral as he advanced. "You took them off because you thought you puked all over them. You didn't. You just puked all over me. *And my goddamn dress shoes.*"

Taking a closer look now that he was right in front of me, blocking out everything else, I saw the stains just visible on the front of his black pants. *It also explained why he was shirtless.*

"Oh." I gulped.

"Yeah, 'oh,'" he said roughly, running a hand through his hair that seemed to move like the finest silk. "Fuck, what time is it?" He turned, digging in the couch and pulling out his cell. His eyes narrowed. "We have to be at the funeral in an hour. You should probably get dressed so we can go. I grabbed your bag from Diane's and put it in the bedroom."

I nodded, too embarrassed to say anything else at the moment as I shuffled toward the door.

"Are you going to change and come back then?"

He half-turned, and I couldn't miss the way his eyes flared as they stared through the rest of my sparsely-clad form. *Stripped in a blink.*

I sucked my lower lip between my teeth. Now that I wasn't so offended by his presence, the effect he had on my body was much harder to ignore.

His gaze left a trail of fuel as it slid up my body and the grating rasp of his voice lit the path on fire.

"Don't have another set of nice clothes," he said with a low, tired voice. "Never thought I'd need a back-up. Never planned on saving you—and being puked on in return."

"Sorry," I mumbled regretfully as he turned and walked toward the kitchen—probably headed for the laundry room. My tongue darted out to wet my lower lip, catching sight of how the back of his pants fit just as well as the front.

"Don't worry about it," he instructed without looking back.

When he opened the door to the garage, I turned back into the bedroom. Grabbing the other fresh set of black attire from my bag, I winced when I found the pile of my clothes from yesterday on the bathroom floor. *Now* the foggy memory of removing them hit me.

Alright, I was wrong about that part—but that didn't mean he'd saved me.

I didn't need a savior. I didn't need anyone. Not then. Not now.

I'd left Carmel at eighteen. Four years before that, Jules was sequestered from me, two years later, my parents were gone, a year after that, my grandmother, and at eighteen, Larry paid for my dream college, freeing me from this place… and from the last close family I had.

And, to survive, I cut off the idea of home like it was a bag of sand tied to my waist. Otherwise, by the time I saw through my tears, it would have drowned me.

No, Eli Downing hadn't saved me. But he had brought a drunk girl home and made sure she was okay. My sigh turned into a small groan. I should be thanking him instead of poking his unreasonably muscled chest with a whisk and accusing him of trying to take advantage of me.

This was what happened when my mind was invaded by emotions I fought to never feel.

Longing. Grief. *Desire.*

Tugging on the fresh clothes, I glanced in the mirror and ran my fingers through the red halo of waves to try to tame them. I needed to thank Eli and then move on. From him. From this place. Especially when he looked at me with a glimmer of responsibility.

Like he needed to take care of me.

My head throbbed and I dragged in a deep breath. He may have been a friend of my grandfather's, but whatever their relationship was, whatever he felt like he *owed*, it wasn't to me.

Eli Downing wasn't beholden to me.

Five

Eli

Bang. Bang. Bang.

The gunshots from the military salute rang like solemn sonic booms. Jarring breaks against calm, ocean-swept air.

The more private crowd that gathered in the graveyard focused on the servicemen as they fired their rifles. But my gaze was solely trained on her.

Laurel.

We'd ridden in silence over to the funeral, her emotional and physical pain straining her delicate features. She'd hadn't moved a muscle the entire service. Not to run. Not to cry. Hardly even to breathe.

Nothing until this moment when she jerked as though the shots were fired directly at her, each one ripping a new hole in her heart.

Her cropped black pants and black blouse shifting as though blown by the breeze. But I was close enough to see the wind had nothing to do with it; it was her small fortress of fortitude that shook under the assault, and my hands tightened where they remained clasped in front of me, doing everything I could to not reach over and comfort her.

Then they were folding the casings into an American flag. A lost life reduced to three buried shots in thirteen folds.

But when they came to present her with the folded flag, she froze, staring at the union stars with her hands handcuffed in front of her.

The next thing I knew, I reached out, murmuring my thanks to the veteran and retrieving the flag from his outstretched hands so the service could conclude. As he walked away, I placed one hand on the small of Laurel's back.

"It's alright," I murmured to her, and we stood like that until everyone filtered back inside the church hall for the small reception.

"How did you know him?" she asked thickly once we were alone.

My jaw tightened as I stared at the open earth where his urn would soon be.

"Larry helped me get on my feet... make a life here... when I moved from San Francisco," I told her, omitting the details about why I left and the exact circumstance of my meeting Larry which were irrelevant to this conversation. "I worked at Roasters for a few years while I built my own business."

"I see." She turned to face me, her expression hardened and withdrawn. "He did that for many people, though. Why does everyone look to you? Why are you here in the front row, next to me? Next to my aunt?"

I grimaced, the truth a ball of acid in my throat. "Because I helped him," I rasped. "Because these last few years were hard... and getting harder... and I was the one who helped him keep everything on track. I was the one who made sure everything with him and Roasters was okay."

And I'd failed on both accounts.

She nodded like my presence made more sense now.

"He was the closest thing I had to family, Laurel," I confessed raggedly. "He treated me like family."

She flinched and leveled me to the ground with her stare. "He was my family," she said tightly. "But I understand. And I'm grateful you were here for him and for everything you've done, Eli, but you don't have to do this. I don't want or need you to do this."

"Do what?" My eyes narrowed.

"This." Her throat bobbed as her hands reached out and took the flag from me. "Helping me… taking care of me… everything… whatever it is you feel like you owe me, because of him, I'm telling you, you don't."

I fumed. "That's not why I'm doing any of this, Laurel."

Her head jerked and she continued like she hadn't heard me, "You don't owe me anything, just like I don't owe you or this town anything. There are no strings attached here. I came for his funeral and now that it's over, I'm leaving. My aunt will get Roasters and everyone can be satisfied it's still in a former-Ocean's hands."

I reached for her shoulders so she couldn't turn away.

"I don't need anyone to take care of me," she insisted, defiantly.

I stepped closer to her, the air growing dense with desperation and desire. "I never said you did, Laurel," I bit out. "But is it so bad to let someone?"

She glared at me, a wordless answer.

"He's gone, Laurel," I continued with a low voice. "For both of us." She tensed. "You're standing here as strong as a statue, as delicate as glass, and just as stubborn as your grandfather. I can't imagine what this is like for you, but I won't apologize for trying to help. It's okay to lean on someone every once in a while."

"No," she choked out as her face splintered with sharp hurt. "No, it's not okay, Eli. My grandfather may have taught you a lot, but let me give you a tip he probably left out—the second you lean on someone, they disappear out from under you."

"Well, let me give you a little tip," I shot right back, my grip tightening, seeing the swell of grief inside her, too scared to break free. "I'm more stubborn than you damn Oceans, and I'm not going anywhere."

Her stance faltered. Her blue eyes grew dark and stormy and drifted down from mine to lock on my lips that had dared to utter such a promise as she swayed against me. Part of her wanted this. Part of her wanted support. Someone else to help her bear the weight.

Part of her wanted me.

"You're right." She nodded. "But I am," she informed me hollowly as the other parts of her, bruised and battered with fear, won out. "Back to L.A. And as soon as possible."

And then she turned and broke from my grasp, heading inside with the flag clasped to her chest as though it were a life raft.

Swallowing a whole string of curses that I wouldn't let loose in front of the dead—especially when they were in regards to his exquisitely mesmerizing but extremely frustrating granddaughter—I squeezed my eyes shut and pinched the bridge of my nose.

What the hell was I going to do?

She was running. To nowhere. To no one. *And I wanted her to run to me.*

"You alright, Eli?"

My eyes popped open to see Ash Tyler approach. *Another broken man who Larry had provided solace.*

Ash had moved out here about six months ago with a severe alcohol problem and several ghosts that haunted him. Larry had given him a place to stay, a place to work, and, most importantly, a weekly Alcoholics Anonymous meeting to attend until he got his addiction under control.

I screened my expression. Larry had been his sponsor—his savior. And, like most of us, Ash had taken his loss hard. I wouldn't let my troubles add to that. I would hold it together for everyone else.

"Yeah." I nodded quickly.

"You sure?" He looked at me skeptically. "You don't look okay."

I speared my fingers through my hair, finally admitting, "Just struggling to help Laurel."

Ash's jaw ticked. "The hardest people to help are those who don't want it."

God, if that wasn't the truth.

I flinched as his hand gripped my shoulder in comfort. "I know, I just—"

"This isn't your fault, Eli," he cut me off. "None of it. Not Larry, and not what happens to Laurel."

I felt the grip around my heart tightening, every beat of my pulse calling him a liar.

"You know when Taylor showed up on your doorstep asking for help?" I asked, alluding to the scene a few months ago when Ash's now-girlfriend appeared on his doorstep, pregnant and needing a place to stay.

He nodded.

"That's how I feel right now. Only, Laurel isn't asking for help, she's fighting to leave when she has no place to go." I exhaled raggedly. "More than that. She's fighting all of this," I told him. "We've all cried. We've all mourned. God, Ash, I haven't seen a single tear from her."

His brow furrowed. "We don't know her. Maybe her relationship with him... wasn't good," he suggested. "I mean, she hasn't come home in so long..."

I shook my head. He was wrong. I knew it like I knew the sun set in the west.

"Even if you're right." He paused and sighed. "You can't help her if she won't take it. Just like you couldn't help him."

I shrugged away from him with a low growl.

Maybe that was why this bothered me so much. Selfishly, I wanted to help Laurel because I couldn't help her grandfather. Not out of obligation, but absolution.

"Maybe leaving is what will help her."

I swallowed hard. "I hope that's not the case."

"Why?"

"Because there are two very large obstacles she can't just leave behind," I told him. "And she doesn't know about them yet."

Laurel

I still felt the burn where Eli's hand pressed on my lower back out by the grave—as though even when he wasn't next to me, he was still supporting me.

I didn't want to take comfort in having him stand next to me during the service. I didn't want to take comfort in him accepting the flag because I was frozen with fear at the finality of the action. And even now, I was only moving steadily because of the ibuprofen Eli had unceremoniously instructed I take before leaving my grandfather's house this morning.

It was so tempting to lean on him.

So tempting to cling to him.

So, I pushed back. Harshly, but out of necessity.

"Laurel?" I turned to face kind green eyes and a small smile attached to a petite yet very pregnant woman. "I'm Taylor Hastings, Ash's girlfriend. I don't know if you've met him yet, but he was very close with your grandfather."

"It's nice to meet you, and I don't think I've met Ash, though I can't be sure," I returned as kindly as I could. "These last few days have been—"

I broke off with an 'oomph' as she pulled me in for a hug and consoled, "I'm so sorry for your loss."

"Thank you."

She drew back, asking, "Will you be in town for long? We're opening a restaurant in a few weeks right on the coast. I know…" She paused. "I know it would mean a lot to Ash for you to be there. He's… umm… dedicating it to Larry."

Of course, he was, I thought blindly as the guilt creeped in like a black fog. Everyone else seemed to have an outlet for their grief except me.

"I don't think I'll be here. I have to leave. I have to get back…"

"I understand." She nodded solemnly.

"Congratulations," I offered, nodding to her stomach, and eager to change the topic to anything else.

"Thank you." She beamed, her hands resting on her bump. "Would you believe I thought it was the end of the world when I found out?" My eyes widened at her unexpected confession. "I was so afraid; it wasn't how I thought my life was going to go." Yet her smile widened. "I came here afraid to face my family, terrified of my future, and fully prepared to follow this path alone. But then being here…"

My breath lodged in my throat. Her story was nothing like mine. Yet it resonated in the deepest parts of me.

"What?" I heard myself press.

"It changed everything. Letting Ash in. Letting myself lean

on him, trust him to take care of me. Take care of us." She chuckled and wiped a stray tear from the corner of her eye, clearly so in love with the man she spoke about. "I didn't expect anything from this place, and here I am, just a few months later, with more than anything I could've asked for."

My throat constricted. My heart pounded in my chest, beating against its cage for me to let it out—*to let it feel.*

But her story wasn't mine. Her story started here, and here was where mine would end.

"That's really wonderful. I'm happy for the two—three of you," I said unsteadily, noting the twinge of jealousy that bloomed. "I wish you all the best."

"Thank you." She wrapped her arms around me once more and murmured, "I wish you all the best, too, Laurel. Wherever that is…"

Her genuine goodwill warmed me, and I found myself hugging her back, a stranger I'd just met, feeling as though we'd been friends for some time.

But that was how loss worked—it exposed vulnerabilities that linked people in ways others took years to find.

When she walked away, I caught Eli's gaze from the other side of the room. He stood next to a blonde male, both men watching our conversation intently. A second later, I realized why when Taylor approached and the man, who must be Ash, pulled her comfortingly to his side.

I looked away.

I didn't like when he watched me because he was the only one who really saw me. Eli was the only one who could see the sadness seeping through my clothes and skin, soaking into my lungs and heart. And he was just waiting for the second I showed signs of drowning so he could jump in and save me.

Swallowing hard, I turned and walked to a table in the

corner where Diane set a small plate of food for me. With a sad smile permanently etched into my face, I was a synchronized swimmer in an ocean of loss, going through every choreographed motion that the crowd expected from me.

"Laurel," Diane called softly as she approached and slid into the chair next to me. "I wanted to introduce you to Mr. Gavin Ross." She turned and motioned for a tall gentleman in an expensively-cut suit to come and take a seat in the remaining empty chair. I pegged him for some kind of professional—*and I was right.* "He is the attorney handling Larry's last will," she explained. "Mr. Ross, this is Larry's granddaughter, Laurel Ocean."

"Miss Ocean, I'm so sorry about your grandfather," he offered with a smooth voice, one I imagined would be pleasant to listen to even as he argued a case in court.

"Thank you," I murmured. "Please, just call me Laurel."

I shivered as warmth crawled up my spine and my eyes flicked to the ember eyes absorbing my every expression. I wanted to scream that just because I might have gotten a little too drunk last night and needed a ride home, needed someone to get me into bed after I threw up on him twice and ruined his only suit, and needed him to take me to the funeral this morning, didn't mean I needed anything else from him.

"Laurel," he began with a tight business-like smile, "I know that this is a very hard time for you, but I wanted to make you aware of the main stipulations in your grandfather's will since I know you live in Los Angeles. I wanted you to be able to make plans accordingly."

What was he talking about?

I folded my arms. "I appreciate that, but I'm not sure what I need to plan for…"

He glanced at Diane and a sense of foreboding drifted over me.

"Miss—Laurel." He cleared his throat with a nervous twitch, looking side to side, before leaning forward and informing me, as though it were the greatest secret, "Your grandfather left his personal property on Coastline Drive to you, as well as the Ocean Roasters business and building."

My mouth dropped open like a fist had closed around my throat, gaping and sputtering at the news I couldn't believe I was hearing—*that I couldn't believe was true.*

"I-I'm sorry," I stammered. "Did you... he did... what?"

I dragged my gaze to Diane but found no comfort in her expression.

I hadn't heard wrong.

But just in case, Mr. Ross repeated, "It's okay. I know this is a lot right now, but I heard you might be leaving soon, so I had to let you know that Larry left it all to you, Laurel." His hands clasped tightly on the table as his lips tightened. "I have the deeds to the properties at my office in town that I can bring to you, or if you'd like to pick them up, I'll just have a few papers for you to sign as well."

He'd left it to me.

The house.

Roasters.

My head shook like I was trying to come up for air against a current that kept dragging me down.

"Why me?" I blurted out, having nothing left to mask my dismay. "Why not my Aunt Jackie? She's his daughter. She lives here," I rambled unreasonably. "She should have it. She should be next."

I felt Diane tense, and I understood her reaction.

My aunt had never wanted nor would ever want anything to do with Roasters—part of me knew that. But she was still his daughter. And when I left… when I told him I couldn't stay here and I couldn't come back, I thought he understood… I thought my grandfather knew she would be the one to inherit it.

"Well," he drawled slowly, "I can't say why he didn't leave it to her. Unfortunately, he never mentioned his reasoning to me. I only know what the document says."

"Does she know?" I found myself asking.

"Not yet," he told me. "I needed to be able to tell you first since you are the primary beneficiary. I will be reaching out to your aunt this coming week."

I exhaled through tight lips. "Of course." I nodded. "I'm sorry. I just wasn't expecting this."

Unbidden, Taylor's words came back to me. *'I didn't expect anything from this place, and here I am, just a few months later, with more than anything I could've asked for.'*

"I can imagine." He appeared to relax a little. "I'm sorry to spring this on you, but I wanted to give you as much notice as possible," he informed me. "What I need won't take long, but there is some paperwork and such that will need to be handled before you go."

Before I go…

How could I go now?

Two buildings.

One business.

And nothing of what I wanted.

"And after I sign them?" I asked.

He blinked at me, taken aback by the question for a moment. "Then they're yours."

Words bubbled up inside me, a product of the reaction between fear and necessity, as I asked calmly, "And if I'd like to sell them?"

Diane froze next to me—the kind of freeze that could start an ice age. I didn't look at her though. *This was my decision, my choice.*

It was Mr. Ross' turn to stare. "Of course, that would be your prerogative, Laurel—"

With a skid of her chair pushing back from the table, Diane interrupted him as she stood, "I'm s-sorry. If you'll excuse me for a moment." I tried to ignore the way she wiped her eyes and walked away from our table and straight toward Eli.

What the hell…

Anger immediately lit inside me. It was none of his business whether I sold my grandfather's house and business or not—and he certainly wasn't going to be able to do anything about it, let alone change my mind.

"You were saying, Mr. Ross?" I encouraged him to continue.

"Gavin, please. But yes, of course, once the deeds to everything are in your name, you are free to do what you wish, and I'd be more than happy to recommend a realtor to handle the sales if you don't already have someone in mind," he continued with hesitant helpfulness.

"Thank you. I would just like to get everything settled so that I can get back to Los Angeles as soon as possible for my job and everything." I winced at how cold that sounded.

I didn't even know why I mentioned my job. My boss told me to take all the time I needed to handle my family's affairs.

"Miss Ocean… Laurel," he corrected himself again. "If I may… I know that you just arrived back in town after being away for some time. I understand that you've made a new life elsewhere, however, you must see how much your grandfather and his business has affected the lives of those here in Carmel Cove."

I bristled, feeling like I was about to be scolded. He didn't know. *No one could know what this town had cost me.* And they all expected me to just come back here and give it more pieces of myself to destroy.

"I just ask that you proceed with caution. Perhaps, you could talk to Eli before you make any decisions. He's a good man and was very close with your grandfather…" He made a move to look over his shoulder at the subject of his statement but then, thinking the better of it, refocused on me. "He's been doing a lot at Roasters over the past few months, and especially after the break-in a few weeks ago—"

My small astonished gasp brought his statement to an abrupt halt.

His face reddened almost to the color of my hair. "Oh, I'm sorry. Did no one… has no one mentioned what happened?"

"No." My head jerked side to side, my eyes still wide in surprise. *A break-in? At Roasters?*

The sharp pang in my chest couldn't mean anything; *I refused to let it.*

It was just a business. *Just a building with my name on it.*

He let out a heavy sigh. "I'm sorry to put this on you. I thought you would have seen… or heard by now…" He pinched the bridge of his nose. "There was a break-in a few weeks ago."

"What happened? Did they find… did they arrest who did it?" I demanded with a slight tremble I tried to hide.

The way his expression soured told me that they hadn't.

"Not yet, unfortunately. I don't think the authorities have put much time into it since, in spite of the destruction, nothing of value was really taken."

"Destruction?" I squeaked out.

In my mind, Carmel Cove had frozen in time the moment I'd crossed the town line. People. Places. Things. All snapshotted in my memory and preserved.

I'd been back all of three days and it was becoming

impossible to ignore how so much of what I knew had changed… *had been destroyed.*

Gavin's strained look told me that destruction wasn't an exaggeration. "A few weeks ago, one of the baristas, Eve, went into work and found the place in complete shambles. The cases, tables, chairs… the photos on the wall…"

My stomach rolled with nausea.

Roasters had been the same for the eighteen years that I'd known it and I had no doubt that my grandfather preserved every square inch of the building even after I was gone. All of those pieces… it was more than just furniture and equipment and photographs… it was a life—*it was his life*—that had been nailed into every beam, painted on every wall, placed in every frame, and brewed into every cup.

It was his life though, not mine. As much as it hurt to think about who would have done such a thing and how much it must have killed him to see it, I wasn't going to change my mind about selling; there was no life for me here.

"It was a bad enough sight that Eli had to keep your grandfather away; they were worried what seeing it like that would do to him."

And now he was gone. Maybe they hadn't kept him away long enough…

"And they don't know who did it?"

"Covington Security has been trying to track down leads since the police let their investigation fizzle, but your grandfather's death put a pause on their progress," he replied.

"Covington… like the plumber?"

"Yes, well, the two older sons. Not the father," he explained. "They have a private security firm in town."

Recalling their stature and demeanor, this information was the least shocking of what the lawyer had to say.

"Don't worry. It's much… much better now," he reassured me

quickly with a wave of his hand. "But there was a lot of damage on top of all the renovations Larry really should have done on the place years ago."

"So, what are you saying?" I asked, my voice a little weaker while trying to process what repercussions this loss was going to have on me. "I can't sell it?"

"No, no." He waved his hand. "You certainly can, it just might be difficult. And you'll probably be able to get more if you repair it first," he tacked on for good measure. "But I would talk to Eli first and see what he has to say. I don't know all the details of the damage or what needs to be done."

Of course. Ask Eli.

Meet Eli.

Talk to Eli.

Let Eli take you home.

Ask Eli to kiss you.

I groaned.

Eli Downing was becoming just as inescapable as the coffee shop I'd inherited.

"I see," I replied hollowly.

"I'm sorry to be the one to lay all this on you, Laurel," he apologized sincerely.

"It's your job," I replied, reaching for one last brave smile. "I appreciate your help. I guess I will be in touch with you this week then to get everything squared away."

His mouth all but disappeared as he nodded and stuck out his hand for me to shake before rising from the chair and leaving me to the first tumultuous moment of the 'after.'

My grandfather was gone and buried. Now began the battle to pick up all the pieces he'd left for me, pieces that were little weights tied to my heart with steel thread, tethering it to a place that would only break it. *Again.*

Did no one understand?

I expected loss from Carmel like I expected night after day. The problem was while everyone else withered under darkness, they looked to me like I was responsible for bringing back the dawn.

But I didn't know how to do that; I only knew how to run from the night.

And now, there was one more thing to hold me here. My heart beat painfully with fear and anger and longing… emotions that I didn't want to have—*that I shouldn't have after all this time trying to escape them.*

As everyone faded away, I whispered a silent apology to the man who'd snuck me my first cup of coffee, the man who brought me sweet treats when he picked me up after school, and the man who'd held me the day my parents died—the day I cried so hard it made me throw up, the day I threw up so violently blood vessels in and around my eyes burst, the day it felt like the world was ripped from underneath my feet.

I apologized to the man who'd only ever shown me stoic strength that I wasn't able to mourn him, and then I prayed for his forgiveness because I was going to be the one to ruin our legacy.

But I couldn't stay here.

I couldn't keep the coffee shop or the house.

I couldn't live in this legacy of loss.

Of course, when I looked up it was to immediately find Eli's *inescapable* gaze with concern spitting from the embers in his eyes.

How I felt around him was one more complication I didn't need—*and one more desire that would leave my reckless heart broken even more.*

Six

Laurel

It was a new day, but my problems had nothing new about them.

"Are you sure you don't want to wait until Monday?" Diane asked as we pulled away from my grandfather's house.

My second night sleeping with ghosts had been just as fitful as the first, only there hadn't been a half-naked handsome stranger on my couch nor a painful hangover when I woke.

"No, I need to do this now," I replied as we approached downtown Carmel.

Diane still had a shadow of tears in her eyes and gnawed on her lower lip to stop herself from bombarding me with questions about why I was going to sell Roasters. *It didn't matter, I still heard them all.*

My heart picked up speed as we turned onto Ocean Avenue. It had been so long...

Break-in.

Destruction.

I winced.

"I'm sorry I wasn't the one to tell you, Laurel," she said with a nervous pitch. "I wanted to prepare you, and I was just trying to find the right time. I didn't realize Mr. Ross would bring it up."

I propped my elbow on the edge of the window and rested my cheek on my hand.

"It's okay," I told her, the irony of this town not lost on me.

On one hand, I was so fragile that information was being doled out in small pieces to help me process. On the other, they believed I was strong enough to blindly remain in a place where the air physically hurt to breathe, and put back together what was broken, just so this town wouldn't have to lose its beloved coffee shop along with the owner.

"I do want to prepare you," she repeated, hazarding a glance at me. "It's pretty bad… what happened…"

"He already told me there was a break-in—"

"Well, yes, there was a break-in. I mean, not really a break-in, of course, because your grandfather, *stubborn old goat*, didn't have a doggone lock on the door—" she broke off with a shake of her head, like there was no point revising that train of thought. "I just want you to be prepared because it's still… a little bit of a mess. The investigation took a backseat with Larry's passing."

"It's fine," I reassured her with a thick voice, watching the unassuming Ocean Roasters sign, with its decorative swirls carved into the deep wood, loom closer and closer.

My stomach lurched forward like the car had run into a brick wall as we pulled into a spot right out front. But no airbags deployed. No safety measures. Nothing to protect me from what happened next.

Diane began to talk again as soon as the car was in park, but I couldn't pay attention. I was still focused on the sign hanging out above the door and over the sidewalk. The wood looked more weathered, and the words that had always been painted gold now looked the color of muddy driftwood.

Again, the lawyer's words reminded me that my grandfather hadn't kept up the maintenance on the building for some time; and I'd bet he hadn't painted the sign since I left for college… *over a decade ago.*

I didn't wait for Diane, whose heels clonked somewhere behind me, as I reached for the doorknob and pulled it open.

Coffee beans.

Their aroma washed over me with bold colors. Rich and sweet strokes with a dash of invigorating alertness painted a picture of the past so vivid it stopped me in my tracks. The shop filled with customers cozying up at tables, chatting at the counter with my grandmother. My grandfather standing behind it, working the espresso machine, a perfect smile lighting up his face when he saw me and exclaimed, '*Ishkey.*' A scene of community and family so alive, I forgot, for a singular split-second, when and where I really was.

I took another deep breath of the coffee-flavored nostalgia—lifetimes of memories brewed into a single building—a single business. Rich and aromatic, it soaked into your veins and, like caffeine, made your heart beat a little quicker, your thoughts come a little faster, the warm familiarity making it seem like anything could be possible.

Anything was possible with coffee.

But with love? With family? I wasn't so sure about those anymore though…

And then I blinked and it was gone. *He was gone.*

And the hole in my chest grew.

Everything was gone. Along with some of the chairs, the clear bakery case, and the pristine espresso machine. Everything about the memory faded into reality as I stepped through the doorway.

Shock tore through my chest. My heart pounded like I was in the middle of a race—a race to escape the sight in front of me—a race to escape my fate.

Only about two tables were upright, making the space seem even emptier. The cushion on the bench that was built in along the wall on the left was completely ripped up and taped back down with duct tape. The bakery case that sat on the long portion of the L-shaped counter on the right was gone—destroyed if the small pile of glass that had yet to be cleaned was any indication.

The wall-papered walls were dented and torn, the paper hanging every couple of feet to make the room look savagely striped.

I couldn't stop a small whimper when I saw all the frames of family photos extending back four generations sitting stacked on the counter instead of where they used to hang on the wall above the bench. The glass broken. The frames marred.

My throat swelled and burned. I brought a hand to my face, but still no tears came. I felt just as broken and hollow as this place. Beaten and bruised from loss. And what tattered remains were left weren't enough to make this—*me*—whole again.

A few more steps brought me in front of the short length of the L-counter where the register was. My fingers gripped on to the end of the counter for support when I finally got a good look at the dual La Pavoni espresso machine behind it.

If the Oceans were the heart of this business, that machine that we'd always called 'Pavi' was the soul—and the soul looked scuffed and scratched and dented. It looked like it had been put through the wringer—and maybe it had, losing the last Ocean who would ever work it.

"He still works."

I jumped with a small screech as a slender woman with long, black hair and pouty lips stared at me through giant, thick tortoiseshell glasses that made her bloodshot brown eyes big. After a quick scan, I saw that she was wearing a long-sleeve tee, pushed up to her elbows, underneath a set of worn denim overalls that were stained with various brown spots.

"Sorry, you scared me," I said with a strangled voice.

"Oh, I'm so sorry. I thought you saw me come through," she explained, looking over her shoulder at the hallway to the back of the shop where she'd come from. "I'm Eve… I met you earlier… I'm not sure if you remember."

As soon as she said it, an image flashed of those same watery eyes, magnified behind large lenses, red from crying as she offered me her condolences.

"Yes, yes I do." I nodded. "Sorry. Just a long day. Just a lot…"

"Of course." She gave me an understanding smile. "Don't apologize. I'm just… I'm glad you're here. I've been working for—" she broke off as her head ducked and she sucked in a steadying breath. "I mean I was working for your grandfather here as a barista when this…"

I relaxed a little further and realized that the brown stains on her clothes made sense if she was working with the coffee machines all day. Before I could say something more, she pressed on.

"He was a good man—a good friend to this whole town. Family, really. He just knew everyone, you know. Always knew what to ask about, what to talk to them about. I mean, there were days people would come in and talk to him and completely forget to order their coffee; it was like it wasn't Monday morning if they didn't stop in and say hi to Larry—" She broke off with a stifled sob.

"Thank you," I said, gently.

I knew what Larry Ocean was to this town. I knew what the Oceans were to this town. They were the family that made everyone—locals and visitors alike—feel like they were coming home every time they stepped into Roasters.

But that was the whole point, wasn't it? They *were* family but no longer. First my parents. Now my grandfather. The idea of our family became just as spread out and diluted as a few coffee beans dropped in the ocean.

"Do you want me to make you a coffee?"

I shook my head even though I could have used one. I was afraid—afraid of what might happen if I drank the coffee from here, like it would be made of magic beans that could change my mind. "No, thank you."

"Okay, well I was just finishing up a few things in the back, if you need anything." She ducked her head.

The back was obviously just a safe space for her to let out the tears she'd been trying to hold back for my sake.

"Thank you," I said as Diane reappeared at my side before I could.

"Hello, Eve," she quickly greeted the other woman quickly as Eve left us alone. "Laurel, were you listening to anything I said?"

She wasn't scolding, she was pleading.

"I'm sorry, I just—"

"Don't apologize," she blubbered and pulled me in for a hug I wasn't expecting, engulfing me against her generous chest which is about where my head fell given how much taller she was than me especially with those heels. "I was just hoping that when you saw it, that you'd reconsider your plans. You know, for your grandfather's sake."

I jerked back, shaking my head 'no.'

I didn't know what she thought was going to happen—that I would walk in here and remember all of the good times, all the days I'd played here with Jules or sat with my parents after church, snacking on a fresh blueberry muffin, or the times that my grandfather sat me on the counter and let me take peoples' orders while he made coffees—and decide to stay.

No.

I walked in here and saw how I'd lost all of that just as surely as Roasters had lost its furniture and pictures and mugs and plates. This place was nothing more than a monumental tombstone to all my losses.

"Diane, I'm sorry, but I can't—" I had no idea what explanation I'd been about to give her, but whatever it was, was cut off by the wonky twang of the bell as the front door opened and a very large man walked in who looked so familiar.

A second later, his twin, my Friendly Giant, followed right behind him.

"M-Mick?" I croaked, looking back and forth between the two of them.

"Hello again, Miss Laurel," he said with a half-smile, pulling off his worn ballcap and tipping his head down in greeting to me. "If you remember my brother, Miles." He nodded to the more stoic-looking, less mountain-like man next to him.

"Ma'am," Miles said with the exact same twang and the exact same nod.

"Nice to meet you," I murmured quietly. "What are you doing here?" I looked to Diane on one side of me and then back to the twin pillars of Southern charm on the other.

"Well." Mick paused to clear his throat. "We were told to head on over here to re-assess what work needs to be done to get Roasters back and ready to rodeo. Been tryin' to get in here for months just to do minor maintenance, but your grandpa… he was as stubborn as a mule—and we had mules on our farm growin' up, Miss Laurel, so I'd venture to say he was more stubborn."

He let out a sad laugh because even good memories hurt. *I knew that. I could have warned him.*

"Larry kept insisting that everything was fine. And then the break-in happened. They let us clean up some while the police investigated, but then Larry…" He ducked his head in quick reverence. "Anyways, we're here now to put this place to rights."

"I appreciate that," I drawled slowly. "But I'm not sure I'll be needing your help. I plan on selling the whole building and business."

Mick took a step back, his large frame shuddering. Meanwhile, his brother turned away to hide a curse that still echoed loud and clear.

I heard a gasp and a quick glance over my shoulder revealed Eve who'd made her way back into the front of the shop to greet the new arrivals only to walk into my blunt statement.

"Of… of course, you can do what you want to do, Laurel," Diane chimed in, trying to diffuse the bomb I'd leveled the entire room with. "I asked them to come." Her hand came up to rub my arm like I was the one trying to convince someone to do something they didn't want to do. "Well, I asked Eli if they could all meet us here to take a look. I thought maybe if you saw the place, that you'd want to fix it up first, and then decide…"

I struggled to hold back a groan.

"To be frank with you, Miss Laurel," Mick began, running his hand along the brim of his hat that was bent in his hands. "There's a lot of work to be done here and not just to spruce it up after the whole break-in business. Ash managed to replace half the roof with some help a few months back, but that was only after there was a major leak in the back. The other part of the roof is still leaking."

He let out a long exhale as he pointed to the wall that had previously held all the photos. With a second look, I realized that there were some stains running down from the ceiling where a faint, irregular brown rim suggested consistent water damage over a long period of time.

As I dragged my gaze back over to the group, I couldn't help but notice how Eve was staring at me, wide-eyed underneath the huge rims of her glasses like I'd just ripped her heart out by announcing my intention to sell the coffee shop. I wanted to scream that whoever bought it would surely want to fix it and keep it.

Why did no one seem to understand the price I would pay by staying here?

A small voice inside my head replied, *Because no one here really knows you, Laurel, and that was how you wanted it.*

"Dollars to donuts, Miss Laurel," my Friendly but not-so-favorite Giant at the moment continued, "as soon as I get in there, underneath the drywall, I'm going to have to look at replacin' the framin' and probably the electrical, too."

I tried to swallow down the truth that was quickly becoming evident to me: for as long as I'd neglected Carmel and my grandfather, so had he neglected the upkeep on Roasters.

"I see," I replied with a tight smile. "But I'm sure that will be disclosed to the buyer and then you can work with the new owner to fix it."

The door dinged again and just like the smell of coffee jump-started my memory, the presence of him ignited my heart. I knew it was Eli before my eyes made it to him.

My inescapable complication.

"Unfortunately, that's not going to be possible, Laurel," he drawled with a hoarse voice, his shadowed gaze catching mine.

This place affected him. *Me* in this place affected him.

"Oh, Eli. I'm so glad you're here," Diane said softly with relief.

I didn't respond to her, instead crossing my arms over my

chest, I shifted my weight on to one leg and raised my chin up in challenge. "Why not? Mr. Ross seemed to think that would be fine earlier."

Okay… that was a little bit of a stretch. He said I would be fine to sell it, he didn't say anything about having the repairs done beforehand.

"Mr. Ross isn't a realtor," Eli drawled as he walked closer to me.

"But you're qualified to make that judgment?" I gaped, the words flying out before I could stop them.

Sure, he'd helped my grandfather, but that didn't mean he knew anything about buildings or selling them…

"Well, I'm a contractor," he replied, his eyes dancing. "So, yes, I would say it's my job to make those judgments."

Dammit.

Even my size five foot was still a mouthful.

I hadn't known what he did—*aside from holding everything about this place together*. My eyes roamed quickly over him, seeing him in a new, frustrating light as more perfect pieces of him clicked into place.

Today, he wore a long-sleeve white t-shirt and what looked like work jeans with the way there were paint stains and a few worn patches on them. Strangely, it made him look no less like a model, only now instead of suits, he was modeling the latest in painter chic. *Like Clark Kent—if Superman had masqueraded as a carpenter instead of a reporter.*

I bit back a groan as my whole body warmed. My boss would have a field day with the look.

Stay rational, Laurel. This wasn't his call either.

"That doesn't—"

"And he isn't an inspector," he continued firmly right over my protest. "I will tell you right now, with the water damage in this building, and the old electrical running through it, there is no way that the shop will pass California's pre-sale building inspection."

As he spoke, he pointed around to more spots behind me, behind the espresso machine and the pastry counter that I hadn't noticed. "You'd have a better chance of California falling into the ocean before you find an inspector willing to risk his license to sell this building in the state it's in."

As he spoke, the pebble that had been skipping across the surface of my stomach inflated into a rock and sank like a boulder.

Everyone else faded from the room and all I saw was the dilapidated remains of my larger-than-life yet all-too-tragic past coalescing into handcuffs around my heart. I knew if I came back here this would happen.

I knew this town wouldn't just let me come and go in peace.

I must have swayed where I stood because the next thing I felt was the small burst of heat from where Eli's hand wrapped around my upper arm, his other gently resting in the small of my lower back.

"It'll be okay, Laurel," he said roughly, as I turned to stare blankly up to him. He didn't know but it would never be okay. "We'll fix everything up to code, and then you can sell it if that's what you want."

That phrase made me nauseous, especially while I tried to sort through the thoughts in my head—the task like trying to filter through a jar of sand looking for one specific crystal.

Shaking my head in denial, I pulled away from him, wrapping myself with my arms like some sort of shield.

Fine.

If I needed to fix this place up, then that was what I would do. But just because it needed to be fixed, didn't mean any of them had to be involved.

"Well, then I guess I don't have much of a choice," I said firmly, making sure my chin was held higher than my hopes because I knew that my chances of making it out of Carmel without more damage to my heart were slim. In fact, if my past was any indication, it was more so guaranteed.

"Thank you for your help, Eli," I said smoothly, taking my hands and planting them on my hips. "But I think Mick, Miles, and I can handle it from here."

I looked over at my friendly giant just in time to see his eyes widen as he began, "Oh, no, Miss Laurel—"

My chest constricted.

"Laurel," Eli spoke softly, stepping in between my betrayed look and its victim. "I'm here because I was the one who took stock of everything before Larry... passed... I'm the one who called those guys because they work for me; they're my carpenters."

No, no, no.

This. All this, right here, was what happened to me in this town at every single turn.

It wasn't enough I'd inherited a business laden with heartbreak. It wasn't enough that business was housed in a building too run-down for me to even be able to legally sell until it was fixed. No, it had to come to this... where Mr. Model Magic —the stranger who'd carried me home from the bar, the man who I'd puked all over—*twice*—and then accused of trying to take advantage of me, the man who looked like he wanted nothing more than to take care of me... *that very man* was the one in charge of the only thing standing between me and my freedom from Carmel Cove.

He was also the man who made my body light up like Clark Griswold's house in Christmas Vacation... twenty-five-thousand twinkling tingles burning with enough desire to take out the whole block.

I shuddered violently and stepped back.

My pap... my parents... always used to say how this town was healing. That, in spite of the influx of tourists, Carmel was a place that healed those who came to live here. I wondered if all that healing came at my expense—at my hurt.

At my heart.

"And what if I decide I don't want to use you or them?" I asked softly so only Eli, who'd shielded me from the rest of the group, could hear. "What if I want to find my own contractor?"

"You're welcome to do that," he said roughly with a quirked smile, and I knew I'd lost the argument before he even continued speaking. "But I worked in this coffee shop for years before I started my business, and I've been in here almost every day for the past year helping Larry. I've already assessed the damage. I know where every problem area is going to be. You want to hire someone else? By the time they get out here and then take the time to get the list that I have, you're looking at least another month and a half before any renovations even begin."

Shit.

"And I'll tell you this, too." He cleared his throat and glanced over his shoulder at the brothers before leveling me with a serious, steadfast stare. "Your grandfather did a lot for me—for everyone here—so everything we do, we don't do for money, we do for him. You hire someone else, you're going to have to pay them and, for a project of this size, you're looking at close to thirty grand, if not more," he informed me calmly. "So, by all means, if you want to waste more time and money—go for it. But if you want it done and you want it done right, then you're going to work with me."

I held his gaze for a few seconds, not trusting myself to say anything at first.

"Well, I very much appreciate it," I finally choked out.

"You're welcome to get started on what you need but I'd like to be kept informed of what you plan on doing and what you find."

I wondered if everyone else felt the wave of relief that rippled off of him like I did.

"Of course," he murmured. "We'll finish up here and then get started first thing Monday morning if you want to stop in we can go over what needs to be accomplished and how long it will take. If there is anything else—"

This time I cut him off with a hand and a smile that didn't reach where it should have. "Thank you, but it's been a long day." I stepped to the side so I could meet Diane's eyes, adding, "I think I'd just like to go home and get some rest."

As soon as I saw her semblance of a nod, I murmured a quick goodbye and fled out into the cool, fall air.

No one else might, but with each step back to Diane's car, I heard the clank of chains around my ankles,

I was obligated to the town to sell the business to someone who would keep it running.

I was obligated to the new owner to fix it up—to restore Roasters to what it was before my world crumbled.

And now, I was obligated to my too handsome contractor who was doing it all for nothing.

Even if I wanted to use someone else, I couldn't. Sure, I had some savings but not nearly the kind of capital required to fix Roasters; I did well but not that well. And I couldn't justify the expense out of stubbornness when Eli would do it for nothing.

My stomach knotted and I flipped the door handle to realize the car was still locked and Diane was still inside the shop making her goodbyes.

With a heavy sigh, I sagged carefully against the side of her old red mustang. My head dropped back to see the darkening clouds above me, moving quickly over the whitewashed sky.

He'd said they were doing it for him—for my grandfather. I knew my pap. I wasn't surprised to know he'd helped a lot of people since I'd left. I knew how much it had hurt him to know he couldn't help me. But Eli looked at me as though it wasn't the only reason he was offering to help.

I shuddered and crossed my legs. I didn't know what he did to me... I was attracted to him, but there was something else he made me feel, something that the protectiveness and concern in his eyes managed to get under my skin and into my soul—and that something had me pushing him away out of instinct because *that* something was the kind of thing this town liked to take from me.

Cruelly. Unexpectedly.

And without a hope of ever fully healing.

Please, don't let this take any more from me.

As though sensing my desperate plea, the heavens opened up and released a deluge of cold irony.

To save this place, it wouldn't cost me anything. *And, at the same time, it could cost me everything.*

Eli

"What are we going to do?" Diane murmured as soon as Laurel disappeared out the door.

My whole body was hard—and not just because I kept remembering what she looked like standing over me this morning wearing nothing but her underwear. I was tense because if I had thought managing Larry's stubbornness in the past few months—months when his mood deteriorated and his patience waned thin, months when he'd slowly stopped taking the antidepressants Dr. Shelly had prescribed—if I thought that had been difficult, I now saw that I had my work cut out for me when it came to his granddaughter.

Those were also the months when I should've been the one to realize he wasn't taking his meds and forced the damn pills down his obstinate throat. Maybe then he'd still be here…

"Is she… is she really going to sell Roasters?" Eve's strangled question softly floated through the silence.

Larry had hired Eve when Ash began construction on his restaurant, knowing he'd need a replacement for the recovering alcoholic when he left to manage his own business full time.

When I first moved to Carmel a decade ago, I'd been the one behind the bar, learning from the great Larry Ocean how to make exceptional espresso and, more importantly, how to make people feel welcome and safe.

I cleared my throat hoping it would remove the emotion lodged in it.

Diane began, "It does seem like she is intent—"

Staring down at the pictures stacked on the counter, I interrupted her gently, "Let's not jump to any conclusions right now. She only just got here. She needs time."

I traced my finger over the top one. It was the photo I always stared at when it hung on the wall on the other side of the room. It was of Larry and Mark and Laurel—three generations—taken just a few months before Laurel's parents, Mark and Fiona, were killed in a boating accident. It was her eyes—their Ocean blue—wide and welcoming. *But no more.* Looking into that gaze a moment ago, all I saw were the walls built up around her heart, high and strong out of necessity. But I wasn't sure if those walls were meant to keep others out or hold her sadness in, though I had a feeling it was both.

"She doesn't want to be here, Eli. You heard her," Diane insisted with a voice that wavered with just as much pain as the rest of us felt. "She's going to hide away until you are done here and then sell the place and not look back. Poor girl is hurting, and I can't say I blame her, I just wish circumstances were different."

Gritting my teeth together, I turned to face the small group. "She's not going to hide away. She's going to be here, every day, watching this place come back to life."

"Why? She won't want to do that."

Maybe... maybe if I could get her here in the shop, around the people who loved her grandfather, maybe then she'd finally let herself heal. If I could just make her realize that this didn't have to be another loss for her, that she could stay here and gain a future with the town that thought of her like family.

Fuck, it was a tall task. But I had to try.

For him.

For her.

I had to try.

As though calling me out on my partial truth, the image of her curled into my chest, too drunk to filter the emotions bleeding from her heart when she begged to not lose anything else to this place, whispered that my mission—*my need*—to get her to stay had some to do with her grandfather, but more to do with the beautiful, broken woman who was scared to come home.

More to do with wanting to be the man who made her feel safe to stay.

And more to do with selfishly not wanting to let her go.

And I didn't give a shit how stubborn or determined she was, I would show Laurel that this place was worth loving.

"She will come if she thinks it will get her closer to leaving. And when she's here, somehow, I'll figure out a way to show her this is where she belongs. With us."

With me.

The thought came unbidden and I shook it off like it was an involuntary twitch that came from my heart but shouldn't suggest anything serious.

Roasters was her home. Carmel was her family. *Now more than ever.*

I wasn't going to let her lose her legacy and the love that came with it, no matter what it took.

Seven

Laurel

I bolted upright on the couch as a loud pop jarred me from where I'd fallen asleep in the middle of catching up on work emails on my iPad. The tablet skidded and thumped onto the floor, unharmed, at my sudden movement.

Something was definitely leaking.

Tossing it back onto the worn cushions, I darted for the kitchen where the loud pop and now swishing sounds were coming from. The noise grew louder as I approached though I didn't see anything immediately.

As soon as I rounded the island, my stomach did a somersault when I saw water running down the seam of the cabinet below the sink, the door vibrating against the pressure. I thought it sounded funny earlier when I'd filled my glass of water from the tap, but figured it was just old pipes.

It was just old pipes… *old pipes ready to burst.*

Without thinking, I bent down and opened the cupboard, only to be greeted with a spray of water right to my face.

Squealing, I stumbled back, my arm coming up to shield my

face just as I slipped on the water already coating the tiled floor and falling directly on my ass, the pooled liquid wasting no time in soaking through my lounge shorts.

"Are you kidding me?" I yelled up at the ceiling, like God, or more likely, my grandfather was listening.

It wasn't bad enough I had a coffee shop which was neck-deep in water damage and overall disarray, but now the house I was staying in—*the house I'd also inherited and had to sell*—just blew a pipe.

With a strangled cry, I grabbed ahold of the counter to help myself stand, wincing at how sore—and wet—my ass was. Pushing the wet strands of hair that clung to my forehead and face back, I took one more good look at the water pouring out onto the floor before the thought hit me that I had no idea what to do.

One might think the thought would have struck sooner—maybe when the spray smashed into my face or water sent me crashing onto my ass, but no. I could apply fashion tape with surgical precision to menswear that *almost* fit right, but how to fix a pipe that was spraying water all over the kitchen. Nope. *Not a clue.*

Running back to the living room, I grabbed my phone and pulled up Diane's number. Just as quickly as I tapped on her name, I ended the call. *What was I thinking?* Diane wouldn't know how to fix a pipe either—she ran an art studio for Pete's sake.

Shit.

I had only one other number in my phone for someone in this town. Someone who'd insisted I put it in my contacts the morning of the funeral—*right after he'd handed me ibuprofen to take for my headache.*

And if I thought realizing my house was flooding, and I

didn't know how to stop it was bad. Realizing that the only person who could help me right now was the very man I was trying to avoid was even worse.

I wished I had George, the plumber's, number. I wished I had time to get his number. I wished I had time to get anyone else's help except for the number I was dialing.

"Hello?" Like I'd just stepped in front of a fire, his voice sent a spray of warmth up my spine.

"Eli?" I croaked. "It's Laurel. I-I have a problem."

Understatement of the month. I had lots of problems. And somehow, I seemed to be reaching to him for each and every one of them.

"What?" His tone immediately deepened into something sharp with concern. "What's wrong? Where are you? Are you okay?"

I groaned. "I'm fine. The house is not. I… I got a glass of water earlier and the next thing I know, there was this loud pop and a waterfall landed in the kitchen," I rambled as my hand waved in all directions like he could see what I was motioning to. "There was water coming out from below the sink, so I opened it and now there's water everywhere and it's not stopping, and I don't know what to do and—"

"Laurel," he cut me off decisively. "Breathe. Do you know how to turn the water off in the house?"

"No." I walked back toward the kitchen and saw the water was now running into the dining room and pooling around the chairs. "Oh my God… it's everywhere."

"Laurel, listen to me." His voice was steady like he had all the answers and knew exactly what to do and even with, what looked to me like flooding, it calmed me. "I want you to go into the basement and follow my instructions, okay?"

"Yeah," I replied thickly, nodding to no one, and hopped

through the puddles that scattered the path to the garage and the basement door.

Over the next few minutes, I tried not to freak out in the small, dark cellar while I followed Eli's instructions, directing me toward the main water valve for the house and told me how to shut it off. I let out a long exhale when I heard the flow of water come to a stop.

I could have hung up—he could have hung up. But he didn't. He stayed on the phone while I went back inside and confirmed the spray had come to a halt. I didn't say much as he calmly told me to just start cleaning up the water, and it felt like barely a minute later when he came bursting through the door.

"You're here." I stood immediately, looking back and forth between him and the mess on the floor.

"You needed me," he replied simply. The way his eyes locked on me made me feel as though the words were anything but simple. "Are you okay?"

He glanced over my sprayed and soaked form.

"Y-yeah. I'm fine," I said a little too unsteadily for my liking. His shoulders sagged with relief and he finally took a look at the damage. "Just irritated."

My head ducked and I wrung out the towel I'd used to soak up some of the water into a bucket.

He stepped around me, his arm brushing mine for barely a second, sending sparks down my body. I reached for the counter to steady myself. I may not know how to fix a pipe, but I knew that water and electricity don't mix and right now, I was wet and he was sparking.

"Larry has a tool bag out in the garage," he said with a strained voice as he craned his neck under the sink. "I'm going to grab it and then, I can get this tightened up for you."

He disappeared and then returned a minute later with the tools and some more towels to mop up the water.

"Put these under you," I said, taking one of the towels and laying it on the floor for him.

He cocked an eyebrow at me, clearly not as concerned about getting his jeans wet as I was, before crouching down with a muffled 'thanks.'

The tool bag clunked when I set it on the counter and pried it open.

"Can you hand me the wrench on top?" His voice echoed in the space underneath the sink.

I was about to ask how he knew the one on top was the right one when I realized that it was the only decent-looking, if not only, wrench in the bag.

When I turned to hand it to him, my body froze at the sight. The way his shirt pulled and bunched over the hard planes of his stomach, the way his arm muscles bulged against the fabric as he reached for the pipe underneath the sink… the twenty-four hours I'd gone without seeing him made my attraction hit harder, not softer as I'd been hoping.

He'd come when I called, all hot and heroic, and I wondered if it would've been safer to let the house be submerged.

"Laurel?"

My gaze dropped, my cheeks warming, as I handed him the wrench and our fingers connected like frayed wires in a puddle of water, the electrical shock instantaneous and intense.

I jerked my hand away, and thankfully, he caught the unsteady tool before it dropped.

"You alright?" he asked again. I swore I could see the embers in his eyes flickering in the shadows of the cupboard like he was some sort of supernatural creature; he would have to be for him to think he could save me.

"Yes," I assured him firmly before grabbing my towel and bucket and moving to clean up the water that had made its way into the dining room. "So, you're a contractor and a plumber?" I tried to make light of a moment that only grew heavier.

His laugh echoed from the cabinet. "Not a plumber, just know how to do the simple things like fix a leaky pipe and jerry-rig the water heater to make sure hot water comes out."

My lips turned up in a smile. "Did my grandfather teach you that?"

"No." His voice strained and I gulped, imagining all those muscles flexing tight as he closed off the leak. "No dad around to do it when I was young, and my mom was… sick a lot. Couldn't afford the real thing, so I learned the good old-fashioned way. Along with some carpentry, automotive, and even electrical. And cooking. Although I'm not sure which of those was more dangerous to the house—attempting to rewire circuits or trying to cook food."

"I'm sorry," I said softly even though upset was the farthest from how he sounded.

"Don't be. Just meant I learned early on that most things in life, no matter how broken, blown, or busted, are still worth fixing… no matter how much damage they seemed to have caused."

My eyes locked on my hand frozen on the damp towel soaking up water. *Was he talking about me?* I felt the undercurrent of longing, of wanting to lay his words over me like a balm, but it was swiftly quelled with the lash of anger that roared defensively through my veins.

Just because he could fix a pipe didn't mean he could fix me— or the curse of loss that hung over my head.

"Larry taught me other important things," he continued wryly. "Like the art of roasting the perfect bean." He grunted. "And how sometimes a good cup of coffee has nothing to do with the brew and everything" —he groaned— "to do with the conversation and compassion it comes with."

I put a fist to my mouth, a cry lodged in my throat.

"Coffee and community," he went on, huffing as the wrench clanked against the metal pipes. "That's what Roasters is all about, right?"

It took every ounce of strength to swallow down the pain and strangle out a reply. "Yeah."

There are two kinds of hurt. There was the kind you could see coming and the kind you could never imagine happening. If I could see it coming, it wouldn't be so bad... to love... to live. *But I couldn't.* I didn't make bad choices. I didn't love people I knew would hurt me. I loved people who were good people, who promised to never leave. Who promised to always be there for me. It wasn't my fault for trusting and loving them, and it wasn't their fault they were gone.

And if it was no one's fault, then there was no explanation. There was nothing I could do to stop it from happening again except never let my heart out of my sight. So, that was what I chose to do.

No. Not chose.

That was what I did.

A few minutes later, with only the clanking of Eli working under the sink, I'd mopped up most of the water, wringing out the excess, and depositing the damp, used towels into the laundry room off of the garage.

Back in the kitchen, the cupboard beneath the sink was closed, the tool bag had disappeared and it would have looked like nothing had happened even though twenty minutes ago, Niagara Falls had been gushing from that very spot.

"Moment of truth," he grunted.

I jumped slightly at his rasped voice from behind me, having gone into the cellar to turn the water valve back on. I felt the barest touch of his hand on my arm as he shifted around me to reach for the sink.

My breath caught.

Not because I was afraid of another flood, but because he was still touching me—*and I'd made no move to remedy it.*

A gentle stream flowed from the sink a moment later.

My shoulders sagged with relief, and I offered him a weak but grateful smile. "Thank you."

"Of course." His eyes captured mine. "I'm always here to help."

And just like that, guilt washed over me. One more problem Eli had to fix. One more thing I owed to him. It was the worst feeling—to feel like I was beholden to him and this town, to my family's legacy when I had nothing left to give it.

Like trying to draw water from a stone, or in this case, pull a solid foundation out of an ocean; it just wasn't possible.

"Don't worry about it," he added as though he could hear my thoughts spilling out and was just as determined to put a wrench in them.

"Well... I didn't know what to do... I really appreciate it. I guess I will see you this week," I offered as a goodbye, and shied back toward the living room.

We may have cleaned up the water, but the mess of emotions it caused were something I didn't want to risk revealing in his presence.

"Laurel." I jumped when I heard my name come from behind me. "It's not your fault," he continued gruffly. "Everything is going to be okay."

I turned to face him and my breath caught, realizing how close he stood. I swallowed over the lump of desire that inflated like a birthday balloon in my throat.

Of course, it wasn't my fault. I knew that, but I didn't feel it. Instead, it seemed like everything was just crumbling around me. *Literally.*

"Pipes are old. Just like the ones at Roasters," he insisted, and I could only nod.

I wanted to cry, and it was the most ridiculous feeling. Days of dealing with death, getting Diane's call, the viewing, a funeral, a grieving community, and not a single damn tear. But *now*, a leaky pipe was what would do me in?

Why now? Why this?

"I know, thank you." I shouldn't have spoken because the impending tears watered my words. "I'm fine. Really. It just scared me. I'm fine."

"*Christ.*" I heard him swear before I felt myself tugged hard into his solid chest.

I should protest. I hardly knew him. Unfortunately, from what I did know, resting against him was the only place that felt safe enough to process some of the pain, knowing he'd protect me. "It's not your fault, Laurel."

He repeated the words over and over again with a gravity that made the sentiment more than just about the stupid pipe. Meanwhile, I stood still, like a petrified animal in his warm embrace.

I didn't hug him back. I didn't even sob. All I could do was let a few streams of tears leak out to relieve some of the pressure building up inside me.

I shouldn't be leaning on him for this—for comfort. I knew better. Leaning on someone only guaranteed a fall when they disappeared from your life.

But I couldn't stop myself.

He was so warm and solid. The thump of his heartbeat underneath my cheek so determined and strong. For a second, I let myself believe there was nothing that could take this man away from me—*as though he were mine or something crazy like that.*

It was probably only a few minutes later, even though it felt longer, before I dragged in a clogged breath and moved gingerly from his embrace. I didn't want to leave it. It felt like so many of the other things about this place—familiar, yet foreign.

"I'm sorr—" My apology fizzled and died on my lips when the hands that held me reached up to cup my face, his fingers pushing the damp hair stuck to my cheeks back behind my ears before his thumbs rubbed reverently over the wet skin, like he was drying off rain from one of the seven wonders of the world.

And that world—the one that kept beating me down—stopped.

It stopped because he made it. *Because he wouldn't let it touch me—hurt me anymore.*

And because he wanted me.

I watched his eyes, the fighting flames inside them shifting between burning restraint and molten lust.

"Don't apologize," he commanded sternly, his jaw ticking with frustration.

I should though. He wasn't responsible for my sadness, and I shouldn't make him feel like he was; the less that tied us together, the easier it would be.

My lips parted as air rushed into my lungs. The rough pad of his thumb strayed low enough to brush over the fullness of my lower lip, making desire the only emotion I could feel.

I really wanted to kiss him.

The thought would have knocked me back if his hands weren't holding my face captive.

I wanted to kiss him. Not as a thank you. Not because I needed it as comfort. I just wanted to be closer to him. I just wanted to share this little broken piece of me.

And I hadn't had that feeling about anyone in a long time.

My tongue flicked out to wet my lip and I asked, knowing it was the second time, "Are you going to kiss me?"

I hardly registered his growl before his mouth crushed mine— hot and possessive and exquisitely overwhelming.

His kiss was a burning flame. Heating. Illuminating. *Cleansing.* It burned away even the strongest insecurities just as easily as it flared the need that pooled between my thighs, warm and wet and aching.

I wanted to kiss him. I *needed* to kiss him. But I didn't know how badly until I was.

I couldn't stop the moan that slipped from my mouth or the way my hands rose and curled into his t-shirt, still damp from the sink water and my tears. I tugged myself tighter against him, squeezing out whatever space was left between our bodies.

I needed to get closer—*closer to where I could feel without loss finding me.*

Flames licked through me as his tongue speared inside my mouth, stroking over mine.

There were so many things wrong with my life at the moment. So many losses and setbacks that made every breath feel like I was trying to breathe oxygen out of water. *And this kiss?* It should've added to that pile of unfortunate circumstances.

I wanted a man I was either going to leave or lose.

Instead, I could finally breathe. And feel. *And need.* For a single safe second.

His fingers slid back from my face and threaded through my hair, tugging on the thick tresses to tip my head back so he could deepen the kiss. I felt his tongue in every corner of my mouth, exploring and claiming each and every inch. I hadn't kissed someone like this in a long time. *And to compare any other kiss to this would be the worst kind of crime.*

His mouth was just as determined as the rest of him—determined to remove any trace of hurt that lingered, determined to give me a safe space to feel... *determined to give me everything if I'd let him.*

One hand slipped from the back of my head to slide down my

back, leaving a trail of goosebumps in its wake, as his tongue stroked along the length of mine. Heat pooled in my core, the ache stoked by the thick length of his erection swelling against my stomach.

I moaned as need filled the hollowness inside me—the need for everything solid and indestructible Eli seemed to be made of.

His groan was low and tortured when I rolled my hips.

This wasn't real. It wasn't lasting. It was only a kiss, and kisses couldn't cure heartache any more than the ocean air could cure illnesses. Still, I clung to every sensation that engulfed me.

"Eli," I whimpered against his mouth. His heart pounded against my hand, mimicking the thump of my own blood through my body.

"Eli," I murmured again against his lips as his hand squeezed my ass, pinning me against his hard cock. "Please…"

I wasn't sure what I was begging for. Kisses? Touching? Sex?

All I knew was I wanted more of it—more of him. In every other instance, he was everything that stood between me and getting away from this place, but in this moment, he was the only thing that let me escape the pain… that let me feel peace.

Harsh and heavy pants from both our lips filled the minimal space between us for a moment, before his eyes flew open, regret and guilt clouding his gaze as he released me abruptly and stepped back.

"*Fuck*," he swore under his breath, running a rough hand through his hair that let one lock fall over the prominent plane of his forehead.

I shivered as a different kind of heat flushed my body.

"I'm s—"

"Don't," he commanded even more harshly this time, rubbing a hand over his mouth. "That was my fault. I shouldn't have done that, especially because you were upset."

So, instead of more of anything, I was left with nothing. *Again*, my heart whispered.

I could only nod. I wanted to tell him no. I didn't want him to stop because being in his arms made all the storms calm. But that was a dangerous thought to have, let alone speak. So, I only nodded, letting the moment of awkward silence drag lazily between us, tethering us through the desire that still charged the air, desperate to break free.

"The pipe should be okay now, but if you have any trouble, just call me. Doesn't matter the time, I'll be here," he promised hoarsely, and my heart squeezed at the offer.

"Thank you."

"I'll see you on Monday." His assertion brought me back to the moment.

I nodded, brushing a strand of hair back from my face as he turned and left. My feet stayed rooted in the same spot and my fingers drifted up, pressing on my swollen lips, ravaged from that kiss, until I heard the click of the front door shutting.

He was gone. And the hollowness began to return.

What was wrong with me?

I'd kissed Eli.

I'd kissed the man who made me want to stay in a place I very much needed to leave.

Sure, some might consider a fling with the handsome contractor a way—*good or questionable*—to deal with grief. But one kiss proved that wouldn't work for me.

One kiss proved any involvement with Eli was dangerous—not because it meant risking another loss, but because the fullness I'd felt was the beginnings of hope—a hope that it would be safe to let someone in… to love again.

I couldn't afford that kind of hope.

Especially when it came within a hundred-mile radius of Carmel Cove.

Eight

Eli

I'd worked my entire life to redefine what 'home' meant to me. The place. The people. The relationships.

I'd come to Carmel Cove homeless—in every sense of the word. And just when it all began to feel secure, when I was starting to think about that final piece of the puzzle—*having someone to share it with*—everything began to unravel.

And now, I worried if I couldn't get Laurel to stay... if I couldn't put Roasters to rights, I'd lose every sense of belonging I'd come to find in this town. And instead of being the one everyone looked to, I'd be the one they turned away from.

The one who hadn't been able to save Larry.

The one who hadn't been able to save Roasters.

The man who couldn't stop thinking about kissing Laurel Ocean.

"Shit." I grunted, a huge plume of dust rolling out from underneath the espresso machine I'd attempted to move away from the back wall.

I'd been at the coffee shop almost every day since the

break-in. We hadn't been able to do much, first because of the investigation, and then, with Larry's death, until we had permission from the new owner. But whatever little I could do calmed my unsettled soul. At least in here, I could put something to rights. I could take away what was destroyed and fix what was broken.

It was a harsh contrast to everything else going on in my life right now.

No matter how hard I tried, it seemed like no matter what I did, it made it worse.

And kissing her definitely made the situation worse.

"Eli?" Eve appeared from the back. "You okay?"

I huffed, my hands planted on my hips, glaring at the stubborn old espresso machine.

"Yeah, just trying to move this so I can get to the wall behind it tomorrow." I glanced at her. "I'll get it. Don't worry about it."

I knew she would try to help.

"You sure?" She adjusted her glasses.

"Yeah," I grunted.

"Alright. Well, I have to head over to the Blooms' house. I'm teaching a class there in about twenty minutes. Just call if you need anything, okay?"

Eve's older sister, Addison Williams, owned a non-profit rehabilitation house for women escaping domestic violence. Blooms provided shelter, food, and most importantly, support for the women, along with programs and opportunities to teach them various skills.

Ash taught them how to cook. Mick and I taught them simple woodworking. Dex and Ace Covington taught them self-defense. And Eve… Eve taught them yoga.

"Yeah." I nodded even though I knew I'd be fine on my own—*always had.*

But alone wasn't something this town did well, as the door dinged with her exit, I heard much heavier footfalls replace her smaller, softer ones, along with a smooth Southern accent.

"Need some help?" Mick's eyes twinkled with amusement as he walked over to me.

"I'm fine," I insisted, even though my muscles screamed in protest.

"Gettin' a head start?"

"Just thought I'd move this away from the wall, so we can start tearing it apart tomorrow," I replied.

He reached out. His large palm splaying on the wall behind the machine. "Could've done that in the morning."

Right. But then I'd be struggling to find something to exert myself and take my frustration out on.

"Trying to clear my head," I admitted, wiping my hands on my dirt and dust-covered work jeans.

"Laurel?"

My jaw tightened. Even just her name had my body recalling the way she melted into my arms, needing the very thing she fought so desperately against.

"That obvious?"

"Obvious that it's her with the building and everything." He folded his massive arms over his chest. "Less obvious that it's because you want her."

My gaze snapped to his, confirming his claim.

I dragged a hand through my hair. "Then how'd you know?" I grumbled.

He chuckled but there was something more serious that lingered in his gaze. "I know what it's like to want somethin' you shouldn't—to want somethin' you can't have." He cleared his throat, and any indication that he was talking about himself disappeared. "Don't we all?"

I stared at him for a minute, wondering who he was thinking about in that moment.

"Yeah, well, wanting something you shouldn't have and kissing something you shouldn't want are two very different things."

His eyebrows popped up. "You kissed Laurel?"

"It was a mistake."

"Then why are you stuck on it?"

My head cocked.

"Mistakes you move on from," he explained. "If you can't, then maybe it wasn't a mistake."

"It was," I assured him. "She already thinks I'm trying to force her into staying. Kissing her only makes that look a thousand times worse. I shouldn't have done it, and I should stay away from her."

I should stay away from her before the need inside me to be the one she finally let go with—the one she finally opened up to and let out everything she so bravely held inside—demanded too much and drove her away.

He scoffed. "Laurel's a smart girl," he told me. "Even after four martinis." He laughed. "She's hurtin', to be sure. We all are. But grief is like drivin' in a fog. Hard to see too much except what's right in front of you. Hard to move fast. And even though you'd think turnin' on those high beams—all the should and shouldn'ts blarin' in your brain of what's expected, what's appropriate—would make the situation easier to navigate, they don't. It's the low light you have to follow." His lips thinned for a second as he nodded. "It's the low glow from in here"—he pushed his thumb into the unmoving muscle of his left chest—"you have to follow to get through… wherever it takes you."

My heart lurched against its cage, eager to agree with him. *Eager to agree I should be following it straight back to Laurel.*

"I don't want to be the reason she leaves," I told him.

He hummed. "You alright bein' the reason she stays?"

The question was a punch to the gut.

"I want to be the reason she's sure she made the right decision, whatever that is." I cleared my throat.

"Will you buy it?"

My eyes flicked to him and then back to the espresso machine. It would almost, if not completely, deplete my savings to buy Roasters.

"If that's what it comes to," I replied tightly.

This was all I had left of the man who'd given me a home, and finally, a definition for that word. And I would do whatever it took to preserve it.

He nodded.

"Alright, well, I guess we better get this thing moved then," he drawled a few seconds later with a confident smirk.

I stepped back as he moved in front of me. The man who weighed a solid two-hundred pounds wrapped his arms on the side of the commercial espresso machine like it was an espresso-making teddy bear, and, with just the slightest hitch in his breath, lifted it and, turning, placed it on the counter behind us.

And he barely broke a sweat.

"I could've done that," I grumbled with a grin.

"Of course." He chuckled, patting my back just as the door dinged again.

We both turned and all three of us—Mick, me, and the newcomer—froze.

"Jules?" I gaped in astonishment at the slender figure of my cousin who stood just inside the doorway with her hand on the knob, as though she were still deciding whether to turn around and bolt.

"Hi, Eli," she greeted softly, her chin dipping with a gentle nod as she folded her hands demurely in front of her. Her gaze shifted to Mick and her lips parted ever so slightly with a hitch.

"Jules, this is Mick Madison. Not sure if you've already met," I introduced them.

She nodded, and I couldn't tell whether it was to indicate that they had, or whether it was in greeting.

"Miss Vandelsen," Mick said, her name thickened with reverence.

"Is everything okay?" I asked and looked to my friend, seeing in his eyes a glimmer of that longing I'd seen before. But by the time I looked between them again, it was gone. "How can I help you?"

Her trance broken, she took a few steps forward, her heels clicking softly on the laminate floor, and I rounded the counter to meet her in the center of the almost-empty room, noting how Mick kept his distance.

"Yes," she assured me with words that appeared to be out of obligation rather than reality. "I'm so sorry to intrude. I just had a few moments to myself, and I wanted to come down here. We..." Her eyes dropped for a second. "We couldn't stay for the reception after the funeral, and I haven't been here since the... incident."

Up close, the bubble of put-together perfection that characterized her, and the entire Vandelsen family, showed hints of fracture and strain.

Wisps of long brown hair escaped the neat bun at the base of her neck. Her eyes, though still done up with makeup, had the faintest shadows of circles underneath them. Even her hands broke their calm hold as her thumb rubbed soothing paths across her skin.

She'd always reminded me of royalty.

Not because many in town referred to her as the Princess of Rock Beach. *Beauty, fortune, and living in a palatial sea-side resort with parents who saw themselves as above the rest lent well to the association*. I saw royalty because I saw someone who was trapped, and forced to appear happy about it. I saw someone who was always under scrutiny—from the outside and within. I saw someone who was a tool of diplomacy—a beautiful and kind one—used by her parents to grow their social empire. And I saw someone who was told she needed to be happy about it just because she was rich.

Except when she came here… to see Larry.

No one had to be anyone but who they were with Larry.

"That's alright," I told her. "It's still a little bit of a mess down here, unfortunately. Probably going to get worse over the next few weeks as we tear it all apart." Her eyes sprung wide, so I clarified, "To fix everything."

Relief flashed across her well-trained features.

Her gaze held mine as she took another step forward and asked hesitantly, "Do you… have you heard anything about the break-in?" She swallowed and looked around nervously.

"Not yet. They're still investigating."

"Of course." Her eyes dropped. "Do you know what's going to happen once you repair everything?"

"I honestly don't know," I told her. "I guess that depends on what happens with the will and the lawyer."

"Oh, of course." She nodded, tearing her gaze away.

"Is there something wrong?"

Her head snapped back to me. "Oh, no," she exclaimed. "I just… I was just working on something… with my grandfather," she replied, hesitantly. "But it's okay. It's not a big deal."

My gaze narrowed on her.

She'd been a frequent visitor to Roasters over the last few months, but I thought it was nothing more than a granddaughter visiting her grandfather. Now that I examined my memories in light of this conversation, there did seem to be something more serious being discussed between them.

"Are you sure?" I asked. "I can talk to Laurel if you want—"

"Oh, no." She flashed a smile and I recognized it as something she shared with her cousin good: the way they both put on a brave face even when something wounded them. "That won't be necessary. It's not a big deal. Please, don't tell her I came, she has enough going on," Jules insisted, maintaining her light expression. "I just wanted to see everything…"

This was the Jules Vandelsen the world saw—where nothing about what she needed was important simply because her family had too much money for her to *need* anything.

"I hope he left it to her," she went on before I could ask anything further, adding with a blush, "I mean, my parents are just so busy, it's better that Laurel gets it."

Translation: She didn't trust her parents not to destroy everything Roasters stood for in this community and all for a profit.

Her expression fell. "I'm sorry." Embarrassment flooded her cheeks, realizing she'd said too much. "I have to get going." She tipped her wrist, quickly glancing at the time on her watch. "Thanks, Eli. For everything." Her expression faltered. "For everything you did for him."

Everything and not enough.

"Of course," I replied, wishing there was more I could do for her. "Are you sure you don't want me to let Laurel know—"

"No. Please." Her eyes flashed with such fierce determination I swayed back, seeing for the first time the fight that lay buried underneath all her finery. "I'll… reach out to my cousin. Thank you," she assured me and then, with a nod of goodbye to me and Mick—who'd remained suspiciously quiet and in the shadows this entire time—she turned to the door.

"Jules?"

She looked back to me.

"If you need anything…" I leveled her with the same hard

stare Larry had been known to have—the one that left no room for argument.

"Thank you," she murmured, the bell chiming once more as she let herself out.

My head tipped to the side, watching as she got into the driver's side of a Rock Beach maintenance truck parked outside.

Had she always driven that?

More intriguing though, was why a woman whose family showed up in a black Rolls Royce to the funeral—one of their many expensive cars they flaunted when they came into town—had chosen to borrow a maintenance truck to come down here?

"You alright?" I turned back to Mick, folding my arms across my chest.

"Yeah." He smiled though it felt as though his gaze lingered on a sight behind me rather than looking at me. "Why?"

I eyed him. "Almost forgot you were there for a minute," I told him and then teased, "Not something that commonly happens."

"Didn't seem like it was any of my business." He turned back toward the wall, lifting the table the espresso machine had been sitting on and moving it to the side.

I hummed but didn't pry, instead asking as I approached him, "How's it looking?"

"Like we've got a lot of work to do."

Nine

Laurel

It was impossible to ignore the stares as I drove through town in my pap's old Nissan truck on Monday morning. I saw the way their expressions turned from confusion and wonder, like maybe him dying had been a bad dream, to recognition and disappointment when they realized it was me inside the cab.

After my announcement at Roasters and the stony silent treatment I received on the drive home, I wasn't about to ask Diane for a ride again.

And I definitely wasn't going to bum a ride from Eli. Not after what happened on Saturday.

Digging through the junk drawer in my grandfather's kitchen, I came across the spare keys to his truck, only to realize once in the driver's seat, that they weren't necessary when I saw the main set resting in the cup-holder of the unlocked vehicle.

Oh, Pap.

Of course, it didn't start on the first attempt, and the only thing I knew about fixing cars was that I shouldn't be the one doing it. After banging on the steering wheel a few times, I swore at the rust-covered pile of bolts, and then kept turning the key until the engine finally started from my sheer determination.

It wasn't a miracle that the truck started. It was just God wanting to see what fate—or my pap—could possibly have in store for me next.

My shoulders sagged when I finally turned into the small drive next to Roasters and parked in the back.

I'd debated whether I was going to come this morning, knowing it meant another interaction with a man my body didn't know how to handle. But the way I saw it, if I was here, the process would move faster.

Pulling down the visor, I checked my appearance again in the mirror. I did the best I could to tame the unruly waves into a ponytail, but I hadn't brought much with me, and without even a hairdryer at the house, any kind of cooperation was a miracle.

And as far as clothes, the selection aside from my two black suits was sadly slim. But then again, I thought I'd be back in L.A. and at work this morning. Instead, I was heading to a broken-down business I somehow owned.

So, I opted for denim overalls that loosely covered a more form-fitting white tee underneath, and my gray sneakers—the only other shoes I had. I figured I could get a solid three outfits out of these and another three with the regular pair of jeans I brought.

A week should be enough to get this place up to code.

With a sigh, I hopped down out of the truck and walked in the back door to the shop to be greeted by Eve's surprised eyes.

"Hey." I stepped cautiously into the storeroom at the back of the building. I remembered how she looked when I said I was going to sell the place yesterday and I wasn't sure what response I was going to be in for now that it was just the two of us.

"Morning, Laurel," she said with a shy smile that completely surprised me. Adjusting her glasses on the bridge of her nose, she pointed over her shoulder to the front of the shop. "They're up front, about to start demo."

I heard the faint rumble of male voices coming from that direction.

My eyes came back to Eve as she began to wipe down the large stove that sat back here opposite the shelves of storage on the other side. "What are you doing?"

She jumped a little and looked at me like I was telling her to stop.

"I just wanted to clean it. Not that anyone is going to be using it to roast the beans now…" Her explanation trailed off sadly. "I don't have to, if you don't want." She looked at me, pushing a strand of hair back behind her eyes that escaped the long braid down her back.

It wasn't worth it. It was just going to be sold.

But I couldn't bring myself to tell her to stop. She looked like she needed to clean it, even if it was all for naught.

"No," I declared with a steadying hand. "You can clean it. I just… I guess I didn't know it was still being used."

She nodded enthusiastically, rubbing the streaked cloth along the front edge of the stove again. "Oh yeah. Larry was back here at least once a week roasting beans; those were the days the lines out front were the longest," she said with a small grin.

"Really?" I found myself asking. "Not the days when he made apple fritters?"

She sucked in a harsh breath and I knew I'd said something wrong. *Crap.*

"He hasn't made those in a long time. I actually don't know how long it's been… I just know a lot of people ask for them but we only sell what we get from Josie over at the bakery."

I shifted uncomfortably, delving my hands into my pockets

as my gaze dropped to the floor. I didn't know why I just assumed that nothing had changed around here since I left—like the town, the coffee shop stayed frozen in time without me here.

The silence stretched my heart muscles uncomfortably.

"I'm going to go see what the damage is," I offered weakly and turned down the narrow hall toward the front room, lost in thought.

"Laurel—"

My sneakers squeaked to a stop when I almost ran into Eli *again* at the threshold of the cafe.

I sucked in a breath, feeling my breasts tingle at his closeness and the memory of our kiss. I licked over my lips, as though a memory could contain a taste.

"Hi," I breathed out.

That kiss wasn't as much of a memory as it was a haunting. It followed me everywhere like a shadow in my thoughts, reminding me of all the things I wanted to feel but was too afraid—*too smart* to.

Neither of us moved as lust charged the air, drawing me to him like a magnet, the emotion barraging against the invisible wall I'd tried to restore around my heart.

He was just a means to an end.

A new piece in the puzzle of my past.

And wanting him wouldn't solve any problems.

Still, he was the first to step back, desire dropping like spilled sand between us. A low rumble emitted from his chest as he rubbed a hand over his mouth with a muttered apology.

I guessed I wasn't the only one trying to cage in what was between us.

Swallowing down the lump of desire in my throat, I noticed he had on the same work jeans as last time I saw him—the ones that fit like they were designer but were made to get down and dirty—along with a muscle-clinging, navy *Madison Construction* tee.

"Mornin', Miss Laurel." Mick's voice, accompanied by his quirked grin appeared to my right.

I tore my eyes from Eli and greeted the friendly giant softly as he wiped his hands on his pants.

"So, what's the damage? What's the plan?" I crossed my arms over my chest, catching Eli's gaze as it flicked to my pushed-up breasts. I should've dropped my arms. Instead, I couldn't help but tighten them.

"Well, Mick is about to tear out that whole corner and the part of the ceiling where the leak is coming in from and see where we stand." He gestured to the wall with one hand.

The giant's grin grew as he picked up a sledgehammer and rested it on his shoulder; this was clearly one of his favorite parts of the job. "'Bout to get loud and dusty in here for a bit. You may wanna scoot in the back until I'm done," he suggested thoughtfully.

Eli looked over to me, expecting me to leave. I arched an eyebrow back at him. I just got here, and I wasn't leaving until I knew just how big of a mess I was dealing with.

Strolling over to the other side of the room, I pushed the pile of picture frames down the counter and hopped on top, watching as Mick ran his fingers over the wall, marking his target before he swung.

The loud bang and subsequent crunch of drywall wasn't as shocking as the pain that hammered into my chest or the way the air rushed from my lungs like Mick had hit me instead of his target. I shook it off. He wasn't tearing the place down, for goodness sake; he was just exposing the problems.

"You okay?"

I turned, hearing Eli's roughened voice beside me. His eyes

told me he'd been watching me, rather than his friend and co-worker, and caught my reaction to the first strike of destruction.

"Yeah, fine," I clipped out with admirable coolness. "Just wasn't expecting it to be so loud is all."

He nodded and crossed his arms over his chest. My fingers curled into the edge of the counter, remembering how it felt to curl them into him. *And wanting to feel it again.*

Warm. Strong. *Unbreakable.*

Mick began to pry off pieces of the wall, exposing more pipes and beams behind it. Meanwhile, Eli kept his attention on me —making my nipples harden into tight peaks and heat settle between my thighs into a coiled ache. I bit my lip, knowing I couldn't rub them together without him seeing.

Without him knowing what he did to me.

I didn't know what was worse—seeing desire or concern in his eyes. Maybe they were equally bad because I shouldn't want either.

But I did… I ached for them both.

"So, they work for you? Or you work with them?" I asked, desperate for anything to think about other than my body's reaction to him. "I see your shirt has their business name on it…"

"Ahh… Yes. To it all," he answered slowly. "I have my own business and they had their own construction thing going on down in Texas before they moved here, but that's really just semantics; we work together for most projects."

"I see." I managed to cross my legs, relieving some discomfort. "Mostly restoring old buildings?"

He dragged a hand through his hair, sending a shiver down my spine. "Actually, a lot of new construction lately. New properties going up on the beach between here and Monterey," he informed me, resting one of his trim hips against the counter only a few inches from my thigh.

"But you were a barista here before that?" I looked over at him with my head tilted to the side. I didn't miss his little slip and it made me wonder what a contractor was doing brewing coffee for a living.

A nostalgic grin curved handsomely up one side of his face. "Yeah. I worked here for a bunch of years paying off my debt to your grandfather."

My clammy hand slipped off the counter as I turned to him, recovering quickly and wiping my palm on the top of my thigh. "Debt?"

The racket Mick made faded in favor of my heart thudding in my ears.

He winced, his smile turning bittersweet at the memory.

"I came to Carmel with nothing but the clothes on my back. Hitchhiked down here on a delivery truck," he drawled slowly and I watched the muscles in his jaw flex and release as he spoke. "If you haven't noticed, Larry doesn't lock anything around here. A habit not even the daily news could break him of."

"Yeah, like his truck," I grumbled under my breath and we shared a small laugh.

It wasn't much, and my heart hurt with the effort, but it was the kind of hurt that felt good—like exercising a muscle to make it stronger.

"He wouldn't even let me install security cameras," he continued with a rougher tone, his expression pulling taut with regret. "I should've just done it anyway. Maybe then we'd have a lead on who broke in and did this…"

My heart flexed even tighter, watching a man I'd only ever seen be sensible and decisive falter under guilt for something that wasn't his decision; he wasn't responsible for my pap's choices.

"It's not your fault," I told him, as though my consolation would help.

He sucked in a harsh breath and the turmoil in his eyes grew worse.

See? My brain chided over the protest in my chest. Don't get involved.

Taking a steadying breath, I retraced my steps back to where the conversation started and asked again, "So, why were you in his debt?"

Eli shifted his weight, giving me an even better view I did *not* need of his ass flexed against his jeans. His grin didn't return, but the tension began to drain from his features.

"I came here with nothing and even though I'd applied to a few places for jobs, I was out of money and hungry. So, when I realized nothing in this place was locked, I started taking money from the cash drawer to buy food. I may have also taken a few pastries along the way."

"You *stole* from him?" I gasped so loudly even Mick paused from his work.

Eli took one look at the expression on my face and let out an unexpected bark of laughter—for him and me. Maybe it should have insulted me, but instead, my chest swelled seeing his face light up with a smile. He might not be superman, but that smile could certainly save the day.

"Yeah," he admitted, chuckling. Then, meeting Mick's curious stare, he hollered, "Get back to work."

"Sorry." I cleared my throat. "Did you... did you just admit to stealing? From my grandfather?" I demanded in disbelief. "*And then he hired you?*"

Maybe my pap was crazy.

"For about three weeks." He nodded. "I kept a record of everything I took; I was going to pay it back." I shot him an 'I'm sure' smirk. "And he didn't stop me until the morning I decided to try and make myself a shot of espresso before heading out."

"What do you mean didn't stop you?" My whole body was turned toward him now, one knee pulled up on the counter, eager to hear the rest of his story.

"He knew I was stealing the whole time." *Of course, he did.* "Caught me staring at Pavi that morning, deep in thought as I was trying to decide which button would turn the damn thing on. He came up behind me and, after doing that disapproving throat-clearing thing he does." I nodded, knowing exactly what he meant. "Said I could take all his money, but when it came to touching his espresso machine, that was where he had to draw the line."

I looked over my shoulder at that very machine where it sat on the counter, battered and well-used. Pavi had served a lot of coffee over many lifetimes. Forget being a fly on the wall, I wanted to be that machine—to see the things it had, to hear the stories told over the cups of coffee it had made... *to have witnessed this story...*

"I apologized and showed him my tally of everything I owed him, promising to pay him back as soon as I could find a job," he continued, turning fully toward me, our faces only inches apart. "It wasn't much, just enough for food and a few things. So, he told me he could either turn me in to the police or he could show me how to work Pavi properly, and I could make coffee until my debt was paid."

That was definitely my pap—always giving people chances to do better for themselves. To turn mistakes into something meaningful.

"So, that's what you did," I concluded, dragging my tongue over my lip before pulling it into my mouth. "But why would no one hire you?"

His brow furrowed in confusion.

"You said you went on interviews for weeks. Why did no

one hire you?" I clarified, wondering how a guy who seemed to be so well-known and revered in this town had stayed jobless.

His face shadowed.

"I didn't have a resume. I'd worked odd-jobs in construction ever since I was... young. But I was always paid off the books. When I came here, I was an outsider. A homeless nobody. I had dirty clothes and showered at the public showers by the beach." He cleared his throat. Meanwhile, desperate words lodged in my throat to know more—to know what happened to him.

Why was he homeless?
Where was his family?
Why did he come here?

Questions I had no business asking of a man whose acquaintance was only a temporary fixture in my life.

"I had no records or proof of my experience. There were too many other candidates who did have all that and looked the part. No one took the time on me... until Larry," he ended quietly.

I couldn't stop the way my heart swelled against my chest that felt five sizes too small. *Because love was our legacy.* Air rushed into my lungs and it tasted salty and cool, just like it had the night my pap told me that.

I shuddered. He knew how to be there for everyone except himself.

Love wasn't my legacy. Not anymore.

A small curse escaped as Eli pushed away from the counter and stalked over to Mick.

And there was the end of that discussion.

A good thing, I assured myself.

It trod too close to my fault lines.

My gaze followed Eli. The man who was the center of everything, who seemed to be attached to every piece of this town. The man with a past as secret as mine was tragic.

He was an enigma.

Something I knew but didn't know. *Like gravity.* I knew it existed and it was the reason my feet were on the ground, but I didn't know the science and all the little facts that made it so.

In the same way, I knew what was essential about Eli, the kind of person he was, the kind of good person my grandfather had taken a chance on. But I didn't know every detail of his past.

He swore as the larger man pointed to the neighboring wall with the bench attached to it, and the pit in my stomach grew larger. I felt like I was watching some hospital show where the doctor went in to do surgery and realized the cancer had spread farther than he realized.

Eli's body tensed up before he nodded, and I knew where the hammer was going to fall even before he turned back to me.

"There's water damage on the framing beams in this wall all the way over to that one," he apprised me with a frustrated sigh, pointing to the bench. "I have a feeling the ones behind the bench are going to be the same, but we've got to take it down to see."

"I see," I replied thickly. *More walls meant more time.* "Do you think that's it?"

Like that wasn't half of the building already.

"I hope so," he rasped. "Anything more and we might not be able to fix it."

The statement hit me in the chest with the same force as Mick as he began smashing into the next wall.

Irreparable.

Unsalvageable.

Lost.

"Eli," he yelled over to us with a huff. "Can you see where the hell Miles is? Tell him I've seen mules move faster than his ass."

Eli nodded, heading outside with his phone to make the call. Taking the moment for myself, I pulled my cell from my pocket and saw I had a voicemail from an unknown Carmel number.

Tapping on the button, I recognized Mr. Ross' voice right away. I'd planned on calling his office today about signing those papers, but according to the voicemail, they wouldn't be ready until Wednesday, and the other parties involved weren't available until Friday. He asked if I could call him back and let him know if that would work.

Other parties. Like my aunt Jackie.

I sighed and stuck my phone back in my pocket.

What was one more delay?

It didn't look like I was going to make it out of here before Friday anyway.

I jumped as Mick smashed another hole through the wall.

As the partial demolition continued, my focus shifted to the stack of photos next to me. I shouldn't touch them, but my hand had a mind of its own, drifting to them as though carried by a deeper tide.

Sitting on top was the same photo from the bathroom at the bar: both of my grandparents with my dad and aunt when they were really young. Beneath that was an old, sepia image of my great-grandfather hanging the *Ocean Roasters* sign in front of the building. They used this one in the paper… in magazines… every time Ocean Roasters or the family-run businesses of Carmel Cove were mentioned, this old, worn photograph was displayed.

I'd seen it so many times, I almost had the sense that I'd been there, watching him hang the wooden plaque, rather than a second-hand observer decades later.

I gulped, sliding it to the side to reveal a more recent picture, one that burned a little more to look at.

It was a picture of Jules and me. We couldn't have been more than five or six at the time, and we were sitting with my mom between us on the bench Mick was currently pulling from the wall, the ripped and worn fabric torn in even more places. My mother was reading *Little Women* to us—our Friday night tradition. Jules' parents always had an event to go to or a party they were hosting, and it was easier to grow their reputation without a daughter in tow. So, Jules and I had a standing sleepover almost every week which started with dinner at my grandparents and then story time here... at Roasters... until my parents closed up for the night.

My chest squeezed with the urge to cry as my fingers shakily brushed over my mom's hair. She had the softest hair and the kindest voice that warmed you from the inside out, like a long sip of hot cocoa that radiates soul-soothing heat when it settles in your stomach.

In the corner of the picture, my dad stood behind the counter, looking over at us but from the look on his face, only seeing my mom.

I noticed that look a lot when I was younger, but I didn't understand it until I was older; it was the look that said life didn't have meaning without her. It was probably a horrible thought to have, but I took comfort in the fact my parents had died together. I didn't know how one would've survived without the other.

My heart skipped a beat, wanting someone to look at me that way, and at the same time, with my track record, hoping no one ever did.

"Laurel?" My head darted up at Eli's voice.

What if he looked at me that way? The thought assaulted me like a wave, cold and unexpected as it crashed into my chest and took me under.

Not happening, Laurel. Don't go there.

Shoving it into the farthest recesses of impossibilities, I quickly rearranged the photos, giving myself a few moments without having to look at him.

"So." I cleared my throat and asked, "If you have to fix or replace the stuff in both walls, how long will that take?"

I turned to face him, air vacuuming into my lungs when he was standing right in front of me.

His eyes narrowed, scrutinizing the hammering of my pulse on the side of my neck. "If it's just those two walls? At least a week. But, depending on how many of the pipes are damaged or leaking, it could take longer. And, we'll only know if that's the extent of it once we get the rest of that wall down. We also need to check the back portion of the roof and add better ventilation for the stove."

I shuddered. *At least was starting to sound a whole lot like a lot more than a week.* I made a mental note to pick up more clothes.

More than a week around Eli... I rubbed my thighs together and made sure that mental note included more underwear.

"Okay," I replied, hopping down from the counter and trying not to betray the weight that was getting harder to bear and the desire that was growing harder to suppress.

"Laurel." He reached for me, and I stepped back.

I didn't want his comfort now. Not after that conversation. Not after the photos. And not after this news.

I couldn't start relying on him now, even though it was exactly what I wanted to do.

"I'm going to go take a look around in the back and see if Eve needs any help," I said, ignoring the way his jaw ticked with frustration.

Shoving my hands into my pockets, I turned before he could say anything more—*before he could make me want anything more.*

Once I was safe in the back of the building, I ambled around the storeroom for a few minutes, running my fingers down the half-filled stacks of to-go cups and lids my grandmother would always let Jules and I help stock.

I unclipped the tops of the remaining containers, sniffing the various raw and roasted beans inside; the different yet equally potent scents of grassy-green coffee beans and nutty roasted ones burned the scent of plaster dust from my nostrils.

Finally, I wandered back to Eve, noticing the stacks of dirt-covered pots and pans sitting on the counter by the stove; some of them I recognized as what my grandfather would use when he roasted the beans. Chewing my bottom lip, I debated for a moment before I reached for a clean cloth and grabbed the skillet sitting on top.

Maybe since I couldn't seem to mourn him, I could at least give him this. Clean and oiled cast-iron, just the way he taught me all those years ago while I'd tried to avoid studying for biology.

Nice and slow, Laurel. No point in rushin'. These pans have been used for a long time, you hear? Not every batch I've made with 'em has turned out good, but sure enough, underneath it all, they've got sturdy souls that don't give up and are ready to try again.

Like most things he taught me about coffee making, I would only realize later how the lesson wasn't really about the coffee or the pan…

I've made too many mistakes, I wanted to tell him as my hand moved in measured circles.

I'd made too many choices to preserve a soul that wasn't sturdy, and I was afraid to try again.

The more I rubbed oil into the pans, the more it felt like I was rubbing away the sadness and hurt from inside me. And, for the first time since I came back to town… since I'd seen or held anything so etched with memories of my pap, I finally felt something strikingly close to peace.

Like floating in the middle of the ocean, it was calm and serene, but it lacked the hopefulness of having the shore in sight.

Maybe it was a sign I needed to hang on for just a little bit longer before I could finally let this place go.

Ten

Eli

"Did you bring food to the house?" I felt her before I heard her, my body tuned to the finest awareness when Laurel was near.

Though I hadn't expected to see her today.

Yesterday, I'd caught the way her shaking hand had risen over her mouth as Mick first ripped into the wall. So reactional, so instinctive, I didn't think she realized her own momentary devastation. Her pained stare as she looked through the photographs stopped me in my tracks; I'd stood outside the door, watching her examine them, wishing there was something I could do to ease the pain she refused to share.

But there was nothing.

She didn't want to need me.

Even as we worked, I kept my eye on her, noticing how she moved around the back of the building, unable to remain in one place for long. *Until the pans.* The way she cleaned and seasoned them, it was like I could see Larry standing right beside her.

And that made the way my body was reacting to her right now all the more unacceptable.

"What food?" I asked, tugging my work gloves off and turning to her.

Laurel's red-gold hair was pulled on top of her head, soft tendrils framing her freckled cheeks that were dusted with the hint of pink. *From exertion, not because of me.* Those bright blue eyes were sharp and demanding, like the morning she'd found me on the couch, ready to caution me rather than accept any show of concern.

"The food at my grand—*my* house last night." Her pink lips pressed together, eyes narrowing into blue blades. "I came home yesterday, and the fridge and freezer were stocked with containers of food. Salad. Lasagna. Chicken Marsala. Chicken Piccata. And there was a huge basket of bread and pastries on the counter."

"Ahh." I nodded, slapping my gloves on my thigh to shake some of the dust off.

We both looked to the door as Mick and Miles walked in, their twin widened stares fading as they murmured a greeting before disappearing into the back so Laurel and I could finish our conversation in privacy.

"So, it was you?"

"No." I flashed a grin. "It wasn't. But I know who it was."

She folded her arms and I winced as my comfortable work jeans grew not-so-comfortable in the front.

"It was everyone, Laurel." I sighed. "The pastries and baked stuff were from Josie. The salad and lasagna were from Mrs. Covington; she always loved your grandmother's recipes for those."

The color faded from her face and she shifted her weight.

"The Marsala was probably Diane, and the Chicken Piccata was from Eve and her sister, Addison," I told her, adding, "But those two I'm not one-hundred percent certain."

She hesitated for a second before replying with a smaller voice, "Why?"

"Why?" I gaped. "Because you're here, Laurel. You're here and you're staying—at least for the moment while we deal with this place." My eyes scanned over her and a vise tightened over my chest with what I saw.

Jesus Christ. It had been so long since anyone had taken care of her, had done something for her without expecting anything in return, she couldn't even recognize it. She'd been the only one to take care of herself for a long time. *Too long.*

"They know this isn't easy for you, Laurel. They just wanted to try and take something off your plate—no pun intended," I said with a low voice, unable to stop myself from reaching out and resting my hand on her shoulder.

Her beautiful face softened as she processed and replied, "But why, Eli?" she repeated with a small shake of her head. "Why would they do that for me when I'm the one…" She trailed off and swallowed hard, her shoulders tightening under my grasp. "Why would they want to help me when they know I'm going to sell this place? When they know I'm planning on leaving?"

I didn't know what was worse: the hurt she felt returning home, or the hate she expected to meet being here.

My exhale was long and forceful. "Whatever you decide to do, Laurel, it doesn't change that you're still family here," I told her. "And they're going to do whatever they can to help."

She looked at me as though I'd grown another head, and it took a minute for it to really sink in and for her to believe me.

"Okay."

"Are you alright?"

Fire flashed in her eyes. "Yeah," she clipped. "I'm fine. So, what can I do to help?"

"Well, Eve isn't here—"

"No, I want to help out here," she broke in boldly. "I want to help get rid of whatever needs to go."

My jaw tightened as her words reverberated through my body.

After what happened yesterday, I didn't expect her to show up today. *I wouldn't expect anyone to show up who'd gone through what she had.*

Yet, here she was, the woman who possessed a strength to carry ten times her weight, standing in front of me, wanting to help tear this place—*and a part of her past*—apart.

But Laurel was equal parts fragile and strong. *Like carbon fiber.* Stronger than steel under certain conditions, but easily fractured under others.

And I refused to be a reason she fractured.

"Okay." I nodded, reluctantly releasing my hold on her shoulder and handing her my pair of gloves. "I don't think we have anything smaller."

She nodded and I watched her hands drown into the black fabric.

"You're going to get dirty," I told her, flinching when her eyes shot to mine. "I just mean, your jeans look like they—"

"Will survive," she finished for me, though I was going to say they looked too nice for this kind of work.

"Okay." *I wasn't going to argue with that look.* "Have you ever torn down a wall before?"

"No, but it can't be that hard." Her weight sunk onto one leg as she reached behind me and grabbed one of the mallets resting against the wall. "Hit and pull."

I chuckled. "Alright there, Laurel the Riveter." I put my hands up. "Let me talk to these guys for one minute, and then I'll show you how. It's not hard, but I don't want you hurting yourself."

I grunted, turning away in pain as she licked over her bottom lip, and yelled for the twins.

Miles' face broke into a huge grin as soon as he appeared. "You gave her a weapon?"

"She wants to help," I retorted, sharing a stare with Mick.

"You know that's goin' to hurt a helluva lot more than a whisk if she turns on you." Miles laughed, and I caught Laurel's eyes popping wide.

I shrugged an apology; this was a small town, and these were my friends.

"I'd put a helmet on if I were you... and maybe a cup," Miles continued as his brother smacked him on the back of his head.

"Don't be a jerk, Miles," Mick chided and then, turning to Laurel, apologized, "Don't mind him. I got all the looks and manners while we were in the womb—"

Miles' bark of laughter cut his brother off. "That's a good one, little brother. And here I thought I was the one who'd gotten the sense of humor."

"Well, lookin' at your face, I'd have to agree," Mick jaunted right back.

I relaxed when I saw a flash of white brighten Laurel's face. *It was hard not to be entertained by these two.*

"Alright, alright." I shook my head and laughed. "You two, start over there." I indicated the wall where the majority of the piping ran through; I needed to see if the ceiling was compromised in that area. "I'm going to let Laurel finish this wall."

While those two continued to taunt each other as they set to work, Laurel and I moved to the other side of the room Mick had just opened up yesterday.

"There aren't too many pipes running through this wall," I told her, placing my palm on the stained wallpaper. "I think most of the damage came from the roof leak which I'll take a look at next week, but for right now, we need to get all of this down and make sure that's the source."

"Okay." She raised her arms and the mallet, about to let loose.

"Whoa." I grabbed over her hands on the handle, a shot of lust sinking straight to my groin at the simple touch.

Her shiver ran through her as her gaze snapped to mine.

"Just let me show you one time," I told her quietly. "Then you can do it all on your own."

That seemed to appease her and she replied, "Okay, what do I do?"

My jaw ticked. I'd wanted to take the mallet from her and show her, but it didn't look like she was relinquishing her grip any time soon.

Holding back my tortured groan, I stepped behind her, reaching one arm around her front so I was grasping the handle over both of her hands.

I squeezed my eyes shut, my body going haywire as it pressed against the back of hers, all warm and soft in ways I shouldn't be thinking about. Not here. Not now. *Not with her.*

But she fit right into me. *And not because she was small.* The way her form tucked snugly into mine seemed like it should've come with an audible click to indicate a perfect match.

"You okay?" I rasped.

I felt her unsteady breath as her back moved against my chest. "I'm good."

Good could mean far too many things right now.

"Told you, you shoulda worn a cup!"

I tensed and grunted, remembering we had an audience— *an audience who recognized my attraction to this woman.*

"Alright." I cleared my throat and forced myself to focus. "You want to hold the mallet up here before you swing." I moved her arms with mine.

"That's not how Mick holds it," she interjected, tipping her head back almost to my shoulder to look at me.

Fuck, maybe I did need a sharp swing to the nuts; it would be less excruciating than this.

Her pink lips parted. A matching rose color blooming in her cheeks. All I could think about was kissing her again. The feel of her mouth against mine. The strokes of her tongue just as bold as the words she spoke.

"Mick is also three times your size and stronger than the rest of us in this room put together," I said tightly, willing her to turn back to the wall so she couldn't see just how painful it was to feel her curves resting against me again, knowing I was touching them but couldn't *touch* them. "He's more likely to hurt the mallet than the mallet is to hurt him."

"Oh."

"So, hold it up here," I went on. "Then, when you swing, make sure you use your whole body, not just your arms, otherwise you're likely to pull something."

As I spoke, I slowly moved the mallet toward the wall, pushing on her back with my upper body so she could feel how it was a whole-body movement.

When we ended, the mallet rested on the wall, and my face was right against her neck. With her hair up, her soft skin was just inches from my lips. I took a deep breath, my mouth watering at the subtle hint of vanilla.

I was too close.

She wasn't wearing perfume. It was her body wash I smelled. *Warm vanilla.*

"I think I've got it," she told me as she pulled the mallet to her.

Before I could step away, she pushed back into me, pressing her ass right into my rock-solid dick, sending sharp stabs of lust into my stomach.

Dammit.

"Yeah," I bit out through locked teeth. "Go slow."

With that instruction, I dropped my arms and spun away, stalking over to the twins to put as much space between Laurel and my unruly cock as I could.

For three hours we worked, and not once did she take a break. Not once did she want to sit or rest her arms. *And not once did she ask for help.*

"Alright, we should break for lunch," I said to the whole group though I was looking at her.

Mick and Miles agreed, pulling off their gloves, eager for some food.

But Laurel didn't stop.

I nodded to the two men to go, and she didn't even pause when they left the building.

"Laurel," I said her name quietly, placing my hand over hers, stalling her next swing and capturing her attention.

Her chest heaved with an exertion she clearly didn't feel, and understanding dawned on me.

When she swung, she was hitting more than just the wall in front of her; she was demolishing all the obstacles she saw in her way. When she picked up and moved the piles of drywall and debris, she was getting rid of everything she thought was broken and unsalvageable in her life.

"You okay?"

"You keep asking that."

I gave her a tight smile. "And I'll keep asking until you want to tell me the truth," I replied.

Her eyes popped wide, blinking a few times as she looked around the room and realized we were alone, before her focus finally fell to me.

She might not want to tell me, but I saw the truth. She wanted to tear this place down because she thought it would set her free.

"I'm fine, and it is the truth," she insisted.

I put my hands up. "Okay, but I'm still going to ask."

"Why?" she demanded.

"Because sometimes the truth changes, Laurel. Sometimes people who were fine become not fine but are too stubborn to say anything." The words erupted from the raw, wounded place in my chest that housed my guilt over Larry, and their vehemence made us both reel back in shock.

The mallet landed on the floor with a loud thump, white dust floating up like a cloud.

"I'm going to get some lunch," she declared, leaving my comment to drift between us with no response. "I'll be back in a little while."

My chin dipped and I remained unmoving until I heard the door close behind her.

"Dammit," I breathed out into the silence, wondering how every time I tried to make things better, they somehow ended up worse.

I ripped down another piece of plaster, groaning as I revealed more water damage to the ceiling.

Christ, Larry. I told you the damn roof needed to be fixed years ago.

"There's still more over here," I grunted.

"Damn." Mick's curse echoed in reply.

My head fell, my shoulders slumping in defeat.

At least Laurel had already left.

She'd come back after lunch and worked with the rest of us until five. Without a break. And without another word to me except for goodbye.

Miles had walked her out to her truck while Mick and I finished up.

"I think this might be the last of it," I said, letting the last piece of old plaster fall from my hands. I could finally see where the softening and staining of the ceiling ended just a few inches away.

Heavy footsteps thudded over to me, announcing Mick's approach.

"What are you goin' to tell her?" He looked up at me with concern to where I stood on the counter; it was easier to reach the ceiling this way rather than on a ladder.

My mouth firmed. "The truth." I dragged in a heavy breath as I crouched and then hopped off the surface back onto the ground. "It's going to take at least three weeks to get this cleaned up. I've got to get back up on the roof. George has to get out here and square away the pipes." My arms motioned around to the room that looked like a war zone. "And then we have to put it all back together."

He nodded. "Alright. We'll put everything else on hold until it's done. We'll get this taken care of, man. Don't worry."

He clapped a reassuring hand on my shoulder as we stared at the rusted and worn pipes crisscrossing through the walls.

"Thanks."

"Maybe it'll be better this way," he suggested with his classic hopefulness. "Give you more time to convince her to stay."

I cleared my throat. "Yeah, I don't think that's going to happen."

"No?" His eyebrow tipped up to match his grin. "The way you two were lookin' at each other earlier…" He trailed off as I shot him a silencing glare.

The last thing that was going to convince Laurel to stay at this point was how she felt about me. If anything, it was only going to drive her away faster.

We both turned as the door to the coffee shop opened and a large man with a half-shaved head, the rest of his hair pulled back in a tight bun, entered the room and imposed a whole different energy on the space.

"Eli," Ace Covington greeted me with a brief nod, his mouth drawn into a characteristically hard line. "Got a minute?"

The former Navy SEAL was the muscle over at Covington Security, the private security firm he'd opened with his brother, Dex, after they'd both left the military. They took on a lot of high-profile cases, but also a lot of local problems the police put on back-burners in order to deal with all the tourists at Big Sur and the issues that came along with them.

I nodded and then shot a quick glance at Mick, who waved me off as he finished packing up his things.

I walked out the back of the building, Ace trailing on my heels.

"Where's Laurel?"

My steps slowed. "Left for the day. Why?"

"Just wondering," Ace rumbled, pushing up the sleeves of his black Henley to his elbows as I turned to face him outside.

Instantly I was on alert. "Did you find out something about the break-in?"

The fact that *nothing* had been stolen was what concerned me the most—*what concerned all of us the most*.

Whoever had done this hadn't taken any money nor had they been interested in any of the valuable pieces of equipment in the building. Unless their sole motive was to push an old man past the brink of what he could stand, whoever the culprit was had been looking for something specific, for a specific purpose… *a specific plot.*

And the dark coil of fear in my stomach burned with the thought that, with Larry gone, Laurel could be the next target.

His jaw ticked. "Blackman's in town."

I shoved a hand through my hair, expletives falling unbidden on my exhale.

Alexander Blackman was the owner of Blackman Brews. He'd approached Larry about purchasing Roasters in the weeks before he died and, when Larry refused, pushed the matter with disrespectful insistence.

"Has Dex found anything else on him?" I pinched the bridge of my nose.

Dex had been looking into Blackman because of how he'd threatened Larry to sell the business. As a former intelligence officer, Dex was in charge of all the tech and information acquisition at Covington. But there wasn't much to find on the slimy asshole who thought it was good business practice to threaten an old man.

"Nothing more than what we already know." He let out a long exhale.

Dex was able to find out Blackman Brews had been created earlier this year and owned nothing more than a few empty warehouses along the coast and a truck with the name plastered on the side which had been seen around town.

"It has to be a shell corporation."

"Right, but we can't harass someone with no proof. And even if we did have proof it's a shell, that doesn't matter if there's no crime to tie him to," Ace ground out. "Look, I want that motherfucker to be guilty as much as you, but it could be a start-up with new angel investors looking to buy a well-known, solid base to jumpstart the business."

My fist tightened at my side and I took a few frustrated steps. I didn't care if he was playing devil's advocate—*or if he had a point*—every day that went without answers for the break-in was one more way I'd failed Larry. First to save his business, then, to save him.

"And what, you think Vandelsen is the investor?" I demanded, scrutinizing him

While trying to initially locate him, Dex received reports that Blackman was seen at the Rock Beach Resort, possibly there to meet with Laurel's uncle, Rich.

Dick.

"It's looking more like it now that he's back there," Ace revealed. "We've been keeping an eye over there in case he showed back up and yesterday, he did."

"Talking to Rich?"

He cleared his throat. "Just staying at the resort is all we can confirm."

I grunted, too displeased to say anything. Not with him, but with the situation.

Blackman looked like the culprit. Acted like the culprit. Hell, he probably smelled like the culprit. But there were too many missing pieces to actively pursue that scenario and confront him, not in the least of which was a very murky motive.

"Why would he destroy the thing he was trying to buy?" I planted my hands on my hips, shaking my head. *If we could just fucking figure that out...* "Did he think that would make Larry want to sell it rather than repair it? It just seems like a far fucking stretch for that to be the case."

And we both knew it.

"We're working on it," Ace assured me. "And we're watching him now that he's back, but I wanted you to know."

He wanted me to be prepared.

"Why did you want to talk to Laurel?" I demanded a little too protectively.

His eyes narrowed ever so slightly. "I wanted to ask if she's been approached by anyone about selling Roasters."

"She hasn't said," I told him. "But she also hasn't met with Gavin yet. So, without the signed papers and the deed in her hand, it's only a close circle who know she's the one inheriting it all."

He grunted, folding his massive arms over his chest. "You should tell her."

"About what?" I tossed at him. "A man who might approach her? Who might be responsible but might also just be opening a new business with her family?" I rubbed my hands over my mouth, pacing in front of him. "She's been through a lot, Ace. Fucking overwhelmed." My head fell with defeat. "Unless you have something concrete, there's no point. Best case? She'll have one more thing on her plate to worry about. Worst case? She'll go looking and demanding answers where there may not be any, or worse, that may put her in harm's way."

"Eli…" His tone was low with warning.

"Ace." My eyes snapped to his. "She doesn't trust me. She doesn't trust anyone here right now. Give it a few days. Give *her* a few days. See what you can find out," I demanded. "And as soon as she meets with Gavin and the news breaks, I'll tell her what little we know. Hopefully, by then, we'll know more."

He eyed me steadily for a solid minute before tipping his head and grunting his assent.

I'd drawn the line. I'd made it clear his job was investigating this sonofabitch. But protecting Laurel? *That was mine.*

Eleven

Laurel

"Hi, I'm looking for Jules—Julia Vandelsen," I said to the woman standing at the front desk in the Rock Beach Resort. At her wary look, I added, "I'm her cousin, Laurel Ocean."

She seemed to relax a little bit at that and excused herself into a back office.

I needed a break. From the house. From Roasters. From everywhere that reminded me of all the things I couldn't have. My family. My pap. My home. *Eli.*

My stomach fluttered.

For two days, I'd helped them tear down the walls at Roasters. Muscles I didn't even know I had ached with the effort I'd used to try and distract myself from the memories those walls held.

But if that wasn't enough of a battle to fight, I had to contend with my traitorous body wanting to cross enemy lines in search of a certain stubborn contractor. Every lingering look. Every brush of his hands. Every offer to help, and every show of concern. For as many old memories as I tore down in that space, *he* filled them with new ones.

And all I knew was I wanted to kiss him again—the man who'd met my grandfather by stealing from him.

The man with all the answers.

A slight smile pricked at the corners of my mouth as I shivered. Even now, the scent of his subtle wood-chipped musk lingered in my brain and sent a warm tingle up my spine.

A woman brushed against my shoulder, her Chanel No. 5 so potent it choked me back to the present.

Thoughts of the past and Eli were dangerous for different reasons on the surface, but at the center, the threat of loss was the same if I didn't keep my distance. So, since my meeting with Mr. Ross this morning had been pushed back until next week because he had a family emergency, I decided it was safest to come here.

To see Jules.

I took another look around the lobby of the golf resort. From the fountain at the entrance to the huge gilded mirrors and thick plush midnight blue carpet speckled with small white dots covering the lobby, I was glad I'd chosen the other suit I'd brought with me because, my other option of jean overalls and a tee would've really made me stick out like a sore thumb among the pastel plaid and country-club-white pants.

A group of young men walked by and my eyes immediately caught the small polo player logo on their shirts. *Spring 2018. Summer 2017. Summer 2016.* If I had more time, I could probably remember the name and exact color of each Ralph Lauren polo they wore. That was what happened when you'd worked at the same company for almost seven years with hardly any social life—spotting styles in the wild became a favorite pastime.

Chewing on the corner of my lip, I turned back to the

counter as the woman reappeared. With another look, I was pretty sure she was wearing a blouse from our Women's Spring 2016 line; I didn't work with that department, but I remembered trying to coordinate with the bold stripes they'd chosen for that season.

"Miss Vandelsen will be right down," she informed me tightly. "However, she has a meeting in thirty minutes."

I nodded, only rolling my eyes as I turned away from her. It was the weekend and her—*our*—grandfather had just died... *The funeral was only last week for crying out loud.* Maybe Uncle Rich could cut her some slack.

But I couldn't judge; everyone grieved differently. Maybe working helped her cope. *Just like leaving home had helped me.*

Looking down, I huffed and rubbed over the dirt mark on the front of my pants. *Stupid truck.* It had given me trouble when I went to start it this morning, only this time, the evil scowl I'd given to the engine bay had me stepping away with scuff marks on the front of my pants.

Truck, one. Laurel, zero.

"Laurel?" I looked up from my frantic rubbing to see Jules gliding toward me.

Today, she wore wide, white dress pants and a matching long-sleeve sheer blouse over a white tank, topped with a sweater tied over her shoulders. Immediately, I noted her hair was pulled back the same way as before—low and tight on her neck, and her face shrouded with makeup and an equally concealing placid expression.

She was beautiful—the perfect model for women's resort fashion, a striking mix of modern style and old-world class—and she looked like she was exactly where she belonged; the perfect princess for this resort palace. But, I'd been around enough models to see beyond the mask, and I'd known Jules for long enough to recognize the weight propelling her measure steps and the sadness highlighted in her eyes.

Maybe I shouldn't have come.

"Hey," I greeted her, wrapping my arms around her shoulders for a hug that turned her body to stone against me. "Sorry, are you busy? I didn't mean to just... run out on you like that the other day."

Her eyes darted to either side of us like she was concerned about who was watching or listening before she cleared her throat and gave a small nod over to the entrance. I fell in alongside her as she walked with her hands clasped tightly in front of her stomach.

"Don't apologize. It was a hard day." She gulped. "I would've come to the reception after the funeral, but my dad... wanted us to get back." Her tone suggested that she hardly felt the excuse was justified. "Eli didn't tell you to come here, did he?"

My brow furrowed. "No. Why?"

Even here, the last place to be bothered by his handsome distraction... and somehow, he'd still found me...

Her chin dipped and she replied very quietly, "I stopped by Roasters the other day. I hadn't been in since the break-in, but I asked Eli not to mention it."

I folded my arms, unwilling to admit I'd been avoiding Eli of late, and instead, asked, "Is everything okay?"

"Of course," she replied so quickly the response could only be one of habit rather than one of truth before she turned the conversation on me. "So, what brings you here?"

My throat tightened. "Well, I don't know how much longer I'll be in town, so I thought maybe we could catch up a little," I said softly. She was really my only family left, aside from her parents who I had no attachment to. No matter what happened in the past, I didn't want to leave this place with any loose ends trailing behind me. "How are you holding up?"

I winced as soon as the words left my mouth.

Our grandfather had just died, she was probably taking it just as well as I was. Then again, Aunt Jackie preferred to associate with the family she'd married into, so who knew how much Jules had seen of our grandfather in the last decade?

"I'm... handling it." She didn't even look at me as she spoke, instead, shifting around me to the sink. "I-I just can't believe it, you know?"

Tears pricked at the corners of her eyes and I was so jealous. *How could she feel this, but I couldn't?*

"Did you see him frequently? Or recently?" I asked softly, aching for someone to give me some clarity.

"I hadn't for a long time. You know how my mom is," she admitted quietly, clearly embarrassed about her mother the way her face flushed as she spoke. "But in the last few months, I was visiting him regularly. He talked about you all the time, you know."

I jerked my gaze up to her green one.

"He missed you a lot," she added, driving the sharp stab home, though she was only trying to be kind.

She glanced around, as though she had somewhere to be... or because she wasn't supposed to be here, with me.

My shoulders sagged. *I shouldn't have come.* I didn't know why I had. We hadn't spoken in years.

"I'm sorry for interrupting your day. I should probably go, they said you have a meeting."

I shivered as a cool breeze brushed against the back of my exposed neck; I'd twisted my hair up into a clip after my shower this morning, and now a few copper strands blew freely across my face as I turned away from her.

"No, please," she begged quickly, her hand gripping my upper arm for just a second before she yanked it back. "I-I know

I don't have long, and my dad is already—" She broke off and shook her head, a slight pink breaking through the pristine foundation on her cheeks. "He's introducing me to someone important. But I have a few minutes. Please, stay," she pleaded.

"Okay..." I acquiesced, and we fell back into a leisurely pace away from the main building. "So, what have you been up to... all this time? I haven't seen you, aside from this weekend, since my parent's funeral."

She and her family had disappeared right after that one, too.

"Just... working. Here. Helping my parents, learning the ropes. Doing what is... necessary... for the business."

"Did you go to school for business, then?" I wondered, thinking back to when we'd only begun to talk in high school about college and then teased lightly, "What happened to nursing?"

If there was one thing I remembered about my cousin, it was her love of science, almost equal to my hate for it, because all she ever dreamed of was becoming a nurse.

A dark shadow crossed over her face as her eyes dropped to the path we were walking around the small golf cart parking lot in front of the massive hotel, the path splitting ahead toward each of the two world-famous golf courses the resort boasted.

"I changed my mind," she explained quietly.

"And went for business?"

I shouldn't be asking. I shouldn't care. We hadn't seen each other in so long and it was going to be back to that hopefully sooner rather than later when I returned to L.A.

"I didn't go to college, Laurel," she finally replied with a dangerous mix of frustration and sadness that shot sparks right up to her hazel eyes as she looked at me.

My steps faltered at her admission—the single flaw in her picture-perfect shell, and the proof, in my mind, that something wasn't right. Not because she hadn't gone to college, but because I knew how much she'd wanted to and being able to afford it certainly wasn't an issue.

Jules had always had her head in a book studying for something—*learning something*. All she'd talked about the summer before our sophomore year was how she couldn't wait to go to college. And then, out of the blue, she'd been shuffled off to private school without so much as a goodbye.

"I thought..." I trailed off, trying to think of the right thing to say. "I thought that was the whole reason you went to boarding school, to better prepare you for college. I thought that was why you never answered my messages." I stopped to stare at her, forcing her to halt, too. "I thought you ignored me because I was a distraction from your schoolwork or something."

She crossed her arms over her chest. "What do you mean? What messages?"

"I emailed you and then wrote you after you switched schools," I informed her slowly, wondering why she appeared to have no idea I'd tried to contact her.

"Oh. Those letters," she brushed off, quickly appearing to recall what I was talking about. "I'm sorry, yes. I should've explained. I-I guess I was just so overwhelmed with the change and the word. School was very consuming, and I couldn't focus on anything else."

I balked.

One time, I'd snuck two apple fritters from a batch my grandmother had made for the church for Jules and me to share. She had a fight with her parents, and I wanted to make her feel better. When my grandfather—*of course*—caught us with sticky fingers and asked whose idea it was, Jules had jumped in and confessed—*lied* that it was her. And right now, she looked just as much a pretty liar as she had that day.

But Jules wasn't a liar unless it came to protecting someone she cared about.

Who was she protecting?

Quickly recovering from her slip, she apprised me, "From there, I had a place—*a business*—I needed to learn to be a part of. I'm an only child; it's my duty to be here and do what's necessary for Rock Beach to survive. College couldn't teach me about that," she scoffed in a way that was almost believable for how many times she'd probably told the same lie. "I would think, of all people, you would understand the importance to some of carrying on a family legacy. Although, you left Carmel, so maybe not."

I heard the bitterness scratching through her voice, but it was only on the surface; she said it because she needed me to let this go and not question her further.

"I made a choice, Jules. I always wanted Roasters… and my future… to be my choice and not an obligation. If my parents hadn't…" I swallowed over the huge lump in my throat.

In L.A., no one asked about my family (except my boss a few times) because no one cared, so I never had to talk about them or their deaths. But here, everyone cared about everything—*too much*.

"I couldn't stay. So, I chose a different future," I argued without the conviction I should've had. "I *needed* to."

Her eyes bored into mine with a sea of emotions that would never reach the shore. Instead, only a few drops of the spray managed to escape from the waves.

"Some of us aren't that lucky," she said so softly that if we hadn't stopped walking, I might not have even heard her.

"You can always make that choice," I replied quietly, noticing a very large man in black stalking over to us, his face so mercilessly stoic it drove a shiver through my body. "You can always choose yourself, no matter what anyone else wants or expects from you," I promised and then confided softly, "That's why I'm selling Roasters, Jules. I have to."

Maybe if I said it enough times, it would scare away any shadows of second thoughts.

She stepped back from me, surprise causing another crack in her composure.

"Laurel, I need to—" she stammered and then broke off abruptly as the giant suit-clad security officer invaded our conversation.

"Miss Vandelsen, you're late," he scolded with a voice that sounded like it came from a machine rather than a man. "Your father is wondering where you are."

A complacent smile appeared on her face even as she tried —and failed —to completely wipe the uneasiness from her eyes.

"Have a safe trip home, Laurel," she wished me genially as though we'd only been talking about the weather. "I'm so sorry about Larry. I'll be sure to give my mother your condolences."

My jaw dropped slightly as Jules nodded to me like it was some sort of formal goodbye before turning and walking back inside the hotel escorted by the mountain man. By every angle, she went willingly and purposely. Maybe it was just my imagination that saw the chains tethering her to this bejeweled jail.

What had I come back to?

What had I missed?

Something wasn't right here, I thought, watching Jules and the man disappear into the resort. Did no one else see? Or maybe they just simply believed what she wanted them to.

Who was I to ask questions? I chided myself. Jules was an adult. She wasn't locked inside this place like a prisoner. She chose to stay.

I'd been gone for so long, hadn't spoken to her for so many years... maybe I was reading too much into her words where there was just a different woman than the one I remembered; maybe that was what happened when I came here—I searched for problems where there were none, expecting them at every turn.

But better safe than sorry.

I lost myself in thought, walking back to the truck. The loud clanking as it turned over worried me for a second, before it rattled to life, and I let out a breath I didn't realize I'd been holding.

This was why I left. Too many questions. Too many attachments.

Too many things to care about that could disappoint me.

Whatever Jules' family issues were, they were *not* my business. I needed to leave the molehill alone and focus on doing whatever I needed to settle my grandfather's affairs and get back to my other life.

The sun was just setting by the time I numbly approached the driveway to my grandfather's—*my* house; the dim dusk gently illuminating the hidden turn.

I'd run every errand I could think of after leaving the resort—anything to keep me busy, because maybe that was the key. I stopped at the grocery store, a local clothing store, checked in on my boss, and answered a few work emails I convinced myself couldn't wait. But inevitably, I'd done everything I could possibly do, which meant coming back to the house was the only thing left...

My house sat on a small slice of heaven—a lush clearing on a cliff at the edge of the ocean, the waves crashed like a continuous round of applause greeting every arrival.

Hidden from the main coastal highway, the poorly-paved drive, exaggerated by the loose suspension of the truck, was long and narrowly wedged against the very edge of the rocky coastal cliffs. The precipitous drop was hidden by the thick, overgrown brush encroaching from either side.

The familiar scrape of branches began to drag along the sides of the old truck before the sound disappeared.

"What…" My eyebrows squished together. *The brush had disappeared.*

Who had—

Rounding the last curve gave me my answer before I could finish the question.

Eli.

My lips tightened as I drove toward his all-too-familiar face. *So much for avoiding him.*

Standing in the clothes he must've worn to Roasters today, judging by the white dust speckled guiltily over them, he hacked away at the overgrowth at the bottom of the drive. His eyes immediately caught mine when he noticed the truck in his periphery, the noise of the electric trimmer drowning out the engine.

His gaze followed me as I parked next to his truck and hopped down from the cab.

"What are you doing?" I yelled just as he cut the motor on the tool.

He stood solidly, pushing up his shirt sleeves over taut forearms and replied, "Cutting back the jungle that's been growing over the drive. Didn't want you driving closer to the cliff in order to avoid it."

I looked up the drive. *I couldn't argue with him.* It wasn't the safest driveway to start, but the foliage only made it worse. One swerve to avoid a branch could send you down the rocks and into the ocean.

"You didn't have to do that," I began, avoiding his eyes. "But thank you."

He nodded, a lock of hair falling loose on his forehead. "I was going to do the bushes around the house next… I've been doing the landscaping here for some time but after the break-in and…" He didn't need to say what I knew came next.

I blanched, my jaw slackening. "He let you?" I glanced around as though looking for proof and then murmured, "He loved doing this stuff…"

My pap had not only been meticulous about taking care of his property, but he'd enjoyed the process. Whole days out of the month were dedicated to keeping everything trimmed and maintained.

"I didn't give him much of a choice." He chuckled. "Especially not after the nasty gash he gave himself on his leg trying to use this thing a few months ago."

With every minute that passed, I fought not to walk right up to this man, curl into his chest, and let go of every hurt I carried. Time and again had shown him to be someone I could lean on—someone I could trust. I shuddered inwardly at the thought, again reminded that being a good person didn't exempt you from dying… *that being a good person didn't mean I couldn't lose him, too.*

"Thank you… for looking after him," I murmured.

He set down the hedge trimmer and tugged off his work gloves. *Who knew such a simple motion could make my body burn?*

The veins in his hands stood out from a long day of demolition and now, yardwork. The skin slightly flushed from exertion. I stared, mesmerized. His hands that knew only how to fix things… maybe if he touched me again, they could fix me, too.

"Don't thank me, Laurel," he rasped, my focus snapping back to his face and eyes that mirrored my own desire.

My lips parted, softly shaking my head.

"You should've seen him out here though." He pointed to

the extension cord leading behind me all the way to the house. Now that I looked, I noticed every few feet was wrapped with electrical tape. "I bought him this for Christmas a few years back—back when he was still doing yardwork—and he cut the cord so many damn times."

I felt a smile break over my face—break through the clouds that hung heavy over any glimpse at happiness.

"I swear, I came over just for the entertainment of it. He'd be out here for fifteen—maybe twenty—minutes and all of a sudden, I'd hear him yell, *'Jesus Christ!'* and the trimmer would go silent." He struggled to speak as his chest rumbled.

And then I was laughing, imagining the scene, hearing the words of frustration as though my pap were standing right in front of me. *And it felt good... so good to remember him this way.*

It was a moment when something more powerful than grief broke through and made me feel light. *Made me feel free.*

"I'd help him patch it up," he continued, his lopsided grin softening the lines of his face, "and another thirty minutes later, *'Jesus Christ!'*"

Deep, heaving laughs erupted from my chest, overtaking the need to breathe with their force.

"Look," he instructed, his hand shook with his own mirth as he lifted up the orange and black striped cord. "It looks like a damn tiger the way I had to keep fixing it with electrical tape."

And then, there were tears.

The last thing I ever expected coming back to Carmel Cove was for the first tears I cried without trying to hide or reason them away to be out of happiness rather than sadness.

Everything about the moment felt as though, in a different life, this was my world. Living here, surrounded by my family and their memory, with this man who fought to take care of me and make me smile.

And that was when my laughter stopped. Instinctively. Protectively. *Fearfully.*

"Laurel?" Eli immediately stepped toward me, his voice deepening.

I should've moved away. Instead, I remained frozen in place, feeling the strength of the ground underneath me, the stillness in the air I breathed. Maybe, if I didn't move, I could let him get just a little closer—fill in just a little bit more of my hollowness. *Just for a few minutes.*

"What's wrong?"

I stared at his chest now just a few short inches in front of me, the scent of fresh-cut foliage and Eli's earthy musk invading my nose and soothing my senses.

I clung to it as I waded through the fog. "I always thought I would see him again."

Even though I'd had no plans to come back, it was an inevitability in my mind that, at some point or another, I'd be back in Carmel... that I'd find my way back home to him.

His arms came around me like the breeze, soft and soothing and something I couldn't escape even if I wanted to.

"It's okay to miss him," he whispered, hoarsely, into my hair. "It's okay to hurt because he's gone. It's okay to be angry and sad. I'm angry, too. I'm angry because I should've done more. I should have forced those meds down his throat just like I forced him to stop doing all of the yardwork."

His words soaked through me, seeping against my skin and into my cells. I wanted to be angry. I wanted to scream at him and demand to know why he left. But I couldn't be angry.

How could I be angry when I had left, too?

"I want to be sad," I admitted with a toneless voice. "But what right do I have to be sad when I was the one who left him?"

I was trapped. Trapped with emotions I had no right to have.

I felt his jaw tense against my scalp, his fingers tightening their hold on the base of my neck. "Laurel, you have every right to be sad. You left because you were hurt. You left because it was what you needed to do in order to heal. That has *nothing* to do with this. You didn't leave because you didn't love him—and he knew that."

Warm hands cupped my face and tipped it up to his.

"He knew that, Laurel," he repeated, his eyes searching mine to see if his words were getting through.

"How?" I asked with a subdued tone.

"Do you know that he loved you?" he demanded.

I wasn't expecting the question, but I managed a nod. In spite of anything and everything else, I didn't doubt my pap loved me.

He pulled back, sliding one hand to cup my cheek and tip my face up. "That's how, sweetheart. Just like you know he chose to leave this world because he was hurting, not because he didn't love you… that's how he knew you wanting to leave this town had nothing to do with how much you loved him."

My chest caved as I buried my face against him.

It hurt so bad to think of him. To let myself wonder about all the things I should've done and should've done differently. No matter what Eli said, I couldn't stop the thoughts—the 'what-ifs.' Maybe if I had done one thing… *maybe if I just hadn't left…* my pap would still be alive.

"Laurel. It's okay to be sad. I'm here."

I drew back, my pulse spinning faster.

I didn't understand this man standing in front of me, holding me. I was on a sinking ship and he continued to bail water over the sides instead of abandoning what was, I was sure, a lost cause.

My eyes drifted to his mouth, and the warmth of my breath lodged in my chest as fuel for my fluttering heart. Confusion and loneliness welded together into a surge of yearning. For as much as I heard his words, I also saw the undeniable desire that lingered on his lips, drawn tight to hold himself back from saying more.

Giving more.

Taking more.

His gaze began to smolder, the warmth overwhelming me and drawing me closer.

My eyelids dipped as I let myself feel all of him, a completely hard and immovably protective male against me.

And hot.

So hot. Unfamiliar heat pulsed through me, stoking the pounding thud of my heart I felt beating in sync with his. I didn't have closeness with people anymore. *Not like this.* Even if I couldn't give him all of me, even if I couldn't open up the well that bubbled inside, maybe I could let him close to me like this. I could let him hold me.

Touch me.

Kiss me.

A shudder ran through me as the ocean breeze blew reality back into my bones, its salty smell a sharp break from the sticky heat woven between us. It was enough to remind me that no closeness was safe. *Especially in Carmel Cove.* Nothing that happened here was transient. It lingered like moss on a tree, slowly growing over the parts of you that stood tall to show the way north... the way that was true... *the way you need to go.*

I couldn't need him like this. I couldn't rely on him to fix the brokenness inside.

And I definitely couldn't risk kissing him again.

I pulled out of his arms and took a few uneven steps back.

"I-I'm sorry." I rubbed my hair back from my face, my body revolting against the loss of warmth. "Thank you. For doing this."

"Laurel—" His gaze implored me not to pull away.

"I'm fine. Really, Eli. I'm fine," I assured him with the 'I'm fine' every single woman on the planet uses at the moment in time when they are definitely anything but fine. "It's just been a long few days. Thank you, again. Have a good night."

I didn't wait for a response before turning, grabbing my things from my truck, and disappearing inside the house.

The knot in my stomach remained for the next hour while the trimmer ran outside.

He respected my privacy and need for space though he continued to work. And that unmistakable defiance declared he was going to be here for me whether I wanted him to be or not.

The knot twisted tighter, taunting me that I did.

I was strong. I'd survived the loss of my parents. I'd had the strength to leave my hometown and everything familiar in order to give myself a fresh start. But whether it was my strength or stubbornness starting to waver, leaning on someone to get through this grew more and more tempting.

And Eli… I shivered.

He stood in front of me like a lighthouse—everything hopeful and reassuring—in the middle of this dark and stormy sea. But I was afraid if I relied on him too heavily, I'd get close enough to realize his light was nothing more than a mirage, and too close to something dangerous I wouldn't be able to avoid.

Twelve

Laurel

After almost two weeks back in Carmel Cove, the amount of uncertainties I was facing seemed to be growing rather than dwindling.

Some *very stubborn* ones even taunted me in my sleep long after the hum of the electric trimmer was gone.

But if there was one thing I knew for certain, it was that repairing Roasters was going to take longer than another week. The water damage had been like a string on a sweater, the more we pulled at the walls, the more damage they unraveled.

Truth be told, it was probably going to take longer than the three weeks Eli had estimated when I arrived at the coffee shop about fifteen minutes ago. *But I wasn't going to tell him that.*

Better to be prepared than disappointed.

"Don't know that there's much left for you to take out, Little Laurel," Mick teased, nudging me with his elbow and shooting me a wink.

The notion of *small but mighty* had become popular between the brothers after my help earlier in the week. While I'd been so focused on forgetting, the twins had been impressed with how much I'd tackled.

"What are you talking about?" Miles chimed in with a smirk. "I think Eli could be knocked down a few pegs, don't you?"

Eli held up his middle finger, pausing in the middle of scribbling a bunch of notes for George when he came to take a look at the plumbing next week.

"Behave yourself, Miles," my Friendly Giant ordered, ever the responsible and respectful brother.

"Yeah? Or what?" He tugged on his gloves like they were boxing gloves and then pretended to punch the air as though ready for a fight.

My head tipped, wondering what kind of entertainment we were in for this morning.

These moments, filled with familiarity and kinship, almost made me forget why I was here... what this was all for.

And what it had cost me.

Even standing in the middle of utter destruction, the room entirely unrecognizable with missing walls and part of the ceiling, exposed beams, decaying pipes, it didn't feel as despairing as it once had. In spite of its wrecked appearance, there was the same comfort and warmth invading this space as when Roasters had been up and running, back when the energy from the people inside was more powerful than what it looked like.

Back when my family had still been alive.

Mick smiled calmly at him. "Or I'll send Eve out here to put you in your place."

Miles' arms fell to his sides and all trace of mirth vanished from his face. "I'm good."

Interesting.

"Did someone call my name?" Eve popped her head in from the hallway, looking around.

Only because of what I just saw did I catch how her gaze quickly skipped over Miles.

"No," he clipped and then turned and walked away.

"Sorry," Mick mumbled as apology for the both of them.

Her brave smile wavered as she turned and disappeared into the back again.

"You holding up okay?" The question drew my attention upward. For a second, I sunk into his possessive gaze, always there waiting... *wanting*... to both kiss and comfort me.

I could see the worry streaked across his face after I'd turned and bolted last night, but it was for the best. I'd felt too many things... with him... things I couldn't understand. *Things I couldn't risk.*

"Yeah, just need something to do," I said steadily, wiping my damp hands on my jeans.

"Unfortunately... or fortunately... because of your help, there's not a whole lot left to do before George takes a look," he said even as his gaze roamed my face, searching for signs of distress. "Eve's determined to tackle cleaning up the espresso machine today if you want to help her."

I winced. "I think it's easier if she cleans it without me."

The pans... the walls... I could handle those. Touching the cool metal of the machine, cleaning out the grinds in there from when my pap was still alive...

Yeah, that wasn't something I was going to be able to handle right now.

Hearing my reluctance, he suggested, "There are also some more books and albums and stuff underneath the counter over there. I don't know what you want to do with them... take them back to the house... or maybe Josie would want some of them..."

I nodded to that. Strange how old photos seemed less threatening than a coffee machine.

"Yeah, I can take a look."

"Here." He held out a mask for me.

While the brothers cleaned up the debris, it was hard to breathe out here without one. Careful not to brush his fingers, I murmured my thanks and tucked the straps around my ears.

I hesitated as I opened the cupboard doors, wondering if I was opening Pandora's box. *Too late now.* A stack of photo albums sat underneath the picture frames from the counter I'd peeked through earlier in the week.

I moved those to the side and reached for the album on top. The soft faux leather cover crinkled and creaked as I peeled it back to reveal faded sepia photos inside. Images of my pap from right before and during the war greeted me. *These were the ones he always looked at with Josie.*

Putting it to the side, I reached for the second album, the cover groaning even louder as I opened it. My fingers gingerly brushed over the plastic film. Photo after photo of my family and me. Memories lost for a long time now floated to the surface.

My breaths slowed as my ribs grew tight with a strange type of homesickness. Not one attached to a physical place, but rather a place in time. *A place in the past.*

I'd forgotten it was the Covington brothers who'd taught me how to ride a bike. I'd forgotten how Josie baked me a Narnia cake for my twelfth birthday. I'd forgotten about Roasters 'Coffee and Carols' event every Christmas Eve when coffee, hot chocolate, and snacks were shared with anyone who came inside while we sang Christmas carols well into the evening.

I laughed because the photo was of everyone singing except for my mom; she had a notoriously bad voice, and everyone knew and loved her for it. Instead, she stood behind the counter pouring coffee into the line of mugs waiting to be served with my dad by her side, handing a filled mug to someone whose face was hidden.

In the front of the crowd, my pap led the community choir with his accordion strapped around his neck. And I stood right next to him with the strand of jingle bells in my hand because it was always my job to jingle. My smile was alive with laughter as we looked at each other; I could almost hear the tune coming out of the photo—just like I could almost feel the love.

A drop of water splattered onto the plastic covering and I looked up, my first thought was a leak had sprung from the ceiling. But the ceiling was clear.

The leak had sprung from me.

Closing the cover reverently, I tucked the album along with the picture frames back into the cupboard and shut the door.

"I'm going to take this one down to Josie," I declared, peeling off my mask.

I didn't wait for acknowledgment before I bolted out the front door, the album under my arm, and took off down the block toward the Carmel Bakery.

The entry bell, similar to the one at Roasters, dinged as I opened the door. Immediately, I was assaulted by the mouth-watering wave of freshly-baked bread infused into the warm air and my steps slowed to savor the scent.

It wasn't always bread that stopped you in your tracks. I could remember times when it was double-chocolate chip cookies or Josie's famous banana-nut muffins. All different yet equally delicious.

I blinked quickly and saw the girl behind the counter watching me strangely.

I recognized her from the funeral—and her resemblance to

Josie. Like digging for something in the bottom of your purse, my mind rapidly pulled out name after name that wasn't what I was looking for until it finally came to me. *Cambria.*

Josie's daughter was younger than me, a quiet girl with pale blond hair that fell below her shoulders, a doll-like face, and subdued green eyes.

"How can I help you?" she asked with a voice as warm and sweet as if it had been baked in the back along with the rest of the pastries. But her smile told a different story; the way it looked like it had been broken and then patched back together with just enough pieces to string it together.

"Hi." I walked up to the counter. "I was umm… wondering if Josie was around? I just have something for her." I looked around, worried Josie wasn't even here.

"She's just in the back, give me one second." Turning, she disappeared through the swinging door, letting in another warm gust of baked bread. *"Mom, Laurel is here to see you."*

Josie appeared through the door a few seconds later, followed by her daughter, and wiped her flour-covered hands on her apron as she greeted me.

"Hi, Laurel," she said, equal measures of surprise and welcome baked into her voice. "Cammie, can you just go back there and keep an eye on the baguettes for me? If you want to work the sourdough while you wait, that would be wonderful."

With a nod to her mom, Cambria pushed through the door again, leaving Josie and me alone.

"Sorry to bother you," I began, lifting the photo album onto the counter. "I wanted to thank you for the basket you left at the house the other day."

"Oh, of course. I tried to put things that were your favorites in there." She beamed with a motherly smile. "I'm sure your tastes have changed, but—"

"Please. It was very thoughtful, and some things haven't changed," I reassured her without thinking, forcing a swallow through my throat that felt tight. "I stopped in because I just came across this up at Roasters, so I thought I would bring it down to you. I figured you might want it."

Her eyes homed in on the album, and she pulled it toward her slowly. "I wasn't sure if it was taken during the break-in," she murmured and blinked rapidly.

I should've told her it was spared and it was all hers and left, but my feet remained planted to the floor like my memories of this town had grown roots to try to keep me here.

Her smile widened as she opened the cover with trembling hands. Eyes shining, she pressed a palm to her heart as relief spread over her powder-dusted features.

"I can't tell you how many times your pap took time out of his day to look through these with me. I loved hearing his stories about my dad," she murmured.

I couldn't understand how. Any and every mention of my parents only brought unimaginable pain.

"Did you not... know him?" It was really the only explanation I could understand. If she hadn't known her father, she couldn't have been hurt by his memory.

"When I was younger, I did. He left for the war when I was a teenager and, unfortunately, didn't make it back." Her eyes flicked to mine. "I was probably about the same age as you when you lost your parents."

I needed to leave.

This was supposed to be for her—about her. Not me.

But those roots had grown deeper. I wanted to be upset because she'd used her past to dredge up my own, and because she was able to look at these photos and smile. Instead, I brimmed with jealousy that somehow her emptiness had been filled while mine had turned into a black hole, sucking in and eliminating anything and anyone who got too close.

"I'm sorry." I reached for the album. "If you don't want this, I'll just take it back. It's not a problem—"

Her hand pressed on top of the pages and held it from me. "Oh, no. Please." My hold relaxed as she looked down at the photos again. "My dad was so excited when him and your pap enlisted. And the stories your pap could tell…" She trailed off with a laugh. "My favorite was the time they chauffeured one of the commanding officers to a different base, but it was so foggy they couldn't see the road. They ended up having to stop and wait until morning to continue, and when morning came and the fog lifted, they realized they'd driven right into the middle of a field."

My chest lurched forward as she continued to page through the album.

"Why would you want to remember all of this?" I couldn't stop myself from asking—from accusing. "Why would you want to remember?"

"Oh, Laurel." The warmth in her eyes killed me. "When I look at these, I don't remember the loss. I remember the love."

I wasn't breathing. In fact, I wasn't sure my heart was even beating when she answered me.

The memory—*the recent one*—of Eli and me laughing last night, remembering my grandfather… it knocked the air right out from my lungs.

That was what she felt.

That was what she meant.

And it was all because of him. Unintentionally… unknowingly… *Because of Eli, I'd remembered the love.*

And the realization petrified me into silence.

"I haven't looked at these photos in a while." She sighed. "After you left, more often than not, I'd stop over at Roasters and ask him to see the pictures in the other album... the ones of you and your parents."

"Why?" I croaked out in disbelief. I could understand wanting to see photos of her father. But we weren't family. "Why would you want to see photos of me?"

"Because I knew your grandfather needed a reason to remember the love," she explained, looking up at me with a sad smile. "He'd spent so many years telling me about my dad when I needed it. When your parents died and you left for school, it was time I returned that kindness. He needed to remember the good times because it was getting harder and harder."

My throat burned like the acid from my stomach was eating its way out of me with each dragging inhale.

I flinched when her hand reached for mine, but I couldn't pull away.

"He loved you so much, Laurel. They all did." Her assurances wrapped around me like a warm impenetrable shield. "He just... didn't know how to make it better for you... or for himself. He thought maybe the space would help you heal. I don't know if he was right or wrong about that, but I know he missed you very much. Every week we'd look through photos. Every week I'd bring over my laptop and we'd look and see how you were doing at school and then we'd follow the news about the company you worked for and the great things you were doing."

I started to shake my head. I didn't want to hear this. I didn't want to know.

"I told him to call you so many times. He just..." She sighed. "Well, you know how Larry could be. Stubborn as the ocean is deep. He knew how much everything about this place hurt you... and if you were finally happy and doing something you loved, he didn't want to bring that hurt back into your life."

I wanted to scream.

What if I wasn't happy?
What if I liked my job but didn't love it?
What if I wasn't supposed to leave?
What if I was supposed to stay?

Like a lead anvil, guilt crashed into my chest without warning.

Those 'what ifs' were on me. I made choices and stuck to them. It was no one's fault other than my own.

"Oh, Laurel." She shut the photo album and clasped my hand in both of hers on top of it. Her hands felt like soft, warm dough as they folded over mine. "You know how stubborn he was. I lost count of how many scrapes and bruises I'd see him with because he'd rather hurt himself than burden someone else by asking for help." Her chest heaved. "Eli did what he could, bless his heart, but the break-in… I think it put him over the edge."

The room fell away and the air thickened until breathing felt like I was trying to inhale molasses into my lungs.

"I should've—"

"This is *not* your fault." She squeezed my hand for emphasis, her warmth fighting desperately to heat the cold guilt pulsing in my fingers. "Your pap loved you and he *never* would have done this if he could have realized what it would do to you. But he couldn't…" Josie paused to wipe a tear from her eye. "He couldn't realize because he was lost. Lost in his darkness… in his depression."

I fought to breathe. I'd never struggled with sadness because I never let myself. I pushed it all away and focused on something else. *Was that what he'd done?* Was that what happened when you pretended to be okay for so long?

"He wasn't himself, Laurel, and you're not to blame for that. How many times did you and I hear from him that life is about giving and receiving? Only half is about the help and the love you give, the other is about the help and love you receive. I think he forgot about that second part. He gave and gave and, for whatever reason, wouldn't take the love so many of us were waiting… trying to give…"

Because that was what depression did.

It took strengths and turned them into weakness. It mutated the mind's thoughts and turned it into a traitor.

It made a man who stubbornly fought to help everyone around him forget how to ask for help himself. It made a man who was so loved believe he had nothing left to live for.

Depression wasn't a disability. *It was a cancer.*

"I'm sorry. I can't—" I gasped as her fingers tightened like a steel vise around mind.

"Grief is the other side of love, Laurel." Her warm perceptive eyes pierced mine. I blinked, and for a brief, insane second, I saw my pap standing in front of me, his worn, weathered face lit by the brightest, comforting smile. "Like sunrise and sunset. You can't have one without the other." *Ishkey.*

The last I heard though it was unspoken as Josie let go of my hand to reach for a tissue, turning away as her shoulders began to shake.

And then I felt it all—the loss, the sadness, the loneliness, the hopelessness. *The love.* And I bolted for the door. She was wrong.

If I stayed, the pain would bring me to my knees. It would break me.

And I was afraid I'd never be able to stand again.

Thirteen

Laurel

Grief was like the ocean. Unpredictable. Inescapable. Some days, the sea was a calm ebb and flow. Others, overwhelming with waves rising and crashing.

But today? Today, it was a riptide. A gentle deceptive tug urging me deeper and deeper until it swept me off my feet and pulled me under.

Today, it was dangerous.

My feet carried me back to Roasters, but I paused in the doorway, seeing no one inside.

Pushing the frayed strands of hair that had escaped my ponytail back from my face, I checked my watch and realized I'd been down at the bakery so long, everyone had gone for lunch. *And they'd left the door unlocked.*

The front room was empty, but there was a light left on in the back.

"Hello?" I yelled even though it was as quiet as a tomb. "Eve?"

My hand shook as I closed the door behind me; this was the first time I'd been in here alone. Each breath felt like air being stabbed into my lungs as past and present warred in front of me. The more we took down of this place, the more memories bled from the walls. My parents. My pap. Everyone I loved had built this place and been built into it in return. And now, it was in shambles and it was all my fault.

If I had stayed, this wouldn't have happened.

If I had stayed, maybe he wouldn't have died.

I halted as the single bulb gleamed across the crafted metal of the espresso machine, shining like new.

An unexpected laugh bubbled up in my throat.

It looked ridiculous. This perfect, glowing machine in the middle of complete destruction.

How could it still be okay?

My throat thickened as I stepped in front of it, even though I knew I wouldn't cry. That only seemed to happen when Eli was around. And I wondered if grieving for someone who wanted to die was worse than for someone who didn't?

Would it be worse to miss someone who wanted to be gone?

"Why?" I asked hollowly, my fingers shaking as they splayed across the metal *La Pavoni* emblem in the center of the machine. "Why did you have to go?"

I asked as though it could reply for him.

But the answer I heard was my own reason for leaving Carmel all those years ago... *Because I couldn't bear the thought of being here any longer, no matter the people who loved me and needed me to stay.*

My eyes squeezed shut, and when they reopened, I noticed the espresso cup sitting on the ledge of the machine.

My head tipped unsteadily. *Had that been there before?*

I reached for it. *Was that coffee in it?*

Just another inch closer confirmed the contents by their strong scent, the warmth of the cup indicating it was just made.

I looked around again. "Is anyone here?" *Still no answer.*

I shouldn't. I knew I shouldn't. Not today. Not after Josie.

Not when love and grief were two sides of the same coin.

But I asked a question into the silence, and this... *this was its answer.*

It was a stupid thing, really, to think a cup of coffee could change anything. *Could change my life.* But it was never just a cup of coffee in this place. *It was a connection.*

Taste, like smell, was one of the strongest sensory connections the brain had to past memories. And like Alice, I'd fallen down this rabbit hole I was desperate to escape, only I didn't need a *Drink Me* sign to encourage me to take one taste.

The rich, potent brew drowned me, engulfed my senses, and took me back.

I jolted as that first swallow spanned years of my life, years in this building with people who I would never see again. Love and loss tangled in a web of new connections, reprogramming the space between my brain and heart that had been wiped clean.

"Laurel?"

My eyes popped open, and a strangled noise escaped. *"Eli?"*

I set the mug down with a loud crash, black filtering into my periphery as I reached for something—anything—to hold on to.

And of course, just like every other time I reached out for something steady and sturdy, I always found him.

"*Jesus.*" He moved into my space, ready to catch me or hold me or kiss me—ready to do whatever I needed... whatever I asked.

His arms locked around me, flattening me against his warm

strength as one hand cupped my cheek. His twin dark flames assessed every inch of my face and he demanded, "What's wrong? What happened?"

My mouth dried up and even though I was staring at him, I wasn't seeing him. My mind was elsewhere, though my body was grounded to him.

"My pap had let me make espresso that night," I told him hollowly, clinging to him as the memories pulled me deeper like the strongest riptide. "He'd helped me roast the beans that morning because I told him I wanted to make my parents coffee before they went out." I tried to swallow but couldn't. My throat was a one-way valve: only words were allowed out.

"They stopped in to say goodnight, all dressed for a charity event. My mom looked so beautiful," I continued with a voice that was hardly recognizable. "They were running late, so they couldn't stay for coffee... for me to tell them." My knees weakened but the arms holding me made sure I didn't sink. "I remember I wasn't even upset. I remember drinking my little cup of coffee, so proud of it... and so sure I would tell them in the morning."

I blinked and Eli's tortured face came into focus.

"But morning never came."

"Laurel..."

My gaze trembled. The aftertaste of the coffee burned my palate and throat. I wanted water or soda or acid... anything to make it go away.

"It tastes like the last time I saw them." *Strong. Bittersweet. Unpalatable.*

"God, I'm sorry, Laurel," he rasped, his fingers wiping over my cheeks as though there were tears to clean. "It's my fault. I just ran next door for a sandwich."

My breath stumbled into my chest. "*You* made this?"

The hammering in my chest seized.

He nodded hesitantly. "Eve cleaned it up this morning. Figured I should see if it still worked."

No. No. No.

My hands that had curled into his shirt unraveled, flattening against his chest as I tried to push him away.

He'd made this. He'd brought me back.

He was responsible.

"It's okay to remember them... to remember him." His arms tightened in an effort to keep me close.

"No, it's not." I shook my head, pulling away.

"Why do you fight it?" He huffed. "I just want to help you. Just like I wanted to help him. And *both* of you are too damn stubborn to just lean a little. Dammit, Laurel, it's okay to not be okay."

"Because!" I yelled, shoving myself out of his reach, pointing an accusing finger at him. "Because to remember them, to remember their loss, I'd have to remember the parts of me they took with them when they left—the parts only they knew." I let out a bitter laugh. "And to tell you the truth, Mr. Know-It-All, without those parts, I don't know if there's anything left of me."

The words were sharp, sudden, unfair.

Just like loss.

"You're wrong." His protest was instantaneous, highlighted by the fierce insistence in his eyes. "I don't know it all, but I do know there is more left of you. More strength. More dreams. More fight."

Each assertion was a punch to my stomach.

"I don't know what pictures you've seen or what stories you were told," I began hollowly, straightening so tall it felt as though there must be a string pulling me upright from the ceiling. "But I can tell you that you don't know me at all."

It wasn't a gauntlet that was thrown, only the truth. But it fell with just as much force.

The way his eyes sparked and flared, the finest heat congealing inside them, felt like he could see right through me. Like he could see right into the closed off parts of my heart. *Like he'd stop at nothing to get to them.*

My arm dropped to my side with a thud and I turned and bolted for the back door.

The photos, the coffee, the memory... *it was all winning.*

And as I fled, I felt the subtle pop of all the lines I'd already attached to him. So many invisible threads of support he'd given when I hadn't even realized it. All working together to form another dangerous link between me and this place —between my heart and this man.

I wasn't even fully seated in the truck before I cranked the key in the ignition. Banging on the steering wheel with my palm a few times, the last accompanied by a strangled cry, I tried to release some of the anger and tension and *everything* threatening to burst inside me.

"Laurel!"

My head jerked up, hearing my name tear angrily from those beautiful lips. *I hated how I wanted to kiss him even when I was mad at him.* Harsh frustration outlined every line of his face as he stalked toward the truck.

My head thudded just as erratically as the old engine trying to run smooth.

Damn man wouldn't give up.

He growled over the roar of my pap's old truck, "Dammit, Laurel, don't do this."

Whatever tree stubbornness came from, we'd both been fed the poisonous fruit.

Pursing my lips, I threw the truck in reverse, slung one arm over the passenger headrest, and shot Eli one last wild 'I'm leaving, and you can't stop me' stare before I backed out of the drive to the tune of his steely stare.

Grief was unreasonable. *Or maybe it was just me.*

Because I was unreasonably upset by the damaged walls being torn down, unreasonably upset by photos of a past I swore I didn't want. Unreasonably upset by a stupid cup of coffee.

But, most of all, unreasonably upset by the gorgeous man who got so easily under my skin and made it seem like it would be the safest thing in the world to trust him… to lean on him and let him in.

But it wasn't safe.

That type of thing was like the Titanic—marketed as indestructible and unsinkable. Until it ran across something it never expected. And when you encountered the unexpected, there was no time to safely evacuate all the pieces of your heart before disaster took your whole life down.

Fourteen

Eli

Goddamn stubborn woman. She was worse than Larry, it was official, I thought to myself as I watched the old truck disappear down the street. *Christ.*

"I always knew you had a way with the ladies," Miles drawled from somewhere behind me.

Turning with a glare, I saw both brothers peering out the back door of the building.

"At least she wasn't holding that mallet when you pissed her off."

Mick smacked the back of his brother's head before maneuvering outside over to me.

"She okay?" he asked slowly.

My heavy sigh carried on the wind as my shoulders dropped. "No."

"You okay?"

I paused. "Are any of us?"

His head dipped slightly. "We will be," he replied and, with a small smile added, "Larry'd have our heads if we weren't."

A harsh exhale escaped. *Well, that was true.*

"You should go." He nodded in the direction the truck had gone.

I wanted to.

God, my feet shifted, *needing* to.

Running a hand through my hair, I swore under my breath. "I have to wait for George to come back."

"If you think we're incapable of handling the plumber, maybe we need to rethink our working arrangement," Miles chimed in.

I stepped to the side, looking past Mick to his smartass brother who eyed me with dark, devious eyes. He was right. *He was just a dick about it.*

All I wanted was to hold her until she knew I wouldn't let go—until she knew it was safe to lean on me even just for a little while.

"You know we'll be fine here," Mick added. "Go get some flowers or chocolate or somethin' and apologize."

"What's he apologizin' for?" Miles scoffed.

Mick grunted and turned on his brother. "Speaking. Hell, breathing. It doesn't matter. When a woman's upset, the first thing you do is apologize. Period."

"That's bullshit."

"Ignore him," Mick instructed.

I chuckled and shook my head.

"Even with an apology, I don't think she wants to see me right now," I confessed. "I made a cup of coffee and she stormed out. Tried to talk to her and she drove off. Not sure what she'll do if I go over there and apologize, but I'm worried it won't be good for me."

"Well, if Larry has a mallet at the house, it won't be." *Dick.*

"You know what I think," Mick began, sending his brother a

pointed stare. "I think the people who need love the most are the ones who push it away the hardest."

Miles' mouth disappeared into a tight line.

Love?

My teeth clenched. I knew what he meant, but my desire for Laurel clouded everything. More than Larry's death. More than Roasters repair. More than anything, she'd consumed my thoughts from the moment I met her.

"And sometimes, the simplest things can make the greatest impact," he finished.

His words hit home. "We all know Larry would agree with that," I mumbled.

We stood quietly for a moment, a low breeze swirling around us from the ocean a few blocks down.

"Start where you are," Mick finally said quietly, and the silence grew heavy.

A few seconds later, Miles continued roughly, "Use what you have."

I looked between them and cleared my throat, finishing hoarsely, "Do what you can."

Start where you are. Use what you have. Do what you can. They were famous words here in Carmel. Famous words Larry engrained into everyone.

He said them so much Mick burned the saying into a slab of stained maple to hang above the espresso machine. A simple reminder. *A simple promise.*

I sighed, resting my hands on my hips and letting my head drop forward. Mick clapped me on the shoulder a second later.

"I know you've got a plan," he told me.

"Oh yeah?" I laughed. "And how do you know that?"

"Because, you're Eli Downing." He gave me a lopsided smile. "You're just like him. You never give up on people who need you."

"Thanks."

"And it's goin' to work," he assured me with another pat.

"You can't know that," I charged.

"Oh, I can." He nodded confidently. "The way you look at her says you won't stop until it does."

With one more pat, he followed his brother inside and closed the door behind him.

Subtle.

Well, I knew where I wasn't wanted. I sure as hell hoped where I was going was where I was needed.

Mick was right about one thing though. I did have a plan.

I pulled out my cell and called in a lifeline.

"Hello?"

"Hey, Ash. You at the restaurant?"

His restaurant was due to open next weekend, so it was a safe bet he was there now.

"Yeah. Putting everything to the test. What's up?" he asked and I heard pans clanking in the background.

"I need a favor." I cleared my throat. "I know it's not Sunday, but I need you to make me some spaghetti and meatballs with Larry's marinara."

His famous Sunday dinner.

There was a pause. "The magic marinara?"

"Yeah."

Another pause. "Damn. Okay. Give me two hours."

"You sure?" I winced, pinching my brow.

"Eli, if you're asking for that meal, I know you're in trouble," he replied. "Don't worry. There's nothing this sauce hasn't been able to fix." I heard the grin in his voice.

"Thanks." I sighed and hung up.

A lot of broken people had found solace at Larry's Sunday dinners. Anyone who needed a meal, an ear to listen, or a shoulder to lean on was welcome—a tradition Ash was going to carry on at his restaurant. *A tradition I hoped Laurel wasn't immune to.*

I squinted up to the sky and murmured, "I'm doing what I can." The sun peeked out from behind a cloud as though shining its approval.

Sometimes, the only thing to do was not give up.

"I hope it's enough."

A few hours later, freshly showered, shaved, and bearing the greatest peace offering of all time—*hot, Italian food*—I pulled down the drive to Larry's house just as the sun was setting.

Even with all the trimming I'd done, the storms passing through left a trail of severed branches that crunched and cracked with warning as I approached.

I dragged in a steadying breath, the scent of homemade marinara sauce from the brown paper bag invaded my nostrils and filled my truck; it was one of those aromas that would linger in here for a couple days.

I debated calling before I showed up. *But where else would she be?* Plus, I doubted she would answer. And as far as trying the house phone... well, Larry had disconnected that line a long time ago, grumpily declaring he was only ever one of two places, if someone wanted to talk to him, they would know where to find him.

Still, relief settled into my bones, warm and hopeful, when I saw his truck parked out front. *She was here.*

Shutting off my truck, I grabbed the bag that weighed far too much to contain food fit for only two people and, putting on my best expression of sincere yet determined remorse, I made for the front door.

Two knocks, no answer. I looked around, surprised I wasn't being chased off the property by a mallet-wielding redhead, and tried again.

Nothing.

Worry came barreling in when she didn't answer the second time.

"Laurel?" I yelled, knocking once more. "It's Eli."

Still silence.

Shit.

With a growl, I twisted the doorknob, knowing a locked door wasn't something that existed in Larry Ocean's world.

"Laurel?" I yelled as I stepped inside, my heart beginning a heavy thud.

A quick scan of the room showed the lights in the kitchen and living room were on. Walking into the living room, I caught a faint whiff of smoke from the old-fashioned, iron fireplace but the fire had been out for a little while and the latched door was closed. Sitting on the pile of blankets on the couch was an old, tattered copy of *The Lion, the Witch, and the Wardrobe* perched on top of a stack of crossword puzzle books.

"Laurel, are you in here?" I called again. "It's Eli. I came to apologize, and I brought dinner."

I went to reach for my phone but stopped when I caught sight of hers lying on the kitchen counter. *So much for that.*

My mind checked off the possibilities. The truck was still here, so she was still here. But with the house empty...

Fuck.

I whipped back toward the door. There was only one place left for her to be.

Out by the cliffs.

Adrenaline pumped like lightning through my veins imagining her walking near them in the dark.

Fuck. Fuck. Fuck.

Setting the bag on the dining table, curses echoing my footsteps, I stalked toward the door. Cold metallic fear coated my hand as I grabbed the doorknob and swung it open.

"*Christ.*" I skidded to a halt.

My chest expelled the word along with the air collected inside it, prepared to yell Laurel's name, when I saw her standing right in front of me. With a low growl, I dug my hands into my hips and accused hoarsely, "You scared the shit out of me."

My eyes did a quick scan over her to make sure she was, in fact, real and alive and okay.

Her vibrant hair was piled high on top of her head, wild from the wind. She'd changed from earlier into a loose white tee, navy shorts, sneakers, and a less-than-relieved glare to see me.

She crossed her arms over her chest and the way it pushed her tits up, her hard nipples poking against the fabric of her shirt.

Fuck. She wasn't wearing a bra.

My dick immediately shot to attention, straining against the front of my jeans. I'd wanted her too badly for too long. And since my punishment for wanting Larry's granddaughter was self-inflicted abstinence, I was ready to explode with just the slightest provocation.

Clenching my teeth, my vision faltered in order to reel my focus back to the reason I was here.

"You shouldn't be out there alone. In the dark," I bit out.

"And you shouldn't be here." She notched her chin up to better pin me with her stare. "I could have you arrested for trespassing."

Her blue irises were no longer stormy. The clouds had cleared to reveal a deep, melancholic hue that hugged darker around the edges.

My arms dropped to my sides as I nodded. "But you won't."

I stepped back so I wasn't completely filling the doorway.

She arched one eyebrow, a defiant flame slicing across her forehead, and asked as she slipped by me. "How are you so sure?"

"Because lawsuits take longer than repairs," I answered wryly.

Her irritated gaze snapped back over her shoulder to me. They broke their hold for a second to scan over me, and I wished I hadn't caught the trace of desire that shot straight to my groin.

Clearing my throat, I ignored the angry ache, watching her turn away, and pressed on, "I brought dinner and an apology."

"I'm not—" Her steps halted at the edge of the kitchen and she whipped around to face me. "What did you bring?"

"Pasta and meatballs," I answered, adding on quietly at the end, "With your grandfather's sauce."

Her mouth parted slightly and I fought not to groan as lust punched me in the gut.

The stain in her cheeks crept lower, down over the white silk of her neck before it disappeared beneath her shirt—a shirt that was almost see-through under the lights. I forced my attention to her face, ignoring the need to know if her blush extended to the tips of her tits and if her nipples were just as rosy.

The air hung suspended on the tipping point. After the memory that ripped her away from me earlier, my proclaimed peace offering was a risk—*a risk of more memories*. But it was one I had to take.

"It smells so good," she said softly, and my eyes widened, wondering if I'd succeeded.

She inhaled deeply, her breasts pushing against her shirt. She breathed in like it was more than air her lungs needed. She breathed like the molecules of memories in the nostalgic aroma could feed her soul.

"I haven't had this meal in a long time." Her throat bobbed as she swallowed. "I don't know if it will be the same."

Sometimes, things didn't have to be the same for them to be just as good, I wanted to tell her. Instead, I nodded and simply tried to hide my relief.

At least, she wasn't kicking me out.

Not yet.

It was a small progress but I would take it.

"I hope you're hungry because I'm pretty sure there's enough food in there for six." I kept my tone light, not wanting to push any more than I already had.

"Well, I don't know about you, but I can definitely eat three people's worth."

She returned my smile and fuck if that brilliant sight wasn't enough to make a man cling to even the smallest thread of hope.

It only took a few minutes to get plates and silverware set since we were both equally familiar with the kitchen. The ungodly amount of spaghetti and meatballs Ash had cooked up was split into two monstrously even piles between us.

And then I waited.

I watched as she rolled up the first forkful, blowing off some of the steam before her eyes slipped to mine.

"Thank you," she murmured.

Simple things. Small steps. *Do what you can.*

"Bon appétit," I said roughly and held my breath.

The moan that slipped effortlessly from her lips as she took her first bite pushed me right to the edge of coming inside my pants. It was unexpected and erotic, and everything made to drive a man insane.

"This sauce is… just like his," she murmured in awe, digging in for another huge bite.

Larry's red sauce was famous around these parts—almost as famous as his coffee. I knew, because I'd seen it made. The labor of love took a few hours, the tomato base cooked slowly on the stove. Basil, parsley, and a dash of sugar all soaking together until it thickened up. The spices mixed with the sweetness and the acidity of the tomatoes melted into heaven on your tongue.

Magic Marinara.

We ate for another few moments in reverential, hungry silence. And as she greedily devoured her plate, I knew I'd made the right call coming here with this.

One last torturous moan shifted into a sigh as the pink tip of her tongue slipped out and slid lazily up her fork.

I choked and shifted my chair, unable to stop myself from imagining the caress on my cock causing it to revolt against my pants.

"He gave Ash the recipe when Ash decided he wanted to open the restaurant," I offered as an explanation... as *anything* to take my mind off of her.

"I didn't think it would be the same."

"It's pretty damn close," I agreed. "But I think it's the effort, not the ingredients, that make it special."

Her face shadowed.

"I'm sorry about earlier, Laurel," I said gruffly, setting my fork on my plate. "I'm sorry about the coffee. I didn't mean to make you upset and I didn't mean to overstep. I do just... want to help."

Even now, the ragged pain on her face when she stared at me from the truck was like a knife through my heart.

She stared at her empty plate, as though the marinara stains could predict her future.

"You shouldn't have to apologize. I overreacted. It's just... hard... being back here. It's hard remembering..." With a hard swallow, her head tipped to the side.

It wasn't everything. It wasn't every hurt or pain she carried. But, for a moment, it was as though she'd pulled off her fighting gloves and exposed the raw, open wounds on her hands—hands that had tried and failed to hold on to so many people who were taken from her.

And I sat in awe of her strength.

Beautiful. Broken. *Beholden.*

"Do you want to talk about it?" I murmured.

Twin blue drops, twenty-thousand-leagues of loss deep looked to me. "How can I? I'm just trying to keep my head above water." She shivered, recollecting herself and added, "Even if I did, I wouldn't know what to say."

My shoulders dropped. I understood.

I understood how there were no words to drain a sea of grief.

"It's going to take time, but you won't swim the ocean like this forever," I filled in when it looked like she couldn't continue. "This is the kind of thing that takes more than a few days… a few weeks… a month to process."

"To move on?" she asked bitterly with a quick shake of her head as though such a thing weren't possible.

I gripped the edge of the chair.

I wanted nothing more than to hold her, to pull her back into my arms and push the stray strands of red from her face and whisper in her ear that everything was going to be okay. But, like someone who'd been starved of food for too long, whose stomach would immediately reject a feast, consoling her when she hadn't allowed herself that comfort in so long would only drive her away.

"You're going to be okay, Laurel," I told her quietly, adding, "You're a strong bean."

"What?" she gaped.

"A strong bean," I repeated.

"He said that to me." She pulled her arms across her as her expression strained cautiously. "The first time I had coffee. He was making some after dinner for himself; he always did before we would sit and do crossword puzzles together. I was maybe about seven or eight, and I asked if I could have a cup." A whisper of a smile crossed her face. "He hesitated and then begrudgingly agreed."

I nodded, vividly imagining the scene.

"I remember how wide my eyes went—wider than the mug he sat in front of me—and I had a grin the size of Texas on my face. I took a huge breath, but only because that's what I'd seen him do so many times." Her eyes glazed over. "I think I'd already decided that I loved it before the first taste hit my tongue."

"And did you?" I chuckled. Coffee was a hard flavor for a kid to like.

"I did…" Her head tipped. "Well, I told him I did, and it was the truth. But I don't think it had anything to do with the taste."

My chest tightened with understanding. "Did he believe you?"

"He laughed just a little and took the mug away," she replied, staring out in a daze. "And then he told me I was a strong bean."

I nodded, repeating the advice I'd heard so many times. "He used to say people were like coffee beans. Different flavors. Different origins. Dark. Blonde. Italian. Colombian. But none of that mattered when you put the bean in some hot water. Whatever was on the inside would come out stronger in the end." I stood and reached for her plate, meeting her gaze. "I know it's hot water coming back here. Being at Roasters. Remembering Larry. It's fucking scalding," I went on, roughly. "But you're a strong bean."

We stayed there, eyes locked for a moment as my statement settled.

She wanted to disagree—*to argue*. Her body was tight. Her brow furrowed. The blue of her irises unsettled. And a few days ago, she probably would have. But not tonight. Because slowly, surely, I was proving to her it was safe to let those walls come down.

What was inside Laurel—beyond the frustration, beyond the pushback, beyond the pent-up grief—was deep-seated loyalty and endless love.

And I wasn't going to give up until she realized she was strong enough to let her feel it once more.

"Why did you come here?" she asked a few seconds later as I carried our plates to the sink.

I looked over my shoulder. "I came to apolo—"

"No, I mean to Carmel Cove."

"Oh." I turned the sink on and began to scrub the dishes clean. "That was as far as the trucker who picked me up was going," I told her, laughing to myself. "He was delivering coffee beans to Roasters."

I remembered that day like it was yesterday. Soda and Red Bull cans littered the truck's cab that had picked me up outside of San Diego and brought me all the way up here.

"You hitchhiked here?" She was next to me, reaching to take the first plate from my grasp, towel in hand.

I nodded. "Almost never stepped foot inside Roasters, too. But the driver threw out his back the night before so he asked if I could help him unload the pounds upon pounds of green coffee beans into the storage room." Handing her the second plate, I flipped off the water and turned to face her, resting my hip against the edge of the sink. "That's how I learned that Larry Ocean doesn't lock anything."

She glanced up and caught my wry grin.

Her movements slowed. "He always said whatever he had—"

"—belonged to the town," I finished with her and our eyes

locked. "Because sometimes people who need help are the ones who don't know how to ask for it... or willingly accept it."

"Wherever you get in life, Mr. Dowling, you don't get there alone," he'd said firmly, like he'd was a teacher who wanted to retire years ago but loved what he did too much to let it go. "While I'd prefer to choose to help someone. Sometimes, that someone doesn't have the luxury of being able to ask. So, I don't lock anythin' around here. Never have, never will. If someone needs somethin' of mine bad enough to take it without askin', then I know they sure must need it more than me."

She inhaled sharply, taking my meaning.

I would help her. Not because Larry and Roasters deserved it, but because she did, too. She deserved to know there were people here she could lean on—*with or without asking.*

"My dad and him always fought about that," she said softly. "I mean, not really fought, but my dad didn't like leaving the shop unlocked every night. Still, nothing ever happened."

Until now. The thought made my fingers tense around my fork. We were going to find the motherfucker who ransacked Roasters. *Whether it was Blackman or whoever he was working for.* They hadn't just destroyed property. They'd ruined the promise between Larry and this town—*to respect the man who'd do anything for them.*

The soft light from above the sink caught the edges of a few runaway strands of red, making them look like threads of flickering fire shielding around her face, beautiful to look at but willing to burn anyone who got too close.

"Laurel," I began, ending with a strangled groan as the pink tip of her tongue darted out to lick the lower swell of her lip.

God, I was so hungry for her.

But I couldn't have her. Not now. Not like this.

Not when she wasn't sure what her life here held.

Her mouth parted and for a second, I thought she was going to kiss me. *And it would've been my downfall.*

Instead, she winced and her nose scrunched up. "What's that smell?"

She turned away, hesitantly moving back toward the dining table. My head cocked to the side, taking a breath. *Did she mean the food?*

I inhaled again, following her direction. My eyes popped wide when I caught the scent. Low and ominous.

Smoke.

"*Fuck*," I growled. "The fireplace."

Fifteen

Eli

"*L*aurel!" I shoved toward her as she rushed into the living room, streaks of smoke escaping from the latched door.

Larry hadn't had the chimney cleaned in years. I'd offered countless times, but he always refused, saying I had more important things I could be doing other than chimney sweep.

"Laurel, don't touch—" I warned angrily as she reached for the door, futile words as her shriek cut them off.

Her hand jerked back in pain, bringing the burning wrought iron door with them and a huge billow of black smoke.

Cursing under my breath, my arm came up to shield my face as I reached blindly for Laurel. Just as I grabbed her shoulder, her small, soot-covered form reeled back into my chest, her frame shaking as she coughed and hacked into her elbow, her softness quaking against me.

"Christ, Laurel," I grunted, gripping the silken flesh of her arms and spinning her behind me. I didn't want her anywhere near that thing; if it was going to harm anyone, it was going to be me. "Stay back."

As she kept coughing, I held my elbow over my mouth as I quickly unlatched the windows facing toward the ocean to let in clean air and take out some of the floating ash. Waving my arm in front of the still spitting fireplace, it took only a few more seconds before enough had cleared for me to see what was going on.

"I thought—" a cough that sounded like it was bringing her lung with it, interrupted her, "—it had died down earlier... before I went outside."

Grunting, I reached for the poker and began prodding inside the soot-covered space. It looked like the rush of air inside had finally stifled whatever embers had caused this mess.

"Fireplace hasn't been used in years," I said, my throat hoarse and scratchy from breathing in the smoky particles. "And I don't know when the chimney was last cleaned." Making sure there was no sign of burning life inside, I hung the poker back up with a heavy exhale. "Looks like you trapped just enough hot embers inside to reignite."

"Oh God..." She trailed off with a low, rough voice. "Could I have..."

My jaw clenched. If she hadn't opened the door, the smoke and debris could've built up enough pressure to make something explode or burst into flames—but when I turned and took a good look at her now that I knew everything was safe, there was no way I was going to tell her that.

"It's fine, Laurel," I said gruffly, poking through the embers one more time as the night breeze sucked out most of the smoke from the room. "Everything is fine."

Propping the iron rod back on its stand, I faced her. She was still looking in horror at the small, blackened fireplace, imagining just how badly this could've gone.

With a low growl, I grabbed a handful of tissues off the coffee table and stood in front of her, blocking her view of the fireplace and forcing those ocean eyes back on me.

"What—" Her question was cut off when the tail of tissue covered her mouth as I began to wipe the soot from her face.

When she'd opened the door, the burst of smoke had given her a mask of ash, mostly covering her forehead and cheekbones. I half-expected her to protest my help, but the shock of what just happened—what *could have* happened—kept her silent as I gently wiped her forehead clean.

Two tissues later, I moved down to her cheekbones, the swells set high on her petite face and at the perfect angle to catch the sun. As I wiped, her freckles, like stars, began to peek out from underneath the smoky sky.

"Thank you," she murmured, peeling her eyes open to look up at me.

I hated how they looked so lost. I hated how Laurel Ocean would tread water in the middle of the sea until it drowned her because she was too afraid to admit she didn't know how to get back to shore—because she was too afraid any life raft might hit an iceberg and sink her down even farther away from safety than she already was.

"Don't worry about it," I said tightly, realizing I'd gotten most of the soot off and was now just rubbing over her face because I wanted to touch her.

I fought the urge to yank her against my chest and wrap her in a hug at the sigh that tumbled from her lips.

"I can't believe I almost burned his house down," she whispered.

"But you didn't. And it was an accident," I insisted, determined to halt her train of thought—*and my own*—of what could've been lost, before adding at my own expense, "At least you didn't steal from him."

Her eyes jerked to mine, a spark of laughter in them and the tug between relief and lust in my body was insane, threatening to rip me apart with each passing moment.

"I still can't believe you were stealing from him," she murmured as a smile tugged at the corners of her full lips, the action forcing her tongue out to moisten them from the smoke that had dried them out.

Desire pumped hotly through my body. All thoughts of the fire vanished and there was nothing else I could focus on except how close she was, how smoky-sweet she smelled—like a campfire on a fall night.

My hand broke ranks and slipped over the edge of the tissue to brush along her soft, bare skin. Her lips drifted apart at my touch, air rushing from her lungs as the spark of laughter in her gaze melted into a pool of need. Now, the only dangerous fire, the only threatening heat, was the one between us—growing larger and more consuming with every breath we took.

I shouldn't.

I really fucking shouldn't.

But all I saw was her. All the hurt I wanted to heal. And then her hand, reaching toward danger. *A moment when anything was possible—and anything could've been lost.*

The thumping of my heart was impossible to ignore. *Do it. Do it. Do it.* Louder with each and every beat.

"Should I be concerned you're going to steal from me, Mr. Downing?" she asked with her eyes trained on my lips, sending a pulse of lust straight down to my aching cock.

I grunted. "I'd never take anything from you that you don't want to give."

My words hung low, suspended in the stillness that replaced the smoke. My fingers trailed to her chin, tipping her face up to mine, and all I could see was every shred of evidence that she wanted to give me this.

The shallow rhythm of her breath. The way heat spread up underneath her freckles. The flick of her lust-scorched gaze over mine.

Do it.

Kiss her.

I held her eyes the entire time as my lips dropped to hers. I wouldn't take a kiss if she didn't want to give it. But if she didn't stop me—there was no stopping me.

And she didn't want to stop me.

She wanted to give me this.

All the pieces were there, the mountains covered with dry and combustible need, and as soon as my lips touched the softness of hers, the wildfire roared to life.

Consuming.

Ravaging.

Unstoppable.

She tasted of laughter and longing, all sweet and smoky, overwhelming my senses and subduing my logic.

Forget magic in the sauce. *There was magic in her.*

My tongue swept hungrily over her lips, groaning when they parted eagerly for me. I'd thought to kiss her tenderly. Softly to soothe her hurts. But as her tongue darted out and demanded mine inside, everything changed.

What I'd thought were calm shores of reverent desire was nothing more than retreating waves of the tsunami of lust building inside me. And the moment of danger that brought us here... it ripped my need forward in a crash that took me under.

"Fuck, Laurel," I growled.

From an old, buried place inside of me, savage survival invaded our kiss. I tore into her mouth like it might never happen again, and she did the same.

Because the threat of losing everything made taking everything the only option.

I licked and stroked every corner of her delicious mouth, tasting tart tomatoes, subtle smoke, and the sweetest flavor of essential urgency. The tissue in my hand fell as I cupped her face, angling it up and threading my fingers back into her fiery waves so I could taste her deeper.

I wanted every inch. To know every inch.

To mark every inch safe from everything except me.

Her small fists that had held on to me countless times since she'd arrived, now gripped my shirt with desperate need, pulling me tighter.

My whole body ached for her. Not just to fuck her but ached to love her in the way her body... her heart... needed but her mind wouldn't allow.

I groaned, irony sharpening my need into the finest, painfully pleasurable point. I'd come to apologize—to make peace after this afternoon. I'd come to show her that this place wasn't going to *take* anything else from her, and yet here I was. Taking.

Stealing.

The first kiss had been her choice. This one... this one was all my doing.

My fingers pulled her hair free from where it was tied up, the strawberry water cascading down. A groan escaped as her hands skated down from my chest and wrapped around to my back, finding their way underneath the edge of my shirt to press directly on my skin.

Letting out a hiss, I pulled her lower lip between my teeth as her pert tits smashed against my chest. I could feel her tight nipples prodding me, begging for attention. It would be so easy to reach up and slide my palm under her shirt, to fit her bare breast into my palm. *To take some more...*

There was nothing between us—no space, no air, no rationality, no reason. Nothing but desire that forced out everything else from the world and my mind but the warm woman in my arms.

The woman who needed me even if this was the only way she was willing to admit it.

The woman I needed even though this was the very last way I should.

Laurel whimpered and arched against me, rolling her hips desperately along my throbbing cock and all traces of thought fled.

Grabbing her ass, I had her up and in my arms in no time. I swallowed her gasp as I spun and pressed her back against the bedroom door that rattled in protest.

Fuck, Larry would murder me if he were here right now.

But I couldn't care.

Not when my hands were cushioned in the soft, firm globes of her ass and the heat of her pussy began to seep through to my cock.

Christ. For how reserved she was with every other emotion, with *this*, she didn't hold back. Her hips rocked against me as insistent and unstoppable as ocean waves, sliding her wet warmth along my pulsing length, her desire steadily soaking through my jeans.

She fit perfectly against me—a piece that had always been missing from this place, I realized had always been missing from me.

Growling, I ground my dick against her warmth. Her lower half pinned to the door, she wrapped her arms around my neck as her mouth begged me for more.

Her skin was warm where my fingers rested along the waist of her shorts. I tried to grip her tighter, like it would stop me from continuing this madness. Instead, her warmth seeped into me, warning that my body would freeze if I didn't feel more.

One hand steadying her greedy hips that arched against my cock, I slid the other underneath her tee, claiming inch after inch of moonlit skin on a path toward her bare, needy tits.

Her stomach shuddered underneath my touch, the muscles clenching in anticipation as I crested over the edge of her ribs. I pulled the breath right out of her when my knuckles grazed the underside of her breast.

"*Fuck...*" White spots burst in my vision when my fingers closed over the soft weight.

Her breast was a warm weight that filled my hand just enough to leave no room for more, and not too much to leave any inches uncovered.

Perfect.

Just like I knew they'd be.

"*Eli...*" she whimpered my name, her hips instantly taut and unmoving as she arched into my hand and pushed her pebbled nipple against my palm.

She let out a small cry in pleasure as my finger closed over her nipple, pinching and teasing the swollen bud until she was writhing in my arms.

"Please..." she begged softly, her voice wavering with her impending orgasm.

"*Fuck, Laurel,*" I rasped as I jammed my cock against her hot center so hard the door groaned and shook in protest.

A low curse rushed from my lips when I felt her small hand delving between us, reaching for the waist of my jeans. Wedging her hips to the door, I grabbed her wrist just before her fingers reached my cock.

One touch and we'd be on the floor with me buried inside her, fucking her like a beast.

"Just you, sweetheart," I growled in warning.

I didn't give her a chance to protest as I forced her hand back to my chest. Slanting my mouth over hers, I swallowed her pleas and fought to give her what she needed. *Everything she needed.*

Steadily, I ground my dick against her, pushing her soaked underwear and shorts to rub against her clit, making her wetter and needier.

But though I lost most of my well-crafted control, my mind disintegrating with each drag of heat along my angry, aching cock, I knew I couldn't—*wouldn't*—fuck her.

No matter how much I wanted to.

No matter that I might not survive the restraint.

It wasn't that I didn't believe she wanted me. Hell, that truth was sworn into every gasp and moan, signed with every arch and grind of her hips, and sealed with the heat pulsing from between her thighs. *She wanted this. She definitely wanted me.*

But she didn't know what she wanted for herself. She was still lost here. Searching. Questioning.

And I wouldn't be one more question. I wouldn't let fucking me be one more thing she'd have cause to regret. *I wouldn't do that to her.*

Kneading her tit until she trembled in my arms, she began to jerk uncontrollably against me, and I knew her orgasm was close. My body tensed in an effort to stop myself from coming like a damn teenager in my pants.

"Let go, Laurel," I demanded harshly against her lips as she fought to breathe.

Her eyes caught mine. Crystal clear and brilliantly bleeding lust.

"Eli..."

"Let me hold you and just let go." And then she exploded.

Her cry as she came was the sweetest thing I'd ever tasted.

I licked and nibbled at her mouth while her body continued to shudder and melt against me. I didn't move as she trembled, her body relaxing and growing limp. I held her like I said I would even though my cock rammed like a caged beast against my jeans, desperate to be inside of her—*desperate for my own release.*

Our breaths mixed and merged in sync, filling the space between us that was barely wide enough to accommodate them. Heavy pants ticked like a clock, counting down to the minute when reality would sink back in and the circumstances that should've kept us apart would start to sever the link between us that fought relentlessly to form.

She shivered as her legs slid slowly down from my hips.

Taking one last second to memorize the silken weight of her tit, my hand returned to her clothing-clad hips to steady her as she got her bearings.

"You okay?" My voice raw with restrained need and self-loathing.

Her gaze swept up to mine, the pink in her cheeks deepening almost to match the redness of her swollen lips.

"Yeah. I'm..." She trailed off and turned her head to the side.

I stepped back, close enough to still reach her if she needed me, but far enough that she could breathe... think... *Far enough that I could try to tamp down my raging lust.*

There'd almost been a house fire, and what did I do?

Kissed her like the only clean air was escaping from her lips and then dry-humped her on the bedroom door. *What the hell was wrong with me?*

She was struggling. Struggling to be here. Struggling to know what to do, who to trust, and what her future held. And my genius fucking idea of helping—of *easing* those burdens was getting her off against my demanding dick. God... I bit into my cheek drawing blood.

You promised to help her, Eli. You promised to look after her.
Wanting her wasn't helping her.
Wanting her was only going to make things worse.

She quickly checked over her clothing, tugging it back to rights before pushing her hands nervously through her messed hair. Possessiveness surged through me, knowing I was responsible for its disarray. When she pulled the weight over her shoulder, my eyes followed it down to her breast, memorizing the outline of her tit, burning the feel of it that lingered like a shadow on my palm into my memory. A memory I would pull up later because there was no way my dick was going to bed quietly.

"Sorry," I offered gruffly, not wanting her to feel awkward or embarrassed. "That's not why I came... I didn't mean..." I held back a curse at my lack of restraint.

"Don't." We both flinched at the harshness of her tone. Her flushed face turned even redder as a tiny hand came up to press on her lips. "It's fine. You should probably go."

Dread was like an ice-cold bucket of water over my head.

This wasn't what I wanted.

I wanted her to feel safe and instead, I was driving her farther away.

"Laurel..."

"It's been a long day. And then the fire... I just—" She broke off with a sigh. "I should go to bed before I do any more damage."

I listened to her reason, but the only thing I saw was the damage I'd done. *Somehow.*

Maybe she needed a night—a night to realize that sleeping with me would've only made this more complicated for her.

"Thank you," she murmured, nodding to the smoke-stained fireplace. "I'll clean everything up and make a note not to use the fireplace anymore."

My body tensed, revolting against her quick recovery—like

she had too much practice dealing with disappointment. I hated that masking hurt had become a habit for her.

And I hated that I was the reason for that hurt.

Especially when I'd only been trying to do the right thing.

She turned and I had no choice but to follow her to the door.

"Thank you for dinner," she said with a small voice, folding her arms across her chest.

It was a clear 'goodbye.'

Shit.

I didn't want to leave her right now—right when she looked like she was so tempted to fall apart. But I'd already pushed too much.

And it was becoming pretty fucking clear I'd pushed too far.

Grabbing my keys from the counter, I paused in front of her, ignoring the pull that felt stronger than gravity to kiss the sorrow from her face.

"I'll see you at Roasters, then?"

She opened the door, the rush of cool air making her shiver as she murmured, "Goodnight, Eli."

I took another long look at her and made a short, simple promise to her and to Larry.

I would do whatever it took to make her whole again… even if that meant letting her walk away.

Walk away from Roasters.

Walk away from Carmel Cove.

Walk away from me.

"Goodnight," I rasped.

I stepped out into the night and, when the door closed behind me, I made a promise to myself that yes, I'd let her walk away… but not before I did ever goddamn thing in my power to keep her here. Where she belonged.

With me.

Sixteen

Laurel

Y*ou're a strong bean.*
 My hand flinched on the doorknob to Roasters as the words stretched the stitches which held my heart in one piece.

Dust crunched under my heels as I stepped inside and sucked in a breath.

I was on my way to meet with Mr. Ross and finalize the details of my grandfather's will, but I couldn't stop myself from coming here first.

Two days since I'd been inside and the damage hit me all over again, only now, it wasn't just the torn down plaster, but the pipes that ran like rusty veins through the walls were pulled out in pieces.

Roasters was on the operating table and needed a heart transplant.

Too bad there wasn't much left of my stitched-together organ to offer... especially after Friday night.

This was what happened when you held grief inside. It ate

away at everything behind the scenes, slowly damaging the structure and integrity behind the façade. The only way to fix it was to take down the walls, rip out what could end up destroying you, and hope to survive with what was left.

There wasn't much left, but I was determined to walk away a survivor. *A strong bean.*

Now more than ever.

Especially when those forty-eight hours dragged into an eternity since I'd last seen Eli, his six-foot, soot-covered muscles strung up on lust, and turmoil raging in his eyes.

And since I'd watched him walk away.

My lungs constricted, the pain of him pulling back just as sharp and unexpected as it had been that night. There were sparks and heat and smoke—and that was all before I almost burned the house down.

I wanted him. I'd wanted him to stay. *For me.*

But that moment when I'd come so close to actually losing the house, that moment when he was standing in front of me, the only thing I knew was that if I didn't kiss him then, I'd lose that, too.

He wasn't mine. In fact, I hardly knew him. *But I didn't want to lose him.*

Through ember-infected air, I'd stared up at the man who was always there. In my thoughts. In my dreams. *In front of me.* And I wanted him no matter what happened. No matter what it could cost me. *I wanted him.*

And the threat of losing one more thing drove me to embrace that. It drove me to feel… to want… *to give into* something that couldn't be lost or water-damaged or stolen or burned. It drove me to sink into the warmth rising in my chest. A feeling that couldn't be ignored like the tide that had finally reached the shore.

It drove me to him.

So, I latched on and took whatever he was willing to give, clinging to him like a buoy in a storm. It felt so good to not hold back, to not crush down and box up my emotions before they got the best of me.

What I didn't realize was how much it would hurt to watch him walk away from them. From me.

I didn't realize it would hurt like a loss.

Of course, he couldn't want me. I was Larry's granddaughter and the one ruining the legacy of this town. I didn't blame him for his reasons. *I couldn't.* I knew he retreated out of respect because that's who he was: the man who took care of things and never took anything for himself. Still, that small reticence flipped my switch from on to off.

Closed off, to be exact.

So, he'd left with his chivalrous shield intact and I recognized the familiar, lesson-learned gash in my chest. *There was nothing for me here in Carmel Cove.*

"Mornin', Little Laurel," Mick greeted me with a half-grin, jarring me from my thoughts.

The man's warmth and kindness were just as imposing as his stature; *I would miss him.*

My stunted smile relaxed seeing he was the only one here at the moment. "Morning, Mick." I stepped toward him. "I just thought I'd stop in... see how everything was going... how was your weekend?"

His head half-cocked to the side, assessing but not interrogating me. "Pretty good. I had to finish up a few woodworking projects," he offered, running over one of the studs inside the exposed wall, before adding at my intrigued expression, "I do custom wood pieces on the side. Mostly decorative stuff, but I enjoy it."

He followed the line of the beam up to the ceiling. "Made one for here. Not sure where it got off to in all the commotion though." He paused. "Keep meanin' to ask Eli."

I flinched. The man with all the answers.

Except when it came to me.

He left me dangling like a question mark. At the end of sorrow. At the end of memories. At the end of desire. "Where… is everyone?"

He eyed me knowingly and my spine straightened. "Miles is taking care of another job and Eli is on his way. Ash needed his help real quick over at the restaurant; he's opening this coming weekend." He paused and knocked on one of the pipes. "And then, George should be here today to get all this back together."

"It can be fixed?" I turned to him.

He couldn't hide his surprise, wondering how Eli hadn't told me. Between the marinara, the fire, and the earth-shattering orgasm that had led to a soul-crushing separation, I'd forgotten to ask about the plumber's assessment.

Mick nodded. "It's goin' to take a bit, but he says he can get everything back in shape," he informed me. "And if George says he can do it, *he can do it.*"

Relief washed over me.

"Good." I gave him a faulty smile.

"You okay?" He looked at me with concern.

"Yeah," I assured him with a nod. "I have to get going though. I have a meeting with the lawyer."

"Oh." He looked to the door. "You don't want to wait for Eli?"

"No." The word was too quick to be anything but questionable.

"Alright," he drawled. "Will we see you later?"

I began to move to the door, turning over my shoulder as I

answered, "Probably not. Once I have everything signed, I need to start getting in touch with real estate agents and get that process started."

I winced, hating to see how my words appeared to so easily wound a man who looked unwoundable.

"Hey, Laurel..."

I paused, looking back to my Friendly Giant.

"We're all family here," he said unexpectedly, emotion overwhelming his form. "We're all heartbroken. We're all grievin'. But when you go through somethin' like this, the best thing... hell, the only thing you can do is lean on your family. So, if there's anythin' we can do—"

"Thank you." With a shaking hand, I reached for the doorknob, a single tear landing on the old brass.

"I'll let Eli know you stopped by."

My steps hesitated as I opened the door. "You don't have to, Mick. I'm fine."

I regretted the words as soon as I said them. They were a lie and Eli would know it.

He knew the 'right' thing had been a mistake the moment he apologized.

I turned and began to walk toward the end of the block. Mr. Ross' office was just across the street. I crossed my arms, protecting myself from the multitude of warm, caring smiles that greeted me during the short walk.

This meeting felt like the beginning of the end. The moment I would set in motion the severance from my past.

But instead of striding confidently through the entrance, I hesitated.

Pausing to look over Ocean Avenue to the coffee shop nestled across the way. I had to admit I didn't know what I would've done if he'd said Roasters was too far gone and the building couldn't be saved.

Maybe if it wasn't too far gone, neither was I.

My tether to this place was fragile and thready. A weak pulse that could be obliterated by the slightest pressure.

But it was still alive. Beating. Strengthening. *Fighting with every breath.*

My skin prickled with sudden warmth and I caught the burning gaze and wind-whipped hair of the man in the eye of my hurricane of heartache. I shivered.

I was convinced I wanted to give this place up.

But it didn't want to give up on me.

And from Eli's expression, neither did he.

"That's it?"

I jumped as Aunt Jackie's shrill question cut through whatever else Mr. Ross was about to say. He'd just finished elaborating all the details of my grandfather's last will which, as I already knew, bequeathed to me the coffee shop and the house, while leaving my aunt with some of his stocks and bonds, and more investment-oriented possessions.

Something I expected her to be pleased with, though she appeared anything but.

Narrow eyes glittered with iridescent irritation as she uncrossed and recrossed her legs, making sure to flatten the wrinkles on her designer skirt. The break in her composure didn't fit with her porcelain put-together persona.

"Were you expecting something different?" Mr. Ross drawled with an unabashed elevated eyebrow at why one of the richest women in the greater San Francisco area was complaining because she'd received *more* money instead of a rundown coffee shop and a house of similar constitution.

Two structures she'd never had any interest in until this very moment.

"No," she said crisply, folding her hands in her lap and shooting him a tight smile from lips that looked to have been enhanced since I last saw her two weeks ago. "It's just that Laurel doesn't live here, and she doesn't really want the coffee shop, do you, dear?"

She assumed my confirmation and continued, "If she did, she wouldn't have moved away. You don't want this place, isn't that right, Laurel?"

My tongue felt like it was digging through sand trying to answer her.

She was right. *Wasn't she?*

But the way she said it... the way she asked... the property was probably worth millions, and she probably wanted to cash in, I surmised. Or maybe she thought they could sell it to some big coffee chain.

Both careless possibilities triggered a defensiveness... a possessiveness... inside me that had been dormant until this moment, and now, all I instinctively wanted was to deny it. I wanted to hold on to everything and never let go if letting it go meant letting it go to her.

"See, Mr. Ross," she said with a voice too saccharine to be anything but cancerous. "I was just hoping to take one thing off my niece's plate during this difficult time."

Aunt Jackie had never been the emotional or full of feeling type of person, and both Mr. Ross and I knew it. In fact, I was sure the Range Rover she'd parked outside had more concern for the environment than she did for others.

Gavin's mouth thinned. "Unfortunately, there is nothing I can do. This is what Mr. Ocean decided and put in his will; it's up to Laurel if she wants to sell everything or not."

I winced. In my defense, he'd revealed my intention to sell.

But it was my intention, so how could I be mad?

Jackie's eyes perked up and her attention snapped to me. "I knew this would be too difficult for you, dear." She patted my hand like she could beat my resignation in deeper. "So, you're going to sell them then?"

"I was… I was planning on selling them, yes," I admitted with much less resolve than I expected of myself.

"Of course, if it's too much right now, you could always hold off on selling for a little while," Mr. Ross interjected, partially because he didn't want my aunt to get what she wanted, and because he was still a part of this community—a community that wanted Roasters to remain in my care.

"It's not," I insisted firmly, my back straightening against the worn wood back of the chair as they pulled me in opposite directions. "But thank you both for your concern."

My aunt tensed briefly beside me before her lips turned up with a smile more acidic than accepting. Mr. Ross nodded and laid a few sheets of paper in front of each of us, topping them with a pen, and indicating where we needed to sign.

The next minute or so passed in awkward silence as what was left to my pap's name was divided between us. My aunt's assessing stare crawled over my skin as Mr. Ross handed me a manila envelope with the deeds to both buildings inside… like I now had something that belonged to her.

When I rose, her arm linked through mine like a snake coiling around me, claiming my immediate attention.

"Laurel, dear, we should talk," she murmured, barely glaring at the lawyer before angling and ushering me through the door into the hall.

"Aunt Jackie—"

"Please, let me speak." It wasn't a request as she continued,

"I know you don't want this, Laurel. You left it once before and it was selfish of my father to dump it back on you now."

I tensed.

"I will be more than happy to buy the coffee shop—even the house from you for a generous price." She patted my arm as though she were doing me the greatest of favors. "How does that sound?"

Like the very last thing I was interested in.

"Why do you want it?" I turned the tables on her. "You walked away from it, too."

Her eyes flashed with something desperate before it instantaneously disappeared. "I did. But that was a long time ago before I was in the position I am now," she said with such conviction that if I hadn't been so skeptical of absolutely everything in this town, I would've believed her. "There wasn't much I could do for you when my brother—your parents died." *You could've not taken my cousin out of my life,* I bit back the argument. "But I can at least alleviate this burden off of your shoulders."

It made no sense. She'd never wanted anything to do with the coffee shop—not growing up and definitely not after she married. And the house? Sure, it was worth a hefty sum because of the location alone, but that was nothing, I was sure, compared to the worth of her and her husband's properties, let alone the revenue that the golf club probably brought in.

"And what do you want to do with it?"

She shrugged, flustered. "Oh, I don't know. It's so old, it's probably not worth repairing anyway. But it's not something you should be worrying about. Just let me take care of it."

Not something worth repairing.

Wrong.

She was wrong.

And I'd sell my soul before I sold this business back to her.

I untangled my arm from hers and stood firmly. "I appreciate that, Aunt Jackie." I braced myself. "But, as of right now, I don't plan on selling Roasters. If it's going to stay in the family, it's going to stay with me."

She couldn't have been as shocked as I was by my own words.

Even if it was a show—a lie—to put her off. I'd told someone I wanted to stay at the moment when I had every reason to go.

Clearing her throat, she forced a smile to her face as she stood poised like a scorpion ready to strike. "I'm sure it's hard to let it go, but we both know that's what you want. You know where to find me when you change your mind."

Shuffling her designer bag to her other arm, she stalked by me. The door barely shut behind her before I heard her on the phone with my uncle Rich.

Her strange behavior was forgotten when I stepped outside and directly into the line of sight of the too-handsome contractor on his phone outside Roasters. Hand on his hip and a scowl on his face, whatever news he heard wasn't good—but it was also forgotten when he saw me.

Wood-burnt eyes rained sparks down my body, and the tingle that started in my lips spread much lower, a familiar ache settling deep in my stomach.

He didn't want me.

At least, not enough...

We stared at each other across the road. A chasm of expectations and longing separating us with no bridge in sight.

Clutching the folder of copies the lawyer had given me, I lifted my chin slightly, taking one full breath of salty air before I turned away, but not before I caught the pained expression on his face.

You pulled away first, I wanted to tell him. *I know better than to reach for you again.*

Seventeen

Laurel

Not even two hours later, there was a sharp rap on my door.

I thought I'd made it clear I wanted space from him. *Maybe he was more stubborn than I gave him credit for.*

Grumbling under my breath, I stood from where I'd been writing an email to update my boss and strode to the front of the house, noting the small wafts of smoky dust that danced around my feet.

The knock repeated and a cold shudder ran up my spine.

Eli was stubborn, but not insistent.

Yanking open the door, I stifled my surprise when it wasn't Eli on the other side.

It was someone I'd never seen before.

"Ms. Ocean?" The wave of pungent cologne hit me first, my years in menswear the only thing saving me from choking on the spot.

Unease rattled through me. He greeted me like he knew me, though we'd never met before.

Even if I didn't remember his face, I would've remembered the debilitating scent.

I blinked up, absorbing the sight of the tall, imposing bald man who took a domineering stance on the stoop. A quick scan showed an expensive black suit—Tom Ford or Valentino if I had to guess—over a black button-down shirt sans tie. He looked professional—professional at what though was debatable; I could see either businessman or killer at that point.

I cleared my throat, the thought making me stand taller.

"Yes..." I replied warily, shifting my weight so there was more of the door between us.

"So sorry to disturb you," he continued with a smile that revealed bright white teeth too oval and feminine and soft for his rigid and sharp stature. It was a strange thing to notice at first but it fit with how his presence made me feel—like the smile was only surface deep and what was beneath was more sinister. "My name is Alexander Blackman. I was hoping you might have a minute for me about your business, Ocean Roasters."

He adjusted his sleeve over a large black and gold watch.

"What about it?" My gaze narrowed.

His smile widened, sensing my discomfort. "I'm the owner of Blackman Brews. We're a California-based coffee chain, and I've been interested in buying your family's business for some time now."

Well, I wouldn't have guessed coffee shop owner—unless it was maybe Starbucks or Dunkin' Donuts—based on the pricey suit and the watch that looked to be made from an entire bar of gold.

"Did Mr. Ross send you?" I queried, trying to figure out how and why he'd shown up today—the day I'd come home with all the paperwork. I remembered Gavin mentioning a realtor before, but not someone actually interested in purchasing.

"Mr.—" He shook his head, clasping his hands in front of him. "No. I'm here because of your grandfather. So sorry for your loss, by the way. Did he not mention anything to you? About me?"

By the way. He looked professional and he said all the right things but with a tone that only felt wrong.

I shuddered and wiped my expression from my face. "About what?"

I played dumb. Mostly because I wasn't about to admit to a stranger than I hadn't spoken to my grandfather before his death.

"I spoke to him on several occasions about selling the business as I'm looking to expand and it seemed like it was getting to be a little too much for him there at the end." He cleared his throat.

I ducked my head briefly before replying, "No. I wasn't aware anyone had approached him about it. Then again, I'm not surprised since he never would have thought about selling."

He smiled again at me with those round teeth like it was supposed to make me feel more comfortable. "I won't take up too much of your time, but word around town is that you *are* interested in selling, so I thought I'd stop over and introduce myself and bring my offer to you."

"I see." I sounded strangled.

He wasn't wrong. That *was* the word around town.

He reached inside his jacket and pulled out a jet-black card with gold emblazoned on the top, *Blackman Brews,* and handed it to me. "I wrote on the back what I offered your grandfather for the place. You're welcome to talk to a realtor or appraiser or anyone you trust, but I think you'll find that it's a more than generous offer."

I took the card from him, careful not to brush his fingers in the process. "Well, Mr. Blackman, there was a lot of structural damage from water leaks and disrepair over the years that was found during the robbery—err break-in." I didn't know what to call it since no one stole anything and, technically, no one broke in since the door was left unlocked. *A destruction of private property?* "So, I'm concentrating on having that repaired first."

He nodded like none of those facts came as a surprise to him.

"Of course. However, the sale could always include a contingency that the building must pass inspection, if you are as eager as I am to move forward."

He had an answer for everything.

Good businessmen always did. *But he didn't seem like a good businessman.*

I should be happy—ecstatic even—that there was a man standing on my doorstep practically begging to buy a building that wasn't even up to code at the moment, a building I'd been desperate to get rid of two weeks ago.

Yet, all I felt was the same defensive hesitation that came over me earlier when I'd had a similar conversation with Aunt Jackie.

Was I really not interested in selling?

I stepped away from the door and straightened my spine. If I could deal with models and fashion designers and the general population of Los Angeles, I could deal with this Mr. Slick.

"Thank you, Mr. Blackman. I still want to run everything by my lawyer and a realtor if the time comes, but I will certainly take your offer into consideration and get back in touch with you if I'm interested."

There was barely a flicker of displeasure in his charcoal eyes, like he expected me to sign over the deed to the building at that very second if it were possible.

I clutched the slippery black business card in my hand and folded my arms.

"Of course," he continued with a voice that was like liquid Mercury, smooth and beautifully fluid, but poisonous if I did anything more than listen. "It was a pleasure meeting you, Ms. Ocean. You remind me a lot of your grandfather." His smile was deadly. "I'm sure you'll be quicker than him to realize when it's past time to let something go."

Was that a threat?

I gulped, feeling the blood drain from my face as he extended a hand. Cold fingers gripped mine in a firm handshake that, if it could've shaken me into doing his bidding, it would have.

My hand dropped to my side as I murmured something along the lines of 'have a nice day' before shutting the door and sagging against it in relief.

What was wrong with me?

For the first time since I'd come back to the town, something I actually wanted—*something that could start to put my life back together*—was dropped in my lap *twice* today, and I recoiled both times.

Two weeks ago, I would've told Mr. Slick to follow me right back into town and show me where to sign on the dotted line. A week ago, I wouldn't be questioning who he was or what he wanted to do with the shop; I wouldn't be thinking about all the people who'd been involved in putting Roasters back together or all the people who'd brought me food and the unspoken offer of support and a shoulder to cry on; and I *definitely* wouldn't be thinking about Mr. Model Magic, who inserted himself into my life where I might not want him even though I needed him, who was helping me—at no cost—get away from this life as soon as I could, and who brought me magic marinara and more-than-magic kisses.

No, I definitely wasn't thinking about him and what his opinion of Mr. Blackman might be.

I'd just begun to push away from the wood as I flipped over the business card to see what this Mr. Blackman thought generations of my family's hard work and reputation were worth.

Ten million dollars.

The scrawled offer sent me reeling back against the door for support. Ten mil—*Ten. Million. Dollars.*

I traced over the writing with the tip of my finger to make sure I'd read it correctly. *Ten million.*

I turned the card back-and-forth, unsure if I was imagining the entire thing, but each time it revealed the same amount. Taking in an unsteady breath, I stared off into the house. I noted the pictures on the walls and the crossword puzzles on the table. The leftovers in the fridge and the fresh bag of coffee Eli had discreetly left the other night.

Simple things.

Simple things that made the biggest difference.

Firming my lips into a determined line, I opened the cupboard under the sink and threw the business card—and his offer—in the trash.

It wasn't a decision to stay, I told myself. It was just a decision to not sell to Blackman.

There was a difference.

And maybe if I repeated it enough times, it would turn true.

Eighteen

Eli

I *shouldn't be here.*
   I was the rational one. The composed one. The one everyone turned to, to deal with hard situations because I could keep my head about me.
   But when it came to Laurel, all of that went out the window.
   No, not out the window—off the goddamn cliffs.
   Nothing of how I felt about her was rational. Nothing of my need for her was composed. And I was going to lose my mind if I continued to stay away.
   Parking at the end of the drive, I turned off my truck; the only light left was the warm glow emanating from Laurel's house.
   I told myself it was the right thing to stay away from the grieving granddaughter of a man I owed everything to. *But I couldn't.* Days apart only proved I'd done the wrong thing by walking away from her. *By making her feel like what we had was a mistake.*
   Days of distraction.
   Hours of irritation.

It didn't matter how much work had to be done. It didn't matter what anyone said—what advice they offered or support they gave. Nothing eased the torment I felt after leaving her the other night—*and walking away from what we both wanted.*

And nothing dulled the pain of seeing the exact same torment written on her face when she came out of Gavin's office; the image of her scarred into my brain.

Her gaze was cloaked with determination—the kind that rose precariously tall, built on sand and stilts; it looked strong and mighty from the top, but from where I stood, I saw it wavered when no one was looking and how easily it could crumble.

Stepping down from my truck, I pushed my desire down deep where it wouldn't cloud my judgment and strode toward the front door, ignoring the rain that dampened my shirt.

With a heavy breath, I knocked firmly on the door that opened a moment later, Laurel appearing with her hair blanketing her shoulders and pink staining her freckled cheeks.

"Eli," she breathed my name and it felt like an all-too-short stroke down my dick that jumped uncooperatively in my pants.

So much for ignoring my desire.

Thankfully, she had one of Larry's old sweatshirts on, so I wasn't taunted with a display of her perky nipples.

The momentary surprise that parted her mouth and warmed my name disappeared as her tongue swiped a cold shoulder back over her lips, "What are you doing here?"

"We need to talk," I replied, stepping toward her until she was forced to back up and let me into the house.

"It's been a long day. I don't think now is the best time," she said, shutting the door and turning on her heel to head for the living room.

It was a subtle cue to show myself out, but I didn't listen. She could damn well throw me out if she really wanted.

I hesitated a moment while following her, noticing how clean the house was as I walked through it. Stacks of dishes had been removed from the cupboards, washed, and now sat on the drying rack. The dining table was wiped and set with placemats I hadn't even seen before. The lights reflected off crystal-clear windows, the floors gleamed, and the carpet looked like new.

Even if this was prompted by the fireplace incident, she'd done more than just clean up from the smoke and ash.

"Laurel..." I drawled with a low voice, watching as she fluffed the pillows on the couch, determined not to look at me. "I'm not leaving until we talk."

"Really?" she balked, standing and planting her weight on one hip. Her gaze pierced me with two bright blue flames of fury. "About what? I already know George can fix the pipes. I already know everything is still on schedule—"

I cut in, "I'm not here because of Roasters. I'm here because of the other night."

Hurt flashed across her face. "In that case, I think you said everything you needed to say, and even if you didn't, I got your message loud and clear. So, you can go."

God, she was so beautiful, even when she was hurt... even when she was mad.

"Dammit, Laurel," I growled. "My message was bullshit." I shoved a hand through my hair, days of tension swirling like a tornado inside me while I tried to remain calm.

"No, you were right to leave. It was a mistake. What happened between us was—"

She squealed in surprise as I closed the space between us, wedging her between my body and the wall, my palms flat on the textured wallpaper on either side of her head as though barring the world from interrupting us.

"I shouldn't have walked away from what happened,"

I rasped. "It wasn't a mistake. It was the furthest thing from a mistake…"

"Then why did you leave?" she demanded, her pulse fluttering against her neck.

"Because I thought it was the right thing," I admitted raggedly. "I thought it was what you deserved—what you needed. I'm trying so damn hard to help you… to help you get through this whatever way you need to. If that means selling. If that means leaving. Whatever the hell it means… and I thought you deserved more than to risk muddling that decision with desire," I told her, pausing before I added with a low, hoarse tone. "And, I thought it was what I owed him—respect enough to not fuck you on the goddamn living room floor like I wanted."

The color in her cheeks darkened, along with the depths of her eyes.

"So then why are you here? Nothing has changed," she insisted breathlessly. "You've done your duty. You can sleep soundly in chivalry now."

A low growl of frustration boiled in my chest.

"I'm here because the last two days I've thought of nothing but you. Nothing, Laurel. Not Roasters. Not Larry. Not how I should try to convince you to stay nor how Larry might kill me if he knew how I felt. No, Laurel. I've thought of nothing but you," I ground out, laying everything bare before her. "And how bad I fucking want you. Not for this town. Not for the business. But all for me."

I felt the sway of her body as it leaned closer to mine, drawn to the raw need I couldn't contain.

I reached over and tucked strands of her hair behind her ear, giving myself inches of excuses to touch her. The barest brush of her cheek against the backs of my knuckles sent off warning flares of lust to every corner of my brain.

"I've thought of what would've happened if I hadn't left, if I hadn't stopped kissing you... if I hadn't stopped touching you..." I groaned, my dick throbbing against my jeans. "And no matter how many reasons I stacked in my corner, they were nothing but a pile of bullshit. The only thing I came here for tonight is you."

My thumbs brushed over her cheeks, moving lower until they caught the edge of her chin and tipped her face to mine.

"Even if it changes nothing?" she pressed, her eyes searching mine through a murky mist of disbelief, expecting me to pull away again. "Even if I still sell Roasters and leave?"

I'd thought the worst thing would be for desire to affect her opinion of Roasters and her future. I was wrong. The worst thing was to hear her now, desperate to know my desire for her was separate from my hope that she'd stay. *Desperate to know if she was one more obligation I was beholden to.*

Time ebbed away, pulling back so slowly until it stopped, and the only sound between us was the soft, unsteady breaths falling from her lips.

"You know that *this—us* hasn't had anything to do with the damn coffee shop for a long fucking time," I swore roughly. "Even if it changes nothing for Roasters... even if you leave..." I paused, the thought searing pain into my chest. "That's like asking if I want to see the sun rise today even if it might not rise tomorrow... There's nothing going to stop me from taking every moment I can get with you." I pressed a kiss to the side of her temple, sliding my mouth over to her ear to finally whisper, "Or from taking every last inch of everything you want to give."

She drew a shuddered breath, her breasts dragging against my chest as her heart hammered in a fierce pace with mine.

Need. Hope. Fear. *Lust.* They all swirled like a vortex in her eyes that blinked open and pulled me deeper. "Are you sure I'm worth the risk?"

"Fuck, Laurel." I crowded her, pressing my body flush against her small soft curves and dragging my lips across her cheek until they were just a breath away from hers. "You're worth everything."

Life and loss, grief and duty… the murky expectations that come with such heavy circumstances faded in the face of the only thing that mattered—whatever was between us was unstoppable.

"So, what are you waiting for?" she murmured hoarsely. "Are you going to kiss me or not?"

"Oh, I'm going to do more than kiss you, sweetheart," I promised as my lips slanted over hers.

The first touch, warm and soft, lasted only for a second before it deepened into something raw and viciously honest. She kissed me like that one point of contact was the only thing of clarity—like it was the only thing for certain that she knew that she wanted, that her heart wanted too badly for her mind to convince her to ignore.

And fuck if I didn't feel the same.

My hands gripped her scalp, bleeding red-gold strands between my fingers as I angled her head and lost myself in her mouth.

Her taste was complex, like the finest coffee, and I wanted to explore every nuance. The notes of sweet. The bursts of bitterness. I devoured her like she was the finest drug with long, savoring strokes of my tongue against hers. Invading every inch of her mouth, the kiss was a foreshadowing—*a promise* that I would do the same to the rest of her body.

Explore it.

Cherish it.

Take it.

Thick, smoky lust leaked from us—from the flames our kiss stoked back to life. Flames that refused to be stifled—refused to be doused no matter how hard we'd tried. When I finally dragged my lips from hers, a voracious need that matched my own reflected in her ocean-blue eyes, just as vibrantly as the sea reflects the sky.

From the first night I held her in my arms, when she begged to not lose anything else, I knew that I'd do anything to give this woman anything she ever asked of me. *Any fucking thing.*

And it had nothing to do with who her grandfather was to me.

It had everything to do with how my body required her with an intensity that rivaled its requirement for oxygen.

"You sure—" I broke off because the question was more than the words I had to ask it.

She needed to be sure. Even if she never spoke about it, I knew being here was like walking on logs that moved and shifted unsteadily in a mire of memories. I didn't want her to cling to me because there was nothing left.

I wanted her to reach for me because she wanted me.

"Eli." She sighed my name, arching against me and letting the last of her defenses fall away. "I need you to stay. I'm tired of fighting how I feel about everything and everyone in this town. And I'm tired of fighting how I feel about you…"

I was slain by the small fingers that clutched into my shirt with the strength of steel and the fortitude that went unmatched.

She was asking me to stay.

This strong woman, so injured by life, who'd lived for so long never asking for help, never asking for a hand to hold or a shoulder to lean on—the woman who'd never felt safe enough to let her emotions out, *safe enough to have the luxury to ask*, was asking me now to stay.

Because she finally felt safe.

My cock jerked against my jeans, desperate to be inside her heat. To feel her wet warmth that tempted me to insanity the other night. To take everything she was offering and make it mine. Treasure it. Keep it safe.

Sealing my lips over hers once more, my groan drowned in the warmth of her mouth.

Her body spoke for her, latching on to mine with every ounce of strength that she possessed. Her tongue whispered against mine how much she wanted me. And mine listened. It licked and stroked, encouraged and pushed her to feel more, to give me more because I would take it. I wanted to. I wanted every beautiful, broken, and uncertain emotion she had. And I would hold her steady until she found what she was looking for.

"I've wanted you like this from the moment I ran into you," she confessed against my mouth as I hoisted her into my arms, her legs wrapping instinctively around my waist.

"I know," I growled, my cock cradled against her heat.

She bit my lip and sucked. "No, you didn't."

I groaned, low and deep. "That night I did." I carried her into the bedroom, kicking the door shut behind me.

"I was drunk, that's why I took off my clothes."

"And is that why you asked if I was going to kiss you?" I growled against her mouth.

Her surprised inhale jerked her hard tits against my chest and a wave of ferocious need rocked through me.

"I did—" she broke off with a squeal as I dropped her onto the bed.

Planting my fists into the mattress on either side, I stuck my face right in front of hers, both of us panting, heaving desire in and out of our chests like it was the new currency our lungs traded in.

"I wanted you that night, too," I rasped, memorizing every soulful fleck in her eyes. "And it was so fucking painful. To want you when I shouldn't." I bumped my nose against hers. "To want to finish stripping you. To want to taste every inch of your skin."

I slid my hands to her hips and then up, grabbing the edge of her shirt and lifting it over her chest.

Her stare held mine, a sexy stalemate as I slid the fabric up over her head.

"I wanted to see if you tasted like moonlight and madness," I growled as I dropped her shirt to the floor.

She shuddered, desire rippling across her body like a breeze over the sea, and her eyes glittered up at me. "So, taste me."

My cock swelled, and my focus held on her face for a few tenuous seconds before it finally fell under the weight of my need to taste the expanse of pristine skin I'd revealed.

"God, Laurel..." I groaned.

I'd seen a lot of beautiful sights living on this coast. Ocean panoramas and sunsets that would make your chest tighten and your mind wonder if such beauty could be real.

But this... *her*...

My knees slammed down onto the unforgiving wood floor, my gaze captive to the sight in front of me.

Her red hair streamed down like falling, flaming stars over her pale shoulders, fading just at the swell of her tits. Pale and creamy, the pert globes stared at me with rosy red peaks. More than the ocean, more than a sunset, my soul wondered not if her beauty was real, but if this moment was.

"W-What did you say?" she stammered, her breasts shaking with her wavering breath.

I didn't answer her right away. *I couldn't.* My attention was enraptured by my hand as it reached out, filling my palm with the warm weight of her snow-white breast. She moaned as I rolled a thumb over her nipple, teasing the peak the way that had driven her insane before.

"Eli..." she whimpered and threw her head back.

I bit into my tongue, drawing blood when her thighs parted on instinct—*with pure ache.*

My other hand gripped her thigh, spreading her legs even wider so I could tip forward between them. Holding her nipple up like it was a fucking prized dessert, my tongue flattened and dragged over the stiff peak.

Hot, sharp lust stabbed through me like the most violent assault and her soft whimper poured salt into the wound.

Latching around the taut peak, I groaned and sucked the sweet, soft bud until she writhed against me. This was what I wanted. Not just to taste her. Not just to give her a safe place to let go. But to make her feel whole.

"You passed out before I could answer," I finally answered hoarsely, dragging my teeth over her sensitive skin. "But I would've told you that once I started, I wouldn't be able to stop."

Her gasp was small but resonated down her body like an earthquake, her tit shoving against my mouth while her hips gyrated against my stomach.

My hand splayed on her thigh slid up over her quivering stomach to cup the firm weight of her other breast, kneading and tugging while I worshipped her with my mouth. She might not be ready to let herself cry from sadness, but from pleasure... she begged to cry from that.

She begged to be consumed by it.

Her little pants and moans drove me insane, past the brink of what my brain was able to process. My body moved with a will of its own—a primal need to make her mine.

My lips licked across to latch on to her other nipple, sucking hard as my fingers drifted lower, toward the wet heat I knew was waiting—*aching* for me.

"Eli, please."

With a growl, I pushed her loose shorts and panties to the side and it only took one swipe of my knuckle over her slit to coat my finger in her slickness and incinerate any last trace of rational thought.

"God, how I've dreamt of this," I confessed, delving two fingers inside her heat.

Her body tightened greedily around me, rippling with need as my thumb rubbed over the hard nub of her clit. With my fingers buried inside her, I curled them into her front wall, pressing against her sweet spot and she jerked violently against me.

I teased her mercilessly, over and over again, sliding my fingers out before sinking them in deep and rubbing inside her. Her desire gushed from her in waves, coating my fingers… coating my palm.

"So wet, sweetheart," I groaned, listening to the slick sounds of her body sucking in my fingers. "So fucking wet."

Taking an immeasurable second, I worked her shorts and panties off her before wrenching her legs wide so my whole hand could pleasure between them.

"Madness," I murmured against her chest, watching her body eat up my fingers. It was the only explanation for how I was able to forestall my own need, drunk on the reaction of her body around me.

I wanted her beyond the brink of sanity. *I needed to.* I fucked her with my fingers until she had no more strength to hold up her walls. Until it was more painful to hold on than it was to let go. To let everything go. *And to give it all to me.*

Need twisted in my gut so hard it ripped the air from my lungs. I found her lust-laden gaze and held it as I kissed down her stomach, slowly fitting my shoulders between her thighs. Her pussy clenched around me, knowing the torment that was coming.

Sinking down, I slipped my fingers from her. I fought the urge to lick them clean, but the only place I wanted to taste her desire was straight from the source—straight from the spring of her sex.

My gaze finally slid to the treasure in front of me.

Pink. Swollen. Glistening.

My cock threatened to explode as my pulse screamed in my ear, pounding a savage beat when I saw her dripping with desire. The heady scent of her need drowned out all thoughts but one: *to taste her.*

"Oh, God. Eli..." she gasped in a breath like I was about to drag her underwater—*like she didn't know when the pleasure would let her come up for air again.*

I closed my mouth over her pussy, and with the first swipe of my tongue along her entrance and up to her clit, she was gone.

Her desire took over with a beautiful violence.

Instantly. Savagely. All-consuming.

Her fingers speared through my hair, locking my mouth against her as she bucked underneath me. I ate at her, swirling around her clit before jamming my tongue as far inside as it could go. All the while, feral growls escaped as she coated my tongue with her need.

Her moonlit skin glistened with sparkling sweat as she shook and shuddered, falling back onto her elbows as she lost the strength to hold herself upright.

"Let me taste you come," I demanded roughly, dragging my teeth over her and pushing one finger back inside to give her body something to hold on to.

"Make me, Eli," she pleaded.

Make her come.

Make her let go.

Closing my lips over her clit, I flicked my tongue over her before sucking hard and sending her shattering over the edge.

She cried out and orgasmed so hard I thought her body might disintegrate into particles smaller than sand under its strength.

I lapped up the waves of her release, relishing every moment all the while my own body threatened to fracture under the strain of wanting her with no relief.

Lifting my head, I found those tempestuous blue eyes that glistened with tears and swirled with savage desire. Her flush was high on her cheekbones, blending the pale skin of her face into the fiery tresses of her hair.

"Eli..." My name was all she ever needed to say for me to know exactly what she wanted.

What we both needed.

I rose up, reaching over my head and tugging my shirt off. Her eyes hungrily drank in the sight of my chest, following my hands to my belt. I didn't drag out the motions. I didn't have fucking time. My cock strained painfully against my jeans even as I undid them, finally bobbing free as I shoved the rest of my clothes to the floor.

When I looked back to her, Laurel's mouth parted with a delicious pout and my dick throbbed, releasing a drop of cum at the thought of pushing between her soft lips. *But not tonight.*

My lip curled, wild with need as I moved over her, her thighs drifting open to accommodate me and her chest rising and falling raggedly in anticipation.

She was so beautiful like this—*magical and vulnerable and all mine.*

"Do you trust me?" I rasped against her cheek, dropping tender kisses on the now-dry streaks from her tears.

I caught her holding her breath before she nodded. "Yes," she murmured, firmly clamping her hand around the back of my neck and pulling my mouth down to hers.

And the cape of chivalry gave way to the beast.

I devoured her mouth as I angled the tip of my cock against her dripping entrance, feeling the heat pulsing, welcoming me inside. Reaching down, I pulled her leg up between us.

There was only one first time. One first time to leave my impression. To make my mark and stake my claim.

Bending her knee between us almost down to her chest, I teased her entrance with the tip of my cock, coating the fat head with her desire until she was rocking up against me.

"Mine," I growled against her mouth as I slammed home.

Home.

It was the perfect fucking word for how she felt around me. Warm. Welcoming. Enveloping.

Her tight pussy stretched around me, scrambling to accommodate the invasion and clenching to draw me deeper.

Our kiss had ceased, fading into harsh pants as I settled deep inside her, trying to rein in the intense urge to come.

"Oh, God..." she gasped with a strangled voice.

Groaning, I took that as her plea to move. My muscles shook as I slid almost the full length of my cock out before driving back into her, sending her arching up into me. But one slow stroke was all I had left before need took over.

I began to thrust into her. Uncontrolled. Unrestrained. And urged on by the wet friction of her clenching around me and the sweet moans of pleasure when I hit her sweet spot with the tip of my cock.

"Laurel..." My face fell into the warm crevice of her neck, her pulse racing against the tip of my nose, as I wished I had the strength to say more. But I had nothing left except instinct.

My teeth sank into the side of her neck as I pumped into her, tearing her body apart with each and every stroke. I tasted the saltiness of her tears as they slipped through my lips, her body so wracked with pleasure—with an intimacy she'd denied it for so long.

I squeezed my eyes shut because I couldn't see any longer. My lips mapped a path to her ear where I begged her, feeling the way every muscle of her pulled taut, her breath stuck inside her lungs as she teetered on the edge… an edge that I was about to fly over.

"Let go," I encouraged roughly. "I've got you."

With one last feral growl, I drove my cock as far as it would go inside her tight, slippery sex and felt my heart stop when she seized around me and screamed my name.

She came with violent submission, trusting me with her body and her pleasure. And it was that earth-shattering privilege that sent me over the edge.

With a roar, I released into her, pumping out hot jets of raw release against her womb as her body clutched mine.

Reality would remind me of our lack of protection later. Right now, my body reveled in knowing there was nothing between us.

With a groan, I collapsed on top of her, her arms caging around me like she was afraid I'd vanish.

"You okay?" I rasped against her ear.

She hummed with sated bliss. "I'm better."

My chest swelled, the simple words holding so much meaning.

Minutes ticked by with our long gasps and hard heartbeats as the world quietly built back up around us.

"I'm on the pill, by the way," she said quietly.

The relief I felt wasn't as great as I thought it would be.

"I should've asked, but to be honest, my dick really didn't give a damn at that moment," I admitted roughly next to her ear, catching the small smile on her pouty lips.

When I found some semblance of strength, I kissed gently along her jawline as I pushed up and slid out of her, heading to the bathroom for a warm washcloth. When I returned, I halted, seeing her sitting up in bed, her hair spilling over her shoulders like red ribbons of an opened gift.

But it was the look in her eyes that forced me to stop—*that brought me to my knees.*

"I'm not leaving," I swore with a low voice.

She'd let herself be vulnerable. She'd let herself feel. *She'd let me in.* And now, her instincts were flaring back to life, reminding her how she'd lost everyone else who'd had that privilege.

Relief flashed as she chewed on her lower lip, admitting softly, "I don't want you to go."

"Good."

A few minutes later, not leaving her sight again, I tugged down the covers and we slid between them.

"I'm not leaving you," I promised again as I pulled her against my chest. Her weary, relieved sigh made my heart thud erratically as she curled in tightly.

I repeated the words a few more times until she drifted to sleep and, as my eyes fell shut, I realized something...

I wasn't leaving her.

But there was no guarantee that she wasn't going to leave me.

Nineteen

Laurel

I'd slept with Eli.

    My contractor.

    My consummate savior.

I groaned, burying my face in my pillow, the long melodic sound pulled from a deliciously sore stretch of muscles used to the very brink of their limits. And while those memories assaulted my body, the rich aroma of freshly brewed coffee invaded my lungs and the sound of shuffling out in the kitchen gave away Eli's location.

I rolled over to find his spot in bed still warm from where he'd held me all night. If I didn't know better, I'd think he was afraid I was going to up and leave without him knowing. This thought pulled a warm shudder through me, quickly quelled with the promise we'd made.

This didn't change anything.

A pre-sex, prenuptial agreement that when everything was sorted, we would part ways.

I would leave and he would stay.

I waited for it—the chastising regret that should have come. When it didn't, I even searched it out. Going through all of the thoughts that should have sprung unbidden in my mind and crippled my heart.

What were you thinking, Laurel?

You're too emotional to be sleeping with anyone.

You're leaving this town, you shouldn't get involved with anyone, especially the man who is captain of the community that wants you to stay.

"Good morning," the sexy rasp was only outdone by the sight of the bare muscled chest it came from. The sheet slipped down over my chest as I sucked in an appreciative breath.

My mouth dried watching his eyes drop to my breasts where my nipples poked against the sheet, awoken by his attention and eager for his touch.

"Morning." My voice was unintentionally low and sultry.

I scooted to the side of the bed, carefully leaning over to grab my tee from off the floor. Giving him a generous view of side boob, I tugged it over my head.

"How'd you sleep?" He had one shoulder propped on the doorframe, watching me intently while I finished dressing. Only then did I stop and drink in the sight of him. Stacked muscles ornamented with strands of veins, culminating in a pair of boxer briefs, pulled tight over his thick erection trapped against his thigh.

My mouth parted, the hunger in my stomach fading for a much lower, more ravenous ache. "Good," I choked out, rising from the bed. "How about you?"

"Don't think I've ever slept so good." There was a lightness to his tone but the headiness in his eyes sent a shiver down my spine.

I had to bite my tongue to stop myself from agreeing with him. "It was nice to wake up next to you, rather than being attacked by you."

I huffed but couldn't stop my smile, any lingering awkwardness after last night completely fading away. "It was only a whisk." I let my eyes drag over him to make a point. "It would take a lot more to damage you."

He smirked. "I made coffee and French toast is in the oven."

"French toast?" My stomach rumbled with excitement.

"My mom's favorite," he confessed. "I made it a lot."

My throat tightened. *Always a steady support.*

"Coffee and breakfast on top of incredible sex," I drawled lightly, arching my eyebrow, and teased, "You wouldn't be trying to convince me to stay, would you?"

It was a joke—and I hoped that my smile said as much as I went to scoot around him, but I didn't make it very far. One arm shot out and hooked around my waist, pulling me to the side until I was pinned between the wall and his body.

"Coffee and breakfast because you had an exhausting night," he growled, his eyes warming me right down to my toes. "If I wanted to convince you to stay, I'd haul your sweet ass right back to that bed where the only thing you'll want to say to me is yes." He pushed his hard length against my stomach, and I felt a rush of moisture seep between my thighs.

"You think I'm easily swayed by sex?" I taunted, ignoring the truth. It was hard to think about leaving the bed, let alone this town, when he had me in his arms.

He chuckled and leaned in close to my ear. "I think it's much simpler than that, sweetheart. Hard for you to go anywhere when my cock is buried nice and deep inside you."

I choked on my desire as he stepped away from me with a confident grin, leaving only the wall to support my shaking legs.

It wasn't simpler. It was far more complex, and we both knew it.

"I'm on the pill."

He acknowledged me with a small nod. "I've never been with someone without using protection before."

I gulped, comforted with confirmation of what my brain already believed. "I haven't either," I confessed softly, averting my eyes as I added, "But somehow all my walls seem to crumble around you."

Last night was more than sex. Last night, I'd let him in, not only in my body, but into the parts of my heart and soul I'd kept private for so long. And this morning, I'd woken sore and sated and in the safe haven of his arms. A place where nothing could hurt me. And it felt good.

Too good.

And I'd realized too late what I'd done. I'd opened the door to feeling. But that door wasn't discriminatory. I couldn't pick and choose which emotions to let in. Now that it was open, I couldn't stop them from piling in and stretching the poorly-patched seams of my battered heart.

I followed him into the kitchen a few seconds later, watching as he filled our mugs.

"If I didn't know him... if I didn't see him roast them... I'd swear Larry roasted his beans with some sort of drug to make them so damn good." He stared at the coffee as he spoke.

"Did he..." I trailed off.

The shake of his head stayed my heart. "I did this batch."

I didn't hesitate when he handed me the mug. I knew the risks... how a small thing like a sip of coffee could trigger such a response. *Especially now, when I felt more vulnerable than before.* But this morning, I wasn't afraid of whatever memories came. Because he was here. *Because he'd stayed.* Because I wasn't alone.

I took a sip and it was bittersweet in every sense of the word.

"How do I move on?" I asked with a small voice, staring into the dark abyss. "I don't know how to move on."

And I needed to move on. I needed to move on if I was going to be able to let go.

Eli stared at me for a long, strained second before setting his mug down and flattening his palms on the counter.

"Do you trust me?"

He'd asked the question before in different scenarios. But no matter what changed about the circumstances, I found my answer never changed.

"Yes."

"Spend the day with me," he demanded.

My pulse stuttered. We'd just slept together, but somehow this request felt more intimate.

"There's nothing for us to do at Roasters. There's nothing left for you to clean here." He extended an arm in show, but I didn't need to look to know I'd scrubbed every inch of this house to the point where we could lick our coffee off the floor without concern. "Spend the day with me, Laurel."

"Doing what?" I held my breath, knowing it somehow held the answer to my original question.

How did I move on?

"Remembering."

I drew in a long breath, heat flooding my body.

He wanted to help me even if it meant making it easier for me to walk away. *Protective and selfless.* And I trusted him, though my heart hammered that it was something more.

"Okay..." I agreed, but then added, "As long as you promise you won't spend it convincing me to stay."

Old habits, like heartaches, died hard...

"Why fashion?" Eli drew my attention away from the water as we walked along the beach, trying to burn off some of the calories we'd just devoured in the form of two Mediterranean sandwiches we'd grabbed for lunch.

I'd expected our morning to take a somber stroll down memory lane, but the last few hours had been anything but.

Our first stop after leaving the house this morning was to pick up donuts to take over to the Blooms' house—a non-profit rehabilitation center for women escaping domestic violence. It was run by Eve's older siblings and all the women were so grateful for the donut delivery—*even if there had been one or two missing from the box.*

Apparently, that was a common occurrence since my grandfather used to do the same thing.

From there, we'd picked up flowers for Ash's new restaurant from the flower shop on Ocean Avenue, Fleurations. The owner, Isla, gave me a bouquet of purple tulips for Roasters. I wanted to tell her the place first needed walls before it could use flowers, but she insisted.

Apparently, my grandfather bought purple tulips every week to put in the front window.

Purple tulips were my grandmother's favorite... and mine.

When we arrived at the unopened restaurant, Ash gave us the grand tour, though Eli was already familiar with the place, revealing the details of his struggle with addiction and how my grandfather helped him. Guilt niggled at my stomach, reminding me that it was going to be dedicated to my grandfather when it opened this coming weekend.

And that I was still in town if I wanted to go.

But not even Taylor mentioned it, keeping our conversation casual and warmly gushing about how her pregnancy was going.

From there, Eli made a stop at Roasters just to appease me, seeing how I'd stared at it the several times we'd driven by.

George had finished with the one set of pipes, so Mick and Miles were back on task getting the drywall into place. It was the first time something was being put back together rather than taken apart.

A small thing, but a big thing.

Eli took my hand when we left, clasping it tight in his as we walked down the main street toward the ocean. He pointed out the new shops, the new businesses, things that had changed over the years. *Over the time I'd been gone.*

It felt... normal.

Being here. With him.

And feeling normal in Carmel Cove was not normal; it hadn't been for a long time.

"It was by accident. I never knew what I wanted to do," I admitted. "Jules... she was always set on being a nurse, but me..." I shrugged, recalling the young, determined version of my cousin. "I was always drifting. And without anything tying me here, I went to school for business management and then drifted to fashion. Guess that just goes to show how much life can change. I ended up in fashion and she ended up at Rock Beach..."

Neither of us where we belonged.

I shouldn't have continued, but somewhere along the way Eli had steadily and stubbornly worked his way inside my defenses to the point where it hurt more to hold it back, than it did to let go.

"That's a lie," I confessed, feeling his eyes lock on me. "I wasn't always drifting." I stared out at the water; we were close enough to where the waves reached my bare toes. "I made my parents coffee that night because I wanted to tell them I'd decided to stay. That I wanted to be a part of Roasters even though I knew I didn't have to be. And then…"

I didn't have to finish. We both knew how that night had ended.

"It was because of him," I went on.

"Your grandfather?"

I nodded. "He'd told me to follow my heart, no matter where it took me. And when I told him my heart led me back there… to take over the business." I paused and let out a rueful but strained laugh. "He shook his head and said he thought I was going to be the first one to escape the crazy coffee gene."

I felt his small chuckle next and realized he'd moved closer to me.

"How do I move on, Eli?" I turned to him, pleading.

The breeze that had been a constant companion for the entire walk settled suddenly.

He reached up and brushed a finger over my cheek, and that was when I realized I was crying.

Grief, like life—like love—affected everyone differently. For some, it was as sudden and as loud as a clap of lightning. For others, it was a steady symphony of sadness, the notes building to a crescendo and tapering off.

But for me, as tears began to leak down my cheeks one after another, Eli catching each and every one along the way, grief was like the sea. It ebbed and flowed patiently at my shore, unabashed about its enormous depths, promising in its calm, and simply waited for me to be ready to step in.

To sink into it.

"I'm sorry," I murmured, shaking my head.

"Don't," he swore. "Don't ever apologize for this. For you. Don't ever apologize for giving me more of you."

My chest caved. He made it sound like 'all of me' was the equivalent of the greatest treasure in the world.

My voice trembled. "I don't know how to move on."

The crushing sorrow might have broken me if not for him. *Eli.*

My lighthouse in the middle of the storm. *He was still here. He was always here.* I watched his heartbeat thudding against his throat, a constant reminder that I wasn't alone right now. It was a subtle and steady, *I'm here, I'm here.*

And I clung to it.

Eli's lips pulled tight as he scanned my face. "This isn't about moving on," he finally replied. "Do people move on from having a baby? At a first birthday or a fifth birthday, do people ask a parent when they are going to 'move on' from the birth of a loved one?"

My head shook.

"So, why do we have to move on when we lose a loved one?" he rasped, his fingers gentle as they continued to sweep over my cheeks. "Laurel, who you are today holds so many pieces of your grandfather. I don't think grief is ever about moving on from those pieces. It's about moving forward."

I shivered and stepped closer to him.

"It's about moving forward and carrying him with you with each step. His memories. His advice. His legacy. His love."

My shoulders began to shake as I waded in deeper.

'Our legacy isn't coffee, Laurel. Our legacy is love.'

"And that love is never lost. It just sometimes changes form." He tucked a wayward strand of hair back behind my ear, the simplest expression of care making my knees weak. "And I learned that when I came here and stole from a cranky old man who made me take a good hard look at the man I was becoming."

"Yeah?" I matched his small smile.

"When my mom died, I lost the only family I had. I'd taken care of her... of us... for years and suddenly, I was alone. I was homeless. I had no purpose. I thought my love died with her."

My chest lurched. I had no trouble imagining the good man

standing beside me having to be a good man before he was done being a boy.

"And then, being here, I realized I could still love her every time I helped someone—every time I used those parts of me shaped by my time with her. It was the same love, just in a different form."

Reaching up, I curled my fists into his shirt. The world around us fell away. It was only him and me. Loss and love. Heartache and hope.

"How was he?" I asked, needing to know. *Needing to hear it from the man who'd known my pap best.* "After I left…"

His eyes flashed with concern, hesitation making his jaw tick.

"You can tell me, Eli," I begged. "I can handle it. I need to handle it."

There was a shift in the tide, and it seemed like even the ocean stilled, waiting with bated breath until the rumble of that warm, smoky voice spilled out over the world.

"He was broken, Laurel." There was a break where my heart matched the tempoed tic of his jaw. "I don't know if there are degrees of broken when it comes to loss like that. His wife. His son. You. I think Larry Ocean was the kind of man who wasn't broken until he was. But he was also the kind of man, from a generation, who wouldn't break no matter how broken he was on the inside."

Even the ocean wouldn't break as he spoke. Just like my pap, it remained perfectly still, unwavering with unmatched fortitude and a darkness buried leagues below the surface.

"He still did all the same things. The gym. The donuts. Everything at Roasters. But after you left, he threw everything he had into helping others heal… because that was the only way for him to still love you. But behind the selfless smoke and mirrors was still a man with a broken heart—a man who wouldn't lean on any of us for help."

My throat felt swollen shut with the guilt and grief.

"Leaving was what you had to do to be okay. He knew that." He forced my gaze to his. He forced me to listen to this part, too. "He knew if you had stayed, it would've destroyed you. And to be there, watching as it destroyed you... that would've killed him long before now."

And then, I was over the edge—an edge I'd clung to with everything I had because there was no one at the bottom to catch me. Until now.

Until Eli.

Suddenly. Unexpectedly. At the edge of the ocean. I crumpled against the wave of sorrow.

"I didn't want to hurt him." I wrapped my arms around my middle, trying to hold myself together. I was lost. Completely and utterly adrift. Tears blinded my eyes and my sobs choked my throat.

"I was so hurt, so stubborn," I rambled as my head turned weakly against his hands, my eyes squeezing shut in pain. "I was so wrong... so wrong. I never told him, Eli. I never told him..."

"Never told him what?" he whispered against my hair as his warmth soaked right through the cold that grief wrought over my body.

"I just..." I sucked in air like it was my last breath. If it was, I was okay with that. I was okay with nothing else after this as long as one person knew the truth before I was gone. "That I loved him. That I never should have left. Now, he'll never know."

And with that, the last of my shields fell. The last of my protection, the final vestiges of my walls were gone. My heart was open and raw, all the missing pieces of it finally exposed.

"Oh, Laurel... he knows, sweetheart. He knows."

The next few minutes, or maybe longer, was a blur. Like standing outside in the middle of a hurricane and trying to see the path fifty feet in front of you, only I was the hurricane and

Eli was the only part of the path I could feel underneath me, against me.

He held me as sob after sob tore out of my chest. I bled my grief onto him. All the hurt and sadness that I'd held in, all the pain and hollowness I'd buried, everything I'd run from so it wouldn't break me—it all broke over me now.

I laid it all on him and he never let go.

I didn't know how long it took, how long it should take, for a decade of sadness and regret to bleed from one's soul. But by the time I stopped crying, his shirt was wetter than my cheeks and my stomach hurt from how forcefully I'd been crying.

It took even longer before I was finally breathing rather than choking in air. Too much sadness for such a small person, it seemed. Truthfully, I wasn't even sure it was all out or if my body just ran out of tears to continue.

But however long it was, Eli was there when it ended. However long it took for me to let go of it all, he would still be there when I was done. He was the rock who withstood my storm of sorrow. He was still there, holding me. Comforting me. *Never leaving.*

Just like he promised.

"Thank you," I murmured thickly.

"You never have to thank me for this," he replied raggedly. "I want all of you, Laurel. Every last beautiful piece."

"Even if they're broken?"

"Then I want every last broken piece. They're all beautiful to me," he insisted with a small smile. "You should know by now that broken doesn't bother me. Broken is just a chance to build something new."

"I feel like there's nothing left to build from," I admitted weakly. "Like the only thing that's filled me up over the years has been hurt, packed down by its own volume and fortified by distance."

And it was a hollowness like I'd never felt before.

His lips pressed gently to mine, grounding the frayed pieces of me that remained. "There is everything left to you, sweetheart." He kissed the corner of my mouth. "Everything you need." And then the other corner. "Everything you need for what's meant to be." His nose brushed mine and my eyes flitted open. "And everything to gain, if you'd just let yourself."

My lips parted with a sharp inhale. "I thought you weren't going to convince me to stay?"

"You don't have to stay, Laurel. I'll never stop you from running if that's what you have to do. But what I have to do" —he bent closer, his words turning into steel—"is be there for you no matter what you choose, to leave… to love." My breath hitched. *Love.* "Because one day, you're going to realize you can't escape love any more than you can escape loss. And that day, I'll be there, waiting patiently, because what we have is worth waiting for, is worth fighting for… is worth losing for."

"Eli…" I drew a stuttered breath.

"But until then, I'd like to take you home and make you dinner." His eyes darkened. "And then make love to you for the rest of the night… if that's alright with you."

I gulped, shivers running rampant up and down my spine.

"Take me home," I told him, crossing a line I swore I'd never cross again.

And, as he wrapped his arm around me and walked me back to his truck, I realized just how dangerous Eli Dowling was to my heart… because even if I left him and this town, he'd still be with me… around me… like water ebbed in and filled even the smallest space between particles of sand, he'd swept in and filled himself into the million tiny spaces between the broken particles of my heart.

Twenty

Laurel

It was a room.

A mess, but a room.

It had been three days since the beach and almost a week since they'd started repairing the pipes. But today... today, the drywall was finally back up, covering the ripped up and repaired plumbing veined through the walls.

Eli and the brothers worked their tails off to get it done as soon as possible—not because they wanted it to be ready to sell but because Eli was doing what he promised: *whatever it took to make this place—and me—whole.*

I folded my arms snugly over my chest.

It wasn't finished. And in some ways, a blank canvas was more frightening than the torn-apart shreds. At least destruction made clear the choices. The blank walls only screamed possibility. *For good or bad.*

And not just here.

For three days, every time I looked in the mirror, I saw steadiness. I saw structure. I saw the shadows under my eyes were less, the light in my gaze was brighter, and how my chest breathed a little deeper without so much weight.

And I saw all my possibilities. Here. At Roasters. *With him.*

And somehow, even the tiniest steps I'd taken in grief, but forward toward healing, were more frightening than the sea of numbness I'd been treading.

There were so many good possibilities for me—friends, family, *love*. But the cold ocean of loss lapped at my feet, a constant reminder of how fragile it all was. *How it could all be taken from me in an instant. Again.*

The bell dinged behind me and I looked over my shoulder to see Josie and Eve walk inside, smiles warmly painted on their faces and their arms full of goods.

"Wow, look at this," Josie sighed. "I just can't believe it."

Josie became a regular face in my life. Even before the album incident, but especially after, she supplied us with breakfast and enough pastries to feed an army each morning, and most afternoons, we stopped there for lunch. In just over the course of a few weeks, seeing her, even if only for a brief minute, became something I'd begun to expect and enjoy—another fixture in the column of normalcy.

"I told you, you were going to be so surprised." Eve grinned, hardly a drop of sadness left in her gaze when she looked around Roasters anymore. *Unless she was looking at Miles.*

Josie reached for my shoulder and gave it a squeeze. "There is no such thing as too far gone, isn't that right?"

I swallowed through the vise around my throat and managed a weak nod, my nose wrinkling with a warm, sugary scent. My brow creased. "What is that…"

Josie's eyes lit up like spotlights. "Apple fritters."

My heart stuttered. "What?" I took another deep drag of the fruity-sweet smell.

"I'm almost positive this was your grammy's recipe…" she added confidently, nodding to Eve to open the pastry box she held, letting a wave of the heady aroma infuse the air.

She grabbed one of the perfectly fried pastries, balancing whatever she carried with her other arm, and handed the sticky treat to me.

There was no arguing with the look on her face. *Not that I made a habit of turning down pastries anyway…*

It was still hot. Almost too hot. *Almost.* But as I bit into the sticky sweetness, the burst of fruit over my tongue, and the scent of apples rushing up my nose, it was both everything I remembered yet something new. I didn't know if it was *exactly* the same as my grammy's, but it was so good it didn't matter.

"It took Cammie and me several tries, but I think we got pretty close even if it's not exactly the same," she said proudly, nodding to Eve who clearly had been forbidden a taste until they'd arrived here.

"It's amazing," I said, my hand covering my mouth that was still full of food.

She put her hand up as though to tell me a secret. "Let me give you a little advice. It's never just about what you have, it's about how you use it. The recipes we tried all had the same ingredients, but how we used them… that was what made all the difference."

"And how did you use them?" Eve chimed in with a satisfied moan. "Laced with crack?"

"Eve!" Josie chided as we all laughed and then asked, "Where's Eli?"

I shivered at the mention of his name.

"Here." The rough molasses of his voice echoed into the space, coating my spine in a layer of inescapable warmth. "Just working on clean up in the back."

"I brought a little—"

"Damn," he broke in. "Are those what I think they are?"

Josie nodded with pride.

His hand found the small of my back as he joined our little group. He always found a way to touch me when we were together. Sometimes to comfort. Sometimes to steady. And sometimes, because the lust burned so electrically in his eyes that he needed to touch me in order to ground it.

Every time we were together—which was almost every waking and non-waking moment of the last few days—I reminded myself of our expiration date. I reminded myself there were no strings—no anchors attached to our relationship. There was nothing but him and me.

Except the more time we spent together, I realized that nothing was everything.

And I wanted everything.

And the tide of fear at my feet grew higher.

"Eli, you've done a wonderful job," she gushed, patting him on the back when he bent forward to greet her with a hug.

"Oh, it's not just me," he replied with a grin. "And not even the twins." He used his thumb to point at me. "This one right here is a force to be reckoned with."

My mouth dropped open and heat flooded my cheeks. "I wouldn't say that…" I mumbled.

The plumbing I'd stayed away from, but other than that, I'd cleaned and organized in the back, spackled and sanded the new drywall, patched the old drywall once we pulled down the wallpaper from the rest of it. And next week, I'd be painting. And then decorating.

And I could finally start the process of selling it… a thought that used to come with relief now made me uneasy.

"Oh, she always was." Josie winked at me.

I'd helped from the start because I wanted it to be done.

Over the weeks though, something had changed. A lot of little things, actually. Little seeds. Harmless. Easily crushed. *Yet determined to bloom.*

"Eli!" Miles yelled from the back, drawing our attention. "What the hell is that amazing smell? Mick keeps insisting it's him and I know for-fucking-sure that's not the truth."

"Apple fritters!"

"Holy shit! Bring some of those back here!"

Eli chuckled, and Josie shooed him and Eve to the back to distribute her treats to the twins.

Heat drained from my body as his fingers disappeared from the small of my back. The two of them walked and talked back into the storage room, leaving Josie and me alone.

"You put a lot into this place, Laurel, and it shows," she told me, pride brimming in her voice.

My mouth dried up. "I didn't... I didn't do much." My protest was weak. "What could I do? I haven't been here very long. And I'm... leaving soon."

I was leaving.

I repeated the words because, like a muscle, the more I exercised my decision to leave, the stronger it would get. Only this muscle was broken because the more I insisted, the weaker it got.

"Laurel, sweetie." She sighed and reached around my shoulder to pull me against her side. "You came here after a decade gone... you came back to the loss of your pap, your family's business in shambles, and, I'm sure, to the memory of your parents. You came back when a lot of people in this world would've cut their losses and stayed away."

I shifted my weight, unsure if I could believe that.

"It looks like now was a good time to bring this over." She gave me a brave smile and extended her arms that held something large wrapped in a towel. "Mick made this." As she unwrapped it, I recalled his mention of it—and how he didn't know where it had gone. "I took it with me during the clean-up to make sure it stayed in good hands."

She handed the richly stained wood plaque, the strong grains etched with my pap's favorite saying.

Start where you are. Use what you have. Do what you can.

"You came back, sweetie. I know it might not seem like much, but you're here, giving of what little you have left." She brushed a hand over her cheek, and I knew she was trying hard not to cry. *So was I.* "And you're doing what you can for Roasters and for us. And that is *more* than enough."

Next I knew, Josie's arms were wrapped around me, the wooden board awkwardly between us.

"We hurt for you when you left, but we still loved you. And we'll still love you if you have to leave again," she whispered, rubbing circles on my back. "Whatever you decide, what matters is that you love yourself for your choice in the end. Follow your heart." Her embrace tightened. "That's all your pap would want."

Her words settled in me just as surely as she held me.

She pulled back as Eli joined us again, discreetly wiping the tears from her eyes as I did the same.

I felt his focus on me, steady and supportive.

"Okay, I should get back to the bakery. I don't want to leave Cammie alone for too long," Josie said to us with a watery smile. "I just wanted to drop these off. I'll see you both tomorrow at the restaurant."

I murmured a heartfelt goodbye even though I hadn't fully decided on whether or not I was going to go to the opening of Ash's restaurant. Josie enveloped me in one more hug before she turned her attention to Eli.

As they talked, I held the wood plaque out in front of me

again to take another look, running my fingers over the smooth grooves in the wood.

I hope I'm doing what I can, Pap…

"You okay?" I looked up to Eli, seeing it was just the two of us once more.

I nodded, scrunching my brow for a second and then replied, "I'm moving forward."

Instead of using the hurts and memories to build another wall around my heart, I used the strong blocks of emotion to create a path into the future, and I took one step at a time.

Eli kissed my forehead, and I sagged into him.

I shouldn't want his warmth or his strength like I did. Even now, I didn't need to lean into him. *I was okay.* But I wanted to feel him. I wanted his arms around me.

And I was really starting to want that constant presence for much longer than the few weeks I was giving myself here…

He hummed, his lips dragging against my hair as he said, "Don't make plans tonight." His voice turned low and ragged as he pulled me against him. His heat and hardness overwhelmed me and the constant ball of need always present in my stomach now flared to life.

I tipped back to look at him and laughed, rubbing my hips against his, feeling the length of him grow. "Why would I make plans? You've commandeered every evening—"

"Commandeered?" He growled, bending down to murmur in my ear, "I didn't realize all those little cries you make as you come all over my cock were complaints."

A delicious shiver ran laps up and down my spine. "Okay…" I agreed with breathless desire. "Maybe commandeered wasn't the right word."

"Don't make plans," he growled again, his lips coming for mine when I pulled back, feeling my phone buzz in my back pocket.

I hesitated, not recognizing the number even though the area code was from Carmel Cove.

I almost sent it to voicemail, but something stopped me. Giving Eli an apologetic glance, I bit my lip and answered, "Hello?"

"Hi, Laurel?" Instantly, I recognized my cousin's voice.

"Jules? Hey. I didn't recognize your number." I met Eli's eyes now that he knew who was on the phone. "What's up?"

"Don't make plans," Eli mouthed with a rough whisper, letting his cinder-filled gaze caress my body with a trail of sparks before he left me to the phone call and strode toward the back of the shop.

"I just… wanted to see if you were still in town or not."

"Yeah. I'm going to be in town for a bit," I told her. *A bit that teetered dangerously close to forever.* "Roasters needed a lot of work but it's finally starting to move along."

"Oh, good." The amount of relief she felt seemed strange for where our relationship was at, especially after our talk at the resort the other week. "Are you busy today? I have some time… free… that I can get away…"

A week or so ago, I wouldn't have been thrilled with the idea of meeting up with Jules considering how strained things were between us. But now, enough little things had changed that I didn't want to walk away from my cousin again. *Especially when her voice barely masked a layer of desperation.*

"Um, sure. Do you want to meet me at the house or in town?" I suggested. "There's a pub a few blocks down from the coffee shop if you want to get some food. Kind of looks Irish but I'm not sure what the name is…"

"The Carmel Pub?" she filled in the blank.

Like magic, the name emblazoned in gold on the dark wood sign flashed in my memory from the night after the memorial. "Yeah, that's it."

"I'd rather—if it's okay," she stammered. "I'd rather meet at the coffee shop."

"Oh." My brows creased, noticing the layer of dust on my sneakers. "It's a little bit of a mess, but if that's okay with—"

"Yeah, I don't mind," she broke in adamantly.

"Then sure," I agreed, brushing more drywall dust off my pants. "I'll be here all afternoon, and I've got some apple fritters."

Because, honestly, who couldn't use an apple fritter right now?

There was a pause and then she said, "I'll see you soon."

When she hung up, I glanced around the empty, hollow shell of a room.

But it wasn't the ingredients that were important—the walls, the floor, the pipes—it was how they were used.

And today, like always, Roasters would be used as a safe space.

Twenty-One

Laurel

"Laurel?" Jules' voice echoed unsteadily from the entry just after the bell chimed.

I'd spent the rest of the afternoon with the twins, Eli, and Eve—until she had to leave to teach a yoga class—cleaning up and rewarding ourselves with more fritters.

And when only Eli and I were left, I told him he could head back to the house, that I was okay to wait for my cousin. I felt his hesitation. In his sharp look and raw kiss. But she'd called me. *She needed me.*

"Hey." I came out to greet her, the apple fritter I'd warmed in the oven for her in my hand.

We stood there for an awkward moment before I stepped close to pull her in for a hug. Her hesitation melted into an embrace that felt like she was clinging to a life raft rather than my warm hello.

"Thanks for waiting," she murmured as she drew back. "My parents wanted to talk to me about the winter events at the resort and I wasn't expecting it."

"Don't worry about it." I extended my hand and offered her the pastry which she accepted with a grateful smile.

I took a quick glance over her. Her hair was pulled back, though not as harshly as the other times I'd seen her. Instead of the white today, she wore black jeans and a black long-sleeve blouse that had a high neck with a bow that tied in the front. But it was her face, the pristine serenity that normally characterized it was gone. Like an old masterpiece, from a distance, the same image was still there. Up close, I saw the fine fractures in her eyes and the faded color in her cheeks.

"Wow," she gasped, her attention shifting to the state of Roasters' resurrection. "It looks…"

"Empty?" I offered with a small laugh.

"I was going to say whole," she replied, underscoring our different personalities. I was perpetually skeptical while she had an unwavering candle of hope. "I can't believe it looks like this… after what happened, I wasn't sure it was going to make it." Her eyes snapped to mine. "Do you know anything? Do they know who was responsible?"

I shook my head. "I've reached out to the police several times, but all they've done is ask if anything was taken, and when I tell them no, they tell me the investigation can't be a priority until then."

"Oh." Her shoulders slumped. "So strange," she muttered, chewing on the inside of her cheek.

I nodded. It was.

Who broke in somewhere just to destroy the place?

"Eli's been on the phone with Covington Security a few times this week," I went on, trying to give her some measure of hope. *And myself.* "They're looking into a few leads, but nothing concrete has turned up."

Eli promised he'd tell me as soon as they found something

solid. Until then, speculation was just one more uncertainty to unsteady my life.

"I'm sure they'll find something." Her brave smile was similar to my own—weighing heavy with perseverance rather than blind courage. "I'm just glad to see it like this," she returned to a more hopeful topic.

"It's not done. We're painting next week and then redoing the counter area. I have to get furniture and the pictures back up. Oh, and the coffee. Can't forget about that."

"It's going to be amazing, Laurel," she murmured with genuine admiration. "Pap would be so happy... so proud."

My eyes averted, still hesitant to believe that. Clearing my throat, I rambled for the next few minutes to tell her all the things that had been ripped apart, repaired, and restored. Meanwhile, she devoured the apple pastry with a satisfied sigh.

As I spoke, the diffuse despair tattooed in her eyes lightened. And what started as a casual conversation, a small thing, turned into something larger when I saw how it eased the troubles she'd come here with.

I went through the paints I'd chosen, the fabric for the bench and the curtains, and my ideas for the new furniture. And for that half an hour, time reversed. We chatted about the future of Roasters like we hadn't lost over a decade in our relationship... our friendship...

Like we both hadn't lost at all.

"I think the blue and lavender is the best; lavender was Gram's favorite color," Jules said with a gentle smile, pointing to the soft plaid I'd picked out for the bench cushion and the window treatments.

"Yeah." I smiled back. "She would love it."

"Remember when we were little, how on Sundays, she let us use soapy cloths like skates to skate around the floor in here to clean it?" Her eyes lit with the memory and we both laughed, recalling how it turned the room into a giant skating rink of suds.

And then her laughter broke off, sadness crashing on to her features.

"Laurel… I called because I needed to tell you the truth." She drew a staggered breath before she continued and leveled the conversation with an unexpected bomb, "I never got your letters."

My head shook in confusion and shock. "What? How? Did I send them—"

"No." She waved a hand, brushing away any suggestion that it was my fault.

"My parents…" Her head fell for a second and then returned with a strange mix of emotions in her eyes. "I just never got them. Even if I had, I doubt they would have let me…" She shuddered. "It doesn't matter. I just wanted to say I'm sorry. I'm sorry I didn't get them. I'm sorry I couldn't be there for you at your parents' funeral; mine thought it would be too traumatic."

My skin crawled. *Her parents had been the roadblock in our relationship.*

I wished I could say I was surprised by her revelation, but I wasn't. I'd never liked my aunt Jackie or my uncle Rich. Not their character. Not their priorities. But mostly, I hated how they treated Jules—like she was only there to serve whatever purpose they deemed important.

"It's okay. It was a long time ago." I reached across the table to squeeze her hand; she shouldn't have to apologize. "I mean, it's not okay…what they did. But it's not your fault."

"I should've done something. I should've spoken up." Her lip quivered as she shook her head in strained self-loathing. "They've always made my choices. They've always spoken for me. And now…"

"Jules, what's going on?" I couldn't stop myself from blurting out. "You can tell me..."

Her expression shuttered and she pulled her hand back from mine, clasping hers in front of her.

"I'm sorry for my outburst the other day. I just... life isn't how I thought it would be, you know?"

Oh, did I know...

"I miss him," she admitted quietly. "I miss Pap. He always had answers."

"Why don't I make us some coffee?" I offered suddenly, feeling like that was what the moment needed. Something warm and familiar and safe.

I'd had coffee several times since the cup Eli had made, but this was the first time I was making it on this machine—*the first time in a long time.*

As the trusty electronics rumbled to life, I asked over my shoulder, "What answers did he have?"

She stayed silent for long moments, her thoughts brewing just as strong as the espresso grounds before they finally began to drip out. "Pap was helping me... figure out a different path for my life."

My brow furrowed. "But I thought you said..."

She'd seemed so confident at the resort the other day that Rock Beach was her life and her future and she looked like she was ready to play the part in its continued growth.

"I know." Her eyes were sharp as they shot up to meet mine. "I said that because I didn't know who was listening."

My hands froze on the knobs as I turned to her with wide eyes. I'd thought our conversation the other day held a strange vibe, but now, that vibe was a blaring siren.

"Jules... what is going on? What do you mean who was listening?" I pushed gently.

She ignored my question, staring past me like she was talking to someone invisible over my shoulder. "For the longest time, I couldn't go see him. My mom, well, you know how they don't... get along. It was clear that visiting him would be a betrayal against her... against them." She shuddered as her arms crossed in front of her. "And if I wanted to do something else with my life, something different than work at the resort, that would be a betrayal, too."

The turmoil she felt reverberated in each word. Her parents made it impossible for her to love herself and them at the same time. They'd given her everything she never wanted and to turn from it, I was sure, they would take as nothing short of complete betrayal.

"I don't want to disappoint them, Laurel," she said softly. "They're my parents and I love them. I just don't... love this."

I searched for words, realizing I hadn't even been paying attention to what I was doing, my hands working the machine from a very old habit I thought was long lost.

"It's not a betrayal to do what makes you happy, Jules." My voice wavered with emotion, the memory of that night out on the cliff assaulting me like a wave crashing on the shore. "You aren't obligated to them. Those who support you, should support whatever decision you make, not guilt you into doing what seems right. There are a million and one ways to do good in this world, Jules. Following in your parent's footsteps isn't the only one."

And I believed them. Not just for her. *But for me.*

"You sound just like him. That's exactly what Pap told me," she murmured with a soft smile that was both wistful and sad, taking the cappuccino from my hand. "And, I guess, leaving is what made you happy?"

Dark liquid pooled in the bottom of my mug. Like the espresso, most of my life had been pressured and scalded by the hot water of loss forced on me. But who I was, was still there. The grinds of what remained of my life still able to produce something strong, something good, *something better* because of what I'd been put through.

I took a moment before I answered, pouring the steamed milk into the coffee. "Leaving is what made me less sad." *Back then...*

"And what about now?"

I took a sip, thinking it would give me a reprieve to decide how to answer.

I couldn't admit to being happier living in L.A. with the new life I'd built. It had been good. I was proud of what I accomplished. I was grateful for the space and strength it had given me to be able to move forward but also to come back.

But I could no longer tell myself that leaving Carmel Cove again would make me less sad.

"I was going to leave again," I confessed. "But now, I'm worried that I'd be happier if I stayed..."

I inhaled the warm, roasted aroma and looked around the space that held so many good memories. *I didn't want to leave it.*

"Why does that worry you?"

I looked at her, wondering how a conversation I'd tried to focus on her had backfired on to me. "What if it's not enough?" I asked, motioning to the space. "What if what I do here isn't enough to make it whole? To bring Roasters back to what it was?"

And that was only skimming the surface.

There was a whole other part of me that wanted to stay because of a man who refused to leave. Leave my side. Leave my house. *Leave my heart.*

She rested her hand on all the pictures and samples we'd been looking at, sprawled out along the counter.

"What if you do?" she returned. "What if you make it better?"

I swallowed hard. "Touché."

The foundation of this building was still strong, it had withstood trials and structural damages just like I had, but here it was, still standing, transforming, rising back up to become better than it was before.

And that could be me. No, that *was* me.

I might not be whole yet. But to get better, involved taking steps. Sometimes there were twelve steps. Sometimes twenty. Sometimes one hundred. But no matter how many there were, they were all in the same direction: *forward*.

And *forward* for me this time around didn't mean going *back* to Los Angeles.

Forward was here. In Carmel Cove. At Roasters.

With Eli.

"Thank you."

Her head tipped to the side. "For what?"

"For asking." A smile flickered over my face as more weight began to rise from my shoulders like dense clouds off the sea. "You know, I think our last conversation all those years ago was about what I was going to do with my life…"

"And look at where we ended up."

"I came here counting the days until I could leave but now…" I paused and swirled the last bit of coffee in the bottom of my mug. "I never expected I'd want to stay."

"I never expected I'd want to leave," she countered so quietly I almost didn't hear her.

I knew she was talking about the resort as her smile faded and she set her empty cup on the counter.

"What do you want to do?"

"I want to go back to school. For nursing." Her eyes

dropped. "Pap was going to help me pay for it. He was helping me go through applications... but maybe this is all a sign that I shouldn't pursue it. You're staying for this family business; I should stay to help mine."

No, I was staying to follow my heart. She was staying because they'd left her no choice.

She shuddered and I never realize how such a slight movement could seem so scary. Like a baby doll in a horror movie—something so innocent should never be so terrifying.

"Why can't you leave?" I pressed, my heart thudding in my chest.

"Where would I go?" she replied simply. Brokenly. "I have no money of my own, no college education, obviously, no friends, no family—" I grunted and she sheepishly conceded that the last was no longer true. "They want me there. It's what they've groomed me for."

There was that shudder again.

"Even if I did leave, what would I do? Where would I go?" she asked with a broken, bitter laugh.

She'd said enough for me to realize what her life was like now. My beautiful, vibrant cousin had become a prisoner in her own home. Maybe not quite with a cell and locks and keys. Maybe not with shackles and guards. But with lack of knowledge, lack of friends or family as a support system, and most importantly, lack of belief in herself.

And I'd never seen chains so imprisoning.

Disbelief stunned my speech and rage thundered through my body.

"How did this happen?"

It was so painful to see how someone who'd always been so determined had ended up in a life like this.

"Slowly," she said carefully, her hands turning to ice in mine.

"Like most horrors that happen in the world, it starts with small, palatable infringements—like going to private school, like being kept from your parents' funeral. A prison isn't built overnight. It's built brick by brick until one day, you decide to go for a walk outside and realize there are bars on every horizon and there's no way out."

"Jules…" My chest tightened as all the air drained from it.

"Pap had been my way out." His death hadn't just been a loss of her past, but also a loss of her future.

"Well, I'm here now," I said forcefully, demanding that my voice be steady. "And I'm not going anywhere. We can figure something out. You could stay with me. Maybe you could work here—" I broke off before I got lost in profuse suggestions. "We'll figure this out. Both of us. Together."

When she looked back at me, her mask of China-doll-like composure was back. *Pained and pristine.*

"I'm sorry. I'm just emotional with him gone." She shook her head, defeated. "Pap was the only person I had left… the only one who would know what to do."

I reached for her hand and squeezed. "I might not know what to do, but Pap wasn't… isn't the only person you have anymore."

What else could I do?

What else could I say except let her know that I was here to help?

"It's not for you to worry about. Not right now." Her hands disentangled from mine. Her whole body protested the truth she'd just admitted. "It's been this way for a long time and maybe now that Pap's gone I'm making everything worse than it is."

"Jules—"

"Please, Laurel," she insisted tightly, clearly rattled by our discussion. "I'm really fine. I'm just still processing it all." Her eyes dropped down to her wrist where her smartwatch lit up with the time. "I have to go. I can't be late for dinner."

"I'm not leaving," I repeated as I followed her to the door. The words sounded far more comfortable on my tongue than the opposite. "I'm going to be here and you know my door is always open, just like his was." I reached for her shoulder and pulled her in for a hug whether she was prepared for it or not. "Whatever you need, Jules, you never have to ask. That's what family is for."

I wanted to do more for her as I watched her walk out of the building, but it was nearly impossible to help someone who didn't want to be helped. All I could do is let her know that whatever she decided, I would be here for her.

Josie was right. Sometimes, the most important thing you can give is your presence… your time. *Your unfailing effort.*

And for now, *being there* would have to be enough until Jules was ready to ask for more.

Twenty-Two

Eli

"You want some help with those, sweetheart?" My hands came to rest gently on Laurel's hips as she leveled one of the picture frames on the wall.

"I think..." Her eyes scrunched, eyeing it up and tipping it this way, then that until she was satisfied. "I'm good."

She stepped back into me, her ass pressing against my cock that was already uncomfortable in my jeans—a common occurrence around her, especially when she was in those yoga pants.

"Looks great." We both took in the sight of the wall holding a single photograph. A wall that had seen every stage of dismantlement and repair in the last month was finally back together, painted, and held the very first frame.

I wasn't sure we'd get this far this week, but something changed for Laurel after we'd gone to the opening of Ash's restaurant, Larry's Lookout. Not changed. *Something that was already there, grew stronger.*

When Ash honored Larry by dedicating the business to him, the determination Laurel had to set this place to rights magnified tenfold, and she'd worked tirelessly to get everything cleaned and sanded and painted so that the very first frame could be replaced on the walls which had sat empty for too long.

Roasters was slowly coming back together—slowly coming back to life. *Just like Laurel.*

"I left the level in the back," she said, turning out of my arms. "I'll be right back."

I nodded and tried to keep my smile from cracking. "Want a coffee?"

She shook her head. "I'm okay. Thanks."

Something else had changed for Laurel. Something that made my heart thump a little harder with fear when she pulled away from me like this.

It was subtle, the way she held herself back. As though she'd reached the end of her rope, flinching back as the tether reminded her not to get too attached. *But only to me.*

"I'll take one, if you're offering," Mick added from the other side of the room, putting the finishing touches on the new countertop that had been installed yesterday.

With a sigh, I walked over to the espresso machine that had been fueling us all week.

"You alright?" he asked with a low voice, pausing from his work.

I hesitated before murmuring over the low hum of the machine. "Just worried about her."

"She's doing better, Eli," he replied sincerely. "We all see it. Sad, of course. But who the hell still isn't?"

I flipped on the grinder. "I don't know. Feels like she's still holding back—pulling back, but maybe I was hoping for too much. Maybe I wanted too much."

"You think she's still goin' to leave?" His genuine surprise made me wonder if I was imagining it.

"No." I let out a sad sigh. "I don't think she's going to leave. I think she wants to stay here."

There was a freedom in grief, in the sadness of letting go of both Larry's loss and her guilt.

Since that day on the beach when she broke down in my arms, Laurel began to build herself back up, using her memories, my memories, this whole town's memories to lay a path to follow. And, for the first time since Larry's death, things started to feel right, especially seeing the coffee house coming back together.

The whole town felt it.

"Then what's the problem?"

"I'm just not sure she wants to stay with me," I told him honestly as water began to press through the grinds.

"What?" He shook his head and laughed at me like I was a fool. "I've never claimed to be the smartest man in the room, but even a blind man could see the way she looks at you."

My mouth thinned into a tight line as I set the small cup of espresso in front of him.

I wanted to disagree.

I wanted to tell him all the times I felt her slip from my arms a few seconds too soon. I wanted to tell him how she gave herself to me every night with complete and utter abandon, but almost as though she needed that mind-bending release to make her forget her mounting reservations.

And I wanted to tell him how each time I tried to pull her closer, to convince myself I was going crazy, she drifted just a little farther away.

"Oh, damn," Mick muttered.

"What?" I looked to him, nodding to the coffee. "Is something wrong with it?"

A slow smile drew across his face. "You love her," he stated boldly with a stunned laugh. "You're in love with her, aren't you?"

My pulse ricocheted.

Was I?

Was I in love with Laurel?

It didn't explain what was happening inside Laurel's mind, but it explained the turmoil rolling inside mine. It explained every unquenchable emotion I had around her. Desire. Possessiveness. Protectiveness.

Love explained everything.

And, most of all, it explained why every slight step she took away felt like the sharpest knife to my chest.

"Eli." One long arm reached over the corner of the counter, a large hand gripping firmly on my shoulder as he continued, "I've seen the way she looks at you."

I swallowed through the tightness in my throat. "And?"

"And if you lost everyone you ever loved like she did, wouldn't it scare the shit out of you to trust that emotion again?"

I froze.

I had lost my family. But not like she had. *Not by unexpected tragedy.*

Before I could reply, Laurel appeared from the back, halting to stare at the two of us.

"Everything okay?" She tucked the level underneath her arm.

I nodded, unsure if my realization made the moment better or worse.

I was in love with Laurel Ocean.

And there was a decently good chance that very fact could put a swift end to us. *To everything.*

"Thanks for the pick-me-up." Mick drained the rest of his espresso, setting the cup on the counter and giving up a lopsided grin before returning his attention to attaching the countertop.

"Everything's fine," I murmured, wanting to believe Mick more than anything. *Needing to.*

Tucking a strand of hair behind her ear, she pulled out her cell.

"Waiting for a call?" I asked, noticing how she stared at it like she could will it to ring.

She shook her head with a heavy sigh. "I just... I've been trying to get ahold of Jules all week. I called her on Monday to see if she wanted to help me pick out new plates and mugs. She answered but said she had to call me right back." She put her phone back in her pocket. "She never did. I just tried her again while I was in the back."

I walked over and put an arm around her shoulder, relieved when she curled into me. Her cousin had been another frequent topic of discussion over the past couple days. Laurel was torn up inside, worried about Jules, worried there was something going on between her and her parents. I didn't blame her. I'd caught bits and pieces from Larry when Jules had been coming to see him; I knew she was trying to get away from Rock Beach and the tinseled and tainted life she led.

"Laurel, if Jules needs help... wants help... she knows where to find you, she knows we are here for whatever she needs. But until that happens..." I trailed off, rubbing the side of her arm.

"I know." She sighed. "I just want to tell her again that I'll help her, that I'll pay for her to go to school."

"We can go up there tomorrow if you don't hear from her." I pressed a kiss to the top of her head. One of my favorite things was how she fit against me. Small, soft, and perfectly sized to tuck right underneath my chin.

And I didn't care how long it took for love to feel safe, I would hold her until then—until she knew I wasn't going to leave.

"Thank you. It's probably fine, I—" she broke off as her phone began to vibrate.

With hopeful eyes, she shoved the level against my chest and reached for her phone.

Laurel

Please, let this be Jules.

I stepped away from Eli's warmth, noting the concern in his rich ember eyes. A switch had flipped inside me after talking to my cousin—a switch that made it impossible for me to leave.

This was my home.

Carmel was my family.

I thought that would be the hardest thing to accept—wanting to stay. *It wasn't.* The hardest thing about wanting to stay was that leaving had put an end date on Eli and me. It created a finality where I didn't have to worry about losing him because we would simply part ways.

But by staying…

Everything my heart truly wanted was suddenly within reach. *And that everything had a name: Eli Downing.*

I saw it in his eyes, felt it in his touch… tasted it in his kiss… he'd hold me forever if I'd let him. And that was the most frightening thing I'd ever felt—having someone who meant so much to me in my life again.

And having someone to lose.

I wanted to be with him. I wanted to stay and create a life here with him. But the fear of losing him was like poison ivy around my heart—letting it feel and beat, but stopping anyone from getting too close.

I didn't think I was capable of a lot of things when I came back to Carmel Cove, but Eli fought to prove me wrong; *he'd fought for me.* And now, I fought to create some distance, wondering if, somewhere along the way, he'd unwittingly convinced me I was capable of love, too.

But if I was, then I was also capable of loss.

Again.

And that thought was the most crushing kind of suffocation of my heart. The problem was, the stupid thing continued to reach for him.

And I was afraid my heart couldn't help itself from falling in love with him.

Ignoring history. Ignoring grief. Ignoring reason.

I was irrationally, irrevocably in love with Eli Downing. And I had no idea what to do about it.

"Hello?" I turned away from him, swallowing the torrent of emotion in my throat, and answered the call eagerly.

A well-spoken, smooth-as-silk voice answered. But it wasn't Jules.

"Miss Ocean, it's Mr. Blackman calling," the man on the other end greeted. "How are you?"

My mouth opened and shut twice before I replied, "Fine. Thank you."

I caught Eli's curious glance over his shoulder; he realized it wasn't my cousin on the line.

"I was wondering if you had enough time to decide to accept my generous offer?" he continued calmly, the question simply one more wall in his maze to steer me exactly where he wanted me. "I see that the renovations to Roasters are coming along quite nicely. With the walls back up, that means it passed the building inspection, so selling the property should be a very easy step for you to take now."

I wasn't sure what concerned me more: that he was keeping a close eye on my business or that he'd somehow gotten my cell phone number.

It didn't matter. I'd made my decision and it was just as well he heard it from me so he could finally move on from trying to buy this business.

"Yes, things are moving along," I began resolutely. "However,

I'm sorry to tell you, Mr. Blackman, but I've changed my mind about the business. I've decided to keep it and reopen it myself, so Roasters is not for sale. Thank you though for your offer."

I looked at Eli and recoiled with the force with which his head whipped up to mine. His face grew hard and immovable. *Enraged.* And a shiver ran up my spine. There was something about this man—something he knew—and whatever it was, I had a feeling it confirmed my instincts: Blackman was a snake.

"Miss Ocean." Blackman's voice until now had been a performance, all the lights making it shine nice and smooth. But now those lights were flipped off, leaving only something dangerous in the dark. "You would do better to reconsider—"

"No," I interjected firmly. I'd fought through enough crap to come back here, to be back here, *to stay back here.* I wasn't going to be bullied by some slimy businessman. "I've made my decision. Roasters is not for sale and, as far as you should be concerned, will never be."

And then I hung up. There was no point in listening to what else he had to say—*and no point in being further creeped out by him.*

I let out a small cry when I looked up to see Eli in front of me, steam coming out of his nostrils.

"Laurel, who was that?" he bit out.

"This guy who wants to by Roasters," I replied, searching for answers in his angry gaze. His whole body snapped straight, and his intense stare paralyzed me with cold fear. "Alexander Blackman. He owns Blackman Brews."

He swore violently, slamming his fist down onto the new countertop, and I jumped at the angry display.

"What's going on? Who is he?" I demanded, noticing how even Mick's gaze was scarily narrow with anger.

"What exactly did he say?" Eli asked with a low voice, and

no matter how hard I wanted to push, I couldn't deviate from answering him. *Not when I saw him like this.*

"He wanted to know if I'd thought about his offer," I began slowly, his barely-restrained anger making me even more concerned about what I apparently didn't know.

"You've spoken to him before?"

I gulped but nodded in confirmation. "Right after I met with the lawyer a few weeks ago." Days and time blurred together under the heat of his stare. "He stopped by the house and offered to buy Roasters from me, and I told him it wasn't ready to be sold because it was still a mess. So, he left his card with an offer—an exorbitant offer, and I told him I'd be in touch if I was interested."

"Motherfucker." His fist pounded into the countertop again.

"I wasn't interested, Eli," I went on quickly trying to abate his anger. "I threw his card away almost immediately. He was a creep."

"Why didn't you tell me? Why didn't you say anything?"

I gaped for a second before folding my arms and straightening up tall.

"First off, stop hitting my new countertop," I told him, holding up a finger. "Second, it was weeks ago, and I didn't tell you because, if you weren't listening, I threw away his card; I wasn't planning on looking into his offer, and I didn't hear from him again." A small huff escaped. "Honestly, I forgot about him until right now."

He rubbed a hand over his mouth, frustration and anger and fear terrorizing his face.

"Do you want to tell me what the hell is going on right now?" I demanded through tight teeth. I'd answered enough questions. It was his turn. "Who is he and why are you so angry?"

His hand fisted and clenched on top of the counter, Mick, who stood on the other side, not looking much more controlled than Eli.

"Laurel, we think that Blackman was involved, and possibly the very person who ransacked Roasters in the first place," Eli rasped.

My heart crashed to a halt, and the fear in my veins exploded in a blast of goosebumps over my body.

My skin crawled. He'd come to my house. He'd offered me money... for a place that he'd tried to destroy. *For my business that he'd try to destroy.*

"What?" I asked with a strangled voice, looking between the two of them. "Why didn't you tell me? Why isn't he" —I waved my arms around as my mind blanked on the word—"*arrested?*"

Eli drew a long breath, shoving his fingers through his hair and tamping his anger down when he saw the immediate effect the news had on me.

"Covington... Ace doesn't have proof," he replied, meeting my gaze. "We don't have evidence it was him, but he approached your grandfather before the break-in to purchase Roasters. When Larry refused, he began harassing him, and when Larry wouldn't put up with it anymore, that's when the robbery occurred."

I shook my head, confused. "But why destroy it if he wanted to buy it?"

His nostrils flared as he gripped the edge of the counter, trying to balance his anger. "It doesn't make sense. Maybe to bully your grandfather. Maybe because of something we're missing..." His jaw ticked and I saw the ripple of tension wave through his body.

"And we don't know anything about him?" Stunned wasn't even a good word for how I felt right now.

"Ace and Dex have been looking, but there's not much to him or his business," he went on. "Could just be new or it could be a shell; they're trying to dig deeper. Blackman disappeared after your grandfather's death, but Ace caught him hanging out at Rock

Beach a few weeks ago, and they've been trying to keep an eye on him since, but, clearly, he's a slippery fucker."

Rage flicked over his features.

So slippery they didn't catch him coming to talk to me.

"But it's him, isn't it?" I asked quietly, searching his eyes.

He tried to be objective. He tried to make sure I understood there was nothing but coincidence and dislike that linked Blackman to what happened at Roasters. But I saw past his politically correct confession to the bitter truth underneath.

They knew the identity of the man who'd tried to destroy my legacy but there was nothing they could do about it.

He answered wordlessly with a pained dip of his head.

"I didn't think he'd come to you," he rasped. "I didn't want to come to you with this until we had proof. Until we knew what his endgame was."

Oh, god. My throat tightened, realizing his implication. *This wasn't over yet.*

"I can't believe this." I shuddered and a second later, Eli's arms were around me.

I curled into him. No matter what was happening, I felt safe in his arms and it was the only thing that calmed my hammering heart.

"I'm sorry," he said gruffly. "I didn't mean to scare you. I just didn't realize he'd approached you. I don't trust him, Laurel. I don't fucking trust him, and to know he was around you when I wasn't there to—" He huffed, refusing to finish the thought.

I looked up to him. "Do you think… he'll do something like that again?"

His gaze became sheltered. "I have no idea. I'll have Ace stop by and install security cameras and locks."

"No." I shook my head. "No locks."

"Laurel—"

"No, Eli. I don't… I won't put locks on the door." I stepped back and crossed my arms in front of me, refusing to budge. "That's not how Roasters was… and it's not how Roasters will be. Not under my watch."

"Laurel," he growled my name. "I'm not talking about forever. Just until we can figure out what his endgame is, until we figure out what his motive is, I need to know you are safe."

I chewed on my lower lip for a minute, not wanting to set that tone for Roasters now that I was going to be the one running it. But at the same time, I didn't want to be stubborn to the point of stupidity.

"I'll start locking the house door, but not here." Pausing, I then conceded, "He can install security cameras though."

A long sigh erupted from his chest. "Either way, I've got to call Ace. He needs to know Blackman approached you. He needs to fucking figure out what that man wants because I won't have him coming after you the way he hounded your grandfather."

The only way to describe his gaze was murderous. Calm and collected Eli Downing was ready to do *whatever* it took to protect me. The thought caused equal measures of fear and safety to pump hotly through my blood.

"Hey," Eli said softly, his fingers catching underneath my chin and lifting my eyes back up to the warmth of his. "It's going to be okay. We're going to figure this out, Laurel. I promise you. I'm not going to let him harm you or this place again."

And what had been a seed of fear in my stomach, a worry about a loss I couldn't control, now sprouted with a vengeance into a very real threat that endangered everything my bruised and battered heart had so eagerly let inside its walls.

Twenty-Three

Laurel

"Hey, Jules. It's Laurel again," I spoke as soon as her voicemail beeped, the door to the bakery shutting behind me with a soft click. "I wanted to try to call you again. I haven't heard from you, so I think Eli and I are going to head up to Rock Beach to check on you. Please call me. If not, I'll see you soon."

Staring at the screen, I tried to will it to ring, but it stayed silent.

In spite of what happened yesterday at the coffee shop, learning about Blackman and the subsequent worry that stained like spilled wine in my brain, it was nothing compared to my concern for my cousin.

Yes, Eli had locked the door to the house last night when we got home. And yes, he'd spent almost half an hour on the phone with Ace as they came up with new security protocols, including remote cameras to be installed outside Roasters this afternoon.

My shoulders slumped as I turned the corner to where I'd parked my truck. Eli had gone over to Covington Security this morning to talk with both Ace and Dex while I ran errands and stopped in to see Diane. I was supposed to meet Eli back at the house before heading to Rock Beach to see Jules.

Tucking my phone back in my purse, I looked up and skidded on the sandy pavement to a halt, my heart crashing into the front of my chest.

"Miss Ocean."

The well-dressed weasel stuck out like a sore thumb. Everyone else on the street pulsed with energy but this man felt like a vacuum, with his black suit, black eyes, and black soul that, if I wasn't careful, would suck the life right out of me.

"We didn't get to finish our conversation yesterday." His large arms crossed over his chest like I was a child to be scolded.

My spine stiffened and my eyes darted around, my pulse thumping heavily when I realized we were alone and he was too close for me to feel confident I could simply turn and walk away without being grabbed.

"I think I said everything I needed to say," I replied, holding his gaze steady and grasping on to the show of fortitude. "I'm keeping the business and staying in town, so Roasters isn't for sale."

I should've stopped there. Kept my mouth shut. Kept my hurt and rage bottled inside.

But I couldn't. Not when this man had preyed on my grief and fear to try and buy a business he'd tried to destroy—*from an old man whose heart didn't need any more harassment.*

"And even if it was, I wouldn't sell it to the likes of you," I seethed, anger racing through my blood. "I know what you did," I spat. "I know how you treated my grandfather."

If a face could embody the concept of malice, it was his the second he heard I was no longer interested in selling.

He stepped closer, reaching out and gripping my upper arm painfully before I could even think about moving back.

What had I done?

My breath grew unsteady, ready to scream. *But not yet.* If there was some way... any way... I could goad information from this scumbag—anything that could help Ace and his guys figure out what Blackman wanted with my coffee shop, I would do it.

For Roasters. For my grandfather. *For me.*

"Miss Ocean." The cool edge to his voice sharpened to the blade of a knife. "Are you sure you've thought this through? I hate to bring up such an unfortunate topic, but your family doesn't have a good history with this town." He paused. "Surviving it, I mean. If you stay, there is nowhere you can go that will be safe." My heart stopped on a dime, lurching the rest of the air from my lungs. *Was he threatening me?* "From their ghosts, of course."

Of course, my ass.

He was threatening me. Ignoring my accusations and threatening me in broad daylight.

This man was more dangerous and determined than I realized. And there had to be far more in his sights than a small family business.

"I think I'll be just fine," I assured him, notching up my chin and yanking my arm from his grasp.

He chuckled, and I refused to let him see how it frightened me.

"Oh, Miss Ocean." Goosebumps covered my skin at the venom in his voice. "I'm going to let you think on your decision for one more night, and I hope to get a call from you tomorrow telling me you've changed your mind. If not, I can't guarantee who else you might lose from your choice."

My heart dropped into my stomach like a steel anchor.

He wasn't just threatening me.

He stepped back and tucked one hand into his pocket,

making sure I could see the gun tucked into the waistband of his pants. My throat constricted and, in the next blink, he brushed by me and disappeared on to the street.

Ice-cold dread pumped through my veins, making my movements slow and clumsy.

He threatened me.
He could have killed me.
He was going to kill someone if I didn't sell.

And all for a coffee shop…

It didn't make any sense. Sure, the property was valuable, and the business, I was sure, could be successful again, but was it worth this? Threats of murder?

I rubbed the sides of my arms to help warm my body that felt incurably cold, the threat of loss seeping in around me like an ice bath of frigid fear.

Who would he take?
Eli? Mick? Jules?
Who would he hurt?
Diane? Eve? Josie?

My lips parted, realizing just how many names… how many people… and how much love had filled my hollow heart.

I had so many things to lose, because I had so many people I loved.

I needed to get out of here. *I needed to feel safe.* I couldn't even bring myself to get out my phone. My emotions were frayed down to a single thread—a single necessity of thought to get back home as fast as I could.

Back to Eli.

Miraculously, my feet carried me to the truck.

I blinked and I was passing the edge of town, the quaint buildings dwindling into the famous cliffside landscape.

He was going to hurt them if I didn't give him Roasters.

I turned on the windshield wipers only to realize it wasn't raining, my vision was only blurred from tears.

"Think, Laurel," I chided harshly. "Focus."

Through the million-mile-per-hour thoughts, I focused in on one. There was no choice. No option.

I had to give him what he wanted.

I'd planned on selling Roasters a few weeks ago anyway, what really could've changed?

I gulped. *Everything.*

I'd tried so hard to not let anyone in. So hard to keep my walls up against an ocean of love I thought would drown me. But I'd been so focused, I'd missed a simple truth.

Love was never lost. It was transformed.

Like water evaporates off the ocean, picked up by clouds and held until the weight was too much, my pap's love had been separated from him, pulled from the sea into the clouds, into the community, and showered back down on me through them.

Through Diane and Josie, Eve and Mick. Through Eli.

I'd fought against the ocean, all the while being drenched by the rain.

They had fought for me. This whole time, they'd helped me, they'd grieved with me, they'd given me space and dealt with my sorrow; *this whole time they'd loved me.*

And if sacrificing a building was what it took to protect them, then I'd do it. *Because Roasters was never about the building.*

I opened the window, needing some air, and a cool, salty breeze blew right in and filled the truck's cabin.

"You were the one who taught me about our legacy," I said to the truck like it was my pap. Or maybe it was the ocean air that prompted me, because if there was anything that could carry the message to him it was that.

"I understood it then, but I *feel* it now. I feel the love you built in this town, the love that stayed in this place and in the people even after you were gone." I shuddered as another gust wrapped around me, encouraging me. "I want you to know that I feel the love you left for me. That even though you're gone, your love for me isn't."

Wiping the string of tears from my face, I let out a small whimper that turned into a cry when the truck jerked and began making a loud rattling noise. Plumes of smoke leaked from the seams in the hood and the dash lit up like a Christmas tree just before everything began to fail.

Now?

Steering to the side of the road, I threw the truck in park and climbed out of it before something exploded.

Gulping in air, I stared at the smoking truck in disbelief.

Why?

Why now?

I flattened my palm on the driver's window and tried to steady my heart.

"I was going to stay," I whispered, as though my pap could hear me. "I was going to stay, Pap." Breaths heaved into my lungs like they were shoveling water from a sinking ship. "And now, someone's going to be hurt because of it." I tipped my head back to look up at the sky. "What do I do?"

I was greeted with a cold splattering raindrop on the tip of my nose.

Fumbling in my pocket, I pulled out my phone and dialed the one man who was always there.

"Hey, sweetheart. I'm five minutes out." His voice always made me feel safe even when I had every reason not to be.

"Eli." My voice faltered.

"What's wrong?" He knew immediately.

"The truck broke down."

He swore. "Are you okay? Where are you?"

"About five miles up from the driveway on the highway," I murmured.

He grunted. "I'll be there in two minutes. Don't stand by the road. Better yet, just wait inside the truck. The tourists drive like assholes."

I didn't even have a chance to reply before he hung up.

Folding my arms, I shuffled to the back of the truck, putting down the gate and climbing to sit on it.

"What do I do?" I repeated to myself.

Just because someone is strong, Laurel, doesn't mean they don't need someone to lean on once in a while. His words always came back to me. A different form, but still there. Always there.

I looked up, hearing tires crunch over the gravel as Eli pulled up behind me. His truck was barely in park before he was stalking over to me, his jeans and tee clinging to every determined step.

"It would have been safer to wait in the truck," he grumbled, stopping in front of me and cupping my face. "What's wrong? It's just a truck, Laurel. Probably just overheated. I can fix it for you—"

"No." I shook my head.

"You don't want it fixed?" His brow creased.

"No, Eli," I whimpered and explained softly, "It's Blackman."

I shivered and squeezed my eyes shut, afraid if I opened them, I'd see him again. But even with them closed, I wasn't spared the image of that bald head and narrow, snake-like slits for eyes.

"What?" His body went rigid. "Where? Here? I swear to God, I'll fucking—"

"No." My palm reached for his chest, finding the steady thump of his heart. "In town." I swallowed through the tightness in my throat.

With a string of curses, Eli looked around before wrapping

an arm around my shoulder and hooking one underneath my legs, hoisting me into his arms. "I'm taking you home."

"I'm fine, Eli," I protested, weakly. "I can walk."

"I know you can," he grunted. "But you shouldn't right now."

I relaxed against the strong shelter of his chest, breathing deep of his familiar spice, unable to stop my small sigh of relief or the way my body began to warm against him, feeling safe.

Curled into the front seat, Eli quickly called a tow for my pap's truck before pulling back out onto the road. His free hand stayed locked with mine the whole time.

"What happened?" he asked, his knuckles whitening on the steering wheel. "What did he say?"

"I told him I had nothing more to say—that I was staying and Roasters wasn't for sale," I began hollowly. "And I told him even if it wasn't, I wouldn't sell to him after what he did."

Eli's nostrils flared.

"He threatened me, Eli." I swallowed down the rise of bile in my throat. "He grabbed me and told me he expected me to change my mind. He told me he expected me to call him tomorrow." A small cry slipped out. "He told me it would be a shame to lose someone else I care about because of my decision to stay."

The truck picked up speed and I was surprised the steering wheel didn't snap straight off the column.

"I knew it. I fucking knew it," he growled as the truck sped toward the house. "I knew that fucker was responsible for the break-in. I knew him approaching you wasn't a coincidence."

I drew an unsteady breath, knowing there was one more thing he needed to know. "And when he went to leave, he made sure I saw his gun."

The string of curses that flew from Eli's lips would've shocked the devil himself.

"I don't understand what is so valuable. What is worth

threatening me for..." I murmured, still in disbelief that I was using the word 'threaten' in reference to myself.

"I'm going to take care of this." He glanced at me as he turned down the driveway. "I'm going to fix this, Laurel."

When he shut the engine off, I told him hollowly, "No. I'm going to fix this. I'm going to give him what he wants."

He glared at me before hopping down and rounding to my side of the truck, yanking open the door.

"No, you're not," he bit out. "You're not going to give that fucker anything."

I slid down from the seat. "Yes, I am," I insisted. I had no choice.

"Dammit, Laurel." His arms caged me in, but I refused to back down. "No, you're not. We're going to figure this out—we're going to figure him out."

I pushed against his chest, anger and fear ripping me apart inside.

"No! We don't have time," I insisted again, raggedly. "There is no time. There's only one choice."

"There is always—"

"Don't you see, Eli?" I begged him. "I don't have a choice and he knows it. I can't—" I gasped in air, the invisible belt around my chest cinching tighter with each inhale. "I can't risk it."

Tears blurred my vision and the prospect of loss made me weak. I didn't want to be weak, but I couldn't stop it. I couldn't help it.

Love without vulnerability is only frivolity.

And through the murkiness, I saw Eli reaching for me.

Always there.

My head shook in denial. "I can't risk any more. I won't risk losing someone else, Eli."

Warm fingers cupped my cheeks, "I won't let him hurt you or anyone—"

"And what about you?" My fist pounded into his chest, but his big body didn't budge under the assault. "Who's going to stop him from hurting you?" I demanded wildly. My head shook and tears slickened my cheeks, forcing him to let go.

"Laurel—"

"No, Eli," I cried frantically, gasping in air. "I can't lose you."

"You won't—"

"I won't risk it," I broke in feverishly, the last of my walls crumbling. "I can't lose you, Eli. I can't lose another person I love."

I gasped and clapped a hand over my mouth.

No.

No, no, no.

I tried to force the word into my heart, but it steadily beat back with a single, sentencing word.

Yes.

And even in this, in what felt like the most vulnerable moment of my life, when I could feel nothing but hurt and grief and pain and regret, I realized a truth I'd fought to disprove. I didn't just realize it, I *knew* it. I knew it like I knew the sun would set on this horizon and that the waves would always crash against the cliffs. I knew it like I knew my lungs would continue to breathe and my heart would continue to beat.

I wasn't supposed to love him, but I did. I'd fallen in love with Eli.

I'd started falling from the moment he cared for me that first night, bringing me home safe, making sure I was alright... even when I vomited all over him. *Twice.*

I'd fallen in love with the way he came to my side, no questions asked, when I needed him.

I'd fallen in love with the way he took care of my family's

business, of the people in this town, and of me with every fiber of his being.

I'd fallen in love with the fireworks that erupted every time he kissed me or the way his touch melted every inch of my body. And I'd fallen in love with the way he held me, like nothing bad could happen to something that felt so right.

I'd fallen for the man who'd kindly, carefully, and consistently shown me over the past several weeks that it was safe to let love in... *that love was worth the risk.*

And the fight against this feeling had been lost a long time ago and denial was as flimsy a shield over the truth as tissue paper to blot out the sun.

He waited those few seconds in stunned silence before closing the space between us and replacing his hands on my cheeks, tipping my gaze to his.

"Laurel," he rasped, the rain beginning to drop with consistent beats now.

It was the wrong time. The wrong moment to admit to loving someone. I knew it. But I couldn't stop it.

When loss threatened everything around me, I couldn't hold back letting him know how much I love him.

That was the risk I wasn't willing to take.

"I'm sorry. I shouldn't have said—" He silenced me with his mouth, punishing my lips with his long, demanding kiss. His tongue wiped away any trace of my apology and left only my confession.

"I told you, sweetheart, don't ever apologize for giving me pieces of you," he growled. "Especially when that piece is your heart... your love."

My eyes widened as I looked at him.

"I love you, Laurel." His gaze bored into mine, safe and sure. "I love you so damn much, and I'm not going anywhere."

My heart hammered in my chest, warmth bleeding into my veins and melting through the fear that left them frozen.

I looked up to the man who would always be there for me, not to fix me, not to heal me, but to give me the love and support knowing I could do those things for myself. He would stand by me and be one of my strengths without demanding to be all of them. He would be there for me to lean on and he would be behind me when I needed to stand on my own. He would be there just like he was right now, loving me strongly and silently, so that no matter when I looked to him—at my highest or my lowest—I would know he was with me. *And that I was loved.*

"I promised you I wouldn't let you lose anything else the first night we met—right here, and you can be damn sure I'm not the kind of man who breaks my promises. We clear?" he demanded roughly, his promise sending a spiral of heat straight down to my stomach.

I nodded and melted against him, the weight and walls around my heart disintegrating. There was still concern for what was going to happen, but the fear that destroyed pieces of my soul, that convinced me the only safe life was the one lived alone, was no match for this man—and for how I felt about him.

"We're going to figure this out. Together." He brushed my hair back from my face, desire burning hotly in his eyes, and growled, "But first, the man who loves you is going to show you just how damn much..."

I sucked in a breath as he lifted me back into his arms, shivering as need zipped straight down to my core and exploded into hungry lust. My arms locked around his neck and my legs wrapped around his waist as he carried me to the house.

I needed everything about this moment.

The world could wait.

The world could wait because love came first.

And, as much as I needed to hear his words, now, I needed to feel him, to be with him. I needed to know, in the most basic way, that he wouldn't leave because he was a part of me.

His mouth covered mine again. With each step, I felt the hard length of him growing between my legs, eager to possess me like the rest of him did—with demanding confidence. Our breaths grew ragged, panting and hungry by the time we reached the door.

The things I came back to Carmel afraid of—tethers I thought were anchors to pull me down, I now realized were fine strings attached to the kind of love that lifted me up like a balloon and let me soar.

"I love you," I murmured as the door slammed behind us.

And then my back was against the door, and Eli's hot mouth was back to possessing mine. Heat exploded in every cell, needing only one thing to survive. *Him.*

I moaned into the kiss, my tongue seeking the firm velvet of his, claiming him for myself. Claiming his kiss. With the kind of desperation that can only be fueled by the threat of loss, our need devoured us. *Our love consumed us.*

I rolled my hips against his, reveling in his tortured groan even as my body turned to mush.

"Fuck, Laurel," he said, gravelly, grinding his erection against me and making me squirm. "The thought of that fucker's hands on you—" he broke off to kiss me roughly again.

The way he held me. The raw rage that scorched underneath each touch. That was his weakness.

"I can't—" He panted harshly, unhinged need to claim warring with aching want to be gentle. "I won't lose you. I'll do anything to keep you safe, but fuck if I can love you slow right now."

He didn't know how to explain, only to show me what the thought did to him—*and what he needed to make it better.*

The man who always held it all together, crumbled at the thought of someone threatening me... hurting me. He crumbled and lost control, needing to prove I was here and all his.

And that vulnerability sent the most delicious thrill through my body. A vulnerability no one else saw because no one else created it. *And that was how I knew his love for me was real and not just frivolity.*

"I need you, Eli," I reassured him, dragging his mouth back to mine. "All I need is you."

His growl assaulted my lips as his tongue laid siege to mine. His fingers dug into my ass, squeezing and pulling the flesh as his fingers searched lower where I needed him. I wiggled, trying to get closer. *Trying to get more.*

"So warm, sweetheart. So wet."

I quaked as he brushed over my sex, desire making my jean shorts damp and rough against my skin.

"Eli..." I pleaded. *Wet and ready and desperate.*

"You sure—" His ragged groan exploded the rest of his question. My hand speared down between us and cupped over his hard length straining against his jeans.

"Please." I tightened my hold over his thickness, savoring the way he ground against my hand with unfiltered need.

After that, there were no more words. Our mouths moved, our bodies spoke, and our hearts screamed... but there were no more words.

Our trail of clothes was a diary of desire leading to the bedroom, telling a tale woven of uninhibited love and lust along the way.

My small moans mirrored his harsh breaths as we ended up in front of the bed. Eli dropped to his knees and stripped me of my panties, ripping them as he yanked them down my leg.

I barely got in a breath—barely a measured

heartbeat—before strong hands gripped my thighs, spreading them wide and bending between them.

"Eli!" The first swipe of his tongue through my sex had me seeing stars.

I gripped his head, needing something to hold me steady—needing to hold him closer.

My legs shook, hardly able to hold myself upright as he devoured me. I shifted back under the insistence of his tongue. The demanding swipes through my flesh made it impossible to sense anything except him. Except his tongue through my slick folds. His lips around my swollen clit.

My knees hit the back of the bed like a ship drifting into harbor amid stormy seas, but I couldn't sit. I couldn't move.

His tongue worked through me until my heart felt ready to beat out of my chest and my limbs felt not my own. My fingers twisted roughly into his hair, tugging him closer as he shifted one of my legs onto his shoulder.

I sank against him, my head tipping back in exquisite pleasure as his tongue dipped inside me, now having greater access to every inch of my core. He teased and tortured me until I forgot anything existed but us.

I needed him. I loved him.

And I wasn't letting go.

It didn't take long. With anxiety and anticipation running through my veins, it didn't take long for desire to use those emotions as fuel and my body went up in flames.

"Don't make a starving man wait for the sweetest thing on earth," he commanded hoarsely. "Come for me, sweetheart."

I screamed his name as I exploded, falling apart and blacking out everything except the pleasure from his mouth. My limbs splintered as his lips drank every drop of my release from my sex for long minutes until a semblance of sense returned to my body.

Sense that made me realize I was no longer standing. Sense that felt the soft mattress against my back. Sense that felt the hard, hot male over me.

"So beautiful," he murmured, dragging his lips over my stomach and latching on to my nipple.

And then the assault on my senses began all over again. This time, with ravenous steadiness.

He loved me and his mouth was determined to brand the truth into every cell.

I arched into him, disintegrating all over again at the steady roll and tumble of his tongue against my breast. Electricity being fed to an already live wire that strung straight down to my core, making my pussy clench and weep all over again.

"I love you." It was a confession and a plea.

He grunted, low and torn as he slid farther up my body, bringing that insatiable mouth to mine. "God, I love you."

My breath caught, locked and loaded in my chest when I felt the fat blunt head of his cock pressing against my entrance.

His lips trailed a path along my jawline while he slid himself along my slick folds, coating himself with my desire like it was a war paint—*confidence in a battle already won.*

"Please..."

He would never deny me. *He couldn't.*

I cried out as he slammed inside me, spearing through tense muscles and taut nerves, and filling each and every last inch of me until I knew nothing but him.

There was no waiting. No time. Nothing but the present as he began to move.

Thrust after thrust after thrust.

Words of love he whispered in my ear coalesced with the desire building where our bodies joined.

Like a firework shot into the sky, my connection to him

blazed a path through the darkness around me, love and desire sparking to leave a burning trail in my wake.

My hands gripped into the muscles of his shoulders, slick with sweat as his hips pumped into mine with breathtaking frenzy.

His mouth ate up my moans as his cock rubbed over that sweet spot inside me. As my body fought for more, so did his. Reaching. Searching. *Loving.* Eli lost all control and every ounce of that righteous and protective anger channeled into animalistic need to possess... to protect... *to love.*

My chest inflated as he drove me higher and higher with each thrust.

Pleasure spiraled through me like a hurricane of need centered solely on him. My lips parted, desperate to cry out his name, but everything choked to a halt as he slid out, pausing for a split-second like he knew what one more thrust would do.

Covering my mouth with his, he slammed his cock deep inside me and took me over the edge, swallowing my cry as I disintegrated in pleasure around him.

Lights and sounds scattered as I fractured, the firework of need exploded into brightly-colored streams of release as my body floated back down to earth in pieces.

I felt him shove and grind up against my womb one last time before he let out a loud groan, his hot cum flooding inside me, my body continuing to clench around him, dragging every last drop from his pulsing cock.

"*Fuck...*" He grunted and collapsed on top of me, and I welcomed the weight of knowing he was with me.

Every breath. Every inch. Every heartbeat.

Slowly, the world rebuilt around us as Eli slid out of me and tipped to the side, taking me with him, and tucking me underneath his arm.

"I love you," he murmured, pressing his mouth lightly on the top of my head.

I peeked up at him, eyes closed, one hand tracing along my arm, the other resting like a paperweight on his chest. "It doesn't seem possible… to love you like I do. As much as I do. And to have found it the way I did…"

It didn't seem possible to love a man so much I'd only met weeks ago under the worst of circumstances.

A small smile tugged on his lips and those ember eyes peeled open, reaching right into my soul. "Grief clarifies what is important. It clarifies what we mean to each other." His fingers skated under my chin, holding me steady as he told me without doubt. "Sometimes those connections are unexpected." *That was certainly the truth.* "And sometimes they are forged with a once-in-a-lifetime kind of lightning that strikes in that unexpected space and changes it forever."

My mouth parted.

"Call it fate. Call it Larry. But never question how I feel about you, Laurel. How much I feel nor how real it is." He pressed a kiss to the tip of my nose. "You are everything to me."

I blinked back tears, at a loss to say anything to adequately describe how I felt. "I love you, Eli. Thank you for never giving up on me."

His smile grew in small measures. "You never gave up on yourself," he replied. "And we" —he paused, his eyes hardening—"aren't giving up on Roasters."

I shivered and nodded. He was right. *There had to be another way.*

"What are we going to do?" I sighed. "And what about Jules?"

We were supposed to be at Rock Beach by now.

He hummed. "We are going to lay here for another few minutes. Then, I'm going to make you scream my name one more time. And after that, I'm going to talk to Ace," he informed me with a wicked grin, adding, "Going to see Jules now might just put her in more danger if Blackman is watching you." He cleared his throat. "He's already been seen at the resort. I don't want to take any chances."

My throat tightened. At least, I knew from my last visit there, that there was security at the resort. Even if they were keeping her locked in, they were keeping my cousin safe.

"Maybe we should let Eve know," I whispered. "And Josie. And Diane. And Mick and Miles. I'm worried about them, too." My gaze dropped. "And you…"

"Hey…" He tipped my chin up to him. "Nothing is going to happen to me. Nothing."

Just like the first day I met him in that hallway, his gaze overwhelmed me. It felt like my heart was standing in front of a fire that would never go out, a fire that would always light up sparks in me, and a fire that would warm the very deepest parts of me, steadily, comfortingly, and securely.

"I love you," I told him in a voice that was barely above a whisper.

His lips crushed mine, firm yet sweet. "I love you, too, Laurel."

Tears pooled in the corners of my eyes as the vulnerability of that love showed through. "I don't want to lose you…"

"You won't lose me, sweetheart. I promise," he rasped, tugging my hips harder against his.

"How do you know? How can you be sure?"

He chuckled and kissed the tip of my nose and then my forehead. "Because you're too damn stubborn to let me go." He chuckled. "And because I'm too damn stubborn to let anything—even death—take me away from you."

My lips tipped up in a small smile and I curled deeper into

his arms. I had to believe him. I had to believe we'd figure out a way to stop Blackman. If I didn't, the alternative would cripple me.

Eli had taught me that both love and loss were equally consuming and equally unavoidable. They drew a line in the sand of life before me. To flee or to fight.

And courage, I realized now, wasn't the absence of fear, but the decision to resist it.

And I would resist it. For love.

Twenty-Four

Eli

"It's drugs."

My hand dropped like lead onto the countertop as Laurel turned from behind me and gasped, "What?"

The harsh square of Ace's jaw ticked as he gave a curt nod. "The Crown Cartel," he said the name like it was the eighth circle of Hell. "They run up and down the west coast dealing with everything from drugs to arms deals to human trafficking. But in this instance, they want to use the coffee shop to smuggle in drugs from Colombia."

We both stared at him.

"To smuggle drugs?" I was in shock.

"Coffee and cocaine. Both come from Colombia. The idea is that the coffee can mask the scent of cocaine when they bring it into the country," Ace explained. "What better way than use a business that has been legitimate for a century? A new business—especially one that looks like a shell—would be subject to greater scrutiny."

Blood thundered in the veins along the side of my head. I

reached for Laurel and tugged her against my side. The tense chill in her body telling me all I needed to know about how the news made her feel.

"My phone was in my hand when your call came through," he said with a shake of his head. "I couldn't fucking believe it. I don't know how Dex found it… I don't want to know what laws he broke… but Blackman is definitely working with the Crown Cartel."

When I'd called him thirty minutes ago, he'd answered with 'how did you know I was about to call you?' Immediately, I knew he had news, and I fucking prayed it was enough to put us a step ahead in Blackman's twisted plan rather than a step behind.

Laurel twisted to face Ace, my arm was still firmly around her waist.

"Before we dive into the million questions I'm sure you don't have all the answers to yet," she broke in, drawing Ace's attention. "I wanted to say thank you, Ace, for everything that you've done for my grandfather and this place after he was gone." She paused as her voice choked slightly. "I'm sure you're going to tell me, just like the rest of them, that it was nothing compared to what he did for you, but that doesn't change the simple fact that you didn't have to do this. You didn't have to take the time nor the risks that I'm sure are stacking up higher than you were prepared for, and I appreciate it more than I can say. Thank you."

I watched the slight lift of his head as my friend tried to mitigate the surprise of both the gratitude and fortitude in Laurel's voice.

He grunted. "Of course. Anything for the Oceans."

Her small smile was fleeting and I squeezed her waist for support.

"So, that's why he's been intent on buying Roasters." Her small hand curled into my chest. "So, the cartel decided they want to use shipments of beans that we get from Colombia to smuggle in cocaine."

Ace nodded. "As a front for their expanding operation."

"This has been going on for several months then. Blackman approached my grandfather to sell, and when he wouldn't, trashed the place." Her brow furrowed. "To threaten him?"

"Most likely to pressure your grandfather into selling, hoping the stress of having to rebuild everything from the inside out would be too much." Ace cleared his throat.

"Wait…" Laurel looked up to me in horror. "All of this is happening now because my grandfather died. If he hadn't, they would still be out of luck. Do you think… you don't think he…" She couldn't finish, looking back and forth between Ace and me.

My chest tightened. "I don't think they had anything to do with Larry's death." I winced, recalling the memory of when I'd found him. *There was no doubt his death was self-inflicted.* "Not directly."

Her blue eyes swirled with turmoil.

Even if Blackman hadn't pulled the trigger, he'd taken advantage of an old, unstable man. He'd destroyed the one thing Larry had clung to—the only lifeline to the family he'd lost. No, he didn't pull the trigger, but it didn't make Blackman any less responsible.

"Based on what I know," Ace broke in. "If Larry hadn't committed suicide, murder wouldn't be too far down on the list of things he would've attempted to move this purchase along." His eyes narrowed on Laurel. "The only thing he wasn't counting on was you."

My chest swelled.

Just because my woman sometimes needed my help didn't mean she wasn't the strongest woman I'd ever known.

"So, tell me what exactly he said to you earlier," Ace requested.

He couldn't see it, but I felt how her spine steeled, turning her body ramrod straight.

Laurel took a few minutes to succinctly tell him what happened in town, how Blackman approached her, how he threatened her, and what he said he wanted.

Ace's face darkened with each statement, swearing when she finished. "*Sonofabitch.*"

She gave me a determined smile before turning to Ace. She planted her hands on the countertop like she was staking her claim, like she was driving the Ocean flag into the ragged ground that was stained with tears and blood.

"How do we stop them?"

Fuck, I loved her.

Even Ace cracked a smile at that. "You leave that up to us, Laurel."

Her head whipped to the side. "Absolutely not. This is my family. My business. *My town.* I refuse to lose any more of it, especially if there was something I could've done."

Both of his hands shot up as a show of resignation topped off with a look of astonishment sent my way. Not many women after being threatened—after having their loved ones threatened—by a member of a drug cartel would be the first to jump to do something about it.

"This is a huge operation we are dealing with here," he began slowly when I didn't contradict her. "Blackman is like the outer ring on a Redwood—there are hundreds of rings after him before you even get close to the center." He bent forward, locking his hands on the table in front of him. "We know he's on their payroll in some way. I don't know if Roasters was only his idea or if he's taking orders from higher up. I don't know if we take him out if there will be a hundred more like him coming down the line. We need to be smart and, more importantly, you need to be safe."

"Okay," she agreed begrudgingly. "But he's expecting me to change my mind by tomorrow—to call him tomorrow."

He huffed, rubbing his fingers along themselves, trying to piece together a plan. Tomorrow wasn't a lot of time—to gather more information nor come up with a way to stop this before Blackman made good on this threat.

I felt Laurel perk up, and I knew what was coming before she even began. "What if I call—"

"*No!*" Both Ace and I spoke at the same time.

"You didn't even hear—"

My hand gripped her shoulder. "Laurel, you're not going to call him. You're not going to lure him out."

"But it makes sense," she insisted, pulling out of my grasp and folding her arms, determination etched into her features. "I'll tell him that I've changed my mind and I'll sell him the building. When we meet to do that... so I can sign over the deed... you can be there to arrest him. What other choice do we have?"

The tic in my jaw was strong and steady. The idea made sense. The idea was a good one. Simple. Effective. *I hated it.*

"I don't like it," Ace interjected, speaking my thoughts. "I don't like it, but I also don't know what other option there is. It's her name on the deed. It's not like I could send someone else."

"Yeah, and what if he just kills her and takes the paper?" I demanded roughly. "Because you have to think about that." I looked to Laurel. "Now that he's threatened you, maybe he's not interested in making this legitimate. We can't rule that out."

"We won't," Ace told me tightly. "We won't rule it out, and we won't let it happen."

I looked between them. I was outnumbered. Both were determined for different reasons, but there was no arguing with them. Especially when I didn't have a better plan.

"I don't like it," I bit out.

Laurel turned in my arms and cupped my face. I could practically hear the ocean of calm echoing in her eyes and still, it didn't get rid of the fear that pierced my heart.

To think that I was the one reassuring her earlier today that she wouldn't lose me, and now, I was the one petrified of losing her.

"It's going to be okay, Eli," she murmured like we were the only two in the room. "I'm going to be okay."

My gaze warred with hers, both loving and hating her strength in that moment. With a deep, uncomfortable sigh, I bent down and kissed her forehead. A reluctant concession.

"So, how is this all going to work?" I turned and demanded of Ace.

If this was going to happen, not only was I going to know each and every step along the way, but I was going to be there the whole damn time.

"Let me get back with Dex and figure out the safest way to make this happen. We'll figure it out tonight and reconvene in the morning. I don't want them to suspect that she's been in contact with us. I don't want them to suspect she knows anything about the drug connection," he said firmly.

We both nodded and the large tattooed man disappeared with the promise to return soon.

As soon as he was gone, Laurel sagged against me, the strength she'd mustered over the past half an hour dissipated now that we were alone. She leaned into me, and I stood there with my arms wrapped tightly around her.

"Thank you," she murmured against my shirt.

"Why are you thanking me?"

Her head tilted up from my chest to look at me. "For letting me do this. For letting me do something to stop this. To save my legacy."

Like I could stop her.

She'd faced every imaginable loss in her life. I wasn't going to be the one to stand in her way from stopping another one.

"Don't thank me, Laurel. Honestly, there's still time for me to change my mind," I grumbled even though we both knew that wasn't happening. "Whether you remember it or not, I promised you the night we met I wouldn't let this town take anything else from you, and that includes this—your decision to do something about it, to try to right a wrong. I'd never be the one to take that from you, even though I wish like all hell there was another way."

"I love you." The words shone from her soul right through her eyes and it was that love that resisted fear.

"I love you, too."

I'd promised her she wouldn't lose anything else from this town. And I prayed I could protect her well enough to keep my word and keep her safe.

Laurel

"You sure you want to do this?" Eli asked for the millionth time.

I nodded and gave him a brave smile even as the nervous sweat seeped from my fingers into that horrible man's black business card. The second one I'd had to touch when he'd left it with me *yesterday.*

Yesterday, the plan seemed simple and sure. Today... now... as I was about to call the number while Eli, Ace, and his brother, Dex, all sat around my dining table... it was overwhelming.

"Yeah," I added as extra reassurance—*for them and myself.*

"You sure you don't want to go through it again?" Ace asked, with zero judgment in his voice if I needed to practice one more time.

"No, I'm good." I nodded and unlocked my cell, tapping in the number.

Determined, I jabbed forcefully on the call button before I could hesitate any longer and held the phone up to my ear.

Those two rings could have been heard on the other side of town for how loud they seemed to me and how silent my companions were. And if looks could murder, Blackman would be dead on the other end of the line right now.

"Miss Ocean." The voice slithered over me, threatening and soft.

Deep breaths, Laurel. He's not here. He can't hurt you.

"Mr. Blackman," I greeted coolly with only the slightest quiver at the end.

"I was hoping to hear from you." He spoke smoothly, like an oil spill on the ocean, the dark and deadly liquid suffocating everything it touched. "Have you thought about what I said?"

Or the way you almost strangled me?

"Yes, I have." I glanced at Ace who was nodding encouragingly. "I've decided you're right. I don't belong here, and I have no idea how to run a coffee shop. I think it's best if I just sell and move on with my life and your offer was very generous."

The moan of satisfaction on the other end of the line made me want to vomit.

"Wonderful," he encouraged.

"I-I don't have the deed," I lied, praying that the shake in my voice came out less than how it sounded to me. "I have to get it from my lawyer on Monday, but then I can meet you at the coffee shop to sign it over."

There was a pause and I held my breath, hoping—praying he believed me.

"I will meet you there at noon."

The breath I hadn't realized was bound in my chest let

loose. "Great. I mean, that works," I stuttered. "See you on Monday."

Just as I was about to pull the phone down, that oily sound smeared over me once more. "Oh, and Miss Ocean? This business is better handled between just the two of us, don't you think? If you choose to bring anyone else into our arrangement, I'm afraid I will have to, too." I could hear the menacing smile on his face. "And I don't think my friends are as nice as yours."

My stomach dropped, bile rising in my throat.

He didn't bother to wait for me to agree before hanging up. He knew he had me.

Eli reached for my hand as soon as I set the phone down, and I latched on to his fingers tightly as I took my first full breath in several minutes.

"Are you alright?" He wouldn't let me look away or share anything until I answered him—until he knew I was okay.

"Yeah." I refused to not be okay. Not now. "Roasters. Noon on Monday." I gulped and looked to Ace. "He… he told me not to bring anyone. He said he'd have to bring someone then, too."

He nodded, and it comforted me to see he must've expected that. "It'll be okay, Laurel. He doesn't know you have someone to bring, aside from Eli. He doesn't know what we know."

"You sure you want to do this?" Eli questioned. "We can find another way."

"I'm okay." I reached for and squeezed his hand.

"Alright, let's go over everything again," Ace suggested, and I agreed. Focusing on the details is what would keep me sane through today and tomorrow, knowing this would all be over come Monday as long as I stuck to the plan.

Even though Ace and Dex walked me through what would happen on Monday when I met with Blackman again.

He went over the wire I was going to be wearing. He

reiterated where he and Dex and Eli would be waiting. He reiterated that the cameras would be watching and capturing everything, too. All I had to do was get on tape either a threat or confession and give him a fake deed and a tracker. By the time he realized it wasn't the real one, the police would be arresting him.

If only Covington could locate where he was. But Dex had checked everywhere. They'd even sent a man over to the resort, but Blackman was nowhere to be found.

We needed to be able to find him *and* solid evidence before we could go to the police. Blackman was important to the organization, and if we could get any information about the extent of the cartel's presence in Carmel Cove, that would be even better.

"Drink." I looked up to see that Eli had made coffee for everyone, the aroma dousing the tension in the room.

Coffee wasn't magic, I reiterated to myself. Just like marinara sauce wasn't magic. Still, as the first sip touched my tongue, I let the lie fall in its tracks and admitted that this was magic—magic like a wardrobe turning into a doorway to Narnia.

Because only magic is able to take something ordinary and make it do the extraordinary.

And this ordinary cup of coffee accomplished the extraordinary task of calming me in the middle of this storm, of giving me strength when it was perfectly legitimate to be afraid, and of making me feel nothing but the love that surrounded me even though I now had everything to lose.

Twenty-Five

Laurel

It felt like only minutes had passed since I'd called Blackman, yet somehow it was Sunday night and in a little over twelve hours, I was going to meet the man who'd threatened me. The man who'd destroyed my family's coffee shop. *The man who'd destroyed the last thread of my grandfather's failing sanity.*

An anger like I'd never felt pooled in my blood, pulling my cells taut with anticipation and anxiety. Each minute was another step across a tightrope to Tuesday, just waiting to get to the other side of the chasm.

Eli was right. Grief clarified what was important in life.

It clarified my place here in my hometown.

It clarified my future at Roasters.

And it clarified my capacity to love—my *need* to love again.

Carmel Cove was where I belonged. *And I belonged here with him.*

"I got it, sweetheart," Eli insisted as I rose to help him clean up from dinner. We'd spent the whole day making magic marinara so we could have spaghetti and meatballs tonight.

It was my pap's traditional Sunday meal, and if I had anything to say about it, it would be ours, too. It was a silly little thing, but I was starting to see all those silly little things as reminders that even though he wasn't here, he wasn't gone.

"Thank you," I murmured, reaching up on my toes, pressing my lips to his.

"You sure you're okay about work?" He arched an eyebrow.

Resting my hip on the edge of the table, I rubbed my hands together. "Yeah. I'm not sure why I was so nervous. I knew Rachel would understand."

In fact, my boss replied to my call informing her of my resignation with a sigh and an *'It's about time I got this call.'*

Maybe because it was her job to see trends before they arrived, she'd picked up enough pieces from my calls and emails over the last several weeks to realize that Carmel Cove was no longer a layover in my life; it was my final stop.

No matter what happened with Blackman and Roasters tomorrow, it didn't change that Carmel was where I needed to be, and I wasn't going to let uncertainty stop me from taking the steps to finally come home. *For good.*

After letting her know I would be back in LA in another week to wrap up what was left of my life there and square away my things, I thanked her for everything that she did for me with tears in my eyes. Even though it hurt to say goodbye to a woman I liked and admired, this was the right move—*the only move*—for me.

Eli gave me a long hard look before nodding and turning back to the sink.

Neither of us brought up the meeting tomorrow. It was the elephant in the room that had already been addressed but stood there, waiting patiently for his time to leave.

Eli had been tense since the moment Ace and Dex and I

agreed on our plan. He didn't have to say anything, it pulsed in every breath. It hummed in every touch.

He was always touching me no matter where we were, whether it was holding my hand at the grocery store or playing with my hair as we tried to work through some of my pap's unfinished crossword puzzles last night.

And in the moments when he couldn't reach me, Eli looked at me with an intensity that, if it could be converted into something physical, the strength of his love would create a magical shield to protect me. But because that wasn't possible, he touched me to let me know he was there to give me strength and at night, he took me to let me know he was mine.

"I'm going to change. I'll meet you on the couch," I murmured, and he shot me a wink that sent the butterflies in my stomach springing to life.

I felt my cheeks heat and the insistent pool of heat lower in my body begin to swell.

I'd never get tired of how this man could make the worries of the world drop like a curtain, leaving only him and me on the center stage of life.

And I'd never stop sending up silent prayers of thanks to my pap for giving me this man to move forward with. Because if I couldn't be grateful for what he left me—the memories, the people, the business, Eli—then what was the point of grief?

Pausing in the living room, I pulled out the book of crossword puzzles we'd been engrossed in last night from the top of the puzzle-book stack. I went to set it on the couch and caught sight of my phone ringing; the sink and the clatter of dishes hid the vibration.

Grabbing it, I hesitated when I saw the caller ID.

Jules.

I glanced at the kitchen. I didn't want to put Jules in any

more danger than she was already, but I hadn't heard from her in so long I was already worried if she was okay.

Pulling my lip between my teeth, I swallowed an apology and prayed I was doing the right thing.

"Hello?" I answered before I could think twice.

"L-Laurel?" My cousin's subdued voice faltered as she replied.

"Hey, what's up?" I sat up straighter on the couch. "Are you okay? I've been trying to get in touch with you for days." I winced, my frayed nerves getting the best of my tone.

"I know, I'm sorry." She paused and I shifted my phone to my other ear. "And I'm sorry to bother you so late," she continued without further explanation of her absence. "I was wondering if you could meet me? To talk…"

"Right now?" My stomach cinched. "Is everything okay?"

Another pause that felt stretched too thin. "No… I mean, I don't know. I can't… I can't talk about it here." Her voice grew softer, weakened with worry and threaded with fear.

"Okay." I nodded, my mind shifting into overdrive, all thoughts of Blackman gone in the face of my suffocating concern for my cousin. "Does it have to do with your family? Are you okay? Are you safe? Do you need me to come there? To get you?"

Questions fired like bullets from my lips. Delusional images of her locked up in a tower flashed through my mind.

"No. I mean, I'm okay, but no, I don't need you to come here," she clarified, sucking in a quick breath. "But can you meet me somewhere? I can't stay here, and you shouldn't come here."

"Of course." There was no question. Even though this had nothing to do with Blackman, I wasn't going to put her off when she sounded like this.

I could hear her uneven breathing through the line and my chest ached.

"I'll meet you at Roasters."

"Absolutely." I rose and bolted for the kitchen. "I'll see you there in ten minutes."

Eli's head whipped to me, eyebrows raised and his hands mid-dry on a plate, as he pinned me with a sharp stare. Holding his gaze, I grabbed my coat from off the hook.

"Please, Laurel. Don't tell anyone. This is... my family. I don't know what to do... who to trust..."

Oh God. It was her family.

"Of course. I'll be there in ten." With my heart hammering, I hung up and leveled with Eli. "It was Jules. Something happened, and I have to go meet her."

"What do you mean? What happened?" he demanded, emptying his hands and approaching me.

"I-I don't know," I admitted. "Honestly, I don't know. It's something with her family and—" I broke off with a huff as I shoved my arms into my jacket sleeves. "I knew it. She practically admitted to being trapped there when I talked to her the other night. I knew I should've stopped her then."

I brushed by him and reached for the door, his truck keys in my hand.

"Laurel..." he chided and then warned roughly, "This isn't a good idea. Not with Blackman out there. I know you're worried about her home situation, but—"

"No buts, Eli." My head swung side to side. "Not now. Not for her."

"I'm not saying no," he ground out, his protectiveness pulsing steadily through the veins in his neck. "I'm just asking if there is any way it can wait until tomorrow night?"

My hand froze on the doorknob as I met his stare for several long seconds. Reaching out, my small hands barely covered half of his biceps as I gripped him and stepped close, telling him softly, "I know he never asked, but I wasn't here to help my pap when he needed it. I can't—I won't put Jules off. Not when she needs me."

There was a long pause, and I could see he never expected a different answer from me even though fear required him to ask.

"Dammit." He huffed, spearing his hand through his hair. He knew like I did this was a cry—*a call* for help. "Then I'm coming with you."

"No." I meant to shake him, but his arms hardly moved with my effort. "This is something with her family—*my family*. And she asked me to come alone."

"Laurel," he growled, and I knew this battle I might not win.

"Please, Eli," I pleaded. "The last time I saw her, she wouldn't tell me everything that was going on and then I didn't hear from her for a week. I don't want to risk you being there... and her feeling like she can't finally tell me the truth."

I moved even closer, putting my body flush to his and searching his gaze. "They've taken away the few people she thought she could rely on. She's alone, Eli. Alone in a palace full of people." My head dropped for a second to take a fortifying breath and continue. "I'll be okay. This has to do with family. Not the business. Not Blackman." I slid my arms around his neck. "Plus, Dex installed the security cameras yesterday, so you can check on us."

Displeasure cracked all of the gorgeous lines on his face as he stood there, tensed like a rubber band about to snap.

"Please."

With a sigh, his forehead dropped to mine and he conceded, "Alright, but just keep me updated, so I don't lose my mind. And I will have Dex check the cameras if you don't."

A small smile pulled up one corner of my lips as I pushed up on my tiptoes to reach him. "I love you."

"I love you, too," he grunted and took my mouth in a demanding, worry-laden kiss. "You have a heart your grandfather would be so proud of."

I shivered with warmth, hoping this was the kind of legacy my pap would be proud of.

Darting out into the crisp, California night, I jogged to Eli's truck. The chilled air had a pre-storm scent, the one that was calm but foreboding. *The one that whispered, 'be careful' with every gust.* But I was too concerned for Jules to heed any kind of warning.

Twenty-Six

Laurel

When I pulled around the back of Roasters, there was a black Cadillac with tinted windows already parked. My already thundering heart picked up speed as I stopped the truck. The goosebumps on my arms should've warned that something wasn't right, but my mind rationalized the expensive black sedan was just the kind of vehicle my uncle would keep in his fleet to drive.

Without another thought, I shut off the truck and left the keys in the cup-holder, beelining for the back door to the coffee shop.

"Jules?" I hollered as I walked through the door, squinting into the dim light in search of my cousin. Met with silence, I pressed through the kitchen and down the short hall to the front of the building. "It's me. Laurel."

Of course, it was, dummy.

I was panicked. Jules sounded so frightened on the phone, and I didn't want to give her any other cause for concern.

"Jules, are you—" I broke off with a gasp as I stepped into the mostly-empty front room.

It was that moment when you wake up from a nightmare with your heart pounding, your eyes wide, and your brain wondering if you're still amidst the danger. But instead of waking up from it, I was falling into it.

"Good evening, Miss Ocean," Alexander Blackman drawled with just as much acidity as the smile that dripped over his face.

Until now, he'd concealed himself well for the public. But tonight... now... he looked every inch the oily devil who'd threatened to harm me and those I care about not even twenty-four hours ago.

"I hope you don't mind that I moved up our meeting." His smirk ticked. "I saw an... opportunity to get this unpleasantness over with."

I heard him, but it was hard to focus because it wasn't his voice or his presence that perpetrated this nightmare. It was the gun he had aimed at my cousin's head as she knelt on the floor next to him.

"Jules, are you okay?" I demanded, ignoring Blackman as I locked my gaze with my cousin's tear-streaked one.

"I-I'm sorry—" she broke off and shuddered as he pressed the muzzle of the gun harder into her skin.

Oh, God.

"Miss Vandelsen is perfectly fine. For now," he replied, jerking her up to stand with a grip that was sure to leave a bruise.

Still, my cousin didn't cry out, though I knew she was in pain. From the looks of her, she'd already been punished for not cooperating with his plan.

The adrenaline pumping through my veins gave me the strangest sense of calm. I knew I was afraid. I knew I was scared to death for my cousin. For myself. But I only had two options: focus on the fear or focus on the solution. Both would take all of my faculties. And both would end with different outcomes.

"What do you want?" I demanded calmly, dragging my eyes back to the black wells of his.

"You know what I want," he seethed.

"And I told you I wouldn't be able to give you the deed until tomorrow *after* I picked it up from the lawyer," I insisted even though it was a lie.

Thwack.

I screamed and lurched forward as Blackman slammed the butt of his gun into the side of Jules' head, her battered form crumbling to the floor with a strangled whimper of pain before turning limp.

Oh my God.

My head throbbed like it had sustained a similar blow.

He'd knocked her out.

My mouth dried up into nothing but sand and shock.

My feet skidded to a halt when the gun swung to aim at me.

"Don't," he warned with a pleasant smile that made my skin crawl—*like he'd gotten enjoyment out of incapacitating my cousin.*

I put my shaking hands up in defeat. Even though there was a gun pointed at me, my focus was on Jules. Her shallow exhales mingled with moans of extreme pain from where her body was sprawled on the floor, blood dripping from the gash in her temple.

Rage now tinted the eerie calm and I prayed that Eli had followed through with his promise to have Dex check the security cameras.

I turned on Blackman and shouted, "I told you I'd give it to you as soon as I got it! Why—"

"Miss Ocean, save yourself the trouble of aggravating me further. I know that Mr. Ross no longer has the deed."

No.

I gulped, dread icing every cell in my body.

No, no, no.

I notched my chin up and threw every ounce of energy into keeping my face a mask of stone. It didn't matter how he knew right now, what mattered was that *he knew*.

"I don't know what you're talking about." Unless he was in that room that day with my aunt and me, he couldn't know that Gavin had given it to me.

Could he?

The sickly-sweet smile dropped from Blackman's face, melted off by the pure evil that lay waiting underneath. His expression was nothing short of deadly as he stepped back and, before the word *'wait'* could escape my lips, his pointed and polished loafer pulled back and slammed directly into my cousin's torso.

"No!" I screamed, unable to stop myself from doubling over as he kicked Jules in the stomach, her silent, tortured scream ripping right through my heart. He'd been looking at me. He'd been aiming the gun at me. I was his problem, not her.

"Please," I begged, tears leaking down my face. "Please, stop. Please, don't hurt her."

I'd come to help her and now she was injured—*bleeding* and unconscious because of me.

"I know he gave it to you, Laurel. And I know you brought the deed here. I know because I have eyes here. I know because the men I work for see everything in this town," he said calmly, the torture he was inflicting on an innocent woman taking nothing from his calm composure. "So, let's try this one last time, Miss Ocean. Give me the deed or I will kill her and you. And then, I will ransack this place *again,* and find it myself."

I sucked a breath.

I'd known, but now I *knew*.

It was him. All along. This was all because of him.

Pain ripped through my chest, tearing my heart in a thousand pieces. I couldn't stop him from hurting Roasters. I couldn't stop him from hurting my pap. But, goddammit, I could stop him from hurting Jules.

No matter what it cost me.

"Okay." I nodded frantically this time, my eyes flicking back to Jules, desperately wishing I could help her. But I couldn't. Which meant I had to find another way to help. Another way to get us out of this situation alive. "Y-You're right. It's here." My head kept bobbing, trying to jostle my thoughts into some sort of action plan. "And it's yours. Just please," I begged. "Please, don't hurt her anymore."

"Smarter than that old man," he sneered. "Now, give it to me. I'm sure it's better that your cousin gets to a doctor sooner rather than later. I try not to discriminate between hitting men versus women. Wouldn't want to be accused of being unfairly sexist."

I gagged, looking away before I vomited.

Focus, Laurel. Focus for Jules.

"Let's go," he snapped; curt words punctuated by the cocking of his gun "I don't have all night."

"Okay." My head jerked to nod as my arms wrapped around me. "Okay, I have it. I'll get it for you. I… I have a container in the back."

I took one last look at Jules, confirming she was still breathing with labored effort, before turning toward the back of the building, and the empty coffee container where I'd stuck the deed.

Even though the room was devoid of furniture, the walls were covered. Paint and photographs and newspaper clippings. Everything that Roasters was hung all around me. And then I caught sight of the wooden plaque Mick re-hung when we finished working on Friday—the one that summarized everything Roasters stood for.

Start where you are. Use what you have. Do what you can.

I swallowed down a sob.

Start where you are.

My steps were slow and measured as I approached the back hall. Not so slow that they drew Blackman's displeasure, but slow enough that I had precious moments to think.

I'm in a tight spot, Pap. My thoughts confessed to him like he could give me the answer.

Use what you have.

I looked around. I was being honest, I didn't have much. Everything out here was empty.

I stumbled slightly as the floor shifted in the hallway, my eyes searching for any object I could possibly use to get Jules and me away safely.

Use what you have...

I passed the espresso machine but burning him with its steam seemed like a longshot.

What else did I have?

My pulse raced. I was running out of time. And I knew once I gave him the deed that was the end of it—and us. I didn't see any scenario where he let Jules or me walk out of here alive.

Dustpan. Broom. I squinted into the dim kitchen. Oven mitts next to the stove. Baking sheet. The skillet—

The cast-iron skillet.

Hope vacuumed into my lungs. *That could work.*

You always said I had skill when it came to using the skillet, Pap. Hopefully it doesn't fail me now.

I shot a quick glance over my shoulder to see Blackman just a few feet behind me.

Do what you can.

Grab the pan.

Do what you can.

Hit the bad guy.

Do what you can.

Grab Jules and run.

I stuck with simple because simple was all my brain could handle right now, and my window of time was short. Hitting Blackman wouldn't kill him, but it would give me time.

Time to get away.

And leave him with the tempting proximity of the deed... of everything he wanted.

I couldn't save them both.

Our legacy is more than brewin' a cup of coffee.

Our legacy is helpin' people, plain and simple.

My throat tightened until breathing anything but short, rough gasps was impossible.

I needed to sacrifice the deed in order to save Jules. I needed to sacrifice Roasters to save my family. And even if I'd made the wrong choice by giving up this place before, there was no doubt that this was the right decision—*the only decision*—now.

I took in a long, deep breath, tasting salt air on the tip of my tongue.

Do what you can.

"It's just in that container over there," I offered, pointing over to the storage area to our left.

As soon as his head turned, I took that split second to spin and grab the skillet off the top of the stove.

Do what you can.

I cried out as I swung the solid weight through the air and connected it with a loud *thwack* to flesh and bone.

And then I ran like hell, praying to God I'd get Jules help in time.

Twenty-Seven

Eli

I grunted and reached for my phone.

Nothing.

No text. No call.

Something wasn't right, I just knew it. I didn't care how unlikely it was that her cousin had something to do with Blackman. I didn't care that, as far as Blackman knew, Laurel was meeting him with the deed tomorrow at which point he'd have everything he wanted. This situation didn't feel right from the second I saw Laurel reach for her coat.

But it had been fifteen minutes and the dark pit in my stomach still wasn't gone. Instead, it was growing.

"Fuck," I growled and dialed Laurel's number.

Voicemail.

Letting loose a curse, I reached for my jacket. This was a mistake. I should've gone with her. Even if I sat in the fucking truck the whole damn time, she shouldn't have gone alone.

My cell vibrated with an incoming call and I answered before I checked the ID, assuming—hoping it was Laurel.

"Laurel?"

"It's Ace," the deep voice returned, surprised. "Where the hell is Laurel?"

A spout of expletives erupted from my mouth. "Roasters. She went to meet her cousin, but something is wrong. She's not answering her phone. I need you to pull up the security cameras," I demanded, adding. "And I need you to come get me and take me there."

"Motherfucker," Ace swore violently and, in that instant, I knew her meeting and Ace's call were connected. And not in a good way.

"Wait, why are you calling me? What the fuck is going on?"

"Blackman knows about us. That tomorrow is a setup." The floor felt like it cracked open beneath me and my heart stopped. *No. No fucking no.* "I'm two minutes from the house. I was on my way to you already to let you guys know. Fuck."

"How the fuck does he know?" I raged, throwing the door open and stalking outside. I had to get to her. Even if I had to fucking walk.

"I had one of my guys keeping an eye on her cousin as soon as Laurel was threatened. I just figured it was better to be safe, especially since we'd spotted Blackman at Rock Beach in the past," he explained with barely controlled anger. "He was about to make one more round for the night when someone knocked him out. When he came to, Jules was gone."

My pulse skyrocketed as his headlights streamed down the driveway.

"But why Jules? And why now? How could he have known that tomorrow was a trap?" Question after question as I opened the passenger door to his truck, ending our call and climbing inside. Ace barely stopped, the truck picking up speed as I closed the door behind me.

"Fuck, I don't know," he said through clenched teeth. "The cartel has connections. Maybe they threatened the lawyer. Or Laurel's aunt. Somehow, he figured out she already has the deed, and he wants to take it from her on his terms."

"But Jules called her," I went on, my hand pulling painfully at my hair as fear ripped my body apart. "Jules wanted to meet her. So, Blackman was already there at the resort. What if he took Jules because she called Laurel? What if he didn't know it was a setup and somehow Jules is connected to all of this?"

Ace's grip fisted around the steering wheel and I was surprised it didn't break off the column.

The silence between us was fragile like dynamite. Possessive, protective rage crammed into a space where one spark was all it would take to make us explode.

Where one hair harmed on Laurel would send me to a place I didn't know existed—a place where I would willingly... *eagerly*... murder a man for touching my woman.

"We're going to save them." I believed him. I knew Ace would do whatever it took to make them safe.

Still, I didn't reply right away. I stared at the hood of the truck as it ate up the road and all the distance between me and the woman I loved.

"And we're going to make him pay."

For Laurel. For Jules. For Roasters. *For Larry.*

Laurel

"Jules, we have to go right now," I groaned, throwing all my weight underneath her shoulder to lift her off the floor. Nausea hit me again, rolling my stomach, when I saw the pooled blood left behind from her head wound.

Her weak, pained whimper as I moved her was drowned out by the angry grunts from Blackman who was all too quickly recovering from my attack. All the blow had done was buy me just a few minutes, maybe only seconds, to get Jules out of here—to get us somewhere safe.

"I'm going to kill you for that, you stupid cunt." His vicious, irate words boomed through the space and through my deafening pulse that thumped in my ears.

I pulled Jules to her feet, ignoring her injured protests, and slung her arm around my shoulders. She could barely stand. Her face was caked in blood, her hair matting into the dark liquid.

"I got you," I whispered, focusing on the task and not the threat; it was the only way we were going to make it out of there. "We have to get out of here. I know it hurts. Just hang on."

I pushed us out the front door of Roasters just as the first shot rang out. I didn't look back to see what he'd hit. It didn't matter as long as it wasn't either of us. The cool burst of air sharpened my senses. I needed to get to a public place—and fast.

Quickly scanning for any building still lit at this time of night, I let out a strangled cry when the first business I could see that was still open was the bar three blocks down.

Three blocks wasn't far. Except when you were carrying the weight of an extra person and there was a man intent on killing you closing in on your heels.

But it was our only hope.

"This way," I instructed, hobbling as fast as I could with Jules slumped against my side. "We just have to get to the bar, Jules," I broke off, needing all my strength to move.

Each deep breath was soaked with the metallic sweetness of Jules' blood and tears slipped from my eyes, knowing how wounded she was.

"Almost there," I reassured us both.

I walked as fast as I could with her stumbling alongside me. My head turned, hearing the door of the coffee shop fly open, the new bell we'd installed dinging violently.

Oh, God.

He hadn't gone after the deed like I'd hoped. He was coming to take care of us first.

Adrenaline pumped like hot fuel through my veins. It dulled the burning in my muscles and gave me a strength I didn't know I possessed.

I pulled Jules over to the edge of the building, practically lifting her with each step until we reached the alleyway on the other side of Diane's studio. I ducked around the corner, spinning Jules with me and sheltering us from Blackman's gaze. *For the moment.*

My chest heaved and I shushed Jules as she moaned in pain against my side.

I needed to think. I needed a new plan.

Blackman was outside. Headed toward us. *We'd never make it to the bar.*

My pulse hammered.

"You stupid cunt." The words cracked like thunder on the silent street. "You won't be able to escape me."

Getting as close to the corner of the building as I dared, I peeked down the road, seeing twin bright beams pull onto Ocean Avenue from the bar's parking lot.

My head tipped back against the brick siding. *If I could get the driver's attention before Blackman got us.*

I heard the expensive tap of his dress shoes pause, probably at the driveway to Roasters. He was wondering if I'd taken her toward the back where I'd parked Eli's truck.

I hadn't. I was afraid if he went out the back of the building, he'd catch us too easily.

His soft chuckle floated through the silence. "You should've just sold it to me when you had the chance. Now, you're the one who's going to pay."

The approaching vehicle grew louder. I looked again, seeing it was a truck still a block away. *But it was my only shot.*

I squeezed my eyes shut, sucking in breaths like I couldn't get enough air, and prayed. If I could distract him long enough, maybe at least Jules would be safe.

Do what you can.

Blackman's shoes clicked closer. A ticking time bomb and split seconds was all I had.

"Don't move, Jules. You hear me? Don't make a sound. It's all going to be okay," I whispered harshly, crouching so I could sit her down and rest her back gently against the side of the building.

My pulse hammered. If heartbeats could have horsepower, mine thundered with a thousand hoofbeats in my ears.

Do what you can.

The light glinting off the emblem on the side of the white truck as it slowed. *Madison Construction.* My heart stopped on a dime.

It was Mick.

There was no time to think. There was only time to do what I could.

I stood and stepped from the alleyway. *"MICK! HELP!"*

My scream was bloodcurdling as it ripped through the silken silence, quickly echoed by the shriek of brakes. Bright red flashed in my peripheral before I ran.

Not away.

Not to the truck.

I ran straight toward the lethal black eyes of the man who wanted to kill me. His gun glinted off the streetlight as he turned toward me, his body partially obscured where he stood in Roasters driveway.

I thought he'd be closer.

I'd hoped, with the element of surprise, I could reach him and knock him down before he could fire.

The space between Blackman and me closed in slow motion. The smell of his cologne hit me first, professional and deadly. The sound of the gun cocking was like a sonic boom.

But when it fired? I heard nothing.

This was it.

I only saw a flash in front of me as my feet skidded to a halt.

I'd done everything I could.

My eyes dropped down.

I hoped it was enough for Mick to be able to save Jules.

My arms fell to my sides as I looked for blood.

But there was nothing. No blood. No pain. No wound.

How was this... My thoughts faded as I looked back to Blackman, half-expecting a second-shot to slam into me.

The half-cocked smile on Blackman's face melted in front of my eyes as he collapsed lifelessly to the ground.

"Laurel!" My name whipped me back to reality. Sounds, sights, movements. Everything returned in an instant.

I turned and saw Mick, the third person in the triangle of him, Blackman, and myself. He stood in front of Roasters, his truck parked cockeyed toward the sidewalk, his kind blue eyes burning with something fierce and a smoking gun in his hand.

"Mick..." My voice was barely a whisper as all the adrenaline flooded out of my body like a bursting dam, leaving me spent and frail.

Like a combination to a lock, all of the numbers clicked into place and revealed what had happened.

I hadn't been shot. Mick had fired on Blackman.

Mick had killed him and saved me.

Gingerly, I stepped toward the heap of black and bleeding

suit, needing to see the wound. *Needing to see for myself that the threat was gone.*

"Are you okay?" My gaze snapped up to Mick standing in front of me, his giant hands reaching for my shoulders as he peered down with worry creasing his brow.

"Yeah, I'm—" I broke off and spun. "Jules!"

Mick's gaze followed mine to see my cousin, sliding herself from around the corner of the building, drawn out by the gunshots.

I reached for him, pleading and pulling him with me. "We have to get her to the hospital. He hit her with the gun. Call 911. We have to—"

Another truck screeched to a stop at the curb. "Laurel!" Eli jumped down from the cab and sprinted toward me.

Mick moved out of the way, dialing 911 as he jogged over to Jules. I caught Ace out of the corner of my eye heading over to where Blackman lay dead on the pavement, pulling out his own cell phone. And then there was nothing else because Eli was there, pulling me into his arms, and making me safe again.

"Eli!" I sobbed, collapsing against him... into his warmth.

It wasn't until I saw him that I knew everything was going to be okay.

Somehow it was all going to be okay.

"Jesus Christ, Laurel. I was so afraid. So fucking afraid, sweetheart." He held me so tightly. So securely. From having a gun pointed at me to being in his arms, I'd gone from vulnerable to safe in a matter of seconds.

"I love you," I murmured against his pounding heart. I needed to tell him.

It was the only thing that mattered.

"Are you okay?" He pulled back and demanded, brushing my hair back from my face, examining me for himself before I could answer. "Are you hurt?"

"No." I swallowed over the lump in my throat. "I'm okay. Mick saved—"

"What the hell were you thinking, going after him like that?" Fear abated into anger—anger that I'd put myself in danger. *Anger that he'd almost lost me.*

"I didn't have a choice." I shook my head, tears spilling easily and fluidly down my cheeks. "I had to do what I could—what I could to save her. She's my only family. She's…" I choked and curled against his chest.

"I know—*fuck*." He let out a ragged sigh and reached for my face, wiping my tears away like only he could. "I know, Laurel. You just scared me. Seeing you run toward him—" I reached up and kissed him, needing to put a physical end to his fears.

"Jules… we have to get her to the hospital." My vision was blurry as I moved us toward where Mick was crouched to the ground, holding my cousin like a rag doll against his chest. "Did you call the ambulance?"

Mick nodded, and I'd never seen his friendly face so enraged before. "What happened?" he asked with a low voice.

"He had her." I glanced at Eli. "He had a gun to her head the moment I walked inside. When I told him I didn't have the deed, he hit her. I had to save her. I had to," I broke off with another sob as the images assaulted me. Eli wrapped me in his arms as every fear and horror I'd held inside suddenly unleashed, safe against the steady beat of his chest against my cheek.

"Mick, what happened?" Eli demanded. "How did you get here?"

"I was down at the bar checkin' on Miles." He paused with a grunt. "I was just gettin' in my truck when I heard a shot. Know that sound anywhere, growin' up in Texas." He let out a wry laugh. "Drove up the street slow to try to see where it was comin' from when I saw the lights on at Roasters, didn't seem right so I was goin' to stop. Then I heard Laurel screamin' like a banshee for help, so I pulled over and grabbed my gun and that's when I saw him about to shoot her. So, I fired."

I felt Eli tense against me. When I looked out from his embrace, I saw Ace standing beside him, his hands on his hips and a hard frown etched across his Viking features.

"Give me your gun," he said with a low voice.

"What?"

"You need to give me your gun and you need to get out of here," Ace insisted with a deadly calm.

"What the hell are you talkin' about? I'm not leavin' her like this." Mick tightened his hold, looking ready to take down anyone who tried to take Jules from him before the ambulance came. The fierce look of protectiveness in his eyes made my breath hitch.

Ace's nostrils flared. "This isn't Texas, Mick. California doesn't give a fuck whose life you saved or what evil you stopped," he bit out with a vicious tone. "You have a license here for your gun?"

Mick's gaze faltered. "In Texas, yeah. Haven't had a chance to apply here since we moved. Haven't needed it."

"Exactly." Ace stepped forward and bent down until he was eye-level with the other man. "You shot someone. You shot someone with a gun you don't have legal right to have. They don't fucking care if the man you killed was the goddamn scum of the earth. They won't care that you prevented two murders tonight. They will care that you used an unlicensed firearm to kill a man."

My blood chilled, the thought that the law would punish a man for saving my life—for killing someone who would have willingly and enthusiastically taken it, made me feel sick all over again.

Sometimes the right thing lived outside of the law.

"Give me your gun and get out of here. I will handle this."

The facts were met with a beat of silence, the sound of approaching sirens getting louder.

"Mick," Eli broke in. "California doesn't care what good you do when that good involves a gun. We'll make sure Jules is okay, I promise. Just get out of here otherwise they will arrest you."

I stepped away from Eli and bent down, reaching for my cousin as I murmured to my friend, "Please, Mick. Do what they say." My lip trembled. "I can't watch them arrest you for saving my life."

I'd never seen such a hard, harsh look on my Friendly Giant's face before—a look that said friendly was all well and good until someone innocent was harmed… then friendly turned fierce.

He took a deep breath before letting out a low, feral growl and shoved his weapon in Ace's direction. Just before he gave me Jules' weight, I caught him murmuring something in her ear, as though he'd been in the middle of a conversation when we'd approached. And, as he shifted her weight over to me, even in her condition, she appeared to not want to let him go.

"Call me as soon as the doctor sees her and let me know how she is," he instructed me softly.

I nodded and watched him go.

Ace wiped the gun as I gave him the rundown of what happened, Mick's actions shifting ownership to the man who was legally allowed to fire a weapon at a bad man. Almost as soon as I was done, the ambulance appeared on the street.

Giving us a nod of confidence and an offer of good luck, Ace waited for the police as Eli and I climbed into the ambulance with Jules. I refused to leave her side and he refused to leave mine.

Twenty-Eight

Laurel

"Is there anything I can get you?" the young nurse, Gwen, at Carmel General asked as I stood outside Jules' hospital room. I'd been there for the past hour and a half, watching… waiting while they ran tests and bandaged her up.

"No, thank you." I gave her a small smile. She'd been so kind and helpful since the moment we got here, even though the hospital was busy for this time of night.

"Here, let me take that from you." She extended a hand for my empty cup. I'd stepped out to grab a drink of water. "She's going to be fine, Miss Ocean." We both looked at Jules as she spoke. "That one is a fighter."

I could only nod. She was right. Jules was a fighter. She'd always been strong and sure and determined. But now, it felt like she wasn't even stepping into the ring. As soon as she was feeling better and out of here, there would be no skirted answers. No dismissed questions or backtracking on bottled-up truths. I was going to get a straight answer as to why she wasn't living the life she wanted, because tonight had proven just how fragile that life could be.

And then, I was going to ask her if she'd ever seen Blackman at the resort—if she knew him.

There were things that didn't add up.

How he knew the lawyer had given me the deed.

Why he'd chosen Jules.

And why he'd taken her from the resort tonight.

But I had to focus on the most important things right now.

She was okay.

Blackman was gone.

"How is she?" I turned to see Eli standing beside me in the spot where Gwen had just been; I hadn't even realized she'd walked away.

He placed his hand on my lower back, warmth suffusing through my body like a blanket of strength.

I looked through the glass door at Jules lying peacefully in the bed.

Her head was bound and even though they'd wiped her face, I could still see the faint stain of blood where it would have been too painful to scrub off right now. The blanket on her covered what I knew was a patchwork of nasty-looking black and purple bruises, wrapped over with more bandages. At least they had given her something for the pain and to help her rest.

"Concussion. Broken rib and a few bruised ones. But as of now, no signs of hemorrhaging in her brain and no sign of internal bleeding." I winced just hearing the list of injuries all over again.

"Christ."

I shivered as he pulled me securely back into his arms, both of us knowing just how much worse it could've been.

"They want to keep her for a few days to make sure there's

no major swelling," I went on, hearing my voice thicken. "The doctor said—" I broke off and swallowed. "He said she might have some memory loss when she wakes and, depending on how the next few days go, it may not come back."

Eli pressed a kiss to my head. "But she will come back, Laurel." He tipped my head up to his. "She is alive because of you."

I looked away. "She almost died because of me."

"No." His low growl made me shiver. "She almost died because of that piece of shit who tried to kill you both."

As I looked into his eyes, I heard the unspoken *'You almost died because of that piece of shit, too.'*

"The craziest part," I told him. "I never thought he'd be there. He was the last thing on my mind the moment she called."

"I'm sure that was his plan. He didn't want you to expect him otherwise you would've acted differently."

I shook my head. "But if you heard what she said... I don't think he made her call me, Eli. I think the call was real. I think her wanting to meet me—to tell me something was real."

"Why?"

"The things she said..." My brow furrowed. "The way she talked about her family." I glanced over my shoulder. "If he'd made her do it, I don't know why she would've mentioned the things she did."

"Unless he really wanted her to make it believable." His hand moved in small circles low on my back. "Laurel, look at all the things he's done to try to take possession of Roasters. To have Jules say things... insinuate things... to make you feel the utmost urgency to meet her is the least of what he was capable of."

I inhaled slowly. I couldn't argue with him. He was right.

But I still didn't believe I was wrong; I still believed Jules called me on her own.

"I guess we'll have to wait and ask her when she wakes up," I murmured, turning to look at my cousin again as though I expected her to sit up any moment. "If she remembers."

"You gave her the chance to remember, sweetheart," he reassured me, nuzzling my head.

"I wasn't going to lose someone else. Not if I could help it," I confessed quietly.

His chest rumbled slightly. "I don't know what I would have done if I'd lost you... if Mick hadn't—"

"But you didn't," I cut him off, tipping my head back to capture his troubled gaze. "And he did."

"Laurel Ocean, you are the strongest woman I've ever met... and possibly the most stubborn..."

I let out a watery laugh as his lips descended on mine. Warm and solid. A spark to the kindling inside me that was dry and desperate to burn after being doused with fear and adrenaline.

I sighed against him, leaning into his cocoon of strength.

"You're the one who taught me love is worth fighting for, even when it involves facing loss along the way."

He grunted. "I'd just rather you didn't face loaded guns pointed at you if at all possible."

I chuckled and buried my head into his chest, feeling like I was finally home.

Tonight, I'd faced my worst fear—another loss. It had come in a way I'd never expected—wrapped in a nice suit and wielding pure malice—and I hadn't faltered. Instead, I fought.

In the middle of everything that happened tonight—the fear, the worry, the uncertainty—I stood tall because of the roots love had grown here. I'd faced loss and conquered it.

And holding on to love amid the most chaotic of circumstances was the most beautiful act of rebellion.

"What did Ace say?" I asked after another minute, knowing

that was who he'd been on the phone with. "What did the police say? Is Roasters…"

"Ace has it under control and only a few minor scrapes at Roasters. Easy fixes." He cleared his throat. "The police questioned him and took his statement." His voice grew quiet. "They are going to want to talk to you. Probably tomorrow."

"Okay." I nodded.

"Are you up for that?"

I knew what he was asking. *Are you up for lying to the police?*

"Yes." My answer was immediate and firm. I didn't care whether or not he had a piece of paper giving him permission to carry a firearm; I wasn't going to risk Mick being punished for saving my life.

"What about her?" I nodded to Jules.

"Did she see Mick?" he asked. "Does she remember seeing Mick?"

I chewed on my lip. I couldn't be sure.

"Let's cross that bridge when we come to it. For right now, we will keep Mick safe and let your cousin recover. They may not even need to talk to her, you never know." He didn't sound too hopeful.

"What about the cartel?" As I peeled away the immediate worries, deep ones emerged. "Are they still going to come after Roasters?"

His mouth pulled tight. "I'm not sure. Neither is Ace. All we can do now is clean up from this mess and hope they look elsewhere rather than continuing to pursue this."

I nodded. "I almost wish Mick wasn't such a good shot so we could've at least gotten some answers."

"Laurel…" Eli growled.

I gave him a half smile. "I know." If Mick wasn't such a good shot, I might be dead. "But you know what I mean…"

"All that matters," he continued, barreling through my unsteady worries, "is that you and Jules are okay. Roasters is fine. And Blackman is gone."

I sighed and nodded. "You're right."

There was no point in worrying about possibilities when we had no reason to—and every reason to be grateful we'd come out of this alive.

"My aunt should be here soon," I said softly.

I'd called her about an hour ago and told her there'd been an accident. She'd said she'd be right over, but, judging by the delay, 'right over' was a term relative to the time it took her to get dolled up.

"We'll stay as long as you want." He nodded, adding with a rasped growl, "But then I'm taking you home and not letting you out of bed for a week."

I laughed as I melted against him, wanting nothing more than to be home and in bed with his body wrapped around mine. *But only after I knew my cousin was okay… only after I*

"Deal." I reached up on my toes for another kiss. "I love you."

"I love you."

"*Oh my God!*" I grimaced at my aunt's shrill voice as it rang down the hospital hall. "Where is she? Where is my daughter?"

I turned and pulled from Eli's embrace to block my Aunt Jackie from the door to Jules' room. I wanted to prepare her for what she was about to see.

Her eyes were swollen and face streaked with tears—a surprising show of emotion for her. My uncle Rich followed several paces behind her, his face also red but with frustration rather than concern. *Probably from dealing with my aunt's hysterics.*

"Laurel, where is she? What happened?" She tried to peer around me. Thankfully, Eli stood firmly at my back to help keep her at bay.

I reached for her hands, white-knuckle-clasped in front of her chest.

"She's okay." I started with the most important fact. "She's going to be fine. But there was an incident. She was coming to meet me at the coffee shop when someone—this man, Blackman, grabbed her from the resort."

The color continued to drain from her face.

"He has been trying to buy Roasters from me and when I declined, he decided to threaten me to get what he wanted," I quickly explained. "And he used Jules to do it."

"What are you talking about? For a damn coffee shop?" Rich scoffed and looked away, scanning the halls as though he expected to see other people here waiting for him.

I ignored him and continued, "He… hurt her pretty badly. She has a concussion, a broken rib, and several bruised ones. They're monitoring her now for any signs of her brain swelling or internal bleeding—"

"Oh my God." She gasped, pulling her hands from my grip like I'd developed leprosy and forcing her way to the door in horror.

She stared at Jules for a long second before she turned, her face contorting as accusation dripped acerbically from her lips. "So, this is *your* fault?" I tensed under the unexpected attack. "Not even in town a few weeks and my daughter is already almost dead because of you."

Heat flared in my cheeks and I felt lightheaded from the charge after everything that had happened to bring us here.

"Are you fucking kidding me?" Eli growled from behind me. "Laurel saved your daughter's life tonight at the risk of her own—"

"Eli," I chided, raising a steadying hand and pleading for him to let me handle this.

His low growl reverberated down my back, his hold tightening protectively.

"Aunt Jackie," I began with an unsteady breath. "I'm sorry for what happened to Jules—more than you will ever know," I told her, praying her harsh comments stemmed from unbelievable hurt rather than truth. "I know she's hurt and I know that's scary, but she's going to be okay. Jules is strong; she's going to be fine." I took a deep breath and told her the rest of what I knew. "The doctor wants to keep her a few days under observation, but he expects her to recover quickly. The only thing he warned was that she might have some short-term memory loss and not recall what happened tonight."

"Oh my God…" Her hand covered her mouth as a strangled wail escaped.

"Jacqueline," my uncle chided under his breath to his wife who was about to go into hysterics.

"I'm so sorry that this happened, Aunt Jackie," I apologized, not because she deserved it, but because Jules did. "If there is anything I can do, anything that Jules needs, please, let me know."

She sniffled and dug into her designer purse for a tissue, jerking away from his touch. "My daughter almost died tonight," she spat bitterly, but I wasn't sure to whom. "You should go," she then added, looking to me. "You should go just like you should've gone weeks ago. If you would have just sold that good-for-nothing place, *none* of this would have happened."

Her accusation shocked and stung as she pushed around me, her heels clanking angrily on the hospital floor as she pushed into Jules' room, leaving me speechless in the hall.

My heart thudded against my chest. Their attitude fit with the atmosphere of the hospital. Cold. Sterile. Cruel. I looked up to my uncle Rich whose expression suggested a similar opinion to that of his wife.

"I'm sorry," I repeated with a slight nod.

He didn't even acknowledge me, about to brush by me when Eli reached out and grabbed his arm.

"I hope you and your wife know that Laurel—*your niece*—risked her life tonight to save your daughter. I can't imagine your concern and stress right now, but I would think twice before either of you say anything like that again to my future wife."

My jaw hit the floor for a second time that night. I would have been less shocked *had* I actually been shot in the course of the events of the evening than hearing Eli refer to me as his future wife.

Rich glared at him for a hard second before blustering and disappearing into the room after his wife, leaving Eli and me alone in the hall.

"Fucking ridiculous," Eli murmured next to me, tension radiating off of him once again. "You okay, sweetheart?"

I gaped at him "You... you just..." I pointed and paused, swinging my gaze between him and where my uncle stood in the room. "You just told him I was your future wife!" I exclaimed with a forceful whisper.

"For several eternity-filled minutes tonight, Laurel, I had to consider I wouldn't reach you in time. That I wouldn't be able to protect you from what Blackman had in store. And ultimately, imagine what my life would be like without you in it," he began with a deep, rasped voice. "Those were the worst fucking minutes of my whole life, and just as clearly as they made me picture life without you, they showed me with perfect clarity that my life needs you in it. By my side. As my wife."

Shivers raced up and down my spine as all unpleasant thoughts about the past faded against the bright light of what our future held.

"So, this isn't me asking you. Not yet," he swore. "But it is me telling you it's going to happen, sweetheart. You. Me. Here. Forever."

My eyes pricked with more tears that eagerly spilled like confetti down my cheeks.

"Eli…"

"I *will* marry you… no matter how many times you throw up on me." Laughter bubbled through my tears. "Nor how many times you try to impale me with a whisk."

"Glad to know that neither a little vomit nor attempted whisking will deter you," I replied wryly, continuing to tease, "So, is this like the time you took my clothes off for me without asking? You're just going to marry me without asking, too?"

"I did not—You took your own clothes off that night!" He growled, and I let out a small squeal as he hauled me tightly into his arms.

"We'd had too much to drink, I guess we'll never know the truth." I giggled.

Our laughter simmered into a kiss and I pulled away to rest my head on his chest, the sting of my aunt's words hurting less in his arms.

"I want to stay," I whispered, looking at Jules. "But I know they don't want me here."

He kissed my head. "There's nothing else you can do for her tonight, Laurel. She's safe. She's in good hands. She needs time to heal, and so do you."

I sighed, stress making my muscles ache in ways I hadn't felt before.

"We'll come back tomorrow."

"Absolutely. We'll come back every day until she's okay to go home."

Until she was okay enough to share the rest of her story with us.

"Thank you."

I watched my aunt and uncle for another second, their harsh expressions a mix of emotions I could only partially decipher. Sending up a silent prayer in my cousin's direction, I molded to Eli's warmth and let him lead me out of the hospital, each step highlighting just how exhausted I was.

I squealed as Eli hoisted me into his arms as soon as we hit the parking lot. "I'm fine." I laughed.

"No, you're mine," he grunted with a devious grin. "And tonight, there will be no question that I'm the one taking off all your clothes."

Need pooled in my stomach. Even though I was exhausted. I needed to be with him more. To kiss him. To feel him. To take his body in mine and savor every moment knowing how close I'd come to losing it all.

"Are you going to ask this time?"

"Nope," he grunted.

I pulled his face to mine and kissed him. "Good."

Twenty-Nine

Eli

"I'm never letting you out of my sight again." I sealed my mouth over hers, kicking the door shut behind us.

Laurel wrapped her arms around my neck, her tongue locking with mine.

Earlier, words had been enough. Earlier, holding her had been enough.

Enough to calm me. To soothe my fears and sate my nerves. But now? Now that we were back at the house and she was all mine there was a need that words couldn't satisfy.

"Eli…" she moaned my name as we pulled our clothes from each other.

Each drop of fabric onto the floor was like another wave crashing against the shore. Fierce. Demanding. Unending.

Naked and panting, I pinned her up against the wall, grinding my cock against the slick heat between her legs and swallowing every whimper of need it elicited.

"Don't ever"—I bit her lip and sucked—"Scare me like that again."

She hummed her agreement, rolling her hips along my erection, coating me with her desire.

Need pulsed through me like an angry devil. Unforgiving and punishing.

She'd been through so much and yet, I wanted to punish her for how she'd scared me at the same time as I wanted to pleasure her for a strength I couldn't help but admire.

"Please, Eli," she begged against my mouth, her nails scoring my back.

Grunting, I wrapped her legs tight around my waist and carried her to the dining table.

Setting her on the edge, I dragged my lips from hers, licking a hot path of unfiltered lust down her neck and on to her chest. I flicked the tip of my tongue over her nipple, her eager gasp making my dick leak, and then continued my way down over her quivering stomach to the hot sweetness between her thighs.

The way her nails scored the wood of the table as I closed my mouth over her wet pussy was music to my ears—a symphony I strung higher and higher with each lick and suck and probe of my tongue against her sex.

It wasn't enough. Not one taste. Not one moan. It wasn't enough until I built her up and made her fall apart screaming my name. It wasn't enough until I felt and tasted her fall apart because it was the only way I knew she was still here. *And still mine.*

"I love you," I said, still licking up her desire. "I'm never letting you go."

"Eli."

I looked up from between her parted legs, her red hair like a blaze against the rich wood.

"I need you."

My straining cock pulsed in agreement, the painful ache

taking a backseat as my mouth took its fill of her body. Now, it was time to fill her with mine.

"Need you, too, sweetheart," I rasped, lifting myself up.

Yanking her hips right to the edge, I stared down at my cock aligning with her pink, swollen entrance, glistening from her release and my mouth.

Groaning, I spread her folds with the reddened tip of my cock, watching as the blunt flesh disappeared into her heat.

"So incredible," I bit out, my eyes squeezing shut with pleasure.

There are moments when words aren't good enough. When loss or the potential for it was too great and too close that relief and desire and the need to anchor yourself to that person in the most animalistic way possible was the only thing that mattered.

That was this moment.

And this was my anchor.

Slowly, I pushed deeper into her tightening muscles.

"Fuck, Laurel, you feel so damn good," I ground out as I sank all the way to the hilt. "Like heaven. Like home. *Like everything.*"

Her pussy clenched as I bumped against her G-spot, sending white spots into my vision. I heard a growl that must have come from me as I began to thrust into her. Steady and demanding turned into hard and possessing as I claimed her—*as she begged me for more.*

She was home. Every goddamn thing about her. Her eyes that were as deep as the ocean, her strength that kept her standing amid more loss than any heart should have to endure, and her love that was so beautiful and overflowing I could hardly breathe.

She cried out my name, gasping for breath as I slammed into her. My fingers dug into the soft skin of her narrow hips, holding them steady so I could fill her completely each and every time.

I couldn't breathe.

"*Fuck*, I love you," I ground out, feeling her start to shake and convulse against me with the start of her orgasm.

I'd come here and found a home in this place, but it wasn't until her that it had become *my* home.

My fingers tweaked her clit in the way she needed, the way I knew would send her over the edge. And a second later, she screamed as another release gushed around my cock, harder and wetter than the first.

Warm and welcoming, she soaked my length and then wrung me out. I groaned low, my cock the only thing guiding me as I drove into her again and again until I lost my mind, my orgasm overtaking each and every one of my senses.

My teeth sunk into the joint where her neck met her shoulder as a roar ripped from my chest and my dick pulsed, shooting streams of cum inside her.

Every level of satisfaction claimed me. Having her. Taking her. But knowing she was all mine, that one took the cake.

"I love you, too," she murmured as I carried her to the bedroom.

Minutes blurred together until she was in my arms underneath the covers, the weight of today finally taking its final toll.

"Thank you."

My chest rumbled. "For what?"

"For not letting me lose anyone else." She laid her hand on my chest.

I grunted. "I think you did that all on your own tonight, sweetheart."

She hummed, sinking closer to sleep. "You're the one who showed me it's worth fighting for."

My grip on her tightened. "Love always is."

"Thank you, Miss Ocean, Mr. Downing." Officer Raymer nodded to us both, flipping his notepad closed. "We'll be in touch if we have any further questions."

We stood inside Roasters, the morning having passed in a steady state of gentle touches and desperate kisses. The aftermath of survival, sweetening each moment of the present.

The Carmel police called for Laurel's statement, so we'd agreed to meet them at Roasters. We'd made an early stop at the hospital, but there was still no change in Jules' condition. They kept her sedated to prevent her brain from overreacting to the trauma.

Tomorrow, the nurse, Gwen said. *Tomorrow she should be through the worst of it.*

After begrudging entrance was granted by the security installed outside Jules' hospital room and a few dark glares from the Vandelsens, Laurel sat with her cousin for a few minutes before we left to come here.

"Thank you." He didn't see it, but I felt Laurel shiver under my arm.

I nodded and shook the man's hand, holding myself steady until the bell signaled his exit from the shop.

"That wasn't as bad as I thought it was going to be," Laurel turned to me and said.

"Yeah? You sure?" I scanned over my woman, searching for signs of distress.

She looked at me. "I know it was the right thing."

I nodded, neither of us speaking out loud the fact that she'd lied to the police in her recounting of last night, switching out Mick's name for Ace.

"I don't think they're going to look into Blackman," I said, roughly, gauging the officer's every response to what Laurel said.

"Maybe we should've told them about the connection to the Cartel." She chewed on her lip.

My head shifted, glancing toward the kitchen as I heard the back door open and shut.

"I think it's better this way. We don't know what their plans are—or if they had plans that extended beyond Blackman. But I think it's better to let Ace and Dex pursue that lead and let them contact law enforcement when they have enough concrete evidence."

She nodded just as Ace stepped into the room.

"It go okay?" His direct question was aimed at Laurel.

"Yeah."

"Good." He reached out and shook my hand. "They didn't seem to question it was me who shot him. Guess they must know by now I do most of the bad-guy shooting in this town." He smirked and we all relaxed a little.

"Any new information?" I asked while we were on the subject.

Ace shook his head. "Dex is still looking, but my guess is the cartel will go elsewhere. Too much attention on Roasters now to make it a viable front. At least in my opinion."

The bell dinged and our attention shifted to Mick as he joined us.

The carefree and friendly spark that he carried was dimmed.

"Mick, are you alright?" Laurel asked, approaching him.

"How is she?" were the first ragged words he spoke.

"Stable." Laurel reached for his shoulder to comfort him. "She's going to be fine."

"God," he swore, rubbing a hand over his mouth. "If the fucker wasn't already dead, I'd fuckin' kill him again for what he did."

The rest of us nodded in silent agreement. Mick stood like a monument of loyalty and concern—but even more so than I'd anticipated.

"Mick, you sure you're—"

"Does she know?" he rasped, cutting me off. "Does she remember it was me?"

Laurel's gaze ducked for a moment. "She's not awake yet, so I don't know. The doctor said she would probably suffer some short-term memory loss and that it may never come back."

"You can't tell her," Ace broke in.

"What?"

"The fewer people know of your involvement the better," he explained firmly. "If she remembers, that's one thing. But if she doesn't, she should get the same story as everyone else. For your safety—"

"I don't give a shit about my safety." My eyes widened at his vehemence.

Ace stepped forward, the two men like giant bulls about to go at it in a ring. "Even more for her safety."

Mick's fists clenched and unclenched at his side for several tense seconds before he sighed and speared his fingers through his hair. "Sorry," he mumbled. "I just feel so helpless."

"Mick, you killed the man who did this to her," Laurel comforted him.

"I know but—"

"No buts. She's going to be okay, and I'm alive because of you."

His shoulders slumped. "So, what do we do now?"

I turned and pointed to the wall behind me. "Only thing we can do. Move forward… starting with patching up those bullet holes and getting this place ready to re-open."

Ace added, "We are still investigating to see if the cartel

has any other connections in Carmel, but right now, it appears Blackman was their only link."

"So, this is over?" Mick rasped.

There was a slight pause, a weight both suspended by relief that Blackman and the threat to Roasters was gone, yet pulled down with worry that there was more to come.

"For now."

"Just feels like there's more to do," he said, planting his hands on his hips and looking around the room.

I walked over to him and placed a comforting hand on his shoulder. "There is always more to do, my friend. Just have to start where you are…"

His eyes jumped to the wooden sign he'd carved for Roasters, and he agreed.

"Jules is safe. She's going to be fine. We'll make sure of that."

He relaxed. "Alright, then we've got some work to do."

Laurel stepped in and hugged him, her small form comical in the way it tried to wrap around his. "I'll make some coffee."

Two days later…

I loved waking her up like this, with gentle kisses down the back of her neck that made her moan in her sleep.

Every moment over the last few days seemed to linger—drawn out and stretched like a piece of yarn. Almost losing the woman I loved put every moment I now had with her into a special kind of focus. *A deep, soul-soothing focus.*

Things had calmed. Roasters was back on track to open. Jules was awake, recovering, and managing the loss of her memory from that night. Laurel managed to speak with her once about what she remembered, but after that, the hospital room was crowded with security and Mrs. Vandelsen, making candid conversation nearly impossible.

My heart ached to see how it tore Laurel up, wanting to help her cousin so badly but not knowing how. But it also steadied it to see how determined she was—the woman who'd come here lost, refusing to tether herself to anyone or anything… that determination now shifted—altered by love.

"Mmm," she moaned and pushed back against me.

We moved forward, the attack at Roasters fading like a bad dream with each day that passed.

Roasters was okay. Jules was okay. That fucker Blackman was dead and Laurel was here, she was staying, and she was mine.

Her lip quivered as she looked up to me. "Is it bad that I'm still worried about Jules?"

"Laurel…" I squeezed her fingers. "It's going to be okay for her, too."

"She's just been through so much… going through so much. I thought I'd just broken through, convinced her that she could take her future for herself, just like I had. She's like a prisoner there, Eli. A pretty, perfect prisoner and the worst part is, after all this, I'm afraid it's only going to convince her that she's right where she belongs."

"Hey," I murmured, tugging her to my side so my arm could wrap around her shoulders. "Jules is a smart girl, you know that. Sometimes, people take tiny steps in one direction without thinking anything of it until one day they wake up and recognize nothing around them. You aren't responsible for making her wake up, sweetheart. All you can do is be there for her when she does and help her find her way back home."

"We're going to help her." It wasn't a question. "Whatever she needs. Whatever she decides. We're going to be there for her."

I thought I couldn't be any more in awe of this woman—the

one who'd come back to face unimaginable loss, the one who rose from the ashes to find her own way back to her heart. She'd then been the one to risk her life, the very last thing she could possibly lose, in order to save her family.

"Of course, we are." I cupped her face. "That's what this place is all about, that's what Larry instilled in all of us, to do what we can to look out for one another."

She sighed in relief. "Thank you."

I kissed her gently. "Don't thank me. Just love me."

"I guess I can do that, too." I felt her smile against my lips.

Her loss might have been as big as the ocean but her love was even greater.

Thirty

Laurel
Two Weeks Later...

"Are you sure this is what you want?" Eli reached for my hand and asked before I could get out of his truck.

We'd just pulled into Roasters and, judging from the cars parked in the back and lining the street, everyone was already inside waiting for us.

I turned and smiled at him, joy bubbling inside me. "Eli, I've had this decision in front of me my entire life. I made the other choice once, I tried *wrong* once. This time, I know this is not only what I want, it's what I need."

He gently squeezed my fingers, and then I was leading the way inside.

A smile bloomed over my face as I walked into the front of the shop. The floors now showed no sign of the dirt and dust that covered them for months, the walls patched and painted in tranquil blues and purples, decorated with photos I hoped would remain for centuries to come.

My ears perked at the sound of the hopper as the scent of freshly ground coffee beans hit my nostrils. I turned to see Eve shoot me a shy grin from where she stood by Pavi who was ready to celebrate this new beginning like the best kind of old friend.

I looked around and didn't just see the memories of my family, I finally saw myself. I saw the girl who'd been too frightened to feel, and the way that love not only overcame that fear of loss, but the way love stopped me from losing myself.

"Thank you, everyone, for coming." My voice wafted confidently over the small crowd.

The Madison brothers, the Covingtons, Eve's brother and sister filled in all the spots between the new tables and chairs we'd put in last week. Diane and Josie sat on the new bench along the wall with Jules situated between them. My stomach tightened. I'd only seen her briefly since her mother checked her out of the hospital against medical advice, deciding she could receive better care and recuperate quicker at home.

Whatever leash she'd been on before was only tightened now, and I struggled to sleep last night thinking she wasn't going to make it.

I'd visited her every day after the shooting, but rarely was I able to get more than a minute or two without my aunt in the room or that giant silent bodyguard of hers who, even in spite of the situation, felt more threatening than he did protective.

And once she'd gone home, it was even worse. When I called, she was unavailable. When I went over to Rock Beach, she was either sleeping or my aunt felt it was too much stress for her to receive visitors. And when she did see me, it was only for a few minutes before she had to go.

I didn't know what I would've done if she didn't make it to Roasters today. But the relief at seeing her now, I knew wouldn't last long.

It was almost impossible to tell the horrors she'd survived as the physical marks from her kidnapping faded. But the way she winced as she turned to talk to Josie and the heaviness in her smile suggested that her bones and spirit were taking longer to recover.

Meanwhile, Mick stood with his arms crossed, his hip resting against the counter as he stared intently at Jules, breaking to greet me with a smile, but swiftly returning back to my cousin. He'd taken what had happened to her hard, and he'd taken the strict instructions to stay away from the hospital even harder.

I watched her look at him with uncertainty and confusion. It was only one quick glance before she averted her eyes and my heart wrenched.

The doctors were right. She didn't remember much about that night. Even some of the time before Blackman took her was lost to her injury. Not being able to recall what happened unsettled her, understandably. It was only at her insistence that my aunt allowed me to tell her what happened that night.

I told her about the gun to her head. About how he threatened and hit her. About how I nailed him with the frying pan to get us out of there. I told her how, when that blow didn't stop him, I'd left her in the alley hoping I could distract him long enough for someone to help her. And finally, I told her how Ace had shown up and shot him.

And she believed it all without a shadow of a doubt from her memory that one piece of that story wasn't true.

As far as the world and she knew, it was Ace who had saved her that night. And I wondered if seeing Mick today would change something—flick a switch of recollection. But those concerns were unfounded as her gaze and her interest didn't linger like it should've for the man who saved our lives.

The only other piece I left out was that she'd been the one

to call me. There was still something that bugged me about what she said, but she wasn't going to remember. Not now, at least.

A loud laugh drew my eyes to the corner of the room where Dex and Ace sat with Miles at one of the other tables, their conversation and laughter dying down as I smiled and moved to the center of the space to address the room.

"I know the past few months has been a rocky road for this town, and especially this place," I continued. "But I wanted to thank each of you for everything that you have done for Roasters and for me... and for my pap."

I cleared my throat at his mention, feeling the tears start to come.

"Once, when I was younger, I told him Roasters was our family's legacy." Eli's hand reached for mine, and I squeezed it tight, searching for strength to keep my voice steady. "And he scolded me." I chuckled. "I think some of you might know what it's like to be scolded by Larry Ocean..."

The soft rumble of laughter from everyone in the room assured me that they all did.

"And then he told me that our legacy wasn't the coffee house or a cup of coffee. Our legacy is being there for the people who needed us—" I broke off and wiped my eyes on my sleeve, mumbling an apology. "I want to thank you because it's all of you who have kept that legacy alive. It's all of you who have not only reminded me of that legacy but have shown it to me at times when I needed it... and at times when I might not have deserved it."

I kept my eyes moving so I didn't linger too long on those who were holding back sobs, my need to cry burning hot in my throat.

"I know that my pap... Larry... may not be here but neither is he gone." Like a deluge, I could hardly see any faces for how thickly the tears suddenly pooled in my eyes. "So, I know that you've all heard the rumors, but I wanted to thank you and tell you in person that, in addition to continuing that legacy, I will also be staying in Carmel Cove and taking over this business… our business. Ocean Roasters will officially see its fifth generation of Oceans."

Instead of stopping, my heart beat stronger. It boomed loudly in my ears, screaming the truth that I'd been afraid to find—to remember.

Our legacy was love.

Tears mingled with laughter at the whoops and clapping from the family that I'd found.

"Oh, sweetheart," Diane exclaimed, the first to approach me and pulled me into her arms, smothering me in her hair-sprayed cloud of hair.

Then came Josie who made me cry all over again, whispering in my ear how proud my pap would be.

Person after person. Hug after watery hug. *Family.*

Slowly, I made my way through the celebrating crowd to Jules who stood with the best attempt at a smile I'd seen in weeks.

"I'm so happy for you, Laurel," she said as I carefully gave her a hug.

"How are you feeling?" I asked immediately, making my own assessment up close. "I've tried to call. Tried to come see you, but your mom keeps putting me off."

After what was said at the hospital, I wasn't going to sugarcoat my interactions with Jackie, not when she'd hidden my concern for Jules before.

"Good. A little better each day." It was that brave smile of hers that really killed me. "I… I know. I'm sorry. It's just taken a lot longer than I thought to start feeling normal again. I still don't remember much about that night."

I grimaced. "I know. Actually, that's one of the things I want to talk to you about. Well, there's a lot of things that I want to talk to you about, like school and working and what *you* want for your life."

It was a lot to dump on her right at that moment but, after not having seen her for a week, truthfully, I was afraid if I didn't at least mention it now, I might never get the chance.

"Thank you," she interrupted and grabbed my hands. "For everything that night, Laurel, thank you. I just… I'm still recovering. It's very strange to have pieces of my life missing and, on top of that, my parents have been even more… protective… lately. I just… need some time before I think about anything else."

Even though she brushed me off, I didn't miss the small flicker of light in her eyes when I brought up school. "Jules," I said insistently, clasping her hands in mine. "Remember, it's your life. It's *your* choice. And it's never too late to start where you are and listen to your heart. I am right here to help you, whatever you need."

She blushed.

"You know you are welcome to stay with me. You can work at the coffee shop to earn money while you get your degree. Anything, Jules. I'll do anything I can to help you." I squeezed her hand and tried to give her a look that said I knew there was something else going on, some other trauma that I wanted to help her out of, if she'd just trust me.

"Thank you." The unspoken '*But I'm not ready for your help yet,*' sitting heavy in the air. "We can talk about it later." When my eyes narrowed, she added, "I promise. Today is about you and Roasters." She nodded over to where Eli was waiting for me to flip the sign on the front door and open it to the crowd of people waiting outside. "Go, enjoy."

"We *will* talk about it later," I said, leveling her with a serious stare.

I hugged the Covington brothers and the Madison twins on my way to the front of the room, reaching Eli with a happy sigh.

"So proud of you, sweetheart," he growled before claiming a quick kiss.

"Thank you for not pushing me… and not giving up on me."

"You're not the only stubborn one around here," he remarked, wryly.

I laughed, pulling us toward the front door.

Pulling his head down to mine for one last kiss, I murmured against his lips, "I love you."

"I love you, too." I didn't just hear his words, I felt them. I felt all of him. His strength and love wrapped around me in a way that I never thought I'd feel safe enough to experience.

Losing someone that you love can change your world. It can change your perspective about who and what is important in life. But in the same way, falling in love can do the same things. I couldn't say if it was rose-colored, but when I looked at the world here, I no longer saw possible tragedy, I only saw possible love.

I flipped the sign that had shown 'Closed' for months now to 'Open' and pulled the door wide. The rush of people was nothing compared to the rush of love that infused every last inch of the space.

This was my home.

How strange that my parents were gone, my grandparents were gone, and yet, I didn't feel any less like a part of a family. *My family.*

Roasters was never about the building. What made it important wasn't the new pipes or perfect walls. It wasn't its location or its coffee. It was the people inside it. It was the Oceans. It was Eli. It was Jules and Diane. It was Eve and Mick and Josie. It was Miles and the Covington brothers. It was the people of Carmel who became family when they walked through the door.

Love is not a thing. Love is an energy. It cannot be destroyed.

Even if the building had been taken from me... at some point, even if these people were taken from me. Love—their love, my love—could not be taken.

Love is not beholden to circumstances like loss or death. Love is beholden to the brave. To those who fight to give it and those vulnerable enough to accept it.

And, as I watched the community file in through the front door that had been closed for months, watched them greet each other with smiles and happy tears, grabbing cups of coffee from the counter where Eve couldn't replenish them fast enough, I realized I was beholden to love.

We all were.

Epilogue

Laurel
Five months later

"Why are you looking at me like that?" My head tipped and I squinted at Eli from across the table. The post-work rush at Roasters had just cleared through and we were sharing our daily afternoon coffee together before heading home and letting Eve close up.

"Just waiting for you to finish your coffee."

I hummed, glancing down at the few more sips of dark liquid left in the bottom of the mug. "You know I like to savor it."

His eyes twinkled as they met mine, spreading warmth through my body.

I liked to savor everything about these little moments. Quiet moments in my coffee shop in my hometown with the man I loved, surrounded by the people who'd become my family over the last several months.

Start where you are. Use what you have. Do what you can.

Staying wasn't the easy choice.

Real loss wasn't like the movies. It wasn't one scene of heart-tearing and gut-wrenching breakdown that completely cleansed my sorrow, allowing me to live happily in the next moment. No, I still hurt. I still missed him with every fiber of my being. But I was still moving forward.

Some days, that sorrow made it hurt. Some days, friendship and family made it flourish. But every day, love made it worth it.

"Well, I'd like to savor you at some point tonight," he grumbled and I chuckled even as I felt my cheeks heat.

"In our new bed?" I arched an eyebrow.

After fixing up Roasters, Eli and the Madison brothers had been busy with new housing projects all along the coast, but finally, they'd had a break which meant their focus had shifted to our house. *My grandfather's house.*

We didn't change much—*We didn't change its character.* But they fixed up a lot that had been neglected and made some additions, including the extra bedroom. We hadn't talked much about kids yet, but there was an unspoken understanding that marriage and a family was where we were heading.

"Absolutely, sweetheart." He grinned.

I took another sip of my coffee and the intensity in his eyes grew.

"Jules said she was going to bring homemade cookies for our double-date on Sunday night," I told him.

We'd continued the habit of spaghetti, meatballs, and magic marinara on Sundays—usually with guests. Many times, with my cousin.

I would always regret not seeing my pap one last time. I would always regret having him gone. But, I would always be grateful to him for giving me this one last gift—of Roasters, of Carmel, and of all the people in it. Because of them, I could move forward without the loss feeling so great.

"Sounds delicious, but not as delicious as your sweet—"

"Eli!" I hissed, covering my mouth to stop myself from laughing as I glanced around, making sure Eve was in the back and hadn't heard him.

He threw his head back and laughed. "Alright, you finished yet?" He bent forward, propping his elbows on the table.

I grinned as I pulled my mug to my lips, draining the last long sip as I held his eyes. As I broke his gaze, my attention caught on something on the inside of my mug, and as I held it out to take a good look, my eyes went wide and I squealed into a mouthful of coffee.

Oh my God.

On the bottom of the porcelain mug, cleverly concealed by the dark brew until it was finished, was glazed the words: *Will you marry me?*

I gulped down the liquid, my hands shaking.

"Is this—Did you—" *Maybe I should've left the coffee in my mouth.*

His smile widened into one carved from pure sunshine as he slid from his seat and down onto one knee.

"Laurel Ocean, from the moment I carried you out of that bar, I knew I never wanted to let you go," he rasped, emotion grating his voice as he pulled out a box from his pocket. "Months ago, I told you I planned on making you my wife. Today's the day I'm asking, sweetheart. And this time, I made sure we were a safe distance from any whisks just in case you got any ideas…"

My hand covered my mouth, tears falling like streamers down my cheeks as I let out the happiest watery laugh.

Eli popped open the lid to the ring box. A bright, glistening pearl stood out between two purple amethysts.

"Will you marry me?"

Between crying and nodding, I managed a garbled, "Yes." Eli reached for my hand and gently slid the beautiful unique ring on my finger before pulling me into his arms.

"I love you."

"I love you, too."

His mouth closed over mine in a long, soul-searing kiss. A promise of love. *Forever.*

And it was only the clapping and cheers that broke us apart, our friends spilling out from the back room of the coffee shop, evidently they'd been waiting there the entire time.

Life wasn't about the destination. And it wasn't about the journey either. It was about the people who were there along the way to support you, to cheer you on, to comfort you, and to love you.

I don't know how long it took—how long for all the congratulations and hugs and happiness to burst and then settle, but as soon as we were alone again, Eli holding the door as I climbed into the passenger seat of his truck, I stared down at the ring once again.

"It's so beautiful." I swiped away another tear as he began to drive us home.

"It was the only thing I could think of when I went to look for a ring… the only thing that seemed to fit," he told me.

"What do you mean?" I tilted my hand, watching as the light caught on the opalescent and iridescent luster of the natural pearl.

"They remind me of you," he answered.

"Because of my inability to tan?" I teased.

He shook his head. "Pearls are created when something unwanted invades the oyster, and so it creates this wall around the invasion and then continues to harden over it, layer after layer."

"This isn't sounding very romantic…" I drawled, reaching for his hand and giving it a squeeze.

"When I look at a pearl, I see something extraordinary and beautiful that was made from something damaging." He pulled my hand to his mouth and kissed the back of it. "Laurel, loss invaded your life. Unwanted. Unyielding. And you took that and became this strong, beautiful woman that I am completely in love with."

My breath caught and built in my lungs, ready to explode right along with my heart.

"I didn't want some perfect diamond. I wanted something to show you everything you are. Strength from hardship. Beauty from disaster. Love from loss."

Tears streamed anew down my face as I climbed over the console to wrap my arms around him. *Thankfully, we were already on the driveway and almost home by that point.*

"I love you." It wasn't enough. Those words weren't enough.

But they never were for the people who meant the most.

"I love you, too, sweetheart." His chest soaked up my tears as he pulled me tight and slowed the truck to a stop.

"Eli, what—" I broke off with a cry as he pulled me onto his lap before opening the door.

"I'm carrying you inside." He gently kissed the wet droplets that lingered on my skin.

"And then you're going to take off my clothes?" I giggled. "Should I grab a whisk on the way?"

He grunted. "I think I'm going to let you strip for me, gorgeous," he murmured against my hair. "And then I'm going to make love to my fiancée."

I tipped my head up and let his lips sink onto mine.

He was right. I'd taken loss because I'd had no choice. It invaded my life like an unwanted intruder. But it hadn't destroyed me. I built myself back up layer after layer after layer, until I came back here. Until I felt safe enough to open my heart back up to the idea of family and home and love.

And now, who I was… what I had… was stronger than the fear of any other loss.

Because, in the end,

Love wins.

Welcome to Carmel Cove

Open-heartedness. Charity. Perseverance.

The foundations of this Pacific-coast town.

I knew from the very start that the setting for this series was going to be a haven—a place where the broken come to heal amongst family and friends (and friends who become family.) A place to find strength and (*of course*) find love.

I hope you've enjoyed Laurel and Eli's story, and the beginning of what will be quite a few books set in this quaint small town.

Speaking of which, I'm thrilled to tell you that the second book, BESPOKEN, will feature Jules and Mick's friends-to-lovers romance!

You can order your copy of BESPOKEN here.
Keep reading to check out the prologue of *Bespoken*!

If you prefer to wait, but don't want to leave Carmel Cove just yet, check out my book, REDEMPTION! A standalone story set in this idyllic town features a few familiar faces! Ash and Taylor's story is an emotional, surprise pregnancy romance set before the events of Beholden and can be read as a complete standalone.

To keep up with the latest book news, exclusives, and updates, be sure to sign up for my mailing list!

Preview of

Bespoken

Prologue

Jules
Thirteen years ago

"Momma?" I called into the Chinese sitting room, glancing around the brightly colored space filled with oriental furniture, the wood ornately carved to look like bamboo shoots, the walls plastered with cherry blossom wallpaper, and almost every surface decorated with tiny Bonsai trees—at least ten of them—meticulously maintained each day.

Once I was sure there were no guests who'd wandered inside despite the 'Closed for a Private Event' sign, I began to worry that maybe she'd said to go to the River Room instead, and I'd made a mistake.

Crap.

I'd been on the phone with Laurel, going over some last-minute notes for our science test tomorrow, when my mother came into my room and told me she wanted to speak to me down here after their party.

No, she definitely said this room.

She and my dad were probably just running late at their meeting. Yes, she'd said it was a New Year's party, but I was old enough to know better.

Rock Beach was the mecca of luxury golf resorts in the state of California. And I believed it even if it hadn't been the first phrase I was taught to say. And just like any prestigious place that drew in anyone from politicians to princes to pop stars, its purpose was more intricate and important than a few putts out on the green.

Like a tree, on the surface, it provided shade and a home for wildlife, but working behind the scenes was the process of turning carbon dioxide into oxygen, a process that enabled life to continue. It was the meetings and conversations and deals that happened here that turned potential into reality and changed lives—in a good way, *of course*.

I never heard all the details—mostly catching bits and pieces of phrases and whispers behind closed doors as I wandered the back hallways from my room down to the kitchen or into the Violet Library, where I liked to study. Most of my friends from school thought it was *so* cool that I lived on a resort. I mean, maybe they were right. Maybe it was cool. Rooms upon rooms, butlers, waiters… I had everyone and everything at my chipped pink fingertips.

Everything except my family.

I plopped down on the largest sofa in the room and pulled out my anatomy coloring book. My very best friend and cousin, Laurel Ocean, had given it to me for my birthday back in August, knowing how much I wanted to go to college to become a nurse. It wasn't until the past week or so that I'd made a lot of headway, being out of school for Christmas and ending up alone most days.

Such a big place. So many people. And still, I was mostly alone when I was here.

It felt like the wrong answer to a math problem. *Two plus two equals one.*

Especially now.

The resort had over one hundred Christmas trees put up and decorated, some even including fake gifts underneath. *A winter wonderland.* But none of them belonged to me, to my family.

I woke up to presents on Christmas morning, but they were unwrapped and stacked neatly in my room for me to look over before breakfast. When I was younger, I asked my mom why we didn't cut down a tree like Laurel's family, and why we didn't wrap presents for each other like all the other kids in my class?

"Because *we are Vandelsens, and we pay people to do that for us, Julia,*" my mother had scoffed and then patted my head. "*And all that paper… all that mess… and wasted time… It's not all it's cracked up to be.*"

She was my mother. *So I believed her.*

I loved my parents. I really did. And from how my classmates coveted my life, I knew I should feel really lucky. I lived in luxury and riches with my parents who'd given me anything I'd ever asked for. And that was why I only ever confessed to Laurel how guilty I felt because all I could seem to focus on was all the things that money *couldn't* buy. Like warm hot chocolate at my grandparents' coffeeshop, Ocean Roasters, after a night of Christmas caroling through the town. Or spending Christmas Eve with my grandparents, aunt and uncle, and Laurel, eating spaghetti and meatballs with my grandfather's magic marinara sauce and unwrapping presents; Laurel had even saved a few ornaments for me to hang on the tree.

There, with them, I felt a glimpse of a different meaning of family, one that I felt guilty for wanting.

But if money couldn't buy it, my parents had no use for it.

"Jules!" I jumped, sending the pencils piled in my lap flying onto the floor as my mom and dad pushed through the door, dressed in shimmering silver and black.

Jackie Vandelsen was beautiful in that way it seemed only rich people could be. Beautiful because of what was attached to the outside of her rather than from a natural goodness inside. And my dad, Rich, was always dressed in case of an emergency interview or photo-op or any other press or marketable opportunity. I'd never seen him not put-together. Maybe because I couldn't recall a time I'd seen him do anything that wasn't for the resort or with the resort in mind.

I'd learned from an early age about the appropriate attire for every holiday, event, outing, and possible social gathering known to man. The knowledge inspired my firm belief that there were more species of social functions than there were animals in the animal kingdom.

"Richard." She turned to my dad. "Perhaps this should wait until morning."

I watched their interaction with wide eyes. They frequently talked about me like I wasn't in the room listening, like it didn't matter because I wasn't going to have a say.

"Jacqueline," my father said curtly. "We've discussed this. It's final. And we have breakfast with the Herons in the morning. Jim is going to be the next mayor, so I don't want us running late. Having his support is going to be crucial for the resort's expansion."

If there was one thing I admired about my father, Rich Vandelsen, it was his dedication to his business. Even though his family had come from money and had owned Rock Beach Golf Club, my father had been the one to turn it into a five-star resort. If there was one thing I wished my father was more of, it was just that... *my father*. He sacrificed a lot to turn this place into what it was, to keep it thriving, and to push toward expansion—and some of those sacrifices were spending time with me. In big ways and small.

My birthday parties were always big, perfectly decorated to the theme for that year, with the best cake and countless gifts— but without my father. It was the same with school events. Sports games. Awards ceremonies. He didn't even have time to try some of the apple fritters my grandmother taught me to make when I'd baked them for a school fundraiser. Instead, he'd just told me to ask my mom for whatever money I was trying to raise and not to worry about actually baking the treats. I'd stood in the doorway, devastated, as he breezed by me with one fritter in my hand, the one I'd saved for him to try.

"Jules." My mother sighed, stepping around my scattered pencils on the floor to sit on the couch beside me. "We need to have a little talk about the future of the resort."

My shoulders slumped slightly as I reached down and gathered the rest of the colors from the floor, prompting my mother to wave at me and say, "Darling, just let housekeeping get that later."

I quickly swiped up the rest of them before she could stop me. I never felt right about having people clean up after me, even if it was part of their job.

"Mama, I know how important the resort is, I promise. You don't have to tell me again."

I set my book down on the marbled coffee table and crossed my legs, linking my hands together to rest on my knee. Even if there was no one else around, there was a certain expectation of decorum when I was in any of the public rooms. Even at this time of night. Even in my pajamas.

"Julia," my father huffed, coming to stand behind my mother, one hand resting on her shoulder, the other on the couch. "I hope you aren't forgetting everything that our business has given you. Every other kid you know would be lucky to have half of what you do, live in the place that you do, experience the things you do."

"Yes, of course, Papa." I nodded insistently, heat rising to my cheeks; I hadn't meant to sound ungrateful. "I know how lucky I am."

There was nothing I knew more of in life. While Laurel would be inheriting my grandparents' coffee house, the Rock Beach Resort was my legacy. Built up from a modest golf course by my father's determination, it was *everything* to my family. I couldn't remember a time when I didn't know the importance of the resort and that, just like my parents, I was expected to do whatever necessary to help it succeed. Rock Beach was my family… my home… of course, I'd do whatever it took to keep it running and make it better.

Still, they reminded me any chance they got. It was their pride and joy and I wanted nothing more than to make them happy—and have it succeed. *Maybe then they could spend a little more time with me.*

"Good." My mom reached over and patted my folded hands, the sentiment feeling colder than comforting because of all her rings that were stacked like miniature platinum and diamond finger-armor. "I should've been more specific. Really, what we want to talk to you about, darling, is your school."

"M-My school?" I squeaked as my head jerked back in surprise. Out of all the things, how could school be a problem? I studied. I did well—all my grades were As. I was in the top of my class. I wasn't taking any chances; I wanted to get into the best nursing program in the state.

"Yes, dear." She glanced up at my father whose eyes stared in my direction but past me. I knew he was already thinking about tomorrow—the meetings, the people, the next steps toward more wealth and status. "We're transferring you to a different school for the rest of the year… for the rest of high school."

Years of social etiquette training masked the jaw-dropping announcement into just the slightest part of my lips.

"W-What?" I asked in soft disbelief. "What school? I-I don't understand."

School felt like my only interaction with real life. This place—with its world class food, fancy furniture, maids, and parties—wasn't real life. School was where my friends were, where Laurel was. It was the gateway to how I got to spend time with the side of my family that my mother most days pretended didn't exist.

Her spine straightened along with her smile. "We're moving you to Our Lady of Mount Carmel for the remainder of high school."

Our Lady of Mount Carmel was a Catholic boarding school about twenty minutes south of Carmel. But twenty miles might as well have been twenty thousand leagues for how effectively it would cut me off from my friends and family.

"Why?" I managed to ask in a calm whisper. Ladies didn't raise their voice, especially in moments of disagreement. Ladies were always calm, collected, and demure.

"Your father and I feel that your education will be much better there, especially without so many distractions." Her smile twitched. "Don't you want the best education you can get, Jules?"

I did.

I couldn't argue that I did.

But school was more than just my education.

"What about my friends?"

"Oh." She waved me off. "You'll make new ones, Jules. Better ones. You'll make the kind of friends that would come here regularly."

I blinked, realizing that I was fighting back tears. *What about Laurel? What about my grandparents? Would I still see them?*

I knew better than to ask. When my parents had married, my mom stayed away from her side of the family, and I still couldn't understand why.

"Of course," I began hesitantly, "I want the best education.

I'm sure that would be an even bigger help on my applications for nursing school and, of course, I want that. But…" My fingers dug into my knee, willing my leg not to shake. "Maybe it would be okay if I just stayed at Carmel High? I'm doing really well and I'm in all the hardest classes," I pressed. "I'm sure that will be good enough."

"Julia." The smile that flickered over my mom's face was brief and patronizing. "I'm sorry, darling, but this isn't a discussion. We're doing what we think is going to be best for your future and your future here at the resort. At Our Lady you will be in school with many of the children whose influential parents frequent the resort. It's absolutely critical that we foster good relationships with these people, don't you agree? Don't you want to help us make sure that Rock Beach does well so you can continue to live such a gilded life?"

No.

The thought came unbidden and instantaneously to my frenzied mind.

"Darling, this isn't just about school—about what's best for you. It's about what's best for the family." There was a duplicitous firmness to her tone, her words strong yet hollow. "Sometimes, we have to sacrifice a little of what we want for the greater good so that no harm befalls the family, yes?"

The silver of her evening dress shimmered in the soft light. It was strange how a single color could transform both lighter and darker—kind of like the facts I was being given. They shifted and twisted under the light until my stomach turned because I was starting to doubt my own mother.

I swallowed hard, contemplating a choice I didn't have. A better school, a better education, and all in all something that would help not only me but my family and Rock Beach. *I couldn't argue.* More than that, my heart screamed that I shouldn't. I should be grateful. I should do this for my family after everything that they'd done for me.

"Of course, Mama," I said softly with a small smile. "Thank you."

"Good girl," my dad injected, patting the couch before eyeing the door. "Alright, now that that's settled, time for bed, Jules, and Jackie, we need to go over tomorrow's agenda."

The goodnight wishes felt foreign and the kisses on my head didn't register. Slowly, with limbs that felt like lumber, I collected my coloring book and pencils and walked back to my room.

It was too late to call Laurel back now. I'd have to break the news to her tomorrow.

When my head hit the pillow, I felt the first tears leak onto the fabric. *Ladies don't cry.*

But I wasn't a lady right now. Right now, I was just a girl who felt like she was losing the only people who really seemed to care about her. And for some reason, that felt like I was losing everything.

This wasn't supposed to happen to rich people. That was the whole point of having wealth, so that nothing bad could happen to you. But the only thing I could think as I drifted off into sad slumber was that something bad *had* happened. No matter who my parents were. No matter where I lived. No matter how few worries in life I had.

That night was the start of a domino of disasters. One slight tipping into the next.

Until one day, I would learn my life was carefully crafted to sparkle like the rarest gem, refracting light but not reflecting the truth.

One day, I would see that all the gilded and fancy things I was conditioned to be grateful for were nothing more than sparkling shackles and bejeweled bars of the cage I'd been raised in.

One day, I would realize that all the money and the shiny things were nothing more than crystalline codes to the world of *what* and not *who* I was—messages I would accept because they came with rationales and excuses from my parents who I loved and trusted to do what was best for me.

One day, I would realize I was bespoken—claimed by my parents and the resort—and worse, that my life was bespoke—tailor-made for a specific purpose and no longer my own.

And on that day, my heart would break to know it was the people I thought loved me who could hurt me the most.

Acknowledgments

To Mr. GQ—I wouldn't trade what we have for anything.

To Brandy and Kassa—Thank you for being gentle with me as I worked through this story… or maybe as this story worked through me.

To Najla—Thank you for always striving to bring my vision perfectly to life.

To Ellie, Rosa, and Stacey—Thank you for making everything about my words sparkle and shine. You are the fairy godmothers in this fairytale.

To all the Bloggers—Thank you. A million times. For every little thing.

To Colleen and Amy—Thank you for choosing this one. I'm proud of all my books, but this one took faith and vulnerability to put out there, and you picked it. And that will always mean the world to me.

To my loyal Readers—Thank you for being there and loving my words, no matter where they take me. But especially thank you for loving the stories that hit so close to home.

Other Works by
DR. REBECCA SHARP

Standalones

Reputation
Redemption
Revolution: A Driven World Novel (Coming Soon)

Carmel Cove Series

Beholden
Bespoken (Coming September 2020)

The Odyssey Duet

The Fall of Troy
The Judgment of Paris

Country Love Collection

Tequila
Ready to Run
Fastest Girl in Town
Last Name

Winter Games Series

Up in the Air
On the Edge
Enjoy the Ride
In Too Deep
Over the Top

Gentlemen's Guild Series

The Artist's Touch
The Sculptor's Seduction
The Painter's Passion

Passion & Perseverance Trilogy
(A Pride and Prejudice Retelling)

First Impressions
Second Chances
Third Time is the Charm

Want to #staysharp with everything that's coming? Join my newsletter!

About the Author

Hey there!

So, you want to know a little bit about me and my writing? Awesome! Even though I write *a lot*... writing about myself always proves to be difficult. I wonder if my 'About Me' could just consist of memes... that would be fantastic!

Alright, let's give this a go. First and foremost, I should warn you that I have a serious obsession with coffee. If you've already found my Instagram, you know this. Other things I love? Wine. Friends (the real ones and the TV show), laughing so hard I cry, painting, snowboarding, cooking, traveling, reading, and, of course, writing. OH, and Disney movies.

Rebecca Sharp is a pen name. One of these days maybe I'll include my real name at the end of a book or something. Anyway, I'm also a dentist living in PA with my amazing husband who we affectionately refer to as Mr. GQ.

Okay, okay. That's enough about me. Let's move onto my books. I (currently) write contemporary and new adult romances. My first book was published in the Fall of 2016 and I haven't slowed down since. I love strong heroines and bad boys that turn out to be good men. There will always be a happy ending because I just can't stomach anything else. Let's see... Happily Ever Afters? Check. Hot alphas? Check. Feisty heroines? Check.

Oh! And I love hearing from readers! I really, really do. I've been so blessed to make so many friendships through this whole Indie author adventure and I would love to meet you and chat with you! How to go about that? Well, you have a ton of options!

If you just want to be emailed with cover reveals, new releases, etc. sign up for my mailing list on my website here. I also host a giveaway in there every month that is exclusive to subscribers, so be sure to check it out: www.drrebeccasharp.com

If you want to see hilarious coffee memes, wine memes, life memes, interspersed with book teasers and info, Follow me on Instagram here: www.instagram.com/drrebeccasharp

If you want all of that good stuff, but on Facebook, as well as the ability to message me privately, go ahead and follow my Facebook page here: www.facebook.com/drrebeccasharp

If you love my work and want the inside scoop on my books, upcoming releases, secret projects, and exclusive giveaways, join my Sexy Little Sharpies reader group here: www.facebook.com/groups/1539118689482683/

And as always, you can follow me on Goodreads (www.goodreads.com/drrebeccasharp) and Amazon (amzn.to/2n8ffbK) to stay updated that way with new releases and info.

I'm pretty sure at any of those places you have the option to message me in some way or another so feel free to do it! You can also just email me directly at author@drrebeccasharp.com!

Happy reading, loves!
xx
Rebecca